Praise for Girls From Centro

M000107399

"Juni Fisher has written a story as bold as breaking news headlines covering the tragic perils of hopeful, honest emigrants lost in border deserts in search of a better life in the United States. The reader will have to turn pages quickly to figure out and follow the maze of conflicting characters, both heroic and evil, in a spell-binding dash to the final five words. There is more than one dramatic movie in this book set in abusive American ranch lands, unholy Catholic orphanages and frightening cults of early day Mormonism."
— Warren Lerude, Pulitzer Prize-winning Journalist

" . . . an engaging and fast-moving ride in the company of memorable characters, both good and bad, across a troubling social, cultural, historical and still timely landscape." — Tom Strelich, *New York Journal of Books*

"These gripping parallel stories are straight up and honest to the bone. I found each character saturated with an authenticity I have rarely run across in border stories. Juni has a savage eye for sharp detail that kind of takes your breath away. It also kind of pisses me off, but that's the envy talking." — Bob Boze Bell, Author, Illustrator and Executive Editor, *True West magazine*

"Juni Fisher's superb tale of love, betrayal, tragedy, and triumph, though set in the recent past, is as vivid and relevant as today's headlines from the Arizona border. Beautifully written and ingeniously structured, it is a slam-dunk winner." — Ranger Doug Green, author and entertainer (Riders In the Sky)

"This may be Fisher's debut novel, but this is not the last we will hear from her. Many people talk about writing a book "someday." This talented author sat down and did it, and did it well. She is a powerful storyteller with an interesting twist of imagination. Readers from all walks of life will find something to love about those girls from Centro who are just trying to get by, trying to make a life. I look forward to having more Fisher books on my shelf." — Amy M Hale, award-winning author of *Rightful Place, Winter of Beauty, The Story Is the Thing,* and *Ordinary Skin: Essays from Willow Springs*

"I was hooked on the six not-rhyming, but poetic, lines introducing Chapter 1 describing Nogales as having 'one ample buttock on Arizona' and 'the other on Sonora.' And, 'the gateway rests between those fleshy parts.' The pithy, vivid prose pictures hinting at the essence of each chapter are alone well worth the price. I don't do tequila shots, but I imagine them being something like that. Getting to know the characters Fisher so skillfully creates is fun and disturbing and ultimately inspirational. I agree with the comparison to *Handmaid's Tale* in another review." — Dave Martin, Record Producer

"Chilling and compelling. I read the entire book in one sitting! A well written book that brings the border and the cultures on either side to life through prose and poetry. Life can be horrific on either side of the border, as the characters slowly discover, and there is a high price to pay for what appeared at first to be freedom. Juni Fisher has written a timely book and it is a must read for anyone watching the border crisis today." — Marcia Matthieu

Other Books by Juni Fisher

Girls From Centro

INDELIBLE LINK

INDELIBLE LINK

LINK

JUNI FISHER

Bink Books
Bedazzled Ink Publishing Company • Fairfield, California

© 2022 Juni Fisher

All rights reserved. No part of this publication may be
reproduced or transmitted in any means,
electronic or mechanical, without permission in
writing from the publisher.

paperback 978-1-949290-80-6

Cover Tattoo Design
by
Melissa Holmes

Cover Design
by

The characters and events in this story are fictitious—except for two, who are
represented with respect and honesty. While the surnames and actions of some
circus folk, both famous and infamous appear, the similarities stop there. Enjoy
the ride and don't worry about it.

Bink Books
a division of
Bedazzled Ink Publishing, LLC
Fairfield, California
http://www.bedazzledink.com

PART 1
Matilda

Circle of Light

SHE SEES THE frayed cuffs of her husband's chambray shirt with eerie clarity as he jumps the boards into the ring, arms outstretched toward her, hands grasping at floating dust, but she can't make sense of the rush of colors that fly past her as she plummets through the circle of light. The music she'd heard a fraction of a second before is now a whistling, crackling assault of sound. She clenches her hands tightly, as if by miracle she'll feel the familiar heft of the trapeze bar. Instead, her nails dig into her palms. Fifteen feet from the tanbark her arms jab involuntarily toward her face. The tattooed bluebird's wing on her wrist flashes past one eye. The scream she hears is her own.

SHE'S STANDING ON her daddy's feet at the New Year's party on the dock in Baton Rouge, and he waltzes in comical, sweeping steps to "The Band Played On." He's singing to her. She's the girl with the strawberry curl in the song, he tells her. Momma is dancing with Gran-pap. Gran-mim's twirly blue silk dress floats around her slender calves as Gran-mim holds someone's baby, swaying and swirling among the dancers. Then the music stops, and Daddy drops her on the dance floor, and she cries out to him.

And now the music she hears is "Stars and Stripes" and she's all alone with a mouthful of tanbark. Someone shouts, "Get that spotlight off. Jesus, get these people out of here."

Oh God. I'm dead.

Parched eyelids shudder apart and white light sears in.

Oh God. I'm not.

Three Weeks After

1958, Fayette, Missouri

SUZETTE CHEVALIER LEANS over her daughter Matilda's hospital bed humming.

That's my song—Get outta my way—I need to be on the ladder. Cas-ey would waltz—

Suzette touches her daughter's twitching cheek and murmurs, "There, there, my sweet."

"The arm and leg and hip will heal, but I can't say—" The doctor shuts off the light box and slides the skull x-ray into the manila sleeve. "Her brain needs time to recover."

Suzette glances at the doctor while he makes a note on his clipboard. She rearranges the travel-rumpled dress she wore when she got on the bus from New Orleans two days ago. "But she'll get better, won't she?"

What's going on? . . . with a strawberry blonde -and-the-band-played-on . . .

The doctor picks up a framed photograph of Matilda in a high-cut leopard print leotard, posing with a dark-haired woman in a corseted gypsy costume and a tall white-faced clown. He turns to the man in the frayed chambray work shirt. "We were at the circus last year. And now this." He shakes his head. "Mr. Kazarian, Mrs. Chevalier, I wish I could tell you more." He sets the photo back among the others on the bedside table.

Wait—what happened?

Bill Kazarian leans forward, his forearms on the arms of the thinly padded chair where he's kept vigil over his unconscious wife for three weeks. The chair groans softly.

"You said there was a specialist in St. Louis . . ."

"Yes. He'll be here next week. The risk of a hemorrhage is still serious. It'll be a while before we know the extent of damage to her—well, her brain functions.

My brain functions? Fire this clown. This one isn't funny.

Bill straightens a photo of his wife on the trapeze platform in her signature pose, one arm over her head, the other hand on her cocked hip. His sassy Matilda.

The doctor slides his penlight into the pocket of his worn, bleached lab coat. "I'll be in again this afternoon. Talk to her. She needs to hear you if she's in there."

Baton Rouge

1958, Fayette, Missouri

"OH LORD, HONEY your daddy was handsome. He was a war hero, remember? And oh, my Michel Chevalier, that was his name, remember? Oh, he could dance." Suzette holds Matilda's splinted fingers. "Your gran-pap Durand didn't like him one bit. Said them Chevaliers was a bunch of rubber lipped red-headed Cajuns and they weren't worth a lick. Yes, he did. He didn't like them Chevaliers, on account they had they own restaurant, not as fancy as his, that's all. But I didn't care."

Matilda can't tell if her own mouth is grimacing or smiling, thinking of her father. How he used to let her wear his Silver Cross medal from the Battle of the Marne in France on her favorite red dress when she was five or six, when they lived in Baton Rouge and she went with him on pirogue tours. She'd hold tight to his pants leg while he poled tourists around, pointing out a gator there, a heron over there, and "away over dere," he'd point a deeply freckled arm at a rotting cypress trunk, "tha's where da Swamp Witch comes out at night, so we's best go on in now." Matilda would hug his legs hard until they'd rounded the bend, terrified that the witch might come out before nightfall.

They'd be back at the dock on the last sliver of yellow light, and Matilda's uncles helped the pretty female guests out of the pirogue "jes' in case you's still swimmy from da boat." Matilda's aunts and grandmother had the pots a-boil and as the guests walked up, they dumped baskets of scrambling crawfish in with cobs of sweet corn and red potatoes.

Little Matilda, blessed with her mother's amber eyes and creamy caramel toned skin, her grandmother's sharply cut Creole cheekbones and nose, and her father's full lips and ginger hair was the after-dinner attraction, making her way from table to table, offering to sing a song or dance for a penny.

"We spoilt you rotten. You was always showing off for folks even when you was jus' a little thing." Suzette tentatively touches Matilda's forehead. "Remember when you made people pay a penny for you to dance? And you'd charge two cents to sing em a song. Didn't matter what they wanted to hear. You always sang "The Band Played On.""

I remember, Momma.

Now her mother's voice fades and she's ten and riding in the pirogue with her father and uncle, and her father is tugging at a loose branch in the water while her uncle poles them through stinking deadfall. The branch recoils from the pull, and her father goes headfirst over the bow. She and her uncle laugh. Her father doesn't come up. Her uncle tells her to stay put and jumps in. He drags her father from the coffee-colored water and struggles to heave him into the pirogue. Matilda pats her father's face, laughing, telling him to stop playing around now.

The bayou tour guide who'd escaped German captors in France at the Battle of the Marne and helped his comrades to safety to earn a Silver Cross couldn't save himself from drowning when a submerged log cracked his head open.

"YOU WAS THE bravest little girl. You never even cried at the funeral."

Matilda remembers the scratchy navy-blue dress and white gloves her grandmother brought out from town. A single layer of crinoline crackled like dry leaves against her bare legs as she sat on the folding chair at the cemetery. The starched white collar rubbed her long, tender neck every time she swallowed a silent sob.

I didn't cry, Momma, because you shook me and told me not to. But you cried up a storm and carried on til they had to take you back to the house. And you didn't let me cry.

"I guess his Silver Cross from the war got buried with him 'cause I never saw it again."

I have Daddy's medal. He gave it to me. I always had it since I was little, Momma. Don't you remember nothin'? What the hell's wrong with you?

Suzette Plays the Track

1939, New Orleans, Louisiana

THE DEPRESSION KILLED off the tourist trade in Baton Rouge, but not horse racing in New Orleans. Gabriel and Cheree Durand sold their ten-seat restaurant and took their widowed daughter Suzette and twelve-year-old Matilda to New Orleans where they bought a foreclosed house just off Gentilly Avenue. Gabriel's new position as head chef at the Fair Grounds Racetrack Club House restaurant opened the door for Suzette to land a job at the Fair Grounds betting windows.

Suzette eased her grief in the company of a string of busboys, gallop riders, and assistant trainers. Luis, a Mexican busboy who brought single carnations snatched from dining room tables to the betting window was among her suitors. Luis was smart enough to take a job at another dining establishment down the road before Suzette's father realized she was pregnant. Suzette weaned her son Looie onto a bottle and left him in her mother's care when the next racing season started.

Within four weeks of the start of the new season, a Texas trainer's nineteen-year-old son was handing his last horse of the morning off to a groom before racing to an empty stall for a roll with Suzette. When his father caught them in the act, he shipped the kid back home. Suzette named that baby Dallas.

The broken-down exercise rider with pock-scarred cheeks and no prospects of ever riding races excused himself to hitch a ride to Evangeline Downs for another job the day Suzette hinted she might be expecting. Evangeline seemed as good a name as any for the daughter Suzette gave birth to the next fall.

The fourth pregnancy in as many years was compliments of the trainer's assistant whose tack room cot she'd been visiting before he headed north to Churchill Downs in April. Of course, Suzette named that son Churchill.

Matilda and her four younger siblings never did get used to the supper table shouting matches between Suzette and her father.

Gabriel's voice shook the windows the night he shouted at Suzette that he didn't raise her up proper to watch her ruin her life and everybody else's because she couldn't control herself. Suzette cried and carried on that it wasn't her fault. After all, she sobbed, she couldn't help who she fell in love with.

Matilda escaped to her room and clicked the door shut. She picked up the *Life Magazine* on her bed and turned to her favorite photographs and story about a circus. The woman's tight-fitting costume was cut so high her hip bones showed. She hung by her ankles from the hands of a handsome man with bulging shoulders and sinewy arms who hung by his knees on a trapeze bar. Another man with hair like patent leather reached toward her from his bar. The woman's eyes locked with the eyes of the man with patent leather hair. A glimmer of light shone on lips Matilda imagined were painted ruby red. The costume looked like a thousand sparkling diamonds. Like magic. Like love.

The next morning, Matilda's grandmother sat crying at the kitchen table with a folded note clenched in her wrinkled hand. "She's gone, honey, she done run off with somebody new, I guess. Says she's not coming back."

Matilda stormed to her mother's room and snatched the closet curtain open. Her mother's suitcase was gone. She would not cry. She would not cry.

PART 2
Eddie

Lucky Eddie

EDDIE LAFONTAINE WAS fourteen when his mother ran off with a Baptist preacher. Eddie started working with his dad, Sonny in the tattoo shop in New Orleans. Eddie filled the air with talk for his deaf father by chatting up new customers, showing them sketches and listening to what they wanted. Sonny added Eddie's wildly detailed designs to his inventory.

Sonny let Eddie wield a tattoo machine on him the first time when Eddie was sixteen and Eddie made the mistakes a kid with a tattoo machine could make, but he had the knack. Eddie had been tattooing in Sonny's shop for eleven years when, at twenty-seven, on a wild-haired whim, he enlisted in the Navy.

'I want to see the world, Pop,' Eddie signed.

Sonny grunted and huffed while his ink-stained hands argued 'Dammit Eddie. Business is good. See the world later.'

'Pop, I go to basic training next week. Then maybe they'll send me to Hawaii. Hey how about Hula girls, Pop. I can do some new designs.' Eddie mimicked cupping breasts and grinned.

'You can look at pictures and draw without getting shot.'

'I won't get shot, Pop, I'm Lucky Eddie.' Eddie pushed up his shirt sleeve, so his tattoo of four aces and "Lucky Eddie" showed. 'You told me I was lucky.'

'Lucky right here, son.' Sonny tapped on the glass counter. 'Lucky here.'

11-15-41
Hey Pop,

Here's some more drawings for you. I showed the guys in my unit the picture of the new front window. They were all talking about how they wanted that for a tattoo. So I hope you use those for tattoos, because that's why I sent them. That hula girl you picked out for the window looks real good and the new lettering almost made me cry. Almost. Thanks for adding that "and Son" part.

I don't guess Drucie has come by. I sent her a post card soon as I got here but didn't hear from her. I'll bet one of those assholes over at the dance hall swooped in on her soon as I was gone. But that's okay. There's plenty of girls here, if you like Hawaiian girls. Man some of these guys go crazy over them. There's gonna be a lotta little half breed kids this time next year.

The weather is real nice. It rains a lot, and it gets hot, but you'd like the beach here. Last weekend this family invited me and some of the guys over for dinner, and they cooked a whole pig right in the sand. There are pigs everywhere. Anyway, it sure was good.

Some of the men from the island have these warrior tattoos I think we could use. I'll do some drawings of them. Theirs are black, but I think we could do them in colors. Things are pretty quiet here. We're going to a movie tonight, so I got to get a shower.

Write back and make the writing girly on the envelope so the other guys will be jealous.

Eddie

November 29, 1941

Hi Son,

Got the sketches. I'll probably put some coconut shells on those girls, since some of our customers are married.

Have not seen Drucie. Maybe she's been busy. I don't know.

I have been going out with a nice lady who moved down here from Caddo Lake. She works at the café, but I also have her working here some and she sure is a big help to me, talking to customers. And she learned how to sign. I think you'd like her. It was her idea to put the hula girls and Lafontaine and Son Tattoo Artistry on the window. She and I repainted the lobby and my studio and yours and the back studio too because she thinks we'll get so busy we'll need another guy to come work here. Maybe she's right. Her name is Mary Ellen. I hope you like her. I sure do.

Business is good, so I need you back. Stay safe and get your ass home.

Love,

Your old Pop

P.S. If you want girly writing get a girlfriend.

Pearl Harbor

December 7, 1941, 07:48

EDDIE LEANED AGAINST a laundry crate to light a cigarette as the first Japanese Kate dropped its torpedo into the sea five thousand feet from the U.S.S. Oklahoma. The company jokester standing ten feet away became a mound of smoking, armless, legless, still-breathing flesh, sans jokes.

The laundry crate blasted sideways eighty feet and hit the water with Eddie grappling for slats. Flames exploded over spreading fuel. Eddie knew he wasn't going to outswim the blue inferno. His hair singed while he calculated how long he might hold his breath.

Eddie filled his lungs and asked God for a little help here, please. God said 'OK, Eddie, here's a Zero nosediving between you and the ship. He's not pulling up.' Eddie rode his crate atop the wave, and escaped death for the second time in less than a minute.

December 7, 1941, 08:12: Eddie's lucky day.

Two fishermen plucked Eddie from the sea and delivered him to the first ambulance at 08:27. Lucky Eddie got twelve pints of blood, morphine, a splint, and a busty nurse. No one told Eddie his leg was too mangled to save.

When the nurse flushed his wounds later, he spewed language his mama would have slapped him for, and the nurse told him he'd be fine while she slid a needle into his vein. From atop his morphine cloud, Eddie missed the doctor telling him the leg would have to come off.

December 12, 1941, 14:00

A nurse helped a drugged-up Eddie to use the bedpan after he woke up from surgery and told him he'd have to learn to do this himself on crutches soon. Eddie looked under the sheet, waited for the nurse to get four cots away, then pulled the sheet over his face while grief washed over him.

The guy next to him who'd lost both legs at the hip, and half an arm watched Eddie with one un-bandaged eye. "We're lucky, Lafontaine. I hear we get shipped out of here with a purple heart."

"Lucky us."

Eddie called the nurse back and pointed to his arm.

"Look, Lafontaine," she whispered, "I can't run over here every time you want morphine."

"Then give me the syringe," Eddie whispered through clenched teeth. "I promise I'll go easy on it." He gave her his best dewy-eyed smile. "I'll tell them I stole it from your tray. I promise." His voice was so faint she had to lean over him to hear. She looked into his face, almost touched her hand to his cheek.

The nurse straightened at the sound of footsteps in the ward and patted Eddie's arm. "I'll be back."

An hour later Eddie's new favorite nurse came to check his bandage and quietly placed something on the sheet alongside Eddie. As Eddie slid his hand over the cool stainless steel and glass syringe, he fell in love.

December 20, 1941
Dear Eddie,

We saw in the papers how the Japs bombed Pearl Harbor. Everybody here is so mad. The Navy sent a letter almost two weeks ago to tell me you were injured. They said you were on a ship and it took a hit, and that your leg was hurt, but you were getting good care. I wrote as soon as I got that letter but it came back yesterday. Maybe I got the address wrong.

I hope you are healing up. I guess with all that was going on, mail is slow, but I hope I hear something. Mary Ellen had a phone put in out in the lobby. She said to tell you to ask for New Orleans and then tell the operator 767 and she'll put you through. I don't know how it works, but that's what she said to tell you. And she says you could ask the operator for Rufus Sinclair's auto shop too. We have breakfast with him most mornings. Everybody asks about you.

Does this leg injury mean they'll let you come home? I sure hope so.

Your Pop

P.S. They said it was your leg that got hurt, but not your hands, so that means you can write back. I mean it.

Eddie Heads Home

A WEARY-EYED NAVY surgeon at the V.A. Hospital in Shreveport took five more inches off Eddie's thigh to stop gangrene from shrapnel the first surgeon missed.

The attending doctor told Eddie, "Your mind has its own pain killers, son. We have to let them work. You don't want to go back to New Orleans to your family needing drugs, do you Lafontaine?"

tell him to screw himself and hand over the goods, the monkey on Eddie's back whispered.

"Oh, no sir, that would be—just awful. I'm just afraid I'll get crazy if one of these nurses bumps my leg. I couldn't live with myself if I hit a woman. I have kind of a temper."

The doctor made a note on Eddie's chart and the nurse with the long Bohemian face glanced at the order, wide-eyed. She swooshed away on white shoes to fill the requisition. "I'm ordering an I.V. morphine drip for your pain, son. Nurse Richards will set you up."

The monkey whispered, *yessssssss.*

Eddie had never sweet talked a girlfriend back home the way he poured it on Nurse Emelia Richards. He told her she had beautiful eyes, like his momma had when she was—and put his hand over his eyes. Emelia assumed he'd stopped short of saying, "alive."

Eddie learned Emelia lived alone, never married. Eddie told her he'd never married either. Waiting for the right girl. Someone with mysterious dark eyes. She caved. Nurse Richards started wearing cologne. Eddie asked if she'd been picking flowers, because she smelled so good.

kiss her, love her, screw her if you have to, the monkey wailed.

A NURSE WHEELED Eddie to the phone to call his family. "They might want to meet you at the train," she said. "Some men call a cab, but I'd think it's better they meet you there, and that they know they'll need room in the car for your wheelchair. And I know it's hard to call. You need help getting the call through?"

Eddie shook his head and wondered if his ears always rang louder than the clanging of the phone on the other end of the line. He scarcely heard his dad's best friend Rufus assure him he'd be there.

The next morning a young doctor pulled Eddie's I.V. out. Eddie's morphine monkey shrieked, *hey hey hey, they're tryin' to kill me.*

Two orderlies helped him into a wheelchair and laid a pair of crutches across his lap. Someone handed him his duffle, a dozen aspirin in a tin, a bologna sandwich, and a purple heart.

Nurse Richards ran all the way to the train station clutching a cloth wrapped package. She leaned over the wheelchair to kiss Eddie on the mouth.

"Oh, now, you shouldn't have gone to any trouble," he said, hoping the rest of the guys hadn't seen the kiss.

"Just a little something for the trip," she cooed.

The three guys closest to Eddie groaned, "Awww."

"Now, don't be jealous, you boys," Nurse Richards said. She whispered in Eddie's ear, "Don't open those cookies in front of everybody."

On the train, Eddie untied the ribbon while the boy across from his seat slept. Atop the tissue paper was a note card with Emelia's address and telephone number. He slipped the note into his shirt pocket, breathed in vanilla and brown sugar, and started to re-wrap the package. A hard edge shifted against the cloth. He lifted crumbling oatmeal cookies and studied two palm-sized cardboard boxes. He stared at the red printing.

> E. R. Squibb and Sons, New York.
> Directions for use.
> Morphine Syrettes-Inject under skin after cleansing site; to relieve pain in severe injury or burns. 15cc.
> May be habit forming.

God love Nurse Richards. God love oatmeal cookies. And E. R. Squibb and Sons. And Jesus and Moses and all of them. Eddie's monkey purred.

EDDIE EMPTIED A morphine syrette into his wrist when Lake Pontchartrain hit his nostrils. He closed his eyes and waited. War-damaged men gathered duffels and crutches as the train groaned to a stop. Eddie leaned against the window to watch fathers, mothers, brothers, wives, and girlfriends come forward solemnly to claim their casualties. A young woman rushed forward to grasp the arm of her man who's lost an eye and part of his jaw. When he turned toward her, she staggered back, hand over her mouth, and fled.

An orderly helped Eddie to the station platform and into the wheelchair. Eddie wheeled to the payphone outside the ticket office and rifled his pocket for a nickel.

"Here, lemme get that for ya, Eddie," the man beside him said. Eddie blinked. His Pop's buddy Rufus stood there, red faced, grinning.

"Hey, Rufe. How ya been?"

"Good, Eddie, better than you, looks like."

"Yeah. They say I'll be back on my foot in no time." Neither laughed. Rufus rested his hand on Eddie's shoulder.

let's have a cookie, buddy boy, Eddie's monkey whispered.

not now you idiot, Eddie's brain whispered back.

Rufus watched, shifting from foot to foot while Eddie held the door frame and struggled into the truck. Rufus set the duffle on Eddie's stump and Eddie sucked air through his teeth. "God, I'm so sorry, Eddie, I'm so—"

"'S okay. I'm fine. Put that chair in the back, will ya?"

Rufus eased the truck out of the station parking, steering around potholes. "Your pop told you he—well, I mean he sent a letter to tell you, right?"

Eddie stared straight ahead. "Why you drivin' like an old man, Rufe? Tell me what?"

"He got married, Eddie."

"Okay. That's good, I guess." He wished Rufus had offered to stop for a couple of beers.

"I guess. I don't know what he sees in her. She talks like she's from Texas or somewhere. Name's Mary Ellen."

"Well in case you forgot, Pop can't hear."

"Right." Rufus drove fifteen miles an hour the rest of the way.

IN BACK OF Lafontaine and Son Tattoo Artistry Rufus held the door while Eddie bumped and rocked the wheelchair over the threshold. Rufus jogged back to the truck for the duffle.

careful asshole, we got cookies in there, the monkey coughed.

"How about we put your stuff in your room, then you can—"

"Yeah. Thanks." Eddie palmed his chair to the second door in the hallway. A wheel scuffed fresh white paint as he angled through the door. The scent of Pine-sol hit him in the face.

Eddie didn't watch Rufus go out and close the door behind him. His eyes were glued to his bed. Glued to the blue striped sheets where he'd given his girl, Drucie a last hurrah the night before he left for basic training. He wondered if the sheets still smelled like Drucie.

He hadn't written to Drucie from the hospital in Honolulu. He hadn't known what to tell her. Maybe she thought he was dead. Maybe that was just as well.

He rubbed his face and turned toward the dresser mirror. He stared at the guy in the uniform looking back at him. The beard stubble didn't hide hollow cheeks and blue-grey circles around his eyes. He squinted at a photo-booth strip stuck in the frame of the mirror from when he and Drucie had gone to the fair, puzzled at Drucie's black nails and lips. Then the grey skin, grey and black clothing, grey and black hair registered. That's how he felt. Grey and black and fingerprint smudged. Bent at the corners.

The door opened behind him. There stood Sonny in his ironed shirt with sleeves rolled to the elbows, grinning like he was glad to see him.

'Hello son,' Sonny signed.

Eddie scraped his lower teeth over his upper lip and nodded. He mouthed "hi, Pop," because either his brain had forgotten how to sign, or it wasn't letting him move his hands.

'Got a guy on the chair. Gotta get back,' Sonny signed.

"Okay," Eddie whispered hoarsely.

Sonny closed the door. Eddie unzipped the duffle and put his package of oatmeal cookies on top of the dresser. He dropped the pants and pajamas into the bottom drawer. Someone had folded and pinned one leg up on each of them. Emelia must've done that when she packed for him. The pity-pack.

He closed his eyes and opened them again an hour later when he heard the back-door squall open. He listened to footfalls in the hallway that weren't his Pop's. Or Rufe's. Or Emelia's.

hey, Eddie. let's you and me party.

"Shaddup ya little asshole," Eddie whispered. The footfalls in the hall came closer.

hurry up, we got time.

"Shaddup. I decide when." Eddie startled himself when he spoke aloud. The footfalls stopped abruptly then began again.

Eddie looked longingly at the ribbon tied package on the dresser before he turned to his duffle for his shaving kit. The monkey moaned in agony while

Eddie ran water in the sink and shaved. Eddie just wanted back into his own skin. He hoped he remembered how.

WHEN EDDIE OPENED the shop door and rolled his wheelchair in, the smell of cigarettes, nerves and sweat pulled him home. Here he knew the score. Here he was an artist, not a serial number in a uniform. Here guys read magazines while they waited. Here he punctured skin with color and wiped it off until the customer had a Lafontaine original tattoo.

In the front studio Eddie saw his dad moving around some guy's leg. The guy's face was white at the temples and chin, red on the cheeks. Eddie moved closer to see: two bare breasted girls in grass skirts bent at the waist, butt cheek to butt cheek. Eddie recognized the design as one he'd sent from Pearl Harbor before the world exploded around him. The guy on the table turned his head. "Hey, Eddie, it's me, Tommy Stang. From the band."

Eddie blinked. "Yeah. Tom. Good to see ya." Eddie gripped the armrests of his chair. Tommy glanced at the folded pants where a leg used to be.

"It's good to see ya, Eddie. Hey, I want to get a heart with an arrow or something on my arm next. You comin' back to work?"

"Yeah. Yeah. I'll be workin'."

Eddie drifted out to the lobby. He breathed in the lingering odor of new paint. Crisp white Venetian blinds hung in the window and a new silver bell had been mounted on the door. New row of chairs against the wall. New glass ashtrays, empty and clean.

Through half-mast window blinds, Eddie watched a woman's legs outside the door. The woman stooped to dip a window scraper in a bucket on the sidewalk. After she'd dumped the water in the gutter, she opened the door and came in.

Well Rufus was right: she wasn't a knock-out, what with the lines around her mouth and eyes, and bushy eyebrows. Hair held back with two bobby pins. But she looked solid. Solid frame. Solid face. Square jaw.

The woman set the bucket beside the counter, walked over, stuck out her hand and looked Eddie in the eye. "I'm Mary Ellen." She let go of Eddie's hand and signed while she talked. "I've been looking forward to meeting you. A lot of customers have asked when you were coming back." Sonny ambled out from the studio and leaned on the glass countertop, watching them.

"The place looks—different . . ." Eddie said.

"I hope we can sign when we talk, so—well, you understand." She signed as she spoke.

"Yeah. Sure."

'Hey' Sonny signed, 'I'll take you both to dinner when we close up. Celebrate you coming home. How about the Oyster House?'

Eddie had a moment of panic. Going out in the neighborhood where he grew up. Wheelchair, folded pant leg. How did that work? What do you wear? Uniform so they all know and don't ask?

'I'll freshen up. We can take my car.' Mary Ellen signed.

Eddie's head was starting to hurt. He fished the tin of aspirin from his shirt pocket. Sonny hurried over with a cone of water from the cooler in the corner.

'I can get stuff myself, Pop.'

'I know you can, but I need to do this right now.'

'Why, Pop?'

'Because I wish I had kept you from going.' Sonny's arms dropped.

'Me too, Pop.'

A WEEK LATER Eddie had one syrette of morphine left. He dialed nurse Emelia Richard's number six times before she answered. She told him she'd send cookies. The monkey bared its teeth over Eddie's jugular vein to watch his blood pulse then whimpered and stroked Eddie's neck.

tell her she's pretty. tell her she smells good.

"I miss the way you smell." Eddie clutched the phone.

"Eddie, truth is, I'm seeing someone and . . ."

tell her you love her you love her you love her

Eddie set the receiver down. He heard the screaming in his head and felt the monkey's claws dig in. His stump ached and twitched. He dialed his old buddy, Tommy Stang. Musicians knew how to get the good stuff.

The monkey let out a long rattling breath.

PART 3
Ink

1942, New Orleans, Louisiana

MATILDA CAME HOME from high school one late spring afternoon her freshman year wearing a sanitary napkin she'd had to mooch from her friend Brenda. Her grandmother gave her a quarter to run to the store for her own box of pads.

She hid the pads under her bed and took out the wooden box that held her father's Silver Cross. She touched the medal and a tattered as a tom-cat's ear five-dollar bill she'd earned for two months of starching Sunday shirts for a neighbor lady. Matilda closed the lid, shoved the box under the bed, tiptoed past her grandmother and out the front door.

Old men on porches and women hanging wash on wire clotheslines greeted her by name for the first five blocks. Then she was in front of the fish market, then the bakery, and then she didn't see a soul she knew on the next street. She stopped in front of a plate glass window with a painting of a woman in a grass skirt that looked like a postcard she'd once seen. The lettering said: "Lafontaine and Son Tattoo Artistry."

A square jawed woman in a flowered dress stood at the counter, turning the pages of a book. The man across the counter moved closer to look, smiled, and tapped a page. The man gave her money. The woman held a curtain aside, and the man went through.

Matilda pulled the door open. The bell on the door frame made a sound as sweet as her gran-mim's good crystal.

The woman called from the back room, "Be right there." Matilda edged toward the open book. She held her breath at the explosion of greens and reds, oranges, yellows, blacks, blues, and purples that flowed over figures of open-mouthed eagles, perched crows, swooping bluebirds, and one delicate hummingbird. She pressed closer to the hummingbird painting and touched the plastic covering on the page. Wings flexed, feathers spread, and the emerald head bent downward to a single butter colored honeysuckle bloom. The beaded curtain chattered, and the smell of straight alcohol followed the woman into the lobby.

"Well, hello, little miss, what can I do for you today?"

Matilda kept her eyes on the hummingbird for fear it would disappear. "This is something they can tattoo?"

"Yes, missy, they sure can. Want to see some more pictures?" The woman turned the pages, commenting that this one was drawn by Sonny, and this one was drawn by Eddie, this one takes about two hours, this one takes a half hour. "You know somebody who wants a tattoo?"

Matilda drew a short breath and brushed her fingertips on the page. "Maybe. What's it cost?"

"The hummingbird is five dollars."

Matilda raised her chin and straightened up until the back of her neck touched her white Peter Pan collar. Her face felt strangely warm. She absently tugged at her panties through her skirt.

A door at the end of the room swung open, and a man in a wheelchair pushed over the low threshold with a thump. From the corner of her eye, Matilda saw a fan of playing cards and "Lucky Eddie" tattooed on his forearm. The woman held the beaded curtain open for the man in the wheelchair to go through, and said, "I'll be right back, honey."

Matilda scurried out the door and sprinted toward home, her tightly curled ginger hair bouncing on her shoulders.

"NOT EVEN IF your mama came in here and said it was okay, kiddo."

Matilda fumed and blushed until her cheeks were two sun ripened peaches.

"You run 'long. When you're old enough to drink come see me." Eddie watched the mop-headed girl's chin quiver.

Matilda slid her ragged five-dollar bill toward Eddie, across the scratched glass display case.

"And don't you be cryin'. Doesn't change my mind. Go on. I don't tattoo kids."

Eddie backed his wheelchair up to the desk behind the counter and jerked his head toward the door.

"I'm not cryin'. The lady said five dollars. I got five dollars." Matilda's throat bobbed when she swallowed. Wide nostrils flared when she glanced at his ink-stained hands and where his hair bristled out over the tops of his ears like it had been shorn off and he hadn't bothered to get a haircut since. Pine-sol didn't hide the cigarette smell of him. She swallowed again.

"How old are you, kiddo?" Eddie lolled his cigarette to one side of his mouth and blew a stream of smoke toward the ceiling.

"Sixteen."

"Like hell you are. Try again."

"Fifteen and a half."

His cigarette ash glowed, then collapsed. She watched it smolder just above the folded pant-leg. His voice dropped four notes. "Ballsy little gal ain't ya? Try again."

"Fourteen." Her eyes stopped at the wisp of smoke on fabric. "Your pants," she said softly. "I'll be fifteen next month."

Eddie batted at the newest burned hole on his pants. "Yeah? What's your name?"

"Why?"

"So I can tell your mama over at the racetrack her little girl was here with five dollars she stole and she's tryin' to get a tattoo. Yeah. I know your mama works there. Seen you there with her. How 'bout that?" He stubbed the cigarette on the top of a beer can strapped to the chair frame and dropped the butt into the triangular hole.

"You're lyin'. She doesn't work there anymore." She pulled the five-dollar bill to the edge of the glass and closed long fingers with chewed nails around it.

"Yeah? Since when?"

"Since she run off. So, you're lyin'."

Eddie lit another cigarette. "I haven't been there in a while. Who takes care of you then? Your daddy?"

Matilda shook her head.

"Your daddy run off too?" Eddie dragged on the cigarette until the paper sputtered around glowing ash. He watched the girl's chin pucker.

She shook her head again.

"I'm sorry, kiddo, 'bout your momma. That's a bad deal. Mine run off too, long time ago. But I don't tattoo kids. I don't want your granddad or the police comin' by to visit. Okay? And don't you go across the street. Them guys over there don't clean their machines good."

Matilda backed away from the counter. The heat rose in her cheeks again. Eddie saw she was pretty the way a greyhound is: all limbs and long neck, long face.

Matilda whirled on her red Mary Janes and yanked twice at the door handle before she figured out she needed to push it open.

"See ya, kiddo," he said to the back of a head of unruly orange hair. He rolled to the picture window to watch her. She didn't even look across the street at Leon's Tattoo Emporium when she turned to hurry back toward Gentilly Avenue. "Atta girl," he muttered.

Cards and Letters

1958, Fayette, Missouri

"HERE'S TWO CARDS. One from your sister"—Bill holds the envelope a foot away from Matilda's closed lids—"and this one's from a Brenda. And there's a letter in it. She says she went to school with you."

Brenda? Brenda sent a letter? I didn't even like her any more after that time she . . .

1942, Fall, New Orleans, Louisiana

CASEY STANG STARTED tenth grade again at seventeen without a self-conscious hair on his black pompadour. He sauntered in on a cloud of smoke and Pinaud's aftershave, barely buttoned into a black bowling shirt that touted "Tommy Stang and the Stingers" and an embroidered saxophone leaning on two bowling pins. Casey was the first boy Matilda had ever seen wearing rolled dungarees over argyle socks and loafers. A wooden match floated from side to side between smooth pale plum lips and a Chesterfield rested behind one ear.

Watching Casey Stang made Matilda shiver like someone had put ice down her blouse.

Casey tapped a chewed pencil on the desk in rhythm while the homeroom teacher blatted on about rules. No leaving school grounds during school hours. No graffiti on lockers or school buildings. No smoking on school grounds. Casey smiled and winked at moon-faced Shirley Sizemore who'd turned to see who was drumming behind her. Matilda watched. Boys never smiled and winked at Shirley.

Shirley's round, flat face turned pink and her upturned almond eyes opened wide when she clapped her chubby fingers over her mouth and spun to face forward.

Brenda Boucher went "pssst" and chucked a folded note that bounced off Matilda's desk and onto the floor. Mrs. Girardi kept droning her homeroom teacher speech about regulations and fire drills and class bells while she walked down the aisle. Matilda inched her foot toward the note right as Mrs. Girardi bent to pick it up.

Mrs. Girardi slid her reading glasses on. "Miss Boucher, if your note is on the floor, no one knows who you're warning not to sit beside or look at Mr. Stang."

Brenda put her hand out for the note, and slumped, red faced amid snickers and catcalls from the back of the room. Mrs. Girardi looked over the top of her glasses at the hecklers. Casey raised his hand.

"Yes, Mr.—"

Casey slid the palm of his hand over his impossibly shining hair. Matilda peeked at his schedule. He was in her Algebra and Chemistry classes.

The first period bell rang. Casey poured himself out of the seat in one fluid motion, then stopped behind Matilda to tap a short drum roll on her chair back. Matilda could have died right then. She looked straight ahead at sweet, simple-minded Shirley who galumphed toward her while Casey drifted out of the room.

"Casey, he's funny, huh?" Shirley sputtered. The armpits of Shirley's pink swiss-dot dress were soaked at eight fourteen in the morning. "His brother plays in a band. I like to dance. Do you like to dance?"

"Sure." Matilda glanced over her shoulder before she rose. "Come on, Shirl. What class you have first?"

Shirley gaped at her schedule. "Gym! Oh boy."

"Okay, later, alligator." Matilda patted Shirley's shoulder. "Be good."

"Hey, Brenda got in trouble, huh? That was funny."

"You're funny too, Shirley."

MATILDA SLID INTO an open seat in the back row for Algebra class. Casey was already at the desk across the aisle. Matilda stared at Casey's tattooed bicep where a black and blue crow perched on a human skull. Her blush spread from her face to the crotch of her cotton panties. She forgot to copy the problems from the blackboard before she went to her next class.

"I THINK HE'S in this class," Brenda said, rotating her chair sideways so she could watch who came into the Chemistry classroom.

"Who?"

"You know who. So, you have to move so Casey can sit by me."

"Hello class, please find a seat for now. You'll be working and studying with an assigned lab partner all semester. When I read your names together, both of you raise your hands, and one of you go sit with the other until all the assignments are made." The Chemistry teacher's rumpled white shirt was buttoned askew under his green plaid necktie.

Casey eased through the door and took the seat beside Stewart Maison. Stewart, in his too-small short sleeve shirt and bowtie mopped his nose with a monogrammed handkerchief.

Brenda raised her hand. "Excuse me."

"Oh, a volunteer. Miss?"

"Boucher. Brenda Boucher. I just, well, in case there's a student who needs tutoring, I can help. I got all A's in Chemistry last year."

"Very well, Miss Boucher. Miss Grayson, where are you?" Violet Grayson's ghostly arm floated up. Violet's pointed teeth were the only thing paler than her skin. "You and Miss Boucher will be together." Matilda traded places with Violet. Brenda shot Matilda a horrified look.

"Mr. Maison, you will be working with—where is Mr. Pace? There."

Stewart Maison shoved his soggy handkerchief into his pocket on his way to sit with Charlie Pace, who'd never owned a handkerchief in his life. Charlie licked his grubby hand and tried to smooth his jaggedly cropped hair.

"Miss Chevalier. Ah, there you are, you will be with—" the brass pencil stopped. The teacher scanned the classroom through smudged glasses. "Well, welcome back Mr. Stang. I hope this semester goes well for you. Miss Chevalier, you and Mr. Stang will be working together."

Brenda's head spun so hard her ponytail hit her cheek. Matilda picked up her books and stumbled into the seat beside Casey and his hair and his lips and his cigarette and his Pinaud's and his skull and crow tattoo. Casey rolled the matchstick languidly across his lips, then clucked and winked at her. Matilda averted her eyes.

"I flunked last year," Casey breathed. "I hope you know how to do this shit."

Matilda looked at her pencil. Casey stretched one arm over his head and stifled a yawn.

"All right, class. Where you are sitting now is where you'll sit. You'll keep the same partner for the semester. You may share notes, but no helping each other during tests. Please open your Chemistry books to the first chapter."

Threadbare cloth textbook covers thudded softly on desktops. Matilda glanced at Casey's book and inclined her head toward it.

"Christ," he said, and flopped the cover open.

The teacher chanted the first page aloud the same way he'd done the past thirteen years. Brenda wrinkled her nose at Velma's lye soap and vinegar scented dress. Stewart honked into his sodden handkerchief. And Matilda did all she could to not peek at Casey. But she peeked anyway.

When the bell rang, Casey flipped his book shut. Matilda clamped her arms to her sides when she realized the sharp sweat tang was her own. The teacher kept talking while students gathered their things. When did he say the first test would be?

"When's the test?" she whispered.

"Friday." Casey was looking right at her. She looked down quickly to write in her notebook.

Students filed out in pairs. Matilda felt like she'd been sitting in melted ice cream.

Casey ambled out the door like nothing was wrong. Like no one was sweating and blushing. Like no one was making anyone's heart pound. Matilda needed to get to the door before Brenda stopped at her desk to shoot daggers with her eyes. It was going to be a long year.

1958, Fayette, Missouri

"BRENDA SAYS SHE heard from somebody you had a little accident. That's what the letter says, a little accident." Bill looks up from the page.

Boucher. That was her last name. She never was too bright.

"I can write to her and tell her it wasn't such a little accident. Maybe you'll want to write to her."

Maybe I won't.

The Crush

1942, New Orleans, Louisiana

MATILDA WATCHED CASEY through the slats on her locker door. A stream of cigarette smoke curled up and drifted left and right behind his sleek black hair like a pair of low-hanging clouds. He slid into his flame-painted car. A Junior girl in a tight sleeveless sweater bounced toward the car on the toes of white oxfords. She leaned in the open window, plucked the cigarette from Casey's hand that rested on the wheel and took a drag, then threw her head back and laughed loudly. She held the cigarette toward him. He took it and tossed it on an arc that sailed over her shoulder. She laughed again and sprang around the front of the car to the passenger side.

Casey put the car in reverse and backed up before she got to the door. She feigned a pout. He looked in the rear-view mirror, smoothed his hair, and continued to back.

"That's Lannie Allen," Brenda said at her back. "She's a cheerleader. I hear she went all the way with him."

Matilda closed her locker and spun the dial. "All the way where?"

Brenda leaned closer and whispered in Matilda's ear. Matilda shifted her books to cover her chest. "How come she don't have a baby then?"

"Oh Lord, Matilda, nobody but your momma gets pregnant ever time." Brenda put her hand over her mouth in mock horror.

"I'm sorry I got assigned to sit with him, Brenda, I wish you'd got him."

"Matilda Chevalier, don't you lie."

"I'm not lying. Somethin' about him makes me sweat."

"You better be careful, Matilda. He's seventeen. You know what that means."

"What's it mean?"

"Oh, good lord. That he'd do to you what he did to Lannie."

"Leave me in the parking lot?"

"Oh, good lord. You know." Brenda arched her eyebrows.

"Well, I ain't like that."

"Oh, if he kisses you, you will be. I would be." Brenda pulled at her bangs. "I'm sittin' by Randy Wallace tomorrow in homeroom. I hear he's a good dancer."

Matilda twitched a half smile and rolled her eyes.

"And there's a dance Friday," Brenda added.

"I heard. You're goin' with Randy?"

"Well, that's the plan. Randy doesn't know yet." Brenda pushed her bangs off her forehead. "Don't you get in that car with Casey."

MATILDA CONCENTRATED ON the instructions while the teacher handed out mimeographed copies of the test. Her pencil scraped and slid for ten minutes before she glanced at Casey, bent over his paper, staring at the first problem.

She straightened her boney shoulders and shifted in her seat. The teacher's back was to the class. Casey looked at the answers she'd written and started writing, then whistled low through his teeth as he copied the final answer.

When class ended, Matilda shoved her books into a pile and made for the door. Casey lengthened his stride to catch up to her. Matilda's hair bounced in time with her skirt hem.

"Hey," he said.

Matilda looked straight ahead and kept walking.

"I said hey."

Matilda coasted to a stop and hugged her books tighter. "You cheated." Her voice shook in a barely audible whisper. Two girls walked by and one of them shot Matilda a withering look.

"Look, kid, I can't flunk Chemistry again."

"Then learn how to do the problems. But don't cheat." She spoke quietly to keep her voice from shaking. Casey leaned forward. She took a step backward. "I can show you how."

"Okay. When?"

"Study hall. I'm going now. I can help you for a little, but I got homework."

"Okay. Where is it?" he said. Matilda jerked her head toward the library building.

THIRTY MINUTES LATER Matilda stopped to look at the clock. "I have homework for other classes."

"You don't do it at home?"

"I have to watch my brothers and sister. And help my grandmother."

"What about your mom?"

"She doesn't live there anymore."

"Oh." Casey closed his notebook. "Hey, I owe you kid." He stood and leaned against the chair. "Wanna dance?"

"Here?"

"Tonight, at the gym. My brother's band's playin'."

"Maybe." Her cheeks felt like they'd melt from the heat.

"Okay. See you tonight."

"But I don't know if—"

He raised his hand slowly and with one finger traced a crescent on her cheek. Matilda flinched. She got that weird feeling again. She hated Brenda for telling her what Casey and that cheerleader had done.

Dance with the Devil

1942, New Orleans, Louisiana

MATILDA SNAGGED HER red chenille skirt on the windowsill and caught her breath, one foot almost to the ground. She heard her little sister Evangeline's bed springs sigh. Evangeline plopped over on her back and resumed her little girl snoring.

Matilda hopped down and brushed her hands over the front of the strawberry embroidered blouse. She hurried out of the back yard, then picked up her pace. She felt like a full-blown bad girl by the time she got to the high school gym.

The bandleader stood at the front of the riser under the basketball hoop with a saxophone hanging from a cord on his neck and black hair spiraling over his forehead. He murmured to the guys in white shirts and neckties behind him and the bass player guffawed. The saxophone player snapped his fingers four beats and raised the sax to his lips. The bass and drum's first notes rumbled across the gym floor like a boat wake on Lake Pontchartrain. The saxophone growled, howled, and rode the wave. Matilda stood to one side of the entry door, barely breathing.

Brenda Boucher sat on a bleacher beside Randy Wallace with her boob pressed against his arm. Randy's face went red to the roots of his slicked-back sandy hair when Brenda stood and lugged him to the middle of the gym floor. Girls and boys clung to each other as if they were freezing. Other couples danced at arm's length, heads tilted as though they were in a Fred Astaire and Ginger Rogers movie.

And then, Matilda stood alone. She eased into a folding chair and smiled grimly at a pimply faced Freshman girl who seemed even more out of place than she was. Matilda pretended interest in the dancers.

She half closed her eyes and her mind slid back to the dock at Baton Rouge where the band played for New Year's Eve. When Daddy waltzed her around with her feet on top of his. When he'd lift her high to twirl at the twirling parts. When the accordion player sang Jole' Blon in Cajun. When Momma danced with Gran-pap, and Gran-mim's silk dress flowed around her like water while she held somebody's baby and swished between the dancers.

In the gym, the first song ended. Dancers clapped politely and wandered toward bleachers to choose new partners.

The music began again. Matilda and the pimply girl sat while other girls were asked to dance and boys who were dropped off by doting mothers found places to hide. A chubby boy with skin like a plucked turkey leaned over the pimply faced Freshman girl, mumbled something, and the girl jumped up so fast her forehead collided with his. He led her to the dance floor. The girl stuck her arm out and clutched his hand.

Matilda slipped out of her chair and into the girl's bathroom where six other girls were fluffing their hair.

"You come with somebody?" a Sophomore girl from her homeroom class asked as she leaned toward the mirror to look at her teeth.

"No. You?" Matilda studied her own face in the mirror.

"I have somebody to dance with. He's just not here yet."

"Oh. That sounds nice." Matilda wished a stall was open so she could hide.

"You got somebody to dance with?" The girl extracted a tube of cherry-red lipstick from her bra and applied the color to her pouty lips.

"Maybe."

"Better get after it. There's three hours, and that gives us about twelve songs an hour to get lucky."

"Get lucky?" Matilda faced the girl.

"To dance. We're behind already. That's why you're hiding in here, right? Nobody asked you the first two songs?"

Matilda brooded. She might be hiding in the girl's room all night.

"Act like you're looking for somebody when we go out. Follow me."

Matilda followed the girl out, watched her wave to someone who wasn't looking her way: the picture of Miss Popular, coming out from fixing her cherry-red lips. Miss Cherry-Red Lips grabbed Matilda's wrist. "Smile. Act like you know people."

Matilda saw Shirley Sizemore across the room and waved. Shirley's face broke into a goofy grin as she lumbered toward them.

"Oh great, you went and invited the ree-tard to come over," Cherry-red Lips spewed.

Matilda turned to her. "Shirley's my friend."

Cherry-red Lips spun away and took her lips with her.

"Hi, Matilda!" Shirley had dribbled water from the fountain on the front of her dress. "You look real pretty. Let's dance."

Matilda glanced at Cherry-red Lips who'd ganged up with some girls in the corner. "Okay, Shirley."

"Hey! I've danced every dance so far. I like to dance. Do you?"

"Yes. I do." Matilda took Shirley's damp hands and tried to lead. Shirley swayed from foot to foot, holding Matilda's hands tightly. Shirley didn't care about being popular. Matilda liked that about her.

Shirley shouted, "Thanks for the dance! I gotta go ask that boy over there." She pointed at a gangly Junior at the other end of the gym, whose neck didn't come close to filling his buttoned shirt collar. Matilda started back to the empty chairs.

He was beside her. "Hi." His voice vibrated in her collarbones. The smell of Pinaud's and hair oil surrounded him. A red bowling shirt said "Casey" on the pocket and his hair reflected blue light from the bandstand. "Saw you dancing with that girl. That was nice."

The band leader called out, "Here's a song for my brother 'cause he thinks they wrote it for him."

"Come on, I asked for this song." He took Matilda's wrist and led her to one side of the gym floor. "You waltz?" He leaned so close all she could see was curled lips.

"Long time ago. With my dad."

The drummer counted, "one-two-three-one-two-three." Casey held his hand out for her and made a comical sweeping bow. Matilda blushed when Tommy Stang and the Stingers started "The Band Played On." The song took her back to when she was five years old, standing on the tops of her father's shoes, dancing to the band on the dock in Baton Rouge.

Her lungs strained for stale gym air as the boy who'd made her first week of school almost unbearable twirled her onto the dance floor. Matilda saw Cherry-red Lips jab a girl beside her. Brenda was hanging on Randy like a drowning person but looked up open mouthed at the vision of Casey Stang waltzing like the star in a dance movie with Matilda, who all of a sudden didn't look so much like an orange-haired scarecrow.

He bent close again as they made a turn. "You know this song?" She nodded. "So, sing it."

Matilda's voice came out in whispery hesitations. "Ca-sey would waltz—" She mumbled the next line, then, "and the band—played—on. He'd waltz—cross the floor—" She held her breath. She couldn't sing "with the girl he adored." She'd just die if she did.

He picked up the song at where Casey's brain was so loaded it nearly exploded and the poor girl would shake with alarm. He laughed. Not at her. Just laughed.

She skipped singing the part where he'd ne'er leave the girl.

"With the strawberry curls," He sang out. She blushed again.

"and the band—played—on," they both sang.

"Dah-Dah-Dah-Dah-Dah," he belted when he and Matilda waltzed past the band stand. Tommy Stang waved his hand in a circle over his head, and the band played on.

1958, Fayette, Missouri

"BRENDA SAYS HERE, 'I hope you write back. Let's get together next time you're in New Orleans. Wait 'til you see my three girls. Yours Truly, Brenda.'" Bill folds the letter and puts it back in the envelope. He props the get-well cards against the framed pictures.

A new nurse's aide comes in with a wash basin and towel, says she's here to give Matilda her bath, but she can come back. Bill indicates for her to go ahead. The aide takes one of the patient's arms out from under the sheet and gasps. Bill is used to gasps. So is Matilda.

Hummingbird Tattoo

1942, New Orleans, Louisiana

"I'M GONNA GO, kid. You stayin'?" Casey and Matilda walked past a gaggle of gawking girls on the bleachers.

"I gotta get home."

"I'll drive you home. Where you live?"

"Off Gentilly. It's okay, I can walk."

"Naw, it's not safe out there at night. Come on."

Casey opened the driver side door and motioned for Matilda to get in. She walked around to the passenger side door and opened it herself. The seat smelled like cigarettes and burnt sugar.

"I NEED TO stop before I drop you off. It'll just be a minute." Casey drove by the racetrack, then down a street where neon lights cast a greenish glow on the pavement. He pulled into an alley and parked beside a Buick in a three car-wide parking lot. "You wait here." A scrawny man in a pork-pie hat stepped out of the alley and fumbled to light a cigarette. "Naw, you better come with me."

Casey led her down a long hallway and pushed the door open. Matilda saw they'd come into the lobby of Lafontaine and Son Tattoo Artistry.

"GOD DAMMIT, I hate this thing." The wood-beaded curtain spattered against the spokes of the wheelchair. Eddie Lafontaine yanked the strands aside. "Casey. Gimmie ten, fifteen minutes. Don't leave." Matilda ducked her head. She didn't want Eddie to tell Casey she'd been there before.

"I'll be back in twenty," Casey began.

"I don't have to go right this minute," Matilda whispered.

Casey eyed her and shook out a cigarette. "This ain't no fast visit."

"It's okay. I don't mind." Matilda picked up the *Better Homes and Gardens* magazine. Eddie clattered back through the beads.

Matilda's heart banged so hard against her ribs she worried Casey would hear it. He ambled over to the glass topped counter, laid his smoke in the ashtray, and spun a design book around.

"Hey, come 'ere," he said with the same sideways look that had embarrassed her the first day of school. "What one you like?"

Matilda went to the counter, turned three pages, and there it was. The hummingbird. The flexed wings, the tiny feathers, the needle-like beak. Emeralds. Rubies. Iridescent. Magic.

"Like it?" Casey picked up his cigarette, tapped it, and put it to his lips.

"Pretty." Her voice was faint. The woman who'd shown designs to Matilda the day she'd bolted out of the shop came from behind the curtain. She smiled at Matilda.

"This here," Casey told the woman.

The woman slid the sheet of paper out of the sleeve in the book. "Five dollars."

"He's already paid," someone grumbled from behind the curtain.

The woman motioned to Casey and Matilda to take a seat. An older man came from behind the curtain, waving and jabbing his hands and the woman did the same back at him, with softer movements.

"That's Sonny Lafontaine," Casey whispered, "best tattoo artist there is. He's deaf so that's how they talk. The guy in the wheelchair, that's his son Eddie. He signs his work. See?" He pushed up the sleeve of the bowling shirt to show the skull and crow. "See, there in the teeth? L E."

Matilda whispered, "How come it's backwards?"

"Backwards?" Casey squinted through his cigarette smoke. "Oh. L E's for Lucky Eddie."

The woman from the counter parted the curtain. "Eddie's ready for you."

"Come on." Casey stood.

"She can stay here with me if she wants to." The woman went to the table to straighten the pile of magazines.

"Naw, come on. Come with me."

Matilda drew back her shoulders and wished it wasn't too late to cross her arms over her flat chest.

"YOU SIT OVER there. I don't need you in the way," Eddie told Matilda.

"No, Eddie, she sits here."

"Where?" Matilda looked at Casey.

"Right here. You like that bird? You're gettin' it. You help me pass Algebra, and I'll get you another one too."

"No, Stang. I don't tattoo kids." Eddie coughed and spat into the beer can taped to the wheelchair.

"No tatt, no dope, Eddie." Casey eyed Eddie.

Eddie sucked his cheeks in, twisted his lips, and glared at Casey. "Asshole. Well, get your ass up here, kid."

Matilda arranged her skirt over her knees and swung onto the chair. Her mouth went dry. She wanted that hummingbird. She wanted that tattoo because Casey Stang wanted to get it for her. She wanted it because he'd danced with her. Maybe he'd kiss her if she had a tattoo.

"Hey, do it where nobody sees, like here." Casey tapped two fingers below his collarbone. Matilda touched the top button on her blouse.

"No. I need that clear off," Eddie said. He slapped a bell on the tray beside the chair. "Mary Ellen! I need you in here." The woman parted the beads and looked in. "Get a robe for—what's your name, kiddo?"

"Matilda."

"Me and Casey are goin' out for a minute. Get that bra off her. I don't want the damn strap in my way."

"Watch your mouth," the woman warned.

Eddie hitched from his rolling stool to his wheelchair in one movement, and he and Casey left.

The woman set a faded cotton kimono on the table. "See?" She undid two buttons at one shoulder to drop a flap. "I made this robe just for ladies." Matilda watched the woman's long hands arranging things on the tray.

"Will it hurt?"

"That's what I hear. You're not dating that guy, are you?"

"No." Matilda wished it wasn't the truth.

"Good. He's not a very good guy. Why are you here with him?"

Matilda told the woman about Chemistry class. And that he'd asked her to dance and wanted to drive her home. But he wasn't her boyfriend.

"OK, but you don't need to be hanging around with a guy like that. You seem like a nice kid. And don't get a tattoo if you don't want to. I'll drive you home if—"

"I want it."

A DOOR SCREECHED open and closed. Eddie rolled in. Casey followed, hands in pockets. The woman patted Matilda's knee. "I'll be right outside."

"Ready kiddo?" Eddie's eyes were softer than before. "I put the design on first, then I do the outline. It'll hurt. I need you to hold real still. You can stop me any time. But you stop me too many times, we're done. Got it?" Matilda nodded. "It's gonna take about an hour. You good?" She nodded.

Eddie hummed "I'll Be Seeing You" while he stenciled the hummingbird. Casey winced when Eddie started the tattoo machine, then backed up to the chair against the wall, unsteady on his loafers, and sat.

Matilda focused on the cracked plaster ceiling for the first three minutes. She blinked a few times while Eddie wiped where he'd cut what felt like a thousand holes in her skin. She felt the vibration in her bones when the machine touched her. Every time the buzzing stopped, she could hear the second hand on the wall clock ticking.

Did he say something to her? Did he tell her not to hold her breath? Maybe. Maybe he did. She drew a deep breath and let it out. The pain was still there, but now it was beside her instead of right over her. The machine stopped and the springs on Eddie's rolling seat sighed. Something rattled and clinked. The whining buzz began again.

Now Eddie was humming some other song she didn't recognize. The sound of the tattoo machine droned like an airplane. Matilda stopped clenching her hands the tenth time the machine stopped and started again. She drifted on a billow of sting and burn and touch.

Eddie wiped below her collarbone again. "Done." He held out a hand mirror.

A brilliant emerald hummingbird with a garnet throat hovered on delicately flared wings below her collar bone. Her breath caught in her chest and she shuddered involuntarily.

"Oh God," she said. She looked toward Casey. He was asleep.

"Don't look at him, look at me, kiddo," Eddie said quietly. He wiped the new tattoo with something cool then tore open a paper wrapped gauze and pressed it over the hummingbird. "Keep this on a couple days. Don't be lookin' at it." His gravelly voice was returning. "Wash it with soap and water next week. Don't rub it. Put a clean gauze pad back on. It'll be pretty healed up in two weeks."

"Okay."

"And kiddo, don't be runnin 'round with this guy. He's a bum. You listenin'?" Matilda nodded absently. She wanted to look at the hummingbird one more time. Eddie pointed at her. "I mean it."

"Okay."

"You're sayin' that but if I see you out with this guy, I'll be mad at you. And you want tattoos, you come here. Nowhere else. You understand?"

Casey stirred and groaned. "Damn, I musta fell asleep. You done? Lemmie see. Oh, it's covered."

"Yeah we're done." Eddie's gravelly voice rumbled close to Matilda's ear. "Remember what I told you."

"Mary Ellen!" Eddie shouted toward the curtain.

CASEY DROPPED HER off where her street met Gentilly, revved the motor, and drove away. Matilda hurried home, keeping to the shadows of hedges and bushes. She was at the edge of the back yard when she heard the grumble of the flame painted car again. Her heart fluttered like tiny wings behind her ribs as she raced to the side of the yard where she could see the street.

She was a hairsbreadth from walking out to the sidewalk when she peered around the side of the house and saw Casey's car illuminated by the streetlamp. She shrank further into the shadows to watch the car stop at Brenda Boucher's house, six doors down. The motor sang the mating call and Brenda answered by hurrying out her front door and into Casey's car. Casey kissed her on the mouth and drove off with Brenda draped on his neck.

Matilda took three steps backward, and walked back to her bedroom window to climb in. She changed into her pajamas in the dark and padded down the hall to the bathroom, where it was safe to turn on a light. She pulled her pajama top open and stared at the gauze. She would not cry.

Tattoo Rush

1942, New Orleans, Louisiana

THE GIRLS IN the gym shower were a-buzz over Matilda's tattoo, first in whispers, then taunting and jeers until the gym teacher came to stand just beyond the spray of the nozzles with her meaty, freckled arms crossed.

Once outside, one of the girls yelled, "Hey, tattooed Matilda!" and collapsed against her gang in gales of laughter. By the last bell the whole school knew Matilda Chevalier had a tattoo.

THE FRIDAY AFTERNOON after first quarter exams, Matilda took five dollars out of her father's medal box, told Gran-mim she was going to study at Brenda's house, and headed to Lafontaine's.

Mary Ellen helped her pick a flower design to fit around her hummingbird, gave her the kimono and sat her in the red chair in Eddie's studio. Eddie came in hollow-cheeked, eyes glittering. He snatched the trace sheet free of the clothespin clipped to the overhead light and went to work. He was a half hour into the tattoo when he shut his machine off to reload an inkpot. "Hey, you show your friends at school this hummingbird?"

"Not on purpose, but they saw it in gym. Ain't my friends. They called me tattooed Matilda."

"Yeah? They say it nice, or mean?"

"Mean."

"Well they're assholes. Your mama see it?"

"I told you. She ran off."

"Oh yeah. With the father of the kids? Every time I saw her she was pregnant."

"Hell no. All different fathers. Looie was the first. His daddy was a Mexican. Then Dallas, daddy was some guy from Texas. I swear to God." She stared at the wrinkles in her skirt for a moment. "Last two she named Evangeline and Churchill because that's where the guys she got pregnant with were goin'."

"Huh. She took all of 'em with her?"

"Hell no. Me and my grandmother take care of 'em."

Matilda welcomed the hammering rush of the tattoo machine. The thousand little wounds in her skin melted the school hallway jeers into a watery puddle.

AN HOUR AND fifteen minutes later the hummingbird dipped its slender beak into an open yellow hibiscus that bloomed amid a bed of fluted leaves. Eddie let out a low whistle. "Damn, I do good work. Hey, who paid, you or lover boy?"

"I paid. I haven't even seen him at school for two weeks."

"Told you that sonofabitch was a bum," Eddie grumbled. "See ya." He rolled into the next room.

Matilda had something better than Casey Stang. She had something all her own, and it was bright and breathtaking. She could look at the tiny bird and the orange hibiscus blossom any time she needed some place to go, far from the world where fathers died and mothers let their kids down. This palm-sized work of art was hers alone and wouldn't fade away like the hickeys on Brenda Boucher's lily-white neck.

1943-44 New Orleans, Louisiana

FOR MATILDA'S NEXT tattoo, her Junior year, Eddie designed a bluebird flying over a spray of cherry blossoms that went from shoulder to elbow. He was wiping her arm with alcohol and touched a bruise on her forearm.

"What happened here?"

"I fell."

"The hell you did. Who did this?"

"Some girls at school. One of 'em said I was a high yella freak. I didn't even know what that meant."

"Yeah? You punch them bitches for sayin' that? Somebody called me something like that I'd punch 'em. You punch 'em in the nose next time they talk bad to you. Be right back, okay, kiddo?"

Matilda nodded.

Eddie rolled to the back room for a smoke before he traced the outline. The pinch of pure Burmese heroin in the glass pipe masked his own pain and rage. The Burmese offered temporary protection from tenacious nightmares of war, and rude, daily reminders of loss. The tattoo machine was his shield.

He returned with hands steady as a surgeon's to outline, to leave his marks.

Matilda had grown to crave the gentle, firm, seemingly uninvolved touch of the tattooist holding flesh taut while the creation of art on her skin added layers of safety to her hidden ache.

Eddie timed his hold on the hit so it would slide through his cells exactly as her breathing slowed when she reached the place he and ink took her.

For Matilda it was just like love, except the hurt was only on the outside. Eddie never let her down.

IN MARCH OF her Senior year, Matilda showed Eddie a magazine photo of Josephine Baker.

"What, you want me to tattoo this picture? Who is that?"

"The skirt. See, it's made out of bananas. She's a famous dancer. Can you do it?"

Eddie reached for his pad and began sketching a narrow-hipped woman.

Matilda leaned closer to watch. "Not her, just the skirt."

"Placement, kiddo, placement." Eddie did the outline and fill on Matilda's right side that day and finished the banana skirt tattoo the next week.

MATILDA BUSSED TABLES after graduation in the restaurant where her grandfather cooked between race seasons, until one of the waitresses quit. The manager gave her five lunch and three dinner shifts a week. Women smiled kindly and asked if she was a dancer. The men who eyed her pale caramel legs as she moved from table to table left the biggest tips.

Matilda turned half her salary and tips over to her grandmother and put the rest in her father's medal box. She took money out to spend on ink, touch, and forgetting.

Eddie's Score

1943, New Orleans, Louisiana

WHEN SONNY AND Mary Ellen bought a house at the edge of the Garden District, Eddie told his father he could make some extra money renting out the extra rooms in back of the shop. Casey Stang was his first renter.

Two weeks later Sonny's old friend Police Chief Dole Fancher had a quota to fill and set up a sting to catch Casey with a new batch of heroin they knew had come in from Florida. Eddie, when asked to let the cops into Casey's room so they could search it, let them into his own room, since he'd moved his own stash into an unused drawer in a little used storage room.

What the police did find in Eddie's room, which they thought was Casey's was Eddie's Purple Heart medal in its box. They brought it out to show Eddie what his tenant had stolen.

"Well, that no good sonofabitch," Eddie said, closing the lid on the box.

"That's his car outside, right?" Fancher waved his pen toward the back door.

"Was. He sold me that car couple weeks back. I bet he has his stash somewhere else in town. He was dumb but not dumb enough to bring that crap in here."

The officers who'd found Eddie's Purple Heart in what they thought was Casey's room exchanged a look.

"We'll go check some other places we've seen him hanging out. And after all you done for your country, that clown steals your Purple Heart." The officer shook his head.

"Thanks, guys. Hey, I got somebody waiting for ink, so if you're done with me . . ." Eddie jabbed a thumb over his shoulder.

A MINUTE LATER Lucky Eddie was on the rolling chair beside Matilda, adjusting the crouching tiger he'd designed to cover her thigh. "How much Mary Ellen charge you?"

"Six and a half bucks. I saw the police car outside. You kill somebody?"

"Yeah? Real funny. Your lover boy got arrested. Told you he was no good."

"He isn't my lover boy. More like your lover boy, since he was livin' with you."

"You're kinda mouthy aren't ya?" He lit a cigarette and squinted at her. "I'm gonna make the colors real bright, in case you ever get a real tan."

"Hey, can you make the tiger's eyes the same color as mine?"

Eddie looked from the design sheet to Matilda's amber eyes. "Yeah. That'll look good."

"Can I have a cigarette?"
"No way, kiddo."

EDDIE SENT MATILDA home three hours later with a fix in the shape of a crouching tiger tattooed on her leg. The drawer of argyle socks in Casey's room coughed up four foil wrapped balls of heroin, two pipes, and a rubber banded roll of twenties. He found the rest of the stash in a shoebox in the trunk of Casey's flame-painted car. Eddie stuffed Casey's clothes in two boxes and left them in the alley.

THE MONKEY TAPPED ragged claws on the dresser, listening for Eddie. The door opened and Jesus Christ in a wheelchair rolled in with a shitload of the good stuff. The monkey lurched at Eddie and humped his leg.

"Hang on you little asshole, got one more thing to do," Eddie whispered and pushed his little buddy aside.

Eddie called his dad's friend Rufus. Would he come get this car and install a hand clutch and brake, and while he's at it, repaint the sides and hood and clean the upholstery? He told Rufus he'd pay cash.

PART 4
Circus

1958, Fayette, Missouri

... BUT HIS BRAIN was so loaded it nearly exploded. Is that what happened to me? Where is everybody? ... and the poor girl would shake with alarm ... where is everybody?

Bill watches his wife's eyelids twitch as she grimaces. He squeezes her hand and her face relaxes. "You know I'm here don't you, baby?"

Is it time to get dressed already? I thought I'd take a nap but now I feel terrible. How long did I sleep?

It's been four and a half weeks.

First Circus

1944, New Orleans, Louisiana

THE LONG-LIMBED TEEN whose cloud of apricot-orange hair provided shade of its own stood under a tree in the Fair Grounds Race Course infield watching two elephants pulling circus tent poles into place.

An enormous blue-black man drove tent stakes with two blows of a nine-pound maul while a well-tanned white man with rolled up shirt sleeves held stakes steady. The big man hummed "Some Day My Prince Will Come" from *Snow White.*

"Maurice. Don't you know another song? 'John Henry' or something?" Gio Fiscalini glanced up at the black man who let his maul rest against his tree trunk size leg while Fiscalini dragged four more stakes out of the wagon.

Maurice guffawed heartily and continued singing. "Some-day we'll meet again. And away to his castle we'll go ..."

"Good God, Maurice." Gio put his hand to his forehead. Maurice beamed at his best friend in the United States, next to his lover Sam Sanger, the elephant trainer.

" ... To be happy forever, I know ..." Maurice switched to a sonorous Shakespearian voice. "It looks as though the locals are showing up. Shall I go frighten that one away?"

Gio glanced toward the tree. "And let them know our strong man Mazubo from deepest darkest Africa is really a Brit and a big twink?" They bawled a short laugh. Gio picked up another stake. "I need another local kid to sell cotton candy for Milana. I'll hire that one if she's still there when we're finished."

"She'd be quite beautiful if one liked the paler skinned mulattos of your country. Or perhaps she is quadroon, with that complexion." Maurice wiped his brow with a monogrammed handkerchief. He flashed Gio a gap-toothed smile. "And if one liked girls. How many more, boss?"

"Two more. And I happen to like girls. Grown up ones. Hey, shouldn't you have an African accent?"

Maurice shifted his grip on the maul. "Perhaps hooting like a savage would be equally appropriate." He struck the stake with practiced precision.

"Lord, what I put up with." Gio hefted another stake. "Last one." The maul sang two notes against the final stake. "See you at breakfast."

"I'll be the big good-looking negro with the plate of pancakes." Maurice sauntered toward the back of the train, swinging his maul like a walking stick.

Fiscalini checked on roustabouts lacing tent sections then had the ticket booth moved, then went back to the side of the tent where he'd seen the girl. She was still there.

"Hello," he called out. She raised a hand. "Gio Fiscalini is my name. This is our circus. Do you like circus?" She nodded. "Well, you should come tonight, then. I need a smart girl to sell cotton candy for my sister. Think you can do that?"

"Maybe. How much you pay?"

"Free admission. Can you work matinee and night shows?"

"I already have a job tomorrow night."

"What do you do?"

"Wait tables."

"How much to hire you away from the restaurant? To work for our circus?"

"I make a dollar a shift, plus tips."

"I'll pay a dollar a show to sell cotton candy."

"Plus tips."

Matilda watched a translucent-skinned woman in a white robe, marabou trimmed slippers and turban make her way to the tent. Gio waited for her eyes to return to him.

"We pay a commission for good sales. I didn't get your name."

"Matilda."

"Well, Matilda, how about a dollar a shift, and ten percent of your sales and you sell all the cotton candy you can sell."

"Do I get a uniform?"

"Yes, my sister Milana will give you a uniform. Is that a yes?"

"Twenty percent," Matilda said evenly.

"If you sell more than three dollars-worth, I'll go fifteen."

Matilda looked toward the tent. "All right."

"Wonderful. Be at the ticket booth this afternoon at five."

Matilda flashed a triumphant smile and dashed home.

AN ELDERLY MAN with papery hands shuffled up to the ticket booth at five, cupped his cauliflower ear to hear Matilda's question and pointed to a faded blue trailer with orange trim where a large woman with coils of jet-black hair struggled to raise a window covering. Matilda hurried over to help prop and secure the panel.

"Thank you, honey, are you helping me tonight?"

"Yes'm. I'm Matilda."

Milana Fiscalini had been selling concessions for the family circus ever since her weight had tipped over the two-hundred and sixty-pound mark, which had coincided with her twenty-ninth birthday a few years back. Before that, she'd worked the dog show, and before that, she'd been an elephant handler, and before that, a rosinback rider, and before that a trapeze flier, and before that the child protégé' on the trapeze with her uncle, father, and aunt.

Milana was content with a niche in the family business that wouldn't leave her arms and legs broken. By thirty-three she was widowed once, divorced once, and abandoned in Tampa by a fast talker. Now, she had a job that made people happy, a winter home in Florida, and sugar. Sugar was the love of her life.

She handed Matilda a blue and orange striped blouse and blue apron. "Cotton candy is ten cents. Can you count change for a dollar?" Matilda demonstrated that she could. "Carry the tray above your head so little kids don't grab at the sticks and make change with one hand. Put dollar bills in your left pocket, change in your right." Matilda glanced at the stack of two-layered wooden trays, each with ten drilled holes. "You come back when the tray is empty and turn in your money but keep a dollar in change. I keep a tally."

Matilda looked around the trailer, clutching the blouse and apron to her chest. "Go in there," Milana pointed at a smaller tent attached to the big top. "That's the women's dressing tent. Bring your things back here. They'll be safe with me."

Two three-foot tall women in the dressing tent cussed like merchant Marines while they pulled black and white striped tights over their round rumps.

A glittering, silver costume with impossibly narrow straps and a deep "V" front and back shimmered like diamonds on a hanger beside a mirror. The bottom half of the garment culminated in a satin lined crotch a scant three inches wide. Matilda slipped out of her blouse and stood in her bra and skirt, staring at the silvery costume.

"Well, will ya look at that, Betty? We got us a new tattooed lady," one of the little women said.

Matilda turned to them. The two women came closer to peer up at her hummingbird, bluebird, and flower covered arms.

"Pretty if you like that kind of thing. Hi. I'm Velma. This here's Betty." Velma's upper and lower incisors were missing on one side.

"Not for me. This body is a temple of God." The bow-legged Betty's drooping left eye fixed on Matilda.

"More like a tent for boy scouts." They howled, hanging on each other.

Matilda turned back toward the dressing table where containers of makeup lay open, smelling of talc, cornstarch, wax, and butter. She hurried to button the blouse. A bulbous nosed man the same size as the two women poked his head in and leered. "Pre-show in thirty minutes, full makeup."

"Pervert," the droopy eyed woman yelped.

MILANA LOADED THREE cotton candy trays and told Matilda she could go to work any time. Matilda headed for the line at the ticket booth.

One of the four ruddy-faced kids waiting in line with their parents jumped up and down.

"Oh, Daddy, can we have cotton candy?"

"How much is cotton candy, miss?"

"Ten cents if you buy from me," Matilda whispered loudly. "Twelve cents from those other girls."

"That's a good deal, dear, get us all one." The even ruddier-faced mother prodded the man, who produced three quarters.

"We'll take two at that price," a handsome blonde boy behind the family of four called out. He gave Matilda a quarter. "Keep the change."

"Miss, I'll take those last two," the round-bellied woman with the equally round bellied, squirming toddler held out two dimes.

Matilda sold three more trays to the people in line, while the other girls who'd shown up to sell stood bewildered at the tent entrance.

While the two little women and the little man raced around the ring playing tag, and the tall white-faced clown in the lime green pantaloons and conical hat bowed gallantly to the women seated in the front row, Matilda offered people who came in empty handed cotton candy at "ten cents instead of fifteen, because you're here early." She promised to honor her price all night. The ninth time she emptied her tray, Milana met her at the entrance with another tray, grinning.

Between the elephant act and the clowns doing a stilt act that ended with one of them falling, Matilda sold another tray. The Flying Fiscalinis were announced as the final act. Sales were brisk until platinum blonde Sally Fiscalini, wearing a white costume with a sheer, skimpy skirt that hugged her slim thighs stepped onto the platform and raised her arm. The crowd went silent while the spotlight followed the star performer across the top of the tent. Matilda watched in awe.

THE NEXT DAY Matilda sold twelve trays for the matinee. Marina sent a roustabout to the supply car for more sugar.

That night Giovanni Fiscalini, Sr. noticed Matilda working the crowd from his trapeze platform and his sixty-four-year-old wandering eye came to life. His brother Antonio sailed away toward the platinum blonde in the shimmering silver costume Matilda had seen in the dressing tent the night before. Antonio caught the woman's wrists at the end of a pirouette and returned her to her bar. Sally landed like a diamond-encrusted bird on her platform, glaring at her husband for not reaching for her hand. Giovanni launched off and traded places with his brother Antonio in mid-air. Antonio landed, then disappeared into the darkness. The spotlight was on Sally and Giovanni.

Matilda watched, holding an empty cotton candy tray to her chest. She was transfixed on the glittering costume. The fabric skimmed over the slight curve of the woman's breasts, held in place by the hopes of wives and mothers in the audience, and pulled precariously low by the wishful thinking of the men beside them. The woman's ankles were in the man's hands. The stouter man came from the shadows again and the woman was passed to him. The woman twisted at the peak of a swing and rotated to face Giovanni on the other bar.

Matilda could barely breathe. She knew the scene from *Life Magazine*. The woman who sparkled like diamonds in the tight-fitting fabric cut so high the hip bones showed sailed toward the man with the chiseled chin. Just like the magazine. The man's eyes on her eyes. Her eyes on his face. Her ruby-red lips catching a glimmer of light. Like rubies. Like diamonds. Like magic.

Second Taste

1944, New Orleans, Louisiana

"NO, POP, SHE'S just a kid. No."

"Come on, Gio, for a little comedy, that's all. Tell her we'll pay her an extra dollar. Get the costume from the cannibal act."

"Pop. We are not doing that act. It's vulgar."

"Just that outfit with the torn skirt. And I need Bill to carry her up, so get his face hair and costume out. Come on. It'll be great."

Gio rested his hands on his hips. "Really Pop? You ask Sally what she thinks?"

"She'll think it's wonderful."

"Liar. Who's gonna sell cotton candy?"

"She'll be selling. The costume can go under the blouse and apron."

Gio stalked off to one of the cars to dig through costume trunks.

MATILDA SOLD COTTON candy the first half of the show and well into the second half, until a man in tattered burlap pants with patches of hair glued to his face came running at her. He bent as he reached her, putting his head to one side of her hips. She gulped in surprise.

"It's okay," he whispered loudly. "Just do what I tell you."

He threw her over his shoulder and aped his way across the ring. She dropped her half-full tray of cotton candy on the tanbark in front of the bleachers. At the trapeze ladder, he started climbing.

"I'm Bill. I won't drop you. Scream. Wave your arms. Just don't kick me." He stopped half-way up, when Gio Fiscalini stepped to the center of the ring, into a single spotlight.

"Ladies, Gentlemen, please, keep your children close. The Borneo Wild Man has escaped. We need complete quiet," Gio announced.

A woman shrieked. Bill jiggled Matilda. "Scream now." Matilda screamed and flapped her arms.

"Good job. Pull the uniform blouse off over your head and hold on to your costume top." Bill kept climbing. "Drop the apron and blouse. I'll grab a bar, and you have to hang on tight to my waist. Act like you're scared. Don't kick. We're going to fly across and back, and then I'll swing you up. Giovanni will grab you by the ankles. Don't kick. He'll need to kind of sling you to get you where he needs you. When he says 'now' you swing your arms up as hard as you can."

A teenage girl in the audience shrieked when the uniform blouse and apron dropped to the tanbark. The tattered top and skirt Matilda had been instructed to wear under the uniform shed strips that floated down into the audience.

"Help me! Help me!" Matilda yelled.

"Doin' great, hon, almost to the top. Don't grab anything up there." Bill kept climbing.

The spotlight swung from Gio to the Borneo Wild Man and Matilda. Gasps and a few laughs from children were hushed by mothers. Men stared up wondering if the girl's tattered blouse would disintegrate at the top of the ladder. Little boys wondered if they'd get to see panties. A drum roll rattled the air. Four clowns raced around under Bill and Matilda with an oversized butterfly net. Another spotlight snapped onto the other platform, and there stood Giovanni Fiscalini Sr., tanned, muscular, and handsome in a one-shouldered leopard-print leotard. The drumroll intensified.

"Okay, hang on. Just hang on," Bill breathed. He lunged off the platform holding the bar. Matilda clung to his waist and got a mouthful of back hair as she let out a bloodcurdling scream that was more real than Bill had anticipated. "Let go of me when he has your ankles."

Fiscalini leapt off his platform, turned over to hang by his knees and extended his hands toward her.

"Let go of me when he has you," Bill said. "He has you. Let go."

Matilda's tumble of curls spilled out of her ponytail holder and streamed around her face as she hung upside down from Giovanni Fiscalini's hands.

Fiscalini said, "Now!" and she swung her arms upward. He switched out one hand from her ankle to grab her arm. She winced. He pulled her up toward his shoulders. "Just let me get you." He pulled again. "Put your arms around my neck." As he swung back and forth Matilda's apricot hair trailed behind her, then covered her face, trailed behind her again, covered her face again.

Giovanni unfolded his legs on an upward arc, tumbled like a sparrow in an updraft, and fell to the net on his back, with Matilda in his arms. He lay still for a moment, and the audience came to life with thunderous applause. The clowns rushed to the side of the net to help Matilda down. Giovanni took a bow while the clowns jogged out of the ring carrying the astonished girl over their heads. Giovanni flipped gracefully out of the net and ran after them, spotlight shining on his greased blue-black hair. The audience continued clapping after he exited.

Eddie Lafontaine was in the audience with Sonny and Mary Ellen. He nudged his father and signed 'How about that? I did the work on that girl. Bet some women come in the shop next week.' Sonny nodded and made the "OK" sign.

The hobo clown with the broom and pan swept up Matilda's uniform blouse and held it up like a prize. The clown handed the garment to Matilda in the wings, along with her apron, which had been rescued by one of the little women. Her change and cotton candy earnings were still in the pockets.

The Borneo Wild Man sat in front of a lighted mirror, peeling hairy patches from his face. Matilda saw that he was not as homely as he'd seemed when he was the shaggy wild thing that had abducted her.

"I lost my hair band." She stood behind him, patting her pockets. "Do you have a rubber band?" The Wild Man smeared cold cream on his face and scrubbed at the last of the rubber cement. He smiled at her reflection in the mirror.

"Sweetheart, if I were you, I'd leave that beautiful hair loose and go make some money for the rest of the night."

Matilda's face turned crimson. She dashed out the back of the tent, put the uniform blouse and apron back on, hurried to Milana's trailer for more cotton candy and sold ten more trays before the end of the show.

She ran all the way home with bruises on her arms and ankles, hair full of wind-knots, and a longing to fly again.

Ooga Booga

1958, Fayette, Missouri

"I'M—I'M SORRY, I didn't mean to stare." The nurse's aide blushes.

"Oh, she's used to people looking at her tattoos. That's what she's famous for," Bill says.

Hey, where's my costume? It was new.

The aide finishes the sponge bath, changes the pillowcase and leaves.

Bill takes his wife's hand. "You want me to tell you about when I fell in love with you, or should I read to you?"

I don't know why I can't make you hear me.

"Okay, I'll tell you."

1944, New Orleans, Louisiana

"HELLO, LITTLE BEAUTY." Matilda looked up from her pile of change. Giovanni Fiscalini looked older at eleven-thirty in the morning than he'd appeared the night before when he was rescuing her from the Borneo Wild Man.

"Hello."

"What is your name dear?" He flashed his showman's smile, looking around the trailer. "Is Milana treating you well?"

"Matilda. Yes."

"And does Matilda Yes have a last name?"

"Chevalier."

"I knew you were French. Do you want to know how I knew?" He leaned against the counter-top, blocking the door.

"I'm not French. My parents were from Baton Rouge."

"Yes, my beauty, many beautiful people of French descent live there." He tilted his head and leaned closer. "Oh, those eyes, Matilda. I want you to do the act we did last night with me for the matinee."

"Sure." She touched her bruised wrist.

"Wonderful. I'll send over a new costume. Today, you'll be my Fair Skinned Nubian Beauty."

"What's that?"

"A lovely name for the way you look." The trailer shifted when three hundred pounds of Milana Fiscalini came up the steps. "Ah, there you are, my sweet." Giovanni kissed his daughter's rouged cheek. "I was just talking with our lovely Matilda here. She's agreed to be in the show this afternoon."

"She has? Look what you did to her arms, Pop." Milana touched a lacquered fingernail to Matilda's wrist.

"I'll see you for the matinee, my beauty." Fiscalini turned to leave.

"Pop, what does Sally think?" Milana folded hefty arms over ribs she hadn't felt in fifteen years.

"Your step-mother does not make decisions about the show." He snapped the collar of his fine cotton shirt up and went toward his railroad car.

"Hon, I'm sorry. My dad's an old letch sometimes."

"Is that like them leeches that suck blood?"

Milana's bosom heaved with her laugh. "Seems the show last night has everybody talking, and ticket sales are good when that happens. That's why he wants you to do the act. But don't think you have to."

One of the little women waddled up the steps to the concession trailer with a paper sack and held it out toward Matilda.

"I got your costume, girlie. Boss says put this on under your uniform. Says wear the slippers in here instead of your shoes. Says leave your hair loose."

MATILDA DUCKED INTO the dressing tent to slip her blouse and skirt off and stepped into the ring in the costume she'd been given to wear with the apron and striped blouse over it. The costume was skin-tight and nude colored, with a skirt that was nothing more than lengths of green taffeta that resembled long strips of dried grass. The Borneo Wild Man in his glued-on face hair ran across the ring toward Matilda. She screamed, threw her empty tray at him, then her apron, then her blouse. He batted them aside, scooped her up, and climbed the ladder with her over his shoulder.

"Nice touch. Here we go," he said.

Matilda cried out in mock terror when he shifted her on his shoulder for better balance.

Giovanni appeared at the edge of the ring in a khaki shirt and pants, and a pith helmet, which he swept from his head as the spotlight swung his way. Bill stopped climbing and yelled in gibberish. Matilda started laughing, which got Bill laughing. He growled to cover it.

"Shhh. Don't make me laugh. You're supposed to be scared. Scream or something."

Matilda shouted in gibberish. A wave of laughter rolled across the crowd.

Giovanni saw what was happening and ad-libbed. "Unhand her you savage!" he shouted from the ladder across the ring. Bill bellowed back in his version of Borneo-ese. When he turned around on the platform to shake his hairy arm at people behind him, Matilda rested her hands on his back, pushed herself up to stare, bug eyed at the adventurer in khaki, shook her fist at him, and jabbered gibberish, stopped to take a deep breath and jabbered some more. The audience went wild.

"Little girl, you just became a star," Bill said under his breath. "Stay on my shoulder, I'll tell you when to slide down." He grabbed the bar and pushed off. "Hoo Hoo Hoo Hoo," he hooted as they swung toward Giovanni.

"Aat Aat Aat Aat," Matilda screeched. She flapped her hands out behind her. The tent filled with whistles and cheers. Fiscalini twirled forward and landed with both feet between his hands, then stood up on the bar as Bill and Matilda flew past him. He made a sweeping motion of relief across his forehead.

Bill swung to the other platform. Matilda pushed her mass of flying curls back with one hand. "Ooga booga booga," she yelled as they landed. Bill took a bow, which put Matilda's feet on the platform, and she pinwheeled one arm wildly. Amid more laughs and cheers from the audience, Bill reached for her arm.

"I'm fine," she whispered.

Bill secured the bar to the platform, hooting and howling as he did.

"Laaadies and Gentlemen, boys and girls," Gio announced from his ringside stand, "Please stay in your seats. He's from the deep, and dangerous jungles of Borneo. The Borrr-neee-ooo Wiiild Maaan." Bill shook his fists at the crowd. "And it looks as though he has met his match." A few catcalls and wolf whistles rang out. "She was discovered by explorers living among a tribe of snow-white apes, in the treetops of Nubia. The Fair-Skinned Nubian Beauty, Miss Matilda."

Matilda stood stock still on the platform as the spotlight shimmered on her face. A kid from school coughed out a mouthful of popcorn. "Hey look! That's Tattooed Matilda!"

Matilda grabbed the ladder and swung around it, put her feet on the rungs and did a Josephine Baker dance like she'd seen in a movie. The tent shook with applause and hooting. Giovanni Fiscalini watched from the platform and gesticulated to ringmaster Gio.

"Hey, what's that?" Gio shouted up. "You want us to keep that wild man up there, so you can come down?"

The elder Fiscalini nodded dramatically.

"Go-baddy boogie waloogie," Matilda chattered. She unhooked the bar while Bill was composing himself and leapt off the platform to swing away from the Borneo Wild Man.

"Shit," Bill said.

Fiscalini reacted by launching toward her.

Matilda realized she had no idea what to do next.

Fiscalini said, "Pump with your legs on the backswing."

She did while he flipped into catching position.

"Now wait." When he was two yards away he said, "Let go," and when she opened her hands, he caught her arms. He kicked out into the shimmering spotlight-drenched air and dropped to the net on his back with Matilda held tight.

The Fair-Skinned Nubian Beauty, Miss Matilda didn't know a thing about trapeze, but it didn't matter. She was the talk of the town. They repeated the jungle rescue act that night in front of a record crowd, including Gran-pap, Gran-mim, Looie, Dallas, Evangeline, and Churchill.

Gran-pap found Gio and Giovanni around the backside of the tent after the show and thanked them for giving his granddaughter a job for the weekend. He didn't care much for the skimpy costume, he said, but he guessed it covered more than it looked like it did.

The older Fiscalini thanked Gabriel Durand for raising such a fine girl. He was used to smoothing the ruffled feathers of fathers, boyfriends, and husbands. Gabriel thanked him for understanding a grandfather's concern, gathered up his family, and took them home. Matilda ran home thirteen dollars richer for the shows and sales.

Bill Kazarian was peeling off facial hair and packing the Borneo Wild Man costume and didn't get to say goodbye to Matilda. His heart cracked just a little, knowing she had gone.

Finding Matilda
1944, On A Circus Train Headed for Lake Charles, Louisiana

"HEY, NOSH, YOU in or not?" Sam Sanger, the elephant trainer for Fiscalini Brothers Circus shuffled a new deck of cards on the makeshift table in the boxcar while his lover Maurice pulled up crates for the other players.

Ignacio relit the stub of his cigar. "Yeah, deal me in. Jokers wild?" He hefted his three-foot two-inch self onto an apple box.

Maurice sighed. "When will you American heathens learn to play bridge. Sammy, my love, you choose the game. You and Eloise were the biggest stars of the weekend." Sam continued shuffling. Maurice snuck a glance at his lover's manicured fingernails.

"But did you watch Bill hauling that pretty quadroon girl up the ladder?" Sam lolled his well-coiffed head toward the rear of the boxcar, with a sly smile. "Hey Bill!" he called over his shoulder, "You playing cards or daydreaming?"

Maurice grinned. "Ah yes, I heard the ruckus and peeked in. She was an exquisite thing, and funny."

Bill Kazarian came in from the back deck and nudged a three-legged stool closer to the table.

Sam began flipping cards toward Maurice, Ignacio, and Bill. "Nosh wants Jokers Wild. Okay with you? Hush my big strong man, I know, you want bridge," he stage-whispered to Maurice, "but you'll have your choice of entertainment later tonight."

"Oh please, will you knock it off? You two'r makin' me sick." Ignacio picked up five cards.

"What's the matter, little man? Lonesome for companionship?" Maurice crinkled his eyes at Ignacio.

"Not unless you got somethin' besides a big pecker in them tight pants."

"OK you two, stop bickering and get your bets on the table." Sam tossed a chip to the middle.

Maurice raised one eyebrow. "Did you get that young lady's name, Bill?"

"Matilda Chevalier." Bill flushed while he straightened his poker chips. Sam and Maurice exchanged a knowing look.

Ignacio grunted. "Hey 'member when me and Velma sent Betty up the ladder in that monkey costume to chase the boss? Sally was so pissed she didn't look at us for a week."

Bill rearranged his cards. "Hey, Maurice, did I ante yet?" Maurice shook his head and Bill flipped a white chip onto the pile.

"You seem a little distracted. Is there something you would like to tell us, Mr. Kazarian?" Maurice pursed his lips. "Oh, don't tell us you are thinking of that girl in New Orleans. Very pretty, but young."

Bill stared at the cards in his hand.

Ignacio set his cigar on the edge of the crate. "Full house, boys, read 'em and weep." He swept a stubby hand over the cards.

Maurice sighed. "I don't believe that girl has even been kissed." He displayed a dazzling grin.

"Now, Maur, don't embarrass Bill. I think he's in love." Sanger shuffled the cards again and pointed at Ignacio. "Oh no, Nosh, you don't take our money and go, we have two more hands to play. Sit."

"Screw you, you big queer," Ignacio grumbled.

"And you're a stumpy freak," Sam chortled. He dealt again.

Bill sighed heavily. "What day we start in Houston?"

"Thursday. We stop for a day in Lake Charles." Maurice watched Bill's face. "You're going back to New Orleans, aren't you Bill?"

"I can catch the train out of Lake Charles, and still get back to Houston. Might have to take a bus part of the way."

"Aw, shit, Bill." Ignacio clenched his teeth on the cigar he'd been nursing. "You can have Betty tonight. She likes hairy guys."

"Stop, Nosh." Maurice put his cards face down on the crate. "How will you find her?"

"Maybe I can find the tattoo place and they'll know where she lives."

"Oh, for heaven's sake," Sam said. "You're serious."

Bill cleared his throat and shoved a red chip toward the center of the crate. Maurice touched Sam's leg to stop him.

"She prob'ly has five boyfriends better lookin' than you and me both, ya big ape." Ignacio leaned forward as though to slap down his cards and farted. "Was that you, Sammy?"

Sam laid down a full house. "Dammit," the little man yapped. "I'm dealing next."

Sam handed Nosh the deck. Maurice flashed Bill a toothy smile. Maurice loved a good romance.

BILL KAZARIAN, IN his best trousers, a white shirt, and tie swung onto the train platform in Lake Charles, Louisiana at eight the next morning with his tattered leather valise. He caught a train headed for New Orleans twenty minutes later.

At the New Orleans Fair Grounds Racetrack train station, he asked the ticket clerk if he knew of a tattoo shop. The clerk didn't. Bill had a moment of despair, then remembered Maurice said he'd overheard the girl saying she worked at a restaurant close by. Bill asked what restaurant was close.

The clerk nodded. "This time of year, Liuzza's By the Track. Real nice."

THE HOSTESS LED Bill to a window table. "Carmen will be your waitress."

"Excuse me, does a girl named Matilda work here?"

"Well, yes. Is that who you'd like?" Bill nodded. His pulse quickened.

The mop of ginger hair was pulled into a tight bun on top of her head and her arms were covered with long sleeves, but there was no mistaking the girl making her way through the early lunch crowd to the solo at the window table was Matilda Chevalier. She flapped her order book open and waited.

"Hello, Matilda."

"Oh, mother of God," she whispered. "What are you doing here?"

"I—well, I had a few days off. I heard this is a good place for lunch."

"What can I get you?" She straightened her shoulders and tapped her pencil on her order pad.

"How about the linguica in marinara."

"Yep. To drink?" He ordered iced tea. She scooted away, brought the tea back with a wry smile and went to take orders from another table. She was back with a plate in five minutes. "Anything else for now?"

"No, thank you. When do you get off?"

"Two."

"May I come back and see you then?"

Matilda's face flushed. "I might have somewhere to go after work."

"I'll wait for you and walk you there, if that's all right." Bill ate lunch, paid his sixty-cent bill, and left a dollar tip. He was waiting outside the restaurant at two.

SHE WALKED BESIDE him in silence until they crossed at Gentilly. "I thought you all were leaving Sunday."

"We did. I got off in Lake Charles and came back."

"What for?"

"For lunch at Liuzza's."

Matilda's eyebrows scrunched together. "Really?"

"No, but it sounded good. I—" He stopped to find words that wouldn't sound ridiculous. He imagined her hair flowing out behind her as they sailed out over the ring. And the tiger tattoo on her thigh.

His brain skidded back to the sidewalk, to the lithe and willowy, close to graceful, almost breast-less girl he'd carried up the ladder. He knew he had to say something pretty quick or he'd lose his nerve. "You sure had the audience going. The guys I work with said you were so funny it was like you'd done an act somewhere else before."

"My Gran-pap wasn't none too happy about it. Why'd you come back to New Orleans? Don't say lunch."

"I've been thinkin' about a tattoo." Bill stuffed his hands in his pockets.

"I know a good place. Want to go?"

"I didn't mean about getting one." Bill blushed as red as Matilda did.

"WHO'S THAT TILDA'S with?" Gabriel leaned into the glass pane in the door. Cheree stilled her crochet hook and looked at him through her quarter inch thick lenses.

"Hello to you too, my sweet." She pushed the lamp arm aside and got to her feet.

"Hello, ma Cher. Tilda is with a man. I've never seen him before."

Cheree looked through her upper glasses at her husband and put out her arms. "Well, yes, I'd love a kiss. Thank you for asking." He put his hands on her arms and pecked her cheek.

"Sorry. Who is the man?"

"I have no idea." Cheree pulled the lace curtain aside to watch her granddaughter leaning against the mailbox. The man stood two feet away from Matilda, hands in pockets, leaning toward her. "I do believe he is going to kiss her."

"I best get out there."

"Gabriel Durand you will do no such thing. She is a young lady. It's high time she had a gentleman caller."

"Gentleman. How's that?" Gabriel stepped to the window to watch.

"He's wearing a proper shirt and a necktie. Sit down, Gabe, let her be."

Gabriel lowered his big frame into his stuffed chair. "Where are the little ones?"

"Lucy from next door took Looie to her house to stay over with her grandson. The rest are in their rooms." Gabriel pushed the arms on his chair and raised his bulk. "Gabe, you sit down. Leave Tilda be." A musical laugh rang from out by the mailbox.

Matilda came in the front door, cheeks pink as peonies. She went to the window and waved at the man who backed away from the porch with his eyes on the window.

"Well, it's about time." Gabriel rolled his head to look at the clock. "You got off work four hours ago, missy."

"Leave her be." Cheree went to the window. "Is he your beau?"

Matilda's forehead made a print on the windowpane.

"Did he kiss you?" Cheree whispered.

Matilda glanced at her grandmother and went back to looking at the speck of white moving down the street.

"Oh, he did, didn't he?"

Gabriel went to the kitchen, banged the cabinets, rattled the refrigerator closed, and came back with three glasses of tea on a tray.

"Who's this boy you've been with?" He glowered at the clock and back at Matilda.

"Just a friend."

"Is that his name?" Gabriel regarded her expectantly.

Matilda held her tea glass in both hands and wondered if the way Bill had talked to her showed on her face. And when he'd asked if he could see her tomorrow, and she'd said yes, did that show? And when he'd said he wanted to take her to lunch tomorrow, and he'd kept his hands in his pockets, and leaned toward her with his eyes open and touched his lips to hers and her lips had tingled and still felt like they were buzzing, did that show too?

"Bill."

"And where is this Bill from?" Gabriel sucked down half his iced tea and clunked the glass onto a crocheted coaster. Cheree tisked at him.

Matilda pressed her lips together and looked at her knees.

"And is this Bill coming around again? Because if he is, I need to meet him."

Matilda's eyes were on her hands. She traced the drop of condensation on her glass of tea with a forefinger she could barely feel.

"Tomorrow. He's taking me to lunch. May I be excused?"

"Yes, sweet," Cheree said softly.

Matilda put her glass in the sink and hurried to her room.

"You let her be," Cheree said, pointing at her husband. "You remember bein' young and in love."

Gabriel drained his iced tea. "That's what worries me."

THEY RODE THE trolley from Fair Grounds to a small restaurant on Bourbon Street the trolley driver suggested. Afterward as they walked to Café Du Monde for beignets and chicory coffee, Bill put a quarter in the violin player's hat, and on their way out, he dropped another in the jar for the pair of blind brothers who played guitar and washboard.

Walking around the square, Bill told her about growing up in California, working for his dad, harvesting grapes to lay on sheets of white paper right on the ground in the vineyard and how they dried into the biggest raisins in the San Joaquin Valley, and she told him about dancing for tips on the dock in Baton Rouge, and about her father dying when he cracked his head on a log in the water, and about moving to New Orleans and about her mother chasing after men who didn't stay put anywhere.

"How old are you, Matilda?"

"Seventeen. Eighteen in November. You?" She stopped to pick up a penny on the street. "Heads. Good luck."

"Twenty-six. I won't feel so lucky when I have to go on to Houston."

"When?"

"I catch the five o'clock bus in the morning. Listen, I'd like to take you to a movie and dinner." He watched her profile for a change of expression. She frowned, and his heart sank.

"I'm s'pposed to work. Maybe I can switch with somebody. You got a nickel?" He fished out a nickel, and she headed for a payphone on the corner. He watched her talking with her hand cupped around the receiver. She hung up and skipped his way. He had no idea the other waitress she'd called to switch shifts couldn't switch shifts, and that she was on thin ice with the manager already, and that she'd get fired if she missed another dinner shift after skipping the weekend before. She bounced to a stop. "All set."

When Bill took Matilda home at eleven that night, Gabriel snatched the door open before they reached the porch steps.

"Hello, sir, you must be Mr. Durand. Bill Kazarian's my name."

Gabriel shook the offered hand reluctantly, glaring at the man whose comical caterpillar eyebrows shaded his dark eyes.

"Oh, won't you come in?" Gabriel gestured with all the gentility he could pretend.

Gabriel sat in his stuffed chair and fired off questions. Matilda and Bill sat on the sofa, not daring to touch. Bill told Gabriel about his childhood home in Reedley, California, and about working for his father.

"I see. And what do you do now, young man?"

Matilda blinked hard. Gabriel leaned forward, waiting.

"I work for a family business, sir." Bill's voice held steady.

"I see. And how is it you have not worked the past two days?" Gabriel watched Bill squirming. "And why is it my granddaughter missed work today and got herself fired because she was with you instead of working her dinner shift?"

"Oh—I didn't,"—Bill faltered, glancing at Matilda then back at Gabriel— "know she—I work Wednesdays through Saturdays most weeks, sir. Mondays and Tuesdays are my days off."

"I see." Gabriel said. "Thank you for bringing our Matilda home. I trust you'll be gone tomorrow then?"

"Yes, sir. Tomorrow."

"Good. Good. Matilda, why don't you go to your room while I show your friend out?"

Matilda took a ragged breath and rose from the sofa. "Bye, Bill. See ya."

"Let's not make any promises you won't be keeping, all right, Tilda?" Gabriel kept his eyes on the man who'd stood when his granddaughter did. Matilda stalked to her room.

Gabriel watched his granddaughter until she'd closed the door. "Bill, do you work here in town?"

"No, sir, I travel for work."

"So, you best get on your way then, hadn't you?" Gabriel didn't look at the hand Bill offered. "I think we already did that, young man."

"Goodbye, then, sir." Bill let himself out the front door. He shuddered off the chilly meeting and thought of the lanky girl who'd dipped her long fingers in powdered sugar at Café Dumond and touched them to the surface of her coffee. And the salted butter scent of her skin when she sat beside him in the dark at the movie, and how her hand felt smooth and warm when he held it.

MATILDA SAT ON her bed staring at the pair of movie ticket stubs and a printed paper napkin from Café Dumond. She put the ticket stubs and napkin in the Silver Cross box, counted her money and closed the lid.

She stuffed her four best blouses, two skirts, three dresses, a pair of dungarees, six pair of panties, her extra bra, and the wooden box into her satchel. Her little sister sat up with a yawn. Matilda placed a finger on Evangeline's lips. "Hush, Evangeline, go back to sleep."

Before dawn, Matilda dropped her cotton nightgown into the satchel, slipped into her new blue sundress, and slid out the window. She was at the bus station at four-fifty with a ticket for the five o'clock to Houston. Bill kissed her cheek and asked if she was sure she wanted to do this. She said she was sure. She got very sure on the bus with her head against his shoulder, dreaming of flying.

Five Weeks After

1958, Fayette, Missouri

AND-THE-POOR-girl-would-shake-with-alarm "Ahhrr mmm." She is startled and bewildered at the sound coming from her mouth. It sounds okay inside her head but comes out like a voice she's never heard. *He'd-n'er-leave the* "Gaah" *What the hell is wrong with me?*

1944, Houston, Texas

IGNACIO WAS URINATING out the side door of the boxcar when Bill and Matilda walked up to the tracks from the bus station. "Hey, Maurice, look-it here. Billy brought Nubian gal."

Bill shot Ignacio a disapproving look. "That's enough Nosh. And button your pants." Ignacio fastened his grubby pants and belched.

Maurice came from the dark end of the car with a dressing table over his shoulder. "Oh my." His eyes crinkled at the corners. "Oh my." He set the table down. "Give me your hands, dear."

Matilda raised her arms and Maurice lifted her in one motion into the boxcar while Bill vaulted in. "Now, what on earth, dear lady? Have you run away from New Orleans to see the sights of Houston?"

"Ya mean the stink of Houston." Ignacio spat a brown stream out the boxcar door.

"Now, my little friend, let's not frighten the young lady away."

"Shit, if this scares her wait'll she meets Sally." Ignacio crawled down the ladder to the ground. Sam Sanger came around the side of the car and let Maurice help him up.

"My God." Sam looked from Bill to Matilda. "What are you going to tell Gio?"

"I'm on my way to talk to him." Bill touched Matilda's arm. "I'll show you to my bunk."

"Perhaps she is more of a lady than to go to your bunk, Mr. Kazarian. Miss—I am Maurice." Maurice bowed at the waist.

Matilda didn't know if she was supposed to bow or curtsy in response. She'd never been around someone this big, or someone who sounded like an English actor in the movies.

"Chevalier. Matilda Chevalier."

"Miss Chevalier might wish to wait with Bernice, while you determine appropriate arrangements, Bill. Come along, dear, I'll introduce you."

Maurice led her over the car couplings to the opposite side of the train. She could still hear Bill's voice, then Sam's in murmurs, then at the next car, the mewling of a cat. The rattle of chickens. The low rumble and trumpet-like snort that resonated in her teeth. A warm grassy aroma floated around one of the cars. Three cars forward, Maurice indicated a set of steps to the back of a railroad car. She climbed up, one hand on the rail, one on the back of her skirt.

Maurice rapped the black door where "Madame Volumptia" was painted in red and gold across the cracking surface.

"Who eez eet?" I low voice hummed through the wood.

"It's Maur, Bernice dear. I have someone for you to meet." The door opened slowly. The woman's housedress strained over her waist-length bosom as she stood in the door, holding a bowl and spoon. "Allow me to introduce you to Miss Chevalier. She's here with Mr. Kazarian and I'd think she'll be more at ease with you while she waits for her beau to make some arrangements." Bernice's plump cheeks pushed her eyes nearly shut as the toothless smile overtook her face.

"Hold on, hold on." She patted the apron pockets for a pair of dentures and slid them into her mouth. "Hello, Miss. I knew a Chevalier once."

"Bernice, our Miss Chevalier is from New Orleans."

The woman's accent became middle American. "Were you from Tennessee before that, dear? The man I knew was in Paris, Tennessee."

"No, ma'am, Baton Rouge."

"I'm Bernice."

"Yes, ma'am."

"Please come in. Maurice, would you like an egg salad sandwich? My chickens have kept up, in spite of the rough ride yesterday."

"Thank you, dear lady, but I have business to attend and must be going." He went down the steps and walked away at a ground covering pace.

"Sit, sit. I'll bet you're hungry." Matilda followed her over the rug-strewn floor to a square wooden table. Bernice patted a chair. "Egg salad," she said, spooning globs of yellow and white into a hollowed bread roll, "is the best thing for when you're tired. Do you like tea, dear?"

Bone-weariness hit Matilda as she watched the woman wrestle for space in the corner where she set a kettle on a two-burner stove.

"In the winter, at our house in Florida, I have a real kitchen. Here you go." She set down a stoneware plate with "Harvey House" printed on the rim in front of Matilda, then plopped an overstuffed roll full of egg salad on the plate. Bernice leaned across the table to look into the teapot. "Sorry, I only have powdered sugar for your tea."

Matilda was grateful that Bernice talked, so she didn't have to. She rested her chin in her hands when Bernice picked up her empty plate, and between the egg salad sandwich and a soggy lump of bread pudding, fell asleep at the table.

Bernice arranged Matilda's arms, gently eased her head down to rest on them and patted the girl's coiled mop of apricot colored hair.

THE BRIDE WORE a travel-creased blue cotton sundress and Bernice's lace tablecloth for a veil. The plump egg salad maker was the matron of honor in her house dress, plus a yellow flowered pillbox hat. The six-foot-seven best man with skin so black his reflection looked purple in the courthouse window snugged up his green silk tie and hummed the Wedding March. The groom, olive-skinned and bushy browed, in a pressed blue shirt and Hawaiian print necktie sported a five o'clock shadow at eleven in the morning.

The bride's hair escaped to wave around the makeshift veil with a life of its own when the couple kissed. The judge's wife filled in a marriage certificate, handed the pen to the bride, and scowled while she stared at the girl's arm tattoos. Matilda signed her name beside Bill's, smiled sweetly at the woman, licked the pen, and handed it back.

GIO SLAPPED HIS palm against his tanned forehead. "Kazarian, have you lost your mind? How old is she? Fifteen? Sixteen?"

"Eighteen pretty soon."

"Jesus Christ."

"What if she could do an act? Put her in a long sleeve leotard and tights if Sally doesn't like the tattoos."

"Sally's got more to not like about that girl than tattoos."

"OK, well, look how good sales were after we did the kidnap thing. When was the last time we oversold in New Orleans?"

"I want you to remember, this is the Fiscalini circus. Dad and Antonio and Milana and me. That's who decides what we do."

"I know. But. She's here now. She's—"

"What if she gets pregnant, Bill? Have you thought about that?"

"But, Gio, if I send her back—"

"You won't get arrested for contributing to the delinquency of a minor."

"Hey, I remember your dad having a girl younger than her in his car one time when Sally went home—"

"My dad doesn't work for me, Bill. Let me think about this. I have to figure out a way to keep Dad in line, or Sally'll shit a brick. God, I'm going to regret this."

"Gio, you won't regret this."

"Oh, I will, Bill."

BETTY AND VELMA were hanging laundry when Ignacio clambered up the steps, smelling of aftershave. He told them he had orders from Gio to move in with them. Velma said he could sleep in her bed first.

As if by divine intervention, Bill and Matilda had a railroad car to themselves on the track that ran along the city park in Houston, Texas. Bill carried his bride and her carpet bag through the door, kissed her forehead, told her to stay put until he came back, and went out to set up for a four-day circus.

MILANA POUNDED ON the door of her father's private car. Sally opened the door in her robe with a layer of pink cream on her face. "Oh, your father's not here, I think he—" Milana pushed past her and plopped her bulk down onto the loveseat. "Well!"

"Afternoon, Sally. We have a new person with the show and you're going to be so nice to her it'll make your eyes hurt."

"Excuse me, Milana, what brought this on?"

"Bill's gotten married."

"Bill? Bill who?"

"You know damn well who Bill is. And if you are the tiniest bit rude or say anything besides 'Hello, how are you?' to his wife, you have me to answer to."

"How dare you come in here and tell me what to do." Sally sneered through cold cream.

"Oh, I will tell you what to do, Sally. And if you can't be nice to Bill's wife, I'm telling my father everything. Everything."

Sally yanked an embroidered hand towel from a pile of string-tied linens and swiped at the face cream. "You wouldn't."

"Oh, I would. I don't know when Bill's wife will start work, but when she—"

"Milana, honestly, I'd know if my husband hired anyone—"

"The girl worked for me in New Orleans. And you are going to be nice. Got it?"

Sally scowled and tossed the pink-stained hand towel toward a chair. "You get out of my car."

Milana rocked to her feet and walked to the door. "Oh, and Sally, this car? This car belongs to my dad and uncle and my brother and me. Remember that."

MATILDA BLUSHED WHEN Bill stood to introduce her during supper. Bare-faced clowns hooted the way they had when she'd danced on the platform the weekend before. Sally raised her chin and wine glass to toast the couple, then drained her glass.

When the bottle at the Fiscalini end of the table was empty Sally walked by Bill and Matilda's seats and stopped to lay a cool white hand on Bill's shoulder while she gushed how lovely his bride was and how she hoped they'd be very happy. "And if you need anything, anything at all, dear," she leaned close to Matilda, "please come see me."

Bill thanked her, refilled his glass, and slid his arm around his bride's waist. Sally floated away in a cloud of white silk and pearls, to where Milana sat with Velma and Betty, across from Bernice and her husband.

"Good evening, ladies, don't you all look beautiful."

The little women tucked their chins, waiting for the insult. Milana put her meaty elbows on the table and rested her chin on her hands. "How lovely of you to stop by," Milana said in a low voice. "Don't overdo it. It's unbecoming."

Sally's face remained immobile. She returned to her husband's side, kissed his cheek, and excused herself.

1944—New Orleans, Louisiana

GABRIEL DURAND ASKED the bewildered-looking man in the lobby if he knew a tall, pale-skinned quadroon girl with a hummingbird and flower tattoo. The man stopped him by holding up an ink-stained finger and tapped a bell on the counter. A pleasant looking woman in a polka-dot dress came from behind a beaded curtain, made a motion with her hand from her lips downward, and turned to Gabriel, signing as she spoke. "Hello. How may we help you today, Mr. . . . ?"

"Durand. My granddaughter has gone missing. Tall, slender, hair this color." He indicated the citrus themed coffee cup that held pens and scissors on the counter. "Now, against my wishes, she had gotten tattoos here. Her name is Matilda." He turned to the man behind the counter again. "She's seventeen."

The man with ink-stained fingers watched the woman's hands, gestured, walked to the door across the room, and disappeared.

"What's the matter, cat got his tongue?" Gabriel asked.

"Mr. Durand, my husband's deaf. He's gone to find his son, Eddie. Eddie's done work on a girl named Matilda. We saw her at the circus last weekend. Would that be her?"

"Yes, I'm grieved to say. Her grandmother and I have been worried sick."

"Of course, Mr. Durand, of course. Sonny'll be back with Eddie shortly, I'm sure."

Sonny came out the hallway doorway, frowning, and made a quick sign from his shoulder across to his belt. The hall door creaked open, and Eddie rolled in, shirt half buttoned, greasy hair hanging in his eyes.

"Matilda's granddad huh? Haven't seen her since—"He screwed his mottled face upward as though searching for a memory on the ceiling, "Sunday. No wait, Monday afternoon."

"I see. And did she say where she was going? Was a man with her?"

"By herself. She run off, you think?"Eddie lit a cigarette, flicked at a tobacco crumb on his shirt, and fumbled with his buttons. In the back hallway, a door opened and closed. The tap of high heels faded away in the hall, then another door opened and closed. "Shit. There goes—" Eddie sucked his cigarette until it flared.

Gabriel's brooding expression darkened. "Did she say anything to you? That she might be going somewhere?"

"No. Maybe she run off with the circus . . ." Eddie's voice dropped at Gabriel's disdainful stare. "Sorry. Nice looking girl like that, I just meant—"A sheen of sweat lit Eddie's face.

"You watch what you say. She's my granddaughter." Gabriel folded his fingers into fists and tucked them under his elbows while he stared at the disheveled man in the wheelchair.

"Yeah. Well, you check with the circus?" Eddie stared back.

"Son, how did you lose your leg?"

"Pearl Harbor."

"Well, I'm sorry to hear that. I've lost something as important to me as your leg was to you. I just want to find her. Thank you for your time." Gabriel nodded to Mary Ellen and went out the door without looking back.

"Wow," Mary Ellen said, watching Gabriel. "Poor guy. You need to get cleaned up, Ed. You smell like—"

"Yeah." Eddie turned his chair around to open the hall door but turned back. "Ya know what, Mary Ellen? My bet's she followed that circus. I bet that guy don't go lookin' where he knows he'd find her."

"GABRIEL, THAT YOU?" Cheree called from the kitchen when she heard the front door. "Now, Looie, you stay here for me will you? And don't you let your brothers touch that stove." She leaned into the living room. "Gabe, Matilda called while you were out."

"Called? From where?"

"Now, Gabe, you sit down, I'll fetch you some ice tea."

"From where?"

"From the kitchen, where else would it be? I'll be right back." Cheree kept talking from the kitchen. Gabriel followed her.

"Cheree, why do you do that? Talk from the other room? I can't understand a word you're—"

"You boys stay here and keep an eye on that pan. If smoke starts comin' up, Looie, you turn than knob there down to three. I'll need to talk to your gran-pap in the living room." She poured tea over ice cubes and motioned to the door. Gabriel went ahead of her and sat heavily. "I said, Matilda called."

"I heard that part. I asked from where? Do I need to go get her?"

"No, she's in Houston. She called to tell us she's went and got married. No, now don't you get yourself all worked up. At least she called. And it's better she's married than—"

"Don't even say it. Damn her. Was it that silly looking white man she brought here?"

"I think he was Armenian, Gabriel."

"Still. She needs to marry her own kind."

"Oh, listen to you, Gabriel Durand." Cheree untied her apron. "Listen to you. What if your mama and daddy had pitched a fit 'cause you married a Creole? Or my parents had when I didn't marry a Creole when I married me a big handsome colored man?"

Gabriel glowered at the floor in front on his armchair. "That's different."

"'Tis not. He seemed like a nice man." Cheree retied her apron. "Supper's ready in fifteen minutes."

"She'll be back pregnant and cryin'." His voice rose when he accented pregnant and cryin' with thumps of his fist on his knees. "And that man'll be nowhere in sight."

"You hush that talk. Little ears in the kitchen don't need to hear that kind of talk. And I'll bet you anything she won't. That girl doesn't know how to cry."

Gabriel sighed in resignation. "I'll bet you she learns."

Five Weeks, Two Days

1958, Fayette, Missouri

DR. HARRIS FROM St. Louis adjusts his eyeglasses to peer at the x-ray clipped to the light box. "You say she's been trying to speak?"

"I wouldn't say speaking. Mostly sounds," the Fayette head nurse says. "Her husband says he thinks she's saying words, but . . ."

I'm saying them. You're just too stupid to hear me.

"Matilda, I'm going to look into your eyes. The light will be bright. Do you understand?"

Her head moves.

"She hears us. That was voluntary movement." Dr. Harris makes a notation. The nurse nods.

1944, Houston, Texas

WHILE MATILDA SOLD concessions at the Saturday matinee show in Houston, Bill got into his Borneo Wild Man costume and the clowns rolled his cage into the ring between Sam Sanger's elephant act and Gio's slack-wire act. Bill slobbered, howled, and reached through the bars for his wife when she passed by the cage with her tray.

The light man swung the spotlight to the cage. Matilda squinted for a moment, then handed Bill a cotton candy. Bill waved the blue cotton candy around his wigged head. Gio turned toward the applause and laughter to see what was going on.

Matilda looked into the spotlight, raised her cotton candy tray over her head, and gyrated like—

1958, Fayette, Missouri

JOSEPHINE BAKER, THAT was her name. I saw her in that movie I snuck into when I was twelve. She was my hero. Wanna see my banana skirt tattoo, mister? Can you take that spotlight off me?

"Her pupil dilation is very good," Dr. McClure says. Matilda hears a pen scratching on paper. "Matilda, can you open your eyes without me helping you?"

The eyelids open halfway, and McClure leans close. "No light this time, I promise. That's very good." He motions for the nurse to lower the Venetian blind. "Follow this with just your eyes, not your head," he says, moving his finger slowly from left to right in front of her open eyes.

"Good. Independent movement, bilateral," he says to the nurse. More pen scratching. "We're going to have your husband and mother back in now and we'll talk about how you're doing."

Oh. I'm in a hospital. Oh. That's where I am. How long have I been—"huuuu?" The doctor pats her hand. "You keep practicing making sounds. That's good." More pen scratching. She closes her eyes again.

A Star Loses Her Shine

1944, Katy, Texas

THE FISCALINI BROTHERS Circus sold forty-five tickets for the Friday night show in Katy, Texas. Sally told Giovanni it was insulting to expect her to perform for forty-five country yokels. Giovanni wondered aloud if the young Mrs. Kazarian might want to do the "Nubian Beauty" act if Sally didn't want to go on. Sally made a face at him.

Two minutes before their act Sally glared at her husband when he told her she'd better be smiling when the spotlight was on her. Saturday morning, the *Katy Gazette* featured a sour-faced Sally Fiscalini, "Star of the Flying Trapeze" on the front page with the caption: "Circus may look like fun, but this star's face says it is not."

Saturday afternoon, there were thirty people in the stands. Sally was incensed.

Sally ordered Bill to get his Borneo Wild Man costume on and to fetch the tear away skirt from the trunk. She'd slip in to sit at the end of the bleachers with a bag of popcorn, she said, and he was to pick her up and carry her up the ladder. Bill assumed the rest of the trapeze troupe knew the plan. They didn't.

As the smattering of applause for the dog act died down, Sally told Bill to give her the count of ten to get to a seat while the audience's attention was on the dog act. Outside, Bill counted "eight, nine, ten," and ran in to grab Sally off the bleacher seat and heave her over his shoulder. The thirty people in the audience who were watching the dogs missed the whole abduction gag.

A simple farm boy in brogan shoes, patched trousers, and his best shirt responded to Sally's scream by lurching from his seat to wrestle the pretty woman away from the hairy man who had hold of her. When the boy pulled at Sally's costume and the bodice ripped, she cursed and slapped his face.

The boy's parents pulled their frightened son away from the circus woman who'd cussed and hit him. They and their five children left in a hurry.

The Katy Feed and Seed store owner shook his head in disgust. He and his three employees and their wives, who'd been treated to lunch and circus tickets left. So did the pastor of the church and his wife, his sister and brother-in law, and his aunt.

The eleven audience members remaining sat in stunned silence to watch Sally shout at Bill to pick her up and do his job or she'd have him fired. Bill glanced up to the platform and saw Giovanni watching, arms folded while Gio hurried the clowns back to the ring for the Keystone Cops act.

Two by two, the rest of the people left the tent muttering about the woman who'd been so ugly to that poor boy. Betty, in her striped Keystone Cops prisoner costume act woke the one remaining man who'd fallen asleep in his seat and pointed to the tent flap.

There were no circus tickets sold in Katy, Texas Saturday night. The reporter who'd taken Sally's photo on Friday waited by the ticket window. Ten minutes to show time he asked the old man in the ticket booth where everyone was. At quarter after six, the old man closed the ticket booth and touched his right eyebrow in salute to the bewildered reporter.

The reporter walked around the tent, and through a loose flap and found clowns talking to Maurice, while Sam, in his tan safari costume forked hay to the elephants. The reporter raised his camera.

Gio stepped toward him. "Please, sir, let's not make this any worse." The photographer pointed his camera toward Maurice and the clowns and pressed the shutter.

THE SHOW DOESN'T GO ON
by Thomas Perry, reporter

Caption for photo: The strong man for the Fiscalini Brothers Circus talks with the clowns, wondering what went wrong.

The ticket booth attendant waited patiently in the afternoon sun, change box ready to sell circus tickets to the citizens of Katy last night, at what should have been the year's best attended event for twenty miles around. But an incident between one of the performers and an audience member, Cletus Harper, son of Clarence and Doris Harper, cast a shadow on the Saturday afternoon performance which caused their friends and neighbors to leave their seats.

"My boy Cletus is only fourteen, and he's a good boy. He didn't know that lady was part of the show. He thought she needed help," said Clarence Harper. Harper had taken his family, including his son Cletus to the circus as a special treat. "I about had to hold Doris down when that lady hit our boy. I never seen anything like it."

Pastor Evanston admitted that after seeing the photo of an angry trapeze performer on yesterday's front page, he and Mrs. Evanston and their guests, San Antonio mayor

Lawrence Sutter and his wife the former Faye Evanston considered not attending. "I wish I had not taken my guests to see such a display," Pastor Evanston said. "How someone can hit a sweet child of God like that Harper boy is between her and the Lord. Our guests were as dismayed as Doris and I were."

It seems that in spite of advertising in this newspaper and posters around town, word of the attack spread among the citizens of Katy, and the town decided to stand with the boy, who does not attend school but is known around town for his gentle nature. Last night, the circus tent was dark.

The Fiscalini Brothers Circus has a contract with Northside Hardware, whose bare lot they leased for three days to present a total of four shows. Owen Brown, owner of Northside Hardware was not available for comment.   T. P

Back at the pastor's parsonage the pastor's sister, Faye Sutter, wife of San Antonio Mayor Lawrence Sutter was livid: first at the shocking display of bad behavior when the scantily clad bleached blonde had slapped the mentally challenged boy, and second that news of the incident might beat her back to the San Antonio Junior League. She'd spearheaded The Junior Leaguer's plan to buy circus tickets for fifty children whose mothers worked for various members as maids and cooks. If this scandal got back to San Antonio, Faye Sutter's chances of moving up from vice president to president the next year would be dashed.

She informed her husband that she and her Junior League were going to do something different for the children for the following weekend, and he'd better not let those circus people even set up their tent in San Antonio.

"Well, dear, I understand your concerns, but the circus has a contract with the city. If you don't tell anyone what happened—"

"My ladies and their families won't be attending, and neither will the children. Or anyone I know." She checked her lipstick in her compact mirror and snapped it shut. "I will not be humiliated in front of the whole Junior League by some low-class ingrate who hits retarded children."

1944, San Antonio, Texas

MAYOR SUTTER MET the Fiscalini train when it pulled into San Antonio to explain there'd been a terrible mistake: the whole fairgrounds had already been reserved by the San Antonio Garden Club for a flower show, and he was so sorry, but he'd have to void the contract.

Gio told his father and Antonio about the mayor's cancellation, and they stood in the supply car, looking out the door at the empty fairgrounds lot.

Giovanni opened his silver cigarette box. He tapped a cigarette on the lid and examined the end of it. "We'll make it up."

"Pop, I have payroll to get out. How do I do that?"

"I'm afraid I can't help. You know I had to buy Sally some things. Tony, can you help with payroll until we get to the next town?"

Antonio had just shaken the last cigarette out of his pack but punched it back in. "Looks like you might need to stop buying so much for—"

Giovanni's eyes flashed. "What I spend on my wife is my business."

"And paying our employees is the family business." Antonio dropped the pack into his shirt pocket and looked at his brother incredulously.

"Son, you'll have to let some of the roustabouts go." Gio and Antonio dropped their heads in unison at Giovanni's suggestion.

"No, Pop, we need everybody we have. Seems like if we need to drop somebody off the payroll right now, it would be your wif—"

"I am still head of this show. You leave Sally out of this!"

"No, G'vanni," Antonio said, "we're all partners in this company. Milana too."

"Aaat!" Giovanni's face clouded. "She's not a partner."

Gio rubbed the back of his neck. "Yeah, Pop, she is."

"Well, she isn't nice to Sally. I don't need to hear what she has to say."

"Pop, that man, the mayor, was in the audience back in Katy. I saw him. We just lost a four-day contract in a good city. Why do you think that is?"

"He said they had a flower show."

Antonio slapped his hand on the boxcar door and slid it open another foot. "See any set up out there for a flower show, G'vanni? They don't want us here and it's because of your wife. You better hope we make it up next week."

"It's Fort Stockton next, Uncle Tony. Not a very big town," Gio said. "We have El Paso after that, and Las Cruces. But, Pop, we can't have her doing that kind of thing again."

"I don't need to hear any more of this. Let's get these water tanks filled and get moving. Tony, run up and let the conductor know there's a change of plans. He needs to get on the wire and make sure we're clear to where is it? Fort Stockton? We'll do a parade there, both elephants. We'll make it up."

"Pop, I need payroll."

"Go sell the black horse, Gio. Take it to town. Make it look good."

Gio looked at his father in disbelief. "Do you want to be here when the mayor sends the police to tell us to move on?"

"Go right now. Take Rosa with you. Sell it to the first dumb farmer that comes along."

ROSA, THE BUXOM, dark-haired rosinback rider dressed in her Gypsy girl costume while her assistant, and sometimes boyfriend Rory groomed the horse. Gio led the horse toward town with Rosa sitting on its broad back, one hand on the surcingle and her legs in front of her to the left side, toes pointed.

It was the new deputy sheriff who spotted them on the side of the road and drove up to ask what they were doing. Gio explained that his dear sister was ill and needed to see a doctor, so he was selling this well-trained circus horse.

Gio lunged the black horse in a circle beside the road. Rosa swung her legs behind her, knelt for two beats and stood up, as elegantly as she ever had in a show. The deputy watched open mouthed. Rosa dropped to a knee and did a leg extension, then purred to the black horse and it stopped. She touched him in front of the surcingle with the side of her foot, and he knelt. She slid off to stand beside him, unhooked the reins from the surcingle, and pulled his head to one side. The horse lay down, then with another pull and cluck, Rosa asked him to sit like a dog.

"Gosh, that's a good-lookin' horse. Smart too." The deputy mopped his face with a red handkerchief. "Think he'd ride good for parades and such? We have a mounted patrol."

"Officer, this horse has been everywhere and has been exposed to everything, having been in the circus. It takes years to get a horse to this level of training. Years." Gio knitted his brows in earnest. "I'm afraid we won't ever be able to get another one trained to where this horse is—but my sister—she's all the family I've got."

"I have a sister too," the deputy said. "You say you want to sell this horse? How much?"

Gio sighed loudly. "I was thinking two hundred dollars."

"What!" Rosa gasped on cue. "Cousin, you know we paid three hundred and fifty for this horse, and he's had two more years of training."

"Yes, dear, but we need to sell Blackie now so my sister can see a doctor." Gio touched Rosa's shoulder. Rosa buried her face in the horse's neck and heaved a sob.

"Miss, listen, don't cry. What do you want for your horse?" The deputy looked at Gio disapprovingly, and back to Rosa.

"It will take me so long to train one as good as my Blackie." She stroked the twenty-year-old gelding's head. "But if you promise to take good care of him, I'll sell him to you for three hundred and fifty dollars."

The deputy put his hand on the horse's neck. "You have a deal, miss. I'll be right back." He turned his car around and drove a quarter mile into town, withdrew money from his bank account, and drove back to where the circus people stood holding the horse, which was grazing as though it was not part of a shady horse deal. He counted out three hundred and fifty dollars while Gio removed the surcingle and bridle and fashioned the lead rope into a halter.

"Would you like me to take your horse to your home for you?" Gio asked.

"No, thank you, I'll lead him home and come back for my car. How old did you say he was?"

"Well, sir, let me think," Rosa began, "I've trained him for two years, and you can't put that kind of training on a horse until it's at least five years old."

"So, about seven? That's a perfect age."

"Yes, seven *is* a perfect age." Rosa tilted her head toward the man. Gio handed over the lead rope.

They watched the sheriff walking toward town, and when the man looked back one last time, Gio waved. Rosa put her hand to her chest and wiped at her eye with the other.

"Nice touch, Rosa."

"Yeah, promise me we won't ever use a blind horse again. I can't tell you how scary that big sonofabitch was, feeling his way around the ring the past ten years."

The crew filled water tanks, loaded the twelve bales of hay the feed store had dropped off before they got news the contract was cancelled. An hour and a half after the circus train rolled into San Antonio, it started toward Fort Stockton.

1944, On the Rails to Fort Stockton, Texas

ELOISE AND MARTA poked hay into their mouths with their trunks while they watched Maurice carrying hay toward them. He held two bales by the wires, alongside his massive thighs—one for each of them, and this pleased their pachyderm senses to no end.

Maurice cut the hay wires as the door opened and Sam came in with Bill's young wife. Matilda's eyes popped open, and Sam knew she'd gotten the shock of ammonia.

"Maur, my darling, we have a visitor."

"So, I see." Maurice boomed, touching his chest when he bowed. "Welcome, Matilda. The girls love visitors who bring treats."

Matilda walked along the short railroad tie wall with Maurice, taking in the heavy, deeply scented hide as she passed the elephant. Marta rumbled softly and lifted her rubbery speckled trunk toward the explosion of curls on top of Matilda's head. Matilda closed her eyes and scrunched her nose while Marta searched her hair.

"Marta, be polite," Sam cautioned. Marta returned to Matilda's face and neck, leaving a smear of hay scented mucous. "I think she'd like to see what you've brought before she decides if she likes you."

Matilda held out an apple. Marta seized it and shoved it toward her triangular mouth. Eloise followed the path of the apple, trying to grasp a sliver of skin and fruit that fell to the straw. "Here, for Eloise." Sam handed Matilda another apple. "Yes, El, she has one for you too. Yes, you are the best girl."

"They're both girls?" Matilda grinned while Eloise snuffed Matilda's clothes for another apple.

"Yes, we only use girls. I had to work with a young bull once." Sam patted Eloise's shoulder then kicked some loose hay closer to the middle of the pile. "Bastard got hold of a clown one night. We love these girls though, don't we, Marta?" Marta put her trunk over his shoulder and sighed. Eloise nosed his pockets. "That's all, El, you ate them all."

The elephants returned to shoving wads of hay into their mouths. Matilda glanced from Sam to Maurice, grinning. "They're so big." She watched the elephants rock on tree trunk legs when the rail car swayed. "How can you make them do stuff when they're so big?"

"Someone else trained them. These girls are fifty years old now. I'm just nicer to them than anybody else has been, and they love me. Oh, and Maur, too." Sam beamed at Maurice, who mashed the hay wire into a tight bundle.

Matilda watched Sam watching his lover. "Are you two married?"

"Oh heavens, sweetheart, no, we can't marry in this country."

Maurice placed the wire in a gunny sack before he went to stand with Sam and Matilda.

"Why, because you're both—"

"Men? Pretty much."

Matilda blushed to the roots of her hair. "Would you if you could?"

"No, I would not be able to marry Sammy. My dear mother would have a heart attack." Maurice pursed his lips toward Sam affectionately.

"Because she doesn't know? I mean . . ."

"No, dear." Maurice's mouth widened. "My mother would just die if I married a white man."

Sam put his hand to his chest and sighed. "See what I put up with for love?"

"HEY, GIO." BILL took the offered chair at the desk in Gio's car. "I think I can work out a bar on a wire to drop down for Sally to lift off the elephant. I'll want two guys on the line hand over hand, you know, make it smooth."

"OK, yeah, that would do it. I don't think Sam's too keen on it, but he'll work on it. We have to have a mechanic on Sally in case something goes wrong so we can get her off the elephant fast." Gio closed the ledger in front of him and picked up his lighter.

Bill shook out two cigarettes. "Sure. Think she'll go for the belt?"

"Too bad if she doesn't. Bernice can work it out in a channel in the costume. We can't have a—"

"Yeah, I know, Gio. Sam's good at keeping things under control."

"Sure. But you know and I know it's an elephant and we don't need that whole Mills clan of hers coming after us if she gets hurt and blames Fiscalini Brothers. And she's pissed at Pop again."

Bill smoothed an eyebrow with a spit-wetted thumb. "When isn't she?"

"TONY, CAN YOU go with me to get measurements for this elephant thing?" Bernice draped her tape measure on her neck.

"Sure. Hey, I don't think Sally'll do that elephant deal more than a show or two before she gets bored. Maybe we can use a rug instead of you having to make a whole new neck pad. This is awful nice of you, Bern."

Bernice leaned forward to kiss her husband's cheek. "I'm not doing this for Sally. I'm doing it for Eloise."

"HEY HEY HEY, wait a minute, where you goin' with that girl?" Velma called.

Sam stopped and leaned into the bunk side of the car where Velma, Betty, and Ignacio shared two mattresses and fought for space among heaps of little clothes. The three of them sat on upturned buckets around a crate top playing poker. Ignacio picked up an extra card when Betty and Velma turned to look at Matilda, Sam, and Maurice.

Ignacio wriggled and picked at his crotch. "Leave that girl here. You fags don't know what to do with her."

Velma snorted and Betty cuffed Ignacio's arm half-heartedly.

"Hey," he said, "don't be a little shit. There's plenty of me to go around."

Maurice leaned around Sam. "Shall I remind you of your manners while you are dangling upside down outside the car again, or will you be a gentleman and apologize to the lady?"

Betty slapped at Ignacio again. "See, asshole?" Betty tossed two white chips on the pile. "Hey, Matilda, you play cards?"

Matilda stepped out from behind Sam. "Well, my Gran-pap and Gran-mim played gin rummy. I know how to play solitaire."

"Ohhh, you play with yourself?" Velma guffawed, "Nosh plays with his self all the time." She and Ignacio pounded on the crate, laughing shrilly.

Maurice took Matilda by the elbow. "Let's get you back to your quarters, my dear. These little wretches were never spanked when their mothers had a chance."

"I'd let you spank me, big boy," Velma purred. Betty put a hand in her armpit and pumped. Ignacio backed toward Velma, loosening his belt.

"Hey, where'd they go?" Betty said to the empty space. "Damnit. We coulda had a foursome and took her money."

Ignacio huffed. "She ain't got any money, dumb shit."

"Nuh uh, you see her sell cotton candy? She's makin' money." Betty laid down a straight and reached for the pile of chips. Velma leaned over to look at the cards and slapped hers down in disgust.

1958, Fayette, Missouri

YOU KEEP SHOVING that baby food in my mouth, I'm gonna spit it at you.

"One more bite, honey. Hey, got a letter from Mim yesterday. Well, looks like Churchill wrote it, 'cause he drew a picture of a dog on it. He's been wantin' a dog. I told him maybe later, maybe if we get our own house." Suzette sets the dish and spoon on the bedside tray. Matilda's eyes follow her mother's movements as she opens the envelope.

1944, 100 Miles outside of Fort Stockton, Texas

BERNICE AND TONY Fiscalini met Sam and Maurice on the back stoop. "I need to measure Eloise for a pad to match Sally's costume." Bernice touched her measuring tape.

"Oh. You're a doll, Bernice," Sam said. "I'm headed back that way."

"And I must work on my costume," Maurice added. "Seems I've gained some weight." He kissed Bernice's hand. "I shall treasure your company another time."

"You need me, Sam? If you don't, I want to get these windows unstuck. Nothing like summer in Texas." Tony jabbed a meaty thumb toward the next car.

"Sammy and I have this." Bernice smiled.

The pair walked through Betty, Velma, and Ignacio's quarters, past a strip poker game that had apparently started three shirts, five socks, and one tiny bra earlier.

ELOISE SEARCHED SAM'S pockets and Bernice's apron while Sam stood on a step ladder to measure her neck. "I have to tell you Bernice, I don't care for this whole idea. I won't have but three days to get El ready."

"I know, Sam." Bernice rubbed the elephant's groping trunk.

"So, even if we get in three days early, how do I rehearse the whole thing? You think Sally's going to come out of her castle to rehearse with Eloise? You don't think so, do you, El?" He scratched Eloise's hook scarred neck. Eloise opened her mouth and reverberated softly. "I need someone to get on her."

"How about a clown?"

"Puleeze."

"How about Matilda?" Bernice draped her measuring tape around her neck.

"Well—yes. Good idea."

"Just ask Bill first, Sammie."

"Oof. Yeah. He is so gaga over her, it's cute. Oh, and, honey, the last thing he needs now is a little knocked up wifey. You have that covered, right?"

"I have her fixed up."

"Right. Hey now that Rosa has run that good for nothing boyfriend off, what's she up to? I heard some activity in her car last night."

"Oh, Sammie, nothing gets by you."

"Oh God, do tell, who's she up to now?" Sam clasped his hand over one shoulder in anticipation.

"Some clown."

"WRENCH PLEASE." BILL stuck a hand from under the generator trailer. Sam handed him a lockjaw plier. "You lose your man license for that, Sam." Bill rolled out to get the wrench. "I'm sure Matilda will think it's great, but what happens when Sally looks out and sees you rehearsing her act with my wife?"

"What's the worst that can happen? Sally gets so mad she leaves and goes back to the Mills show?"

Bill slid back under the generator. "Just take care of my wife, Sam. She's— you know." He slid back out. "She's the moon and the stars to me."

1944, New Orleans, Louisiana

'ANY MAIL FOR me?' Eddie signed. Sonny flipped through the stack and held up a postcard with a picture of a longhorn steer beside an oil derrick.

Eddie read the back and chuckled, then signed to Sonny, 'Well, now I know why Matilda hasn't been in.' Sonny gave him a questioning look.

'She says she went off with a guy from the circus and they got married. Goofy kid.'

'Wonder if her grandfather knows.' Sonny signed.

'Don't look at me, Pop. Ain't for me to tell him.'

EDDIE TOLD TOMMY Stang he'd have to put the tattoo of the ship he wanted on his back.

"Why can't you put it here?" Tommy touched his neck.

"'Cause it looks like hell when you put on a suit and tie, trust me. Roll over big boy, this won't take long."

"Real funny. Hey, did I tell ya? Casey's gonna be in the slammer a damn long time."

"Yeah? I'll be go to hell. How long?" Eddie flipped the design sheet over.

"Year and a half, I think. Says he got the shakes in there real bad the first couple weeks. He says he's gonna go clean."

"Yeah? So, how's that work? He smells it on you, he'll be right back."

"Naw, I don't smoke it," Tommy said. "Messes up my voice."

Eddie glanced at Tommy's left arm, took his wrist, and rotated the arm outward. The needle scars were hidden in the tattoo of a palm tree at the crook of Tommy's elbow.

"Well, sonofabitch." Eddie breathed.

"So much sweeter, Eddie. I swear. We can trade if you want to. Show you how."

"Naw, Stang. I don't need that. I don't. Damn, pal."

"Okay, well, it's no big deal. Doesn't stink up your clothes."

Eddie picked up the front of his shirt and sniffed it. "This stink?"

"Yeah. Dead giveaway."

Eddie finished the ship on Tommy's pale back just before his monkey woke up and grunted. Tommy handed Eddie a tin box instead of cash for the tattoo.

THE MONKEY SLAPPED Eddie's forehead until one eyelid lifted, then peered into the flaccid pupil. *Anybody comin' out? Time for breakfast, time for tea, time for lunch, time for me,* and licked the other eyelid. The eye shuddered open. *Hello hello hello I'm dying asshole. I feel sick, buddy boy. I think I'm gonna puke. Feel this, pal.* It poked a shattered fingernail into Eddie's ear. Eddie batted at it.

"No. I ain't gonna do that right now."

What did you say, buddy boy? What what whaaat. Wake up honey baby, let's have some fun. The monkey grabbed Eddie's trachea and humped his neck. *How you like it, buddy boy? Open up that big ol vein, lemmie stick it in.*

"Please."

Holdin' out on me buddy boy? You know I looove youuu. Make a baby, that's what we do, make a baby. I'm the daddy.

Eddie swatted at his chest and neck. Anything to make the tingling stop. He put his palms on the sides of his face, then pressed them over his ears. Something was screeching. Whatever was pushing on his jugular vein, he wanted that to stop too. He rolled a bloodshot eye at the alarm clock. Three in the morning. He closed his eyes again and lay panting in the dark like a dying dog.

The monkey shrieked again. Shat in his mouth. Eddie rolled over, puked into the coffee can by the bed. The sheets stank of old vomit and sweat and monkey shit. Eddie sat up, looked, bleary eyed at the dresser across the room.

Just this one time. Just this one more time, then no more. Just this one more. He hopped over one legged. His monkey rode the scarred stump, gasping. *Oh buddy oh buddy I'm about to, I'm about to, oh yeah baby, oh yeah baby, come to me. Come to me. Me. Me. Me.*

Six Weeks After

1958, Fayette, Missouri

YOU RUN OFF and left me and Looie and Dallas and Evangeline and Churchill, Momma. You never even said goodbye. Kids at school made fun of me because of you. Only friend I had after high school was a guy at the tattoo place. Did you know that, "muh-muh?"

Bill arrives freshly showered and shaved, with coffee and sandwiches. His mother-in-law reports, "Bill! She said, 'Momma.'"

"IT'S DIFFICULT TO say how long these kinds of injuries take," Dr. Harris from St. Louis says. "Has she spoken since she said 'Momma' last week?"

Matilda's mother shakes her head.

"Mr. Kazarian, how about you? Is she saying words?"

I'm right here. Ask me. Want to hear me sing? Cas-ey would waltz with a straw-jerry pie . . .

"Not really words, but we talk every day, don't we, honey?" Bill says, stroking Matilda's arm. "I know she hears me."

Andy van played . . .

The doctor makes a note on his clipboard. "So, she is responding—"

"Ask her yourself, doc. Before you got here, we talked about the first year she was in the show. Ask her."

. . . onnn . . . Heee married the curl with the draw-berry girl . . .

"All right, Matilda," the doctor says, adjusting his glasses, "what color was your costume?" He watches her face. Matilda's mother leans forward.

"She had a lot of different costumes, doc. Honey, tell him what you wore when you first helped Sam with the elephants. What color was it?"

That nasty white drum major jacket that smelled like moth balls? "B-buh-buh" *Bernice dusted it with chalk and it was always puffing like it was smokin' and made me sneeze.*

The doctor cocks his head. "Matilda, are you saying blue?"

I said white. Are you deaf? Andy gandy-band stayed gone . . .

Dr. Harris says. "Next week we'll do more tests—"

Shaddup I'm tryin' to sing. What color. I said that already. "Wwiide"

"Doc," Bill interrupts, "she said white. The costume was white."

1944, Fort Stockton, Texas

GIOVANNI FISCALINI HOPPED off the train in a pale blue silk shirt and linen trousers to greet the Fort Stockton city manager and explain they were ahead of schedule because he'd given up his contract in San Antonio for a fundraiser for an orphan's home, and it was only right to give to those who needed help the most. Sally glided out a moment later in a matching pale blue silk dress with a strand of pearls at her throat, flashing her showtime smile. Giovanni sprinted over to help her down.

"How do you do. I'm Sally Fiscalini. How lovely of you to come meet us. Darling, you do have those tickets ready for Mr.—"

"Hale. Bud Hale. City manager. And justice of the peace." The whip-lean bronzed man extended his hand. Sally placed her fingers in his hand and slipped them away to touch her pearls before Hale could close his hand.

"Darling," she said, not taking her eyes off the man's face, "You didn't warn me how handsome the city manager would be. How *ever* will I keep my mind on my act?"

Bud Hale blushed. Bud's lady friend Louise from church had never mentioned his looks, just the calluses on his hands from working his ten acres of cantaloupes and carrots.

"Ah, you see, Mr. Hale, my wife is a hopeless admirer of good looks. No wonder she wanted us to hurry to your town."

"Well, you're sure welcome to set up things early. Not much goes on here, so I imagine everybody in town'll come by to have a look."

"We'll be very glad to see them. Very glad. I'll send my son Gio to your office later. He handles all the arrangements, you understand." The two men shook hands again. Hale headed for his truck, and the Fiscalinis went back to their coach.

Giovanni re-combed his hair. "I have things to do. Are you staying here?"

"I need Bernice to come do my fitting. She's dragging her feet on purpose. She knows I want that costume." Sally opened the silver cigarette box beside her emerald brocade chair. Giovanni flicked the wheel of the heavy crystal lighter for her. Sally blew a thin stream of smoke over their heads. "I know you understand, darling, how awful that last show in that horrible town was for me. I'm so glad we're far away from those dumb yokels, aren't you?"

"My dear, I never said I understood." Giovanni turned away from her. "But if you dislike the audience so much, perhaps you need to not perform for a while."

Her dark brows gnashed together. "What are you talking about? I love the audience." She narrowed her eyes and flicked the cigarette over a glass ashtray.

"No, my dear, you love adoration." Giovanni kept his back to her. Sally stood on the Persian rug in their lavish coach in her expensive new dress and shoes, smoking her imported cigarette. Giovanni left the door open and walked the length of the train.

A few minutes later, he knocked at Tony and Bernice's car. Bernice opened the door. "Hi, G'vanni, Tony's over helping Milana, I think."

"That's fine. I came to see you. Sally wants to know about her costume. Is it done?"

"Almost. She asked for a lot of bead work."

"Of course, she did," he said wearily. "When Tony comes back—"

"I'll tell him you're looking for him. Are you all right, G'vanni? You look pale. Would you like some toast? Tea? Egg salad sandwich?"

"No, thank you. Will you go see Sally with the costume as soon as it's done?"

"No, she needs to come here."

"Please, Bernice, if you can go to her, just once. Please."

"G'vanni, how long have you known me? Forty-five years? When did I ever go to anybody's car for a fitting? She can come here like everybody else." She touched his arm. "You look terrible. Sit down. I'll make tea."

"No, I have to get the rousties and clowns to work. There's too much to do." He put the back of his forearm on his cheek and looked at the sweat on the sleeve.

"Sit. Just for a minute." Bernice took his arm and led him to her overstuffed chair by the window.

"Only a minute. I just—only a minute—then ..." His black brows slumped in sleep. Bernice looked at her brother-in-law, the man everyone said in whispers was the good looking Fiscalini brother. She only saw a tired, grey skinned old man with dyed black hair.

MATILDA RAN BESIDE the train to the bull car with two apples. Maurice and three roustabouts pulled the ramp from under the car and positioned it on a railroad tie.

A trumpet-like snort sounded inside the car. "Easy, Eloise, easy," Sam warned. Marta rocked back and forth, chuffing. Maurice jumped on the ramp and declared it stable with a thumbs up. Sam eased Eloise out of the car.

Eloise blurted when the shy Marta put one foot tentatively on the ramp. "That's a girl, that's a girl." Sam walked beside her as she picked her way down. Matilda watched, breathless.

THE BAGGAGE HORSES swished at flies that came from all over town to inspect new smells and dung brought in by the train. Tony helped the clowns load a wagon and move it around to the other side of the park where he'd picked a spot. "Put those panels in a circle by those trees, boys. Fourteen panels will be enough. See where that grass is green? There. Yes. That'll be in the shade in the afternoon. Put a trough there." He mopped his shining face with a bandana.

Gio walked over to Tony, looked around, and nodded. "You're thinking horse rides, right?"

"Yeah." Tony pushed his bandana into a back pocket. "We can use the blue pads. I say we put some clowns in clean shirts and have 'em put just noses on. We still got all those foam noses in a box somewhere, right? Sell tickets and noses. Set Milana up beside the ticket booth. Gordy and Shill can get the sno-cone grinder out."

"Good. I'll be in the tent helping Bill. He's working out the rigging for the elephant lift for Sally." Gio glanced around. "Be fine with me if he told me it wouldn't work."

KIDS CAME ON foot and bicycles to watch the circus being built. Milana was ready for them, and sold them sno-cones for a dime, cups of colored sugar water for a nickel. She sold popcorn for a dime but only filled bags to two thirds and folded the tops over. "There you go, sweetie, easier to carry this way."

Betty promised to mind her mouth and flatulence for a ten percent sales commission. She walked around among the kids, talking up the wares in a British accent. Kids ran home to raid piggy banks and hurried back to buy something to spoil their dinner. "It was from this little bitty woman and she said she's related to the king of England," they told their mothers.

Rosa and three clowns in clean shirts and red noses led the four baggage horses in circles. Two kids to a horse for a quarter, fifteen cents to ride alone. Most of the kids bought a red clown nose for another dime. "It's a real clown nose, from the circus," they informed their fathers at supper.

Mothers and children rode the carousel for a nickel during the day. Bill had the second generator up and running again so they could run outside lights at night. Roughnecks with oil stains on their boots and beer on their breath whooped wildly and rode the carousel after dark for a dime, three rides for a quarter. Those that managed to fall off their painted mounts never argued at being charged to get back on them.

The cross on a cinderblock and plywood church near the city park advertised it as the Freewill Church of the Pentecost. Tony struck a deal with the preacher to have a special church service in the circus tent, for a small percentage, of course. Didn't thirty percent of the offering sound fair? After all, it was a large tent. Sunday service for the Freewillers became a tent revival for regulars, roughnecks, and enrapt farmers eager to be forgiven for sins they couldn't remember committing.

Milana wore her white dress, low cut to entice reluctant followers to drop pennies in the tin bowl for a Dixie-cupful of red communion sugar water.

The Fiscalinis gave the roustabouts and clowns Monday off in shifts so they could go into town. Cafes were happy for the extra business, and the five and dime owner who didn't know he was getting shoplifted by an errant clown was thrilled at the number of shoppers. He even let those nice circus people put up posters outside his store.

Velma and Betty spotted the neon COLD _EER sign a half mile off. They dressed up and headed toward the watering hole in the afternoon. The two of them caused a pretty good stir, walking on the side of the road and hitching their dresses up at passing cars and pickups. A couple of oilfield boys from Arkansas drove by, put on the brakes, and turned around for a better look.

For the price of a couple of beers the Arkansas boys had their little dates primed for sport. They didn't care if it wasn't even dark yet when those drunk little circus gals hiked up their dresses and rode them like government mules in the bed of the pickup out behind the bar.

SAM, MAURICE, AND Matilda paraded Eloise and Marta to the dirt banked livestock tank a quarter mile to the south, where the elephants rolled and lolled and sprayed water to their hearts' delight.

The quadroon girl with apricot-orange hair, the girl who got tattoos when she was a sophomore, the girl who left the dance with Casey Stang but didn't end up knocked up much less get kissed, the girl who wanted away from the mix and match family her mother had created and abandoned, for once, fit in. Among the misfits on the circus train Matilda had found her family.

BILL HAD THE rigging set up for Sally to rehearse the elephant lift. Giovanni paced around, looking at each cable and bar as though he'd never seen them before. Sally didn't come to the tent at all on Monday, or on Tuesday morning when Sam worked with Eloise. Sam asked if he could use Matilda to get the timing worked out with a rider.

At more than fifty years of age, and forty years of circus wear and tear, putting her feet on the platform seemed like enough to Eloise. She grunted and waited for an apple before she raised her trunk and Sam decided it was all right with him.

With Matilda on Eloise, Sam showed her where to hold, and to lean back until the elephant lifted her shoulders to get on the platform, and then to lean forward. Sam had Matilda raise her arm, and Bill marked his distance to lower the bar to her.

When Bill and Sam were confident the rigging was ready to test, Giovanni went to get Sally, who insisted she'd be fine come showtime. She didn't need to rehearse. Giovanni came back with the verdict.

"OK, well, can we try it with Matilda?" Sam asked.

Matilda grinned and raised both arms. Bill couldn't have refused her if he'd wanted to. He lifted Matilda off and held her just above Eloise's neck for a few seconds before he set her back down. Maurice came in looking for Milana and stayed to watch.

"Matilda, dear," Giovanni said, "let's try it again, and while you're over the elephant, swing your legs."

"Hey, no, she's not trained to do aerials," Bill interrupted.

Maurice walked over to Bill. "Let's put the mechanic on her, Bill. You and I can manage that and the lift."

By ten thirty the elephant was as ready as she was going to be. Giovanni sat down and lit his fifth cigarette from his fourth.

"What do you think, boss, think that will do for the Missus?" Maurice asked.

Giovanni looked up at Maurice, startled.

"You OK, boss?" Maurice walked over and gently rested a hand on Giovanni's shoulder. "Boss?"

"Yes, yes, that looks fine." He rose, swayed on his feet, and went out the back of the tent.

"He's not OK," Sam said, motioning to Bill to come over. "Gio might need to see this and rehearse it since his father's not feeling well. Maybe you better go get him."

Five minutes later, Gio watched the old elephant pace in with the girl on her back, stop at the right spot, put her front feet on the platform, and raise her trunk for an apple. Bill ran the lift to zip Matilda upward, then lowered her to the floor.

"Looks fine, Sammy, but is the elephant going to stay there or go out?"

"Out. I'll run her through it, Gio. We were getting the lift, you understand."

"Yes. If it were me, I'd leave her there, but you know Sally wants to be the only star."

"Yes sir, I mean, yes, I will run her through it."

"Ok, I know you will. Where's Pop?"

Maurice pointed in the direction of the coach.

"DID YOU HAVE fun, Matilda?" Sam asked while he scratched around Eloise's ear opening.

"Oh, I did." Matilda blushed when Bill put his arm around her shoulders and kissed her temple.

"I wish we could train you to do the whole act. Eloise already likes you," Sam said.

Bill gave Sam a warning head tilt as Sally Fiscalini strode into the ring wearing canary-yellow leotard and tights with a flutter skirt tied at the waist.

Bill escorted his grinning, glowing wife back to their car.

"WE HAD TO get the elephant doing the lift. It's for your own safety, Mrs. Fiscalini," Sam said, "and fortunately Matilda was willing to help."

"And I suppose you haven't been told I've worked with elephants all my life. My father had—"

"Sally, Sam's doing what I told him to do. And you haven't worked with elephants in years." Gio nodded to Sam who tapped Eloise's shoulder and started out of the ring.

"I'll have you know I was a star attraction when I was riding elephants. And you have some common girl as what, my understudy? Really, Gio, you are getting as daft as your fa—"

"Please stop, Sally. I have a show to put on whether you show up for rehearsals or not."

"Well, I never!" Sally huffed.

"No, you never do." Sally swung a fist at Gio's face. He caught her wrist. "Sally, stop. Just stop. Go back to your car. We're done with rehearsals. They have it worked out. Sam will cue you. And you will do this act with a mechanic, and I'm not hearing any arguments."

"We'll see about that." Sally's face twisted as she stormed out.

Gio watched her pass his father's coach and climb the steps to Bernice and Antonio's. She knocked, the door opened, and Sally went in.

BERNICE HANDED THE glass-beaded red and green striped costume over. A moment later Sally screeched from behind the screen, "I need help in here. Fix this!" She stood with her hands on a chair back, waiting for Bernice to pull her corset tighter. "How can I breathe in this? You must have got my measurements wrong."

"Oh, for Christ's sake, Sally. No, I didn't. You gained weight." Sally put her hands over her face and began to cry. "Stop with all the tears. I know better."

"Bernice, I'm—I'm—"

"Lord, how far along this time?"

"I—I—"

"Is it Giovanni's?" Bernice put her hands on her wide hips and stood back from her sister-in-law. Sally slid the costume off her hips and let it drop to the floor. She pulled her yellow leotard back up and tied her skirt higher than usual.

"Please, Bernice, can you put a panel in around the zipper? I just need some time."

"Sally—we can't wait. What are you, three months along?"

Sally smoothed her hair and nodded.

"Then it's now or never. You're not performing this week. I don't care what you tell your husband."

GIO WATCHED SALLY leave Bernice and Antonio's coach and hurry to his father's car.

Bernice stood on her stoop with her tape measure hanging from her neck, shook her head at Gio, and went back inside.

Sally told Giovanni she'd twisted her knee and didn't think she could perform. She shooed her husband out once she was in bed with the ice filled red rubber bag. She'd be fine, she insisted, just needed rest. Told him to go play cards with the boys and to leave her alone through dinnertime.

GIOVANNI WAS SITTING down for coffee in the pie car when Bernice entered her brother-in-law's car with her black leather doctor's bag. When Bernice left an hour later, Sally rested on clean sheets, trussed up with four sanitary napkins, and wasn't pregnant.

At the desk in Gio's coach, Gio and Tony worked up a new show. They agreed they could do an all-male trapeze act and do more with the horses, but it was a shame they couldn't do the elephant act.

Sally was fast asleep with a fresh bag of ice on her uninjured knee when Giovanni came from supper. He looked in on her, then put on his silk pajamas, lay on the couch at the other end of the coach and tried to remember the last time his wife had been happy.

ROSA TOLD GIO she was ready to perform the horse-to-horse backflip layout she'd learned when she was working with the Zoppé show. Gio told Schatz to resuscitate the longer Keystone Cops act and have the doctor act ready, and they'd have Maurice put on the two headed giant outfit so Velma and Betty could ride on his big shoulders with their heads poking out the oversized neck hole. The added acts provided the ten minutes of fill time they needed.

The next morning Gio and Tony let Sam know they'd have to scrap the elephant lift for this show.

"Guys," Sam appealed, "what if we put Matilda on and let her do the lift? And Tony, you can just pick her up, pass her off, or put her on the boards. Eloise needs to do the whole thing in the tent with the crowd. And Matilda can do it."

"I don't know, Sam. Gio, what do you think?" Tony dumped sugar into his third cup of coffee and stirred vigorously.

Gio shrugged. "If we do that, poor Dad'll have to listen to Sally bitch. If Sally's knee is healed up by the time we get to El Paso, she'll do the lift there."

Tony leaned forward. "Nothing's wrong with her knee, Gio."

"Really. What's the matter, her costume didn't fit?"

Tony whispered, "No, just like in Boston last year. Bernice helped her out again."

"Does Pop know that?" Gio watched the dining car for tipped heads and listening ears.

"No. And maybe he should. It's not like Bernice doesn't have enough to do fixing up people that get hurt and keeping Ignacio and his concubines from breeding."

"Well, from what I hear walking around at night, they're breeding." Gio mopped the bottom of his cup with a paper napkin.

"Right. Well, at least not making more of them."

"Let's get Matilda in the ring helping Sammy for a few nights. I don't want to put that much on her just yet."

SAM RAN A finger around the rim of his coffee cup. "Bill, would you let Matilda be my assistant? She'd mainly stand there and look nice. I think in this cow town, she might go over better than my Maurice in a loincloth."

"Fine with me. She loves those elephants. I'll ask her. But no jungle outfit, okay? Some of these guys in this town are kinda rough." He looked to Gio and Tony for approval. "Maybe Bernice has something she can put her in. I want her to feel pretty."

"She's pretty, Bill," Sam said quietly.

"I know, Sam, but she doesn't know."

RORY CHAPMAN HAD charmed his way into Rosa's bed when the show played Atlanta, Georgia in early spring. He'd told her he was a bareback rider and he'd worked for the Hanneford Circus, and as soon as his leg was fully healed from a spiral fracture he'd gotten coming down from a three-layer pyramid when the inside horse had stumbled, he was going to be a big help to her show. Since Rory had been with Fiscalinis, all he'd done was groom horses. He was always in the wrong place when it was time to leg Rosa up for the act.

Rosa figured out in the first month that Rory was lying about his experience with horse acts and had probably wormed his way onto the train to escape trouble somewhere else. Over the next month Rosa grew tired of his ever-changing story and had run him out of her bed, which was good news for Schatz, with whom Rosa had a long-standing arrangement. Rory schlepped his way into the roustabout car to bunk. Gio put Rory on crew pay but told his long-time guys to keep an eye on him.

Rory offered a cigarette to Sally one day in Georgia, while everyone else still assumed his story about being a performer healing from an injury was true. While Giovanni and Gio were off picking up groceries Sally had him slip through the door of Giovanni's and her car. She sent him away twenty minutes later.

Milana had observed Rory leaving the car with the back of his shirt-tail flapping and filed the information away.

WHILE ROSA REHEARSED the horse-to-horse layout with Giovanni and Tony watching, Rory hurried to Sally's car where she was reported to be recovering from her sprained knee. He knocked on the window. Sally opened the curtain and shrieked at him to get the hell away from her. He jumped down, turned to go, and ran right smack into Milana. Milana didn't need to say a thing.

Rory packed his duffle bag and in less than a half hour was in town at a café telling locals he had plenty of experience breaking colts and knew about cattle, too, since his family had a ranch in New Mexico. By the time Rory hitched a ride to Midland, the woman who gave the nice looking clean-shaven young man a lift was convinced he was the horse trainer for Ringling Brothers circus, sent to Texas to purchase some matching horses for his new act.

Tony heard from Milana that she'd caught Rory at Sally's window and was disappointed the punk had bailed so soon. He'd sure hoped for a chance to rough him up.

SAM'S THURSDAY NIGHT elephant act included his new, willowy female assistant in white trousers, a white drum major's jacket and a tall white top hat that hid her tightly wound bun of orange curls. Matilda handed hoops and balls to Sanger, Master of Elephants, and fed apple halves to Eloise and Marta. She held Sam's hand to take the bow with him, then trotted beside Marta as she followed Eloise out of the ring.

Bill patted Matilda's arm when they passed each other: her on her way out, him in makeup, going in dressed as an old bewildered-looking clown with a shovel to pick up elephant dung while he double checked everything for Gio, Tony, and Giovanni's Flying Fiscalinis act. Giovanni didn't do his signature double rotation that night, and nobody in Fort Stockton knew the difference.

FOR THE FRIDAY matinee, Gio and Tony decided to go with Sam's idea, which was to send Matilda in on Eloise to perform the lift. Sam suggested she wear a green leotard and green tights to accent her hair color. Since she'd be wearing the mechanic, Maurice and Bill could be ready to pluck her off the elephant if anything went wrong.

The music began. Eloise hesitated at the entrance, then charged past the spot where they'd practiced the lift.

Bill called "Off." He and Maurice pulled the mechanic rope and Matilda squeaked in surprise when she was yanked into the air but spread her arms and trusted her husband. The momentum carried her in an arc around the ring.

"I'm putting her down across the ring away from that elephant," Bill whispered hoarsely. They kept her aloft for another circle. Matilda frog-kicked like a swimmer. The audience howled. Sam cued Eloise to do a trunk stand to get regain her attention.

But all eyes were on the girl in green, who swam in the air like a skinny Esther Williams, landed at a staggering run, twirled, and waved both hands at the laughing, clapping crowd. Matilda unclipped the cable from the mechanic, blew Bill and Maurice a kiss, took a bow, and ran out.

Bill found Matilda in the backyard, with her hands over her face. "Oh, sweetheart, you did great anyway. Please don't cry. They loved you. You did perfect."

Matilda wasn't crying. She was ecstatic. "Can we do it again?"

Changing of the Stars
1944, Fort Stockton to El Paso, Texas

THE NEXT NIGHT, Gio let Matilda pick the song she wanted. When Bill and Maurice lifted her from the elephant's neck and flew her around the ring she swam and flapped to "The Band Played On." The crowd loved her.

On the way to El Paso, everyone in the crew was still talking about that funny wife of Bill Kazarian's and her wildly waving mass of curls, flying around the ring getting all the laughs.

When the train stopped in El Paso, while Giovanni buttered Sally's toast, she told him her knee was much better and she'd be ready to perform when they got to Las Cruces and that she wasn't about to let Bill's scrawny wife steal her spotlight.

1944, El Paso, Texas

"GODDAMMIT, BERNICE, YOU pull this thing tighter." Sally reached around and yanked at the corset strings.

"Don't you take it out on me, Sally."

"You fix this goddamn costume. I'm wearing it."

Bernice had already added one-inch panels of black fabric on both sides of the red and green beaded costume to get Sally into it. Sally decided she'd wear fishnet tights with it, and Bernice suggested she wear flesh-colored tights under them until she got back in shape. Sally wheeled to glare at Bernice, who folded her arms and returned the stare.

Giovanni told Gio and Sam that Sally would do the elephant lift, but Gio and Sam were firm there'd be no such thing until Sally had actually rehearsed. Giovanni told Sally and Sally stormed out to find Gio and order him to make Sam get the elephant ready or else.

Gio said, "Or else what?"

Sally yelled at Sam next. Sam told her he wasn't going to let her on the elephant until Gio cleared it. She screamed that she'd have him fired. He told her that was fine.

RIGHT AFTER THE San Antonio cancellation Gio had sent a letter to the president of the El Paso Rotary Club about how wonderfully generous it would be for the factory owners in town to treat the families of their workers to opening night at the circus. Every member of the El Paso Rotary bought ten tickets in advance for Thursday night.

The Elks Lodge got a letter about the merits of Friday night and a bundle of tickets, and the Moose Lodge members, not to be outdone, bought Saturday matinee and night show tickets. El Paso opened Thursday night to a full house.

At intermission, Sally came into the backyard looking for Bill and told him to get things set up for her elephant finale.

"No, Mrs. Fiscalini, I can't do that. Gio and Sam already told me you're not doing the act."

"What's going on?" Gio asked when he walked by on his way to help Rosa and Schatz with two teams of horses.

"I'm riding that elephant, or I'm not going on at all!"

"Really, Sally, don't say things like that. We were fine without you all last week."

Sally stomped to her coach and slammed the door shut behind her.

Gio turned to Sam and Maurice. "Maurice, get the elephant ready. Bill, go get Matilda in her costume. She's doing the lift."

THE NEXT WEEK during the first night in Las Cruces the underarm of one sleeve of Matilda's green leotard ripped. In the morning, she ran the leotard over to Bernice's car.

Bernice clucked at the rip and said, "Give me a minute, sweetheart. You want toast? There's toast and jam on the table." After ten minutes at the sewing machine, Bernice handed her the green leotard, sans sleeves, with thin rolled straps, and a deep cut neckline. "Might as well show off those pretty tattoos."

When Matilda was dressed for the Friday night show, Bill stood behind her, looking at her reflection.

"Holy simoly, honey. Look how good the green looks with those flowers, and here." He shifted the strap higher on her shoulder. The hummingbird tattoo seemed to glow. "Look at you."

Matilda stared at her reflection.

THAT NIGHT BERNICE watched Matilda being lifted from the elephant's neck, saw her sail over the ring, observed the clumsy—maybe a purposely clumsy—bow. She noted how the people in the audience craned their necks to watch the frizzy-haired girl run out, waving and grinning, and heard them murmuring about the tattoos.

Bernice went to Bill after the show. "How do you feel about us showing off more of your wife's tattoos?"

He shrugged. "If she wants to."

"Good. I have an idea. Have her get that green leotard over to me tonight."

THE NEXT MORNING while Sally sulked in the coach, Bernice reworked the green leotard: a single strap on one side, and the leg holes cut nearly to the waist. She spread a line of toupee' glue on the edges to keep the costume from slipping.

"Really?" Matilda wondered, looking in the mirror.

"Yes, really. Honey, you got something special. Let's use it."

THE AUDIENCE GASPED when Matilda rode out on Eloise, shoulder and thigh tattoos showing. They clapped wildly at the lift, fly, and landing. They roared when she took a bow. Giovanni said nothing to Sally when he went back to his coach that night and found her in the tub with a magazine.

Antonio hugged Bernice hard. "Did you see? Did you hear? Your costume was perfect for her."

Matilda and Bill sat cross-legged on their bed that night, tracing patterns on each other's skin. He touched the hummingbird tenderly.

She blinked at him. "I want more."

"I know."

GIO LAY ON his bed, having already sent that night's circus follower home. He'd seen the shift from the audience when Matilda came out with her ink on display. He started planning a new act. He was going to teach that funny, skinny tattooed girl to be a flyer.

1958, Fayette, Missouri

". . . AND OH, EVERYBODY was talkin' about you after Bernice fixed that old green costume up to show off your tattoos. Remember that?"

I was scared to death that leotard was gonna slide off and embarrass me and you both. "Buh-buhn"

"That's right. Bernice. She called yesterday. She and Tony want to come see you when you're ready. You'd like that, wouldn't you?" Bill says, pushing her hair off her forehead.

Tell Bernice to come see me. You tell her I need her. I need some egg salad.

"Hey, if the doctor says it's okay, maybe we can mash up some of her egg salad for you. I'll bet you'd like that."

1944, Las Cruces, New Mexico

"LOOK AT THIS. Wouldn't this be pretty as a tattoo?" Matilda draped a half yard of Hawaiian print fabric from Bernice over her thigh. "As long as we're here today, I could get this done."

"Pretty. Won't you have a bandage?"

"Yeah. Bernice can sew one leg of a pair of tights on that side."

"You don't want to wait 'til we can get back to New Orleans and have your other guy do it?"

"Naw, I don't want to wait. Eddie'll understand."

"Whatever you want, honey. I'm headed to town now. I can ask around about a tattoo parlor."

"I'll just go with you."

AT LOU'S TATTOO in Las Cruces, a woman with full sleeve crosses and roses designed a hip to knee garland of lavender, magenta, and pink flowers to replicate the fabric and matched the color of the leaves to the emerald leotard Matilda took along. Four hours of fresh ink were exactly what Matilda needed.

SALLY ORDERED HER husband to take her into town for a new hairdo. Giovanni suggested she ask Bernice to cut her hair. Sally threw her hairbrush and hand mirror against the wall, put on a new dress and shoes, snatched up her matching pocketbook, and walked toward the main drag. She slid into a phone booth to make a collect long-distance call to Florida.

"Daddy? Where's our train right now? Where in Utah? Oh yes, Heber City. Of course. Where next? Where? Good lord, when did we start playing Salt Lake City? What dates? Because, Daddy, I'm coming back. Because I'm leaving Giovanni. Because. I just am. Daddy—no—stop. I don't want to try. Tell them I'll meet them in Salt Lake. What station stop is that? Never mind, I'll find them. Thanks, Daddy."

Back at the Fiscalini train, everyone on the train heard the shouting when Giovanni came in to find Sally packing her suitcases and trunks. Maurice and Schatz waited outside, chuckling at the river of obscenities that gushed from open windows, then happily carried Sally's things to the train platform.

And just like that, the Flying Fiscalinis were ready for a new female flyer.

The Desert

1944, Lafontaine's, New Orleans, Louisiana

EDDIE'S MONKEY TAPPED its ragged claws on the dresser and waited, hunched over the dresser drawer where Eddie kept his kit. *Where are you, buddy boy? Come back and take care of me me me.*

More for me. More for Eddie. More for me. How's 'bout it, Eddie? Daddy-o's poontaine thinks she's real smart. She says my Eddie stinks. Dumb bitch. Hurry back, stinky buddy boy.

The door opened. His Lord and Savior rolled in.

1958, Fayette, Missouri

SOMETHING'S WRONG WITH *my leg, Bill. I can't move it. I can't point my toe. I've got shows to do.*

"Oh, and when they take the pins out of that leg," Bill says as he massages her ankle, "they say it'll be stiff, but I'll help you get it working good again. We'll make you good as new."

I think I'm talking to you, but "whaaaa" *doesn't anything comes* "owwww?"

"Is it your leg or head that hurts you the most, honey?"

1944, Benson, Arizona

WHEN THE TRAIN pulled into Benson, Arizona, Tony tried to get the lot extended to Sunday, so Bernice's daughter Christine would have an extra chance to come and bring her five kids, but the preacher of the Riverside Church of Christ was not about to split his door with the circus for Sunday. Christine didn't come anyway, just like she hadn't the past ten years. Bernice said it didn't matter. Tony knew better.

The preacher did allow them to keep the tent up until Monday night which gave Gio and Tony a day to teach Matilda a simple catch on the trapeze. While Bill worked the mechanic, Giovanni sat in a folding chair, smoking one cigarette after another.

"Gio! Her extension! She has to get both legs extended. Matilda, dear, show me that you can point your toes. Good. Now do that in the air instead of looking like a duck landing on a pond."

Matilda pushed off again. "But keep your legs together. There. Knees! Knees! You can't fall, your husband has you."

WHEN ROSA WAS laced into her gypsy girl costume, grown men sucked air through their teeth and hope their wives didn't notice. The shining black hair, lush, full lips, and her ever-changing beauty mark made Rosa the woman men secretly wanted to meet after the show. They'd fantasize her tossing back a drink and grabbing them by the hand for a roll in the straw they imagined surrounded her sleek horses in a private railroad car. Rosa's dramatic horse to horse layout was the highlight of the first half of every show.

But it was Matilda, the long-limbed, coffee with heavy cream-skinned girl with the mass of pale apricot-colored curls and tattoos from shoulders to forearms and covering both thighs, that made the newspapers. One reporter called her a "nice looking colored girl; so rare in the circus." Some speculated the tattoos weren't real. Some speculated her hair was bleached, or a wig. What Tattooed Matilda lacked in trapeze skills, she made up in her ability to ad-lib when things didn't go as planned.

IN TUCSON, MATILDA performed the lift from Eloise and executed two simple passes between Gio and Tony. Giovanni posed on the platform but never left the boards.

After their first show in Tucson, Bernice took an egg salad sandwich and tea to her brother-in-law's car.

"Thank you, Bernice, you are nice to bring this. I'm sorry for all the things my wife said to you. She is—what's the word I want?"

"A bitch and you're better off without her?" Bernice poured tea from a thermos and set the cup down firmly.

Giovanni looked up, startled. "Ah, but my Sally was so beautiful. How could I resist? I just don't know why she was always so—well, you know. I see you and Tony. So . . ." He sipped his tea.

"Peaceful? Happy? I love you dearly, G'vanni, but you keep getting married to women your eyes tell you to marry without seeing that your heart should have a say."

Gio tapped on the door. "Pop," he began.

Bernice held up the thermos.

"No tea, thanks. Bernice, you stay, I need you here too. Pop, I want you to see a doctor. Something isn't right. Let's find a doctor tomorrow. I'll send Rosa with you. She needs to see a doctor too."

Bernice's head snapped around. Gio waved two fingers at her. She understood.

Giovanni sighed deeply and put one hand to his temple. "Gio, I'm tired. I'll be fine in a few days."

Gio and Bernice moved their chairs closer. Tony came in and stood behind his wife.

"We're getting Pop to a doctor tomorrow, Tony," Gio said quietly.

"Good idea. You listen to my wife and your son. Milana and I agree."

"Why does everyone think I need a doctor? My heart is broken. My wife left me. I'm all alone."

"Brother," Tony shook his head, "you were alone when Sally was here."

OUTSIDE THE DOCTOR'S office, Giovanni told Rosa to tell the doctor she was his wife. Rosa laughed. Rosa told the doctor she was Giovanni's daughter.

"Your father's heart is weak. I'll write a prescription for some medication. Now, Mr. Fiscalini, I want you to eat more leafy vegetables and cut down on the wine. And no more smoking."

GIO WENT TO Giovanni's coach and took the wine bottles out of the bar while his father slept. When Giovanni came out later in the afternoon to watch rehearsals, Milana handed him a paper cup of water.

"No, dear. Be a good girl and get me some wine." He handed the cup back.

"No, Poppy, doctor's orders."

"Gio! You come down here. You fire that damned Rosa. How dare she tell everyone about my going to the doctor."

Gio came down the ladder. "Pop. Stop. We're trying to help you."

The elder Fiscalini stood, slapped the cup of water out of his daughter's hand and stamped out of the tent.

1944, Indio, California

GIOVANNI'S COMPLEXION HAD grown greyer and waxier by the time they reached Indio. Gio and Tony wondered if they ought to take him in a hospital and leave Milana with him while they went on to Los Angeles. Giovanni wouldn't hear of it. He dressed for every performance but didn't perform. He came to dinner in the backyard before night shows and pushed food across his plate in slow, deliberate motions. Milana took to sitting with him to get him to eat. He demanded she bring him wine. She gave him grape juice. He threw the glasses across the table at the clowns.

THEIR NEXT SHOW was in the outer parking lot at the Santa Anita racetrack for a three-nighter. While the tents went up, Rosa went to see an old racehorse trainer friend, hoping he'd have a solid, sound pony horse she could train as a trick riding horse because if there was ever a time for her to do three acts a night, it was now, before she turned forty. She forked over forty-five dollars and came back riding a glass-eyed piebald with a halter and lead rope. Schatz took one look at the horse and muttered, "Good Lord." But the gelding seemed gentle enough, and Rosa told Schatz if the horse had been a track pony there wasn't anything that would undo him.

Sure enough, the piebald was unflappable in the tent when Rosa started him on a lunge line. That was, until Sam entered with one of the elephants, and the poor horse looked for a fast escape right over Rosa, jumped the side rail, and galloped out the back flap.

While Rosa iced her bruised shoulder and face, Schatz caught the horse and led it to the training barns, where a gallop boy pointed to the barn the former owner of the horse occupied. Schatz got Rosa's forty-five dollars back and the trainer, who'd thought he might have an opportunity to visit Rosa that night, got the message that his appearance at the circus tent would not be met with enthusiasm.

The trainer's assistant had shown up two days earlier with a new lady friend, a woman who had latched on to him when he'd offered her a ride from Louisville, Kentucky to New Orleans. The woman said her family was there, and that she was going to get her old betting window job back at Fair Grounds. He'd let her out at the office with her suitcase and went on to deliver some horses on the backstretch row, thinking he'd never see Suzette Chevalier again.

Two hours later, when he was finished loading horses to take to southern California, he found Suzette in the truck with her suitcase.

SUZETTE SAT ON the bleachers in the circus tent beside her boyfriend. She laughed at the clowns, gasped at the size of the two-headed giant, clapped for the heavily made-up rosinback rider and for the dog act. She listened breathlessly, while the announcer conveyed the tale of the exotic Nubian princess who'd been raised among apes. How, after her capture, no one could keep the child from swinging from clothes lines and chandeliers. How she had to be taught English to keep her from hooting like a savage. How they had to go looking for her when her primal desire for tattoos took over.

And Suzette gripped her boyfriend's arm so hard she left fingernail marks when her daughter, Matilda, rode in on an elephant.

Suzette sent her boyfriend back to the barn after the show, saying she'd seen someone she used to know and wanted to say hello in private.

"UMM. MOMMA." MATILDA'S voice was barely audible over the din of roustabouts cleaning under the bleachers.

"Hello, Matilda. My goodness you've grown. I saw Momma and Daddy a couple weeks ago and they said you'd run off. My goodness, child. My goodness."

"Momma. What are you doin' here?" Matilda gulped down other words she couldn't say. She would not cry. She would not cry.

Bill saw the stricken look on Matilda's face and headed over.

"Everything okay here?"

Suzette turned to him. "Excuse me?"

"I was asking my wife. Bill Kazarian." He extended a hand. "And you are?"

Suzette put her hand in his and smiled coyly. Matilda cringed. "I babysat your wife when she was little. Well, look at the time. I must be going. So good to see you, Matilda."

Suzette walked out the back gate. Matilda let out a rattling breath when Bill touched her arm.

"Who was that?"

"My mother." Matilda pulled away from Bill and headed to their car.

"SO, THIS IS what, a medal of honor?" The round-bellied man in the white undershirt put his glasses on to peer at the medal in the wooden box. Tattoos of roulette tables and dice covered his arms.

"Silver Cross. My daddy's. Got it in the First World War. Can you do it?" Matilda lifted her father's medal and lay it on the sketch pad between them. She self-consciously tugged at the bandeau top she'd worn under an open blouse.

"Sure. Show me where." He dug around in a pencil cup.

Matilda tapped to the left of her sternum. "Can you fit the cross part underneath these flowers? Like it belongs there?"

"Yep, can do. Want me to leave some room beside it, you know, for something else someday?" Matilda nodded enthusiastically. "What if I do a border of leaves so it goes with this other work?" She nodded again. "Good work, by the way. Anybody around here?"

"Naw, a guy I know in New Orleans."

"What guy?"

"Lucky Eddie. He did a bunch of my ink."

The man raised one scruffy eyebrow. "Lafontaine?" Matilda's eyes widened, and she nodded. "Son of a gun. I knew his dad. Deaf guy? Sonny?" She nodded again.

"I'll be damned. His uncle taught both of us. Long time ago. He sends a Christmas card. Damn shame 'bout Eddie's leg. So," he sketched quickly, "what about this?"

Matilda glanced down at the sketch pad and her mouth spread into a wide smile. "Let's do it."

1958, Fayette, Missouri, six weeks after

"WELL, WE CAN certainly take the arm cast off now. I'll do an x-ray of the leg while we're at it. I don't want to remove those pins until I know the bones have healed completely," Dr. McClure says.

"I think she'll like the cast off so she can move her arm. She's moving her good leg and arching her foot," Bill says earnestly, "aren't you, honey?" He slides his square hand onto his wife's forearm and strokes it tenderly. She opens her eyes and turns her head toward his voice.

You tell him. I need both legs to work. You tell him.

"I know this sounds crazy, doc, but I understand her," Bill says, "and it bothers her that she can't move her leg."

1944, Santa Barbara, California

THE FISCALINI BROTHERS Circus wasn't granted a permit to do a parade in Santa Barbara, but there was no ordinance that said the troupe couldn't walk to the public beach for a swim.

It was Bernice's idea, taking the elephants and horses to the ocean, with Matilda riding Eloise in a raspberry-colored two-piece costume. Sam and Maurice donned matching tiger print loincloth costumes to guide the elephants down the pine tree lined lane and over the bridge that spanned Highway 101.

Rosa waited a few minutes for Matilda, Sam, and Maurice to get on their way before she went out wearing a white halter top and shorts, riding the white Percheron. Schatz wore a matching Hawaiian pattern shirt and shorts, white face makeup, and his conical hat to follow Rosa, leading the two grey Percherons.

Giovanni, Antonio, and Gio paraded out a minute later in tight fitting trunks, black hair oiled to a spit shine. Schatz had the clowns wear swim trunks but put on face makeup.

"Whattabout us?" Velma piped, "We wear trunks too?"

"You show them tits to everybody anyway," Ignacio hooted.

Ignacio, Betty, and Velma went next, tussling and wrestling over a beach ball and bucket. Bill wore the Borneo Wildman wig, sunglasses, and loincloth to ape his way out in front of the dogs, trainer, and five clowns.

The traffic jam on highway 101 backed up for a mile each direction.

While the elephants splashed and rolled in the Pacific, Rosa roman rode the two grey horses up and down the beach at a trot, sending sheets of water up as she swung the team out into the waves. The crowd of onlookers grew.

When they'd been on the beach an hour, Gio signaled for the troupe to line up, and they started back, with Matilda and Eloise in the lead. More than a hundred onlookers followed. Milana and the elderly ticket booth tender were ready for the onslaught. Opening night was sold out before noon.

Giovanni and Antonio's sister Gloria, their flyer before she'd fallen in love with a rancher and left the show, drove down from Cambria with her husband for a pre-show dinner. Gloria kissed cheeks and exclaimed how she'd missed everyone, whether she'd met them or not.

She held Matilda's hands in hers. "Well isn't Bill the luckiest man? Just look how pretty you are. When's the baby due?"

Bill choked and sputtered while Tony clapped his back.

Matilda blushed from her shoulders up and gawked, pop-eyed at the tall, pony-tailed, and sharp featured woman. "Oh, sweetie, I know these things. Right, Bernice?" Bernice shook her head. "Well, soon enough." Gloria slid over to visit Velma and Betty.

Bernice leaned close to Matilda and whispered, "Don't let that bother you. My sister-in-law says that to every woman she likes."

PERFORMANCES SOLD OUT in Santa Barbara. Rosa received roses every night from a deeply tanned man in a seersucker suit. Giovanni went up for the trapeze act and did some calls and gesticulations to the other performers since Gloria was there. Concessions sales were brisk because Milana told the local girls she'd hired to wear shorts and bathing suit tops.

The Santa Barbara audiences chanted Matilda's name and she responded by doing impromptu Josephine Baker dances on the platform. Bernice watched from the back and planned Matilda's next costume.

The Sunday newspaper featured photos of Rosa with the horses and Matilda on the elephant. When Bill brought the paper to breakfast to show his wife, Matilda touched the photos, and read the captions: "Beautiful Equestrian Ballerina, Rosa, and Trapeze Star, Tattooed Matilda." She scanned the pie car for Rosa and Schatz and handed the paper toward them.

"Well how about that!" Rosa said.

Gio leaned across the table to take the paper from Rosa. "Time to make new posters."

BILL TOLD MATILDA the next stops were at the fairgrounds in Tulare, California, then Fresno.

"Isn't that close to where you're from?"

"Yes."

"You gonna call your family?"

"I don't know. Maybe."

"They're your folks. I want to meet them."

"Honey, you don't know them."

1944, New Orleans, Louisiana

"ANOTHER POSTCARD FROM Matilda, Eddie." Mary Ellen dropped the card on Eddie's sketch table.

"Yeah? What's she say?"

Mary Ellen held the card up so Eddie could see the photograph of the beach and harbor.

> Dear Eddie,
>   We are in Santa Barbara California and we took the elephants to the beach. They sure did like it. Have you ever been there? Bill says we'll be in some place called Toolarry next, then the next town is Fresno, close to his family so I guess I'll meet them. I don't think I'll be back to New Orleans for a while. I hope things are good there.
>   See you later,
>   Your friend Matilda

Mary Ellen tucked the postcard in the frame on the corkboard on the studio wall alongside a half dozen other postcards from Matilda. "Sounds like she's having a good time. I can't imagine living on a train like that."

"Yeah. I hope that guy's good to her. She's a good kid, no thanks to her mother. Now that was a piece of work. Purty, but trashy. Then some of those asshole kids were shitty to her at school. I don't think she really had any friends here."

"She had you. She could've gone anywhere for tattoos."

Eddie flashed his mother-in-law a smile. "Yeah? I told her not to."

The Family

1944, Fresno, California

"AND THIS IS Matilda, the girl you saw on the trapeze." Bill rocked on his heels, took a hand out of his pocket, and motioned for Matilda to come over where his family stood after the Sunday matinee in Fresno.

"Well, that was some show you put on, miss." Bill's brother and pregnant sister-in-law pressed closer.

"How much does that elephant weigh?" The bristly headed ten-year-old boy who wriggled behind Bill's sister turned his face up toward Matilda. "Hey, has it ever stomped on you? How much does it eat?"

Bill's sister exhaled. "I'm sorry. My son, Joe," she patted the boy's head, "asks a lot of questions."

The kid peered around his mother's arm. "Hey are you colored or are you—"

"Joe! How many times do I have to tell you?"

"But Mommm."

"I'm sorry." Bill's sister gripped her son's arm tightly. "We sure loved your part in the show. I heard somebody say you were new to the circus. Is that right?"

Matilda blushed. She waited for Bill to say, "This is my wife, Matilda." Bill said nothing.

"I started with the show early summer." Matilda looked to Bill to take the cue.

"Well, thanks for the tickets. We sure had a nice time." Bill's sister glanced around at the family. "We'd better get going. Nice to meet you, miss."

Bill walked his family out without inviting Matilda to go along.

Matilda waved at the curious boy who turned at the tent opening for one last look.

MATILDA WAS DUNKING a leotard in a bucket of rinse water for the fifth time when Bill came in after dark, unbuttoning his shirt. "What'd they say when you told 'em?"

He pulled on a t-shirt. "I didn't have a chance to tell them. Hey, I'll be back in a minute, I need to talk to Gio." He stopped at the door. "Good show today."

MATILDA LISTENED TO the door close and hung the leotard on the clothesline across the living room of the car. Her throat ached. Her face burned with humiliation. She wondered if he was ashamed of her looks, or if it was her tattoos. She would not cry. She would not cry. She put on her nightgown, faced the wall, and pretended to be asleep when he came to bed. She thanked God he didn't touch her. She would not cry.

THE TROUPE STAYED over an extra day in Fresno to restock the pie car and wait for a load of elephant and horse hay. Bill said he had some errands to run. Rosa and Schatz came by to get Matilda, and the three of them walked along the side of the road toward the movie theater six blocks from the fairgrounds.

Rosa cleared her throat. "Bill goin' to see his kid today?" Her face went dark at Matilda's look of surprise. "Oh shit. Sonofabitch didn't tell you."

"His family came last night. His sister brought her son." Matilda slowed her pace.

"How'd that go? Meeting his family?" Rosa looked at Schatz sharply when he nudged her arm.

"Fine. I—he—" Matilda's voice went to dust in her mouth. Rosa frowned and pressed closer. Matilda stopped. Puffs of dust settled on her shoe tops.

"Bill forgot to tell you something," Rosa's voice dropped to a harsh whisper, "didn't he?" Matilda swallowed the taste of bile.

Schatz squeezed Rosa's hand. "Rosa, it's not our business."

Matilda turned around and headed toward the train.

"Damnit, now look. You go on. I'll talk to her. We'll meet you at the theater."

"I'm fine. You don't need to go with me," Matilda called without looking back.

Rosa shot Schatz a knowing look, turned toward town, and hurried to catch up with Sam and Maurice.

"LISTEN, MATILDA, ROSA got worried when she saw Bill talking to his family, and didn't see them, you know, looking surprised and happy."

"Yeah, well, he didn't tell them I was his wife, that's for sure."

"Rosa was more worried about the other."

"Well, does he have a kid?"

"Might not be what you think, you know? Well, I don't know what you think."

They walked another minute in silence. Matilda caught a sob before it got to her collarbones and shoved it back down into her aching chest. "Schatz?"

"Uh huh."

"You gonna tell me?"

"You need to ask Bill, honey."

"No. I'm asking you because he already didn't tell me. So, you tell me."

"Rosa says Gio says he does."

"*What?*" She stopped at the side of the road and looked around. No one was around to hear. "*What?*"

"I don't know what to say, hon." Schatz faced Matilda and placed a hand on her shoulder. His long face went soft and his eyes welled. Matilda's features rumpled into furrows.

"Oh, honey, I'm so sorry." Schatz patted her shoulders and looked up and down the street. "Oh, don't cry. Let's go on to that movie. Come on." He had no idea what to do with an upset woman, much less one who'd just gotten her young heart whacked up the side of the head.

"I'm not cryin'. But he lied?"

"Wait, it's not quite like that. Rosa says Gio told her Bill said his wife took the baby and left him. He's never seen the kid once in something like seven years."

"Oh, that makes it a lot better. A lot better." Matilda was incredulous.

"God, I'm so sorry, hon. Let's go to the movie. I'll make Rosa keep her mouth shut. She shouldn't have been the one who told you."

"'S OK, Schatz, it's not your fault. Or Rosa's." Matilda pulled her chest inward to feel for her heart. It was still there, pounding blood through her veins. "I don't know what to do, Schatz. I don't know what to do."

"Come on. We'll get three popcorns. Three cokes. Come on. It'll all be okay."

"*How does it be okay?*" Matilda balled her fists and stared at six-foot-six, gentle-faced Schatz. His fine hair lay slack against his head, like he had just wet and combed it. She wished it would bristle up. She wished he'd be mad with her. "Why is this happening?"

Schatz took her by the arms and whispered, "You're in the circus, baby girl. Full of clowns."

1944—Bill's Annulment

"SO, I SIGN and then what happens?" Bill's damp shirt and suit coat clung to him.

"Once you've signed, the annulment is granted. You're no longer married to Crystal." The lawyer opened the drawer in front of him and produced a pen.

"What's this part about fraud?" Sweat trickled down Bill's back.

"There has to be just cause, Mr. Kazarian. That was the cause Mrs. Kazarian listed. We don't ask."

Bill read the paper on the desk again without picking it up. The fountain pen lay across the letterhead.

"I filed for a divorce back then. Why didn't it work?"

"She didn't respond to the petition. Did no one tell you there was more to do than that?"

"I guess not. I was too scared to come back. Her brothers said they'd kill me if I did. What about the boy? What was that other thing?"

"When you sign this other paper, Crystal will have sole custody. She doesn't want money from you, Mr. Kazarian. I don't know why but consider yourself lucky. Some women—well . . ."

WHEN BILL WAS nineteen, he'd finally given in to the incessant kissing and groping by black-haired, busty Crystal, the over-ripe daughter of a neighboring farmer. She came to him crying shortly afterwards, saying he'd gotten her pregnant. Said her father and brothers would kill him if they found out she wasn't "pure." Crystal's mother got to put on a wedding. Bill's father yelled at him for not keeping his horse in the barn.

Bill's in-laws were in his business from day one. Always wanting to know the price his dad had gotten for raisins, for equipment they sold. Always asking when he was going to build their Crystal a better house.

Crystal delivered a full-sized baby boy five months after the wedding, and six-and-a-half months after the first time she'd dropped her drawers on the seat of Bill's truck. Bill marveled at the size of the baby Crystal swore was premature.

She told him she wanted to hurry and get pregnant again a month after the baby was born. She wanted to be pregnant all the time, she said. Bill tried to reason with her. He was only nineteen and she was only eighteen, he said. Shouldn't they wait before they had another baby? Crystal went running back to her parents.

He went to his in-law's house to ask her if her leaving meant she wanted a divorce. She screamed, "Yes!" and slammed the door. Her brothers paid a call after that. Bill got away with two black eyes, a broken tooth, and a warning from Crystal's brothers that he'd better get out of town. He didn't need to be told twice.

BILL READ THE part of the document about fraud again. "This part here, she says I'm sterile. How can she say that if we had a baby?"

"Listen, Bill, I can't say this in an official capacity, but I'm telling you man to man, you should take this deal. Crystal's parents want this. She wants this. She wants to marry someone else."

"Who?" Bill's face flushed.

"Listen. Just take the deal. You can write to her sometime and ask to see the boy if you want. Of course, she can say no. You're sure he's yours?"

"What do you mean?"

"Look, off the record, I've known her family a long time. My son had been dating her too. Between you and me, I'm glad she didn't put the finger on my son. That kid wasn't born premature. And he doesn't have your black hair, I can tell you that. I'm sorry. I think you got a bad deal, but that kid might just as well be my grandson. Or somebody else's. You're better off than that schmuck her mother has her set up with. Off the record."

Bill signed the annulment. He peeled off his clammy jacket outside the office and hailed a cab. He was sure glad his dad had pulled him aside and given him the letter saying where he needed to go to sign the papers. Yessir, he was sure glad of that. He'd take Matilda out for a night on the town. And he'd have to make up an excuse, like he loved her so much he wanted to marry her all over again. He could do that. That was the truest thing he knew.

BILL WASHED UP and put on a clean shirt. Matilda, Rosa, and Schatz would be getting out of the movie in around thirty minutes, he figured.

He stuffed the towels in the laundry bag and remade the bed. Dusted the chest of drawers and the mirror over it. If Matilda got home early enough, maybe a cab driver would know where to find a justice of the peace. Did he need a marriage license ahead of time? He couldn't remember. But they'd be in Nevada in a few days, and he knew from going along to a wedding in Reno once that they could get a license and get married the same day there. That's what he'd do. He'd marry Matilda again in Nevada.

At four o'clock he watched Schatz go by. He looked up the tracks and saw Rosa leaving Bernice and Tony's coach. He stuck his head out. "Where's my wife?"

Rosa stopped with her hands on her hips. "Which one, Bill? The last one, or the one that just got her heart broke?"

"Rosa, you didn't."

"Somebody had to tell her, Bill. Jesus."

"Did she come back with you?"

"She didn't get as far as the theater." Rosa walked on toward the horse car.

Bill jogged down to the elephant car. Sam and Maurice weren't there. He went to Bernice and Tony's car and knocked. Bernice came to the door with a finger to her lips.

"Tony's taking a nap. I never get him to take a nap."

"You seen Matilda?"

"No. But I guess Rosa told her why you went off to town in a hurry today. Good God, Bill."

"I signed the annulment papers today. I swear, Bernice, I just—"

"I didn't know you hadn't done that a long time ago, Billy." Bernice stepped out onto the landing and closed the door behind her.

"I didn't know it wasn't over and done 'til yesterday. And now Rosa went and told Matilda."

Bernice wrapped her hand on the railing and counted to three. "Shame on you, Bill. Don't you blame Rosa. She's not the one who was already married." Her face burned pink to the roots of her hair.

"I know. I know. I don't know why I—"

"Good Lord, Bill, you had me go stand with you to get married and I didn't know that whole deal was a sham."

"It wasn't like that, Bernice. It wasn't. You know I—"

"That poor girl. I hope she'll forgive you. I wouldn't."

"I can't find her, Bernice."

"Did you look for her stuff?"

"Oh shit." He vaulted to the ground and jogged back to his coach. In the tiny closet five wire hangers lay on the floor. He yanked open the three drawers in the painted chest beside the closet. Empty. Her satchel was gone. He opened the ancient steamer trunk at the end of the bed. Bill sank onto the clean sheets and stared at the pile of Matilda's costumes.

1944—Bus Station

THE BALD, LIVER spotted man at the ticket counter adjusted his greasy horn-rimmed glasses to peer at Bill. "Son, there's not another passenger train until tomorrow."

"I'm looking for a woman. Kind of orange looking hair?"

"Redhead? There was a cute little redhead here this morning."

"Would have been this afternoon, in the last hour. Tall woman. Kinky hair out to here." Bill indicated with his hands. "More orange than red. She has tattoos."

"Hooo, she was here. Tattoos all over her arms. Legs too. Looked like she belonged in a circus. Say, she wanted to know about a train outta here too. She wanted by the law or something?"

"Which way did she go?"

"She went to the bus station. Bus leaves every two hours going south, every two hours going north."

"Which way?" Bill looked around.

"Toward the gol-danged bus station. I told you."

"Which way *is* the station?"

"Why didn't you just ask me that in the first place? That-a-way." The old man jabbed a finger to the left of the door.

Bill hurried to the next corner, then jogged to follow a Continental Trailways bus that turned the corner two blocks ahead. He hoped like hell it was coming in, instead of leaving.

BILL WALKED CAUTIOUSLY across the bus station. Matilda shared a bench with a white-haired woman and a lidded basket that rocked and emitted unhappy cat sounds. The white-haired woman was rambling about how Fuzzy didn't like to ride in the basket, but it was better than leaving him all alone when she went to visit her sister in Bakersfield.

Matilda glanced at the basket. "Fuzzy sounds mad."

Bill walked around the end of the bench. "Matilda, honey, let me explain."

"Explain?"

"Honey, it's not like you think. I didn't know I had to do more paperwork—"

"Paperwork? You didn't even tell me you were married."

"Is he your boyfriend? He's married?" The white-haired woman moved her basket-full of howling Fuzzy and scooted down to make room on the bench for the new entertainment, right there in the Fresno bus station.

"No, ma'am, not my boyfriend. He and I got married a couple months ago. Today I found out he was already married." Matilda didn't look at Bill.

"Matilda, will you please let me explain?" Bill pleaded.

"You got ten minutes. Then I'm gettin' on a bus."

THE BUS DOORS wheezed shut behind passengers headed for Bakersfield and Los Angeles. As the transmission barked and clunked into first gear, the woman who'd packed her yowling cat to go to her sister's waved cheerfully from her window seat.

"That cat pissed all over that basket and this bench." Matilda pointed at a puddle. She didn't move over to make room for Bill.

"Matilda, I have the papers back at the train. I swear. That's why I had to go to town today. I thought I was divorced a long time ago, and that was stupid of me. I didn't know there was more to do 'til my folks showed up last night. That's why I didn't tell them about you. About us. Because I'd just found out—"

"You're married."

"Yes, I was married. Not for long, but I was. And she doesn't ever want to see me again."

"Can't say I blame her." Matilda watched the tail end of the bus.

"Honey, listen, it was—I was pretty stupid. She wanted a divorce, so I filed for a divorce. Her brothers about beat me to death. And I got on the next train out of town. I swear I didn't know there was more to do. I'm—so sorry."

Matilda ran a finger along the cluster of vines and flowers on her forearm and kept her eyes on the corner where she'd last seen the bus. "I paid for that bus ticket."

"I'll pay for it."

"I might just want another ticket."

"Come home with me. We'll be in Nevada tomorrow. I'll marry you right. I'll marry you every day if you let me."

Matilda was still watching the corner. "I left my grandparents and my brothers and my sister. I left them to be with you." She rose from the bench and picked up her carpet bag. Bill reached for it, but she held the handle tight.

"I'll make it right, Matilda. I'll make it right. I promise you right now. I'll love you forever. I will. I never said that to nobody before. I'm saying it now— no, don't wave your hand at me like that. I'm saying it out loud." Bill's voice boomed out and a group of high school-age boys turned to look. "I love you, Matilda. Marry me."

One of the boys dropped to one knee in front of another boy and put his hands on his heart. The standing boy put his hands on his face and pantomimed "yes."

"It's a little late for that." Matilda raised her chin. "I want to see the papers. Damn you. And you owe me for a bus ticket."

Nevada Wedding

1958, Fayette, Missouri

"REMEMBER THAT TIME you packed your suitcase and left? I thought I'd never find you. Remember? We got married twice," Bill says after the nurse left with half consumed bowls of pureed peaches and creamed corn.

Oh, I remember. You sat in cat piss on that bench. I bet now you wish you'd never found me.

1944, Reno, Nevada

IN DOWNTOWN RENO, Bill grabbed Matilda's hand and took her to a little white wedding chapel down the street. Maurice and Sam were their witnesses. Just as the wedding march started Rosa and Schatz slipped through the lattice doors and sat down in the front row. Rosa said she wanted to make sure it got done right.

The second night in Reno, Giovanni bowed out of dressing for the show and said he'd run the mechanic for Matilda's lift act. Maurice glanced at Gio. Gio shook his head "no" but Giovanni elbowed his way to stand in front of Maurice and stubbornly held the mechanic rope.

Matilda rode in dressed in her new bright pink, high cut, one sleeved costume with quarter inch wide strips of fabric between bodice and bottom. Eloise paced rhythmically toward her mark. From the platform, Gio saw Matilda's expression change from showman's smile, to a "keep smiling even if you don't know what's going wrong here" smile. Matilda gasped when she was snatched off the elephant, lowered to the high ridge of the back, and then left dangling in the air as the elephant continued around the ring.

Bill raced toward Maurice. Maurice cradled the pale, unconscious Giovanni Fiscalini in the crook of his arm.

A hush fell over the audience when the huge black-skinned man picked up the elderly man as though he were a child and ran toward the back of the tent. Bill gave Matilda a hard, steady pull, and she responded by arching her long back and spiraling as she was pulled upward. She looked to each platform for Gio or Tony to pick her up from there, but they were already hurrying down the ladders on either side of the net. Matilda swung her legs and aimed for the platform. She landed, held an arm high and blew a kiss to the audience. From the corner of her eye, she saw Bernice twirl a finger toward her from the curtains, and knew it was up to her to go on with something. She took the bar and launched from the platform. She heard Bill's sharp whistle and saw that Rosa, still in her rosinback costume had climbed the opposite side and was holding a bar.

Matilda and Rosa locked eyes. Rosa pumped the bar once and sent it to Matilda. Matilda let go of her bar and floated across the dust and smoke-stained air for an eternity before her hands found the second bar. She rotated smoothly to reverse directions. She saw Rosa on her way down the ladder. Matilda twisted and pushed for her platform. Another whistle sang out as she landed. Tony was coming back up.

"Take off," he called. Down in the ring, Sam trotted beside Eloise. Tony unhooked the lift rig and swung it toward Matilda. "Back on the elephant and take it out."

Matilda slowed her arc, legs pointing straight down, while Sam positioned Eloise. She let go before her toes had reached the elephant's back. When her calves hit the mighty neck, she squeezed them together to slow her drop. Eloise paced smartly out, trunk searching for the apple Sam held. The tent went dark as they reached the curtain. The lights came on as the soundman started "Stars and Stripes." That was when Sam, Bill, Rosa, and the clowns knew Giovanni's condition was serious.

"Fiscalini Brothers Circus thanks you for coming, and remember we have four more shows in beautiful Reno, Nevada. Good night, and dream of the circus!"

The cotton candy girls worked the crowd as they left, selling what Milana had made up before she'd left her trailer to go to her father's side.

Gio waited for Tony to get in the truck, then hurried to catch up with the ambulance.

STILL OIL-SHINED from the show, Maurice sat on a step stool in the backyard with his hands pressed together between his mighty thighs. He'd been crying.

Bill knelt in front of Maurice. "I think he had a heart attack. Was that what it looked like, Maur?"

"Yes, I think so. I was mad at him for being in my way, and for grabbing the rope. That's what yanked Matilda off Eloise when he went down. I wish I'd known what was happening. I wish I —he didn't know what he was doing."

"It's not your fault, sweetheart." Sam brushed a hand on Maurice's chest.

Matilda pressed her lips together. "How come the sound man put on that other music, like everything was okay?"

"That's the song he's supposed to put on if something goes wrong," Sam said, "and everybody's supposed to come running. You hope your whole life you never hear *Stars and Stripes* when you work in circus."

Bill stood. "Let's get this all shut down. Come on, guys, get the gates closed up. Somebody—you, Betty, you and Velma. You go lock up Milana's trailer. Make sure the cotton candy spinner is turned off. We don't want to burn it up. Matilda, will you go see if Bernice went with them? If she did, close her booth up." The two little women, still in makeup, headed to the concession trailers and Matilda trotted for the midway.

"He looked dead when they put him in the ambulance," Ignacio offered.

Sam whipped around. "Don't say that, Nosh."

"Well he did."

The Show Goes On

ANTONIO CAME BACK to the train at six the next morning for a change of clothes.

Bernice sat at the tiny table in her nightgown. "How long will he be in the hospital?"

"I don't know. The doctor said it was pretty bad."

The crew was at breakfast when Antonio walked in and stood at the end of the long table in the center of the pie car to tell the roustabouts and clowns what he knew: that Giovanni had suffered a stroke and was still unconscious. He asked Velma if she could take over the concessions for Milana for the rest of the run.

"Do I get paid extra?"

Ignacio grunted. "Vel, you're such a bitch."

"If she doesn't want to help, I will." Betty waddled over to stand near Antonio.

"Thanks, Betty," Antonio rubbed the stubble on his cheek. "Gio and I are going back to the hospital." He dabbed his eyes with his handkerchief, then blew his nose.

"Will he be all right, Tony?" Maurice folded his huge hands and leaned forward.

"The doctor doesn't know yet." Antonio looked down the table at the crew. A solemn clown stood to take his plate to the wash basin. Two others followed.

Betty put her small, pudgy hand over Antonio's where it rested on the table.

"I'll take care of Milana's trailer, boss. Don't you worry. Go get some sleep."

AT THE HOSPITAL Gio told his sister he'd get them a cab back to the train so they could rest. Milana stared at him, bleary-eyed, and shook her head. She would not leave her father with strangers.

Rosa and Schatz said they could stretch the rosinback act out an extra five minutes, and the clowns could do an extra run-around throwing popcorn, so Schatz had time to get the new roman riding team ready behind the curtain while Rosa did a costume change.

Sam agreed that Eloise could go around the ring several times with Matilda aboard before the lift. Gio suggested he and Tony wear the leopard print swimsuits they'd worn in Santa Barbara, and they'd have Bill climb to a platform wearing his Borneo Wild Man hair to reach and jabber every time Matilda swung close.

People did what they needed to do, because circus goes on.

Seven Weeks After

1958, Fayette, Missouri

"SON, YOU'RE WELCOME to park your trailer out at our place if that trailer park's too noisy. I can run some electricity out from the shed for you. Whatever you need, you tell me." The sheriff of Howard County, Missouri stands in the hospital room door, unsure if he should come in wearing his holster and gun. He's been by a half dozen times since the accident, but his wife has come every day with meals for Matilda's husband and mother.

I know who this is, don't I? I've heard that voice. He was there, wasn't he? If you and Momma won't tell me what happened to me, maybe he will.

"Is there any—change?" The sheriff shuffles uncomfortably. He knows he's asking an intimate question of a man whose wife is in a coma.

"There is. She knows I'm here, and she tries to talk, don't you, honey? She and I appreciate you coming by." Bill touches Matilda's forehead.

If he wants to do somethin' he can tell me—

"Is there anything else I can do to help?"

"Well, sheriff, I've been here for six—no seven weeks, not working. If you know of any work I could do, anything, I need to be—"

Seven weeks? What? Where have I been?

"Well, when my wife heard from your mother-in-law you'd sold your house in Florida to pay the hospital, she and her church ladies started raising money. She set up some jars at the bank and the gas stations, and all the stores in town, and clear down to Columbia. Everybody knows Nadine, see. She set up an account for you with the hospital. She—well, we both thought it might help."

"I—I don't know what to say." Bill and the sheriff shake hands the way men will do.

You sold our house? Matilda turns her head toward Bill's voice. A dry sob comes up but is unable to escape her lips.

PART 5
Need

Bottom of the Barrel

Dear Eddie, Mary Ellen and Mr. Lafontaine,

This post card is a picture of the bay in Sarasota. That's in Florida, where Bill's house is. I guess we will be here until the first of March. There's lots of circus and carnival people who live here. One lady on our block has hair all over her, and her husband has scales, I swear to God. The lady Rosa who has the horses, she got two new ones. She had to because some of them she had were old.

I was going to take a bus home to New Orleans and see my grandparents but we're doing rehearsals here already for next year, so I guess I'll be there in May or June. So, I'll come over. Don't get mad at me. I got some other tattoos while we were traveling, and there's a place here I go to, but they look good. You'll see. Merry Christmas.

Your friend Matilda

Dear Matilda,

Thanks so much for your note and Christmas card. I read it to Eddie while he was working on a tattoo and showed him the front of the card. He says to tell you he'd rather be there for the winter than here. He's been pretty busy, so I thought I'd write and let you know we got your card. We have lots of business, seems like people always want tattoos. Merry Christmas to you and your husband from all of us.

Warmly,

Mary Ellen Lafontaine

1945, February, Lafontaine's, New Orleans, Louisiana

'WHAT'S WRONG WITH you?' Sonny signed. Eddie mashed his cigarette on top of the full ashtray on the nightstand.

"Leave me alone." Eddie rolled onto his back.

'What's the matter, are you drunk?' Sonny signed. He looked down at his son who lay on a stained mattress with yellowed, reeking sheets slumped at the foot of the bed. He reached for the tin box beside Eddie's stump before

Eddie could grab it. Sonny stared at the syringe and needle, the spoon, the wads of wax paper, the lighter. He dropped it on the mattress.

'Leave me alone.' Eddie signed with shaking hands. 'I'm in pain. I need it for pain.' He waved a hand at his stump in disgust.

'Then we go to the V.A. and get a doctor to help you. But not this. Not this.' Sonny's face grew red with silent rage. 'Are you trying to get arrested? Like your no-good friend?'

"I don't care," Eddie moaned. Sonny swung at his son and punched him in the chest.

'I care.'

Sonny went to Mary Ellen. 'You call the Veterans Hospital. Eddie needs a doctor.' Mary Ellen put her hand on Sonny's face and looked into his grey eyes. He grimaced. 'He's been using heroin. Did you know that?'

Mary Ellen stared at the appointment book for a second, then nodded.

Sonny breathed out in a small explosion. 'How come I didn't know?'

'Sonny, maybe you didn't want to know.'

Sonny pressed his lips together. 'He has to stop.'

'I know someone. But not the Veterans Hospital. All right? They might call the cops.'

'He can't keep doing this.'

'Leave that to me, Sonny. I'll call someone.'

THE MONKEY WAS wide awake, frantic, scrambling for a better toehold. *get up get up, buddy boy. bitch is on the phone. somebody's coming to hurt us, buddy boy. get up. get us outta here. dumb bitch. we oughta kill her. come on let's go. go get us a little somethin'.*

The monkey yanked a handful of hair off its scrawny ribs and shoved it in Eddie's mouth. Eddie coughed and felt for the glass on the nightstand. The glass was half full of puke. The monkey groped in the puke and shoved a handful in Eddie's nose. Eddie gagged and overfilled the glass with more puke.

come on. get a shirt, buddy boy. go nekked. go go go. i'll guard the door.

Eddie drug on a stained shirt and lurched into his wheelchair. He had five dollars in his pants pocket. He rolled out the back door. The monkey grinned.

"IN THE NAME of the Father and Jesus Christ, I cast you out, Satan." The skeletal woman's hairpins vibrated loose as she trembled, pressing her hands against the door in the hallway. "You hear me, Satan? You vile devil, you cannot have that child of God!"

"Sister Wilmalene . . ." Mary Ellen whispered.

"Shush. Be careful, sister, Lucifer can enter your body through your mouth," Wilmalene rasped. "You hear me Satan? God himself is waiting out here. You come out of there! Or are you a coward?" Her querulous voice rose with every breath.

Mary Ellen gripped the vial of water she'd been instructed to hold, feeling more ridiculous every second.

"Show your face Satan!" Wilmalene's bandy arms bent 'til her forearms rested against the door. Her thin, tight lips were an inch from the yellowed paint.

"What the hell are you two doing?" Eddie had rolled up behind Mary Ellen, who jumped forward and knocked the bag of bones in the high-necked dress away from the door. Mary Ellen grabbed the woman's arm to keep her from falling.

Wilmalene sagged in Mary Ellen's grip. "Go ahead and fight, Satan. You can't win. We are stronger than you. We are servants of Gaaaaaaaawwwwd!" She sank to the floor, and Mary Ellen propped her against the wall.

Eddie rolled closer. "Impressive. That for me?"

"Eddie, I was trying to help."

"Jesus, Mary Ellen, did Satan kill her?" Eddie eyed the woman on the floor.

"Eddie, stop it. She's a faith healer. She's here to help you. Please."

"Mary Ellen, will you do something for me?" Eddie lit a cigarette and blew a stream of smoke to one side of Mary Ellen and the collapsed faith healer. "Stay outta my business. Oh. I didn't notice. Did Satan come out? If he didn't maybe you oughta come in and look around. Might be under the bed." He pushed his door open and wheeled into his room. "Jesus Christ! Looks like hell in here."

Mary Ellen knelt beside the woman on the floor and helped her up.

"Oh, precious Jesus," Wilmalene whispered, "Did I cast the demon out? Did I speak in tongues? Did I?" She leaned against Mary Ellen's side.

Eddie opened his arms wide and gaped ghoulishly at the woman. "I'm still here, baby." He shoved the door shut.

"Come on, Sister Wilmalene. I'll drive you home."

"When I come back, I can pull him out through the keyhole and send him back to hell. You hear me, Satan?" Wilmalene's thin voice echoed off the walls.

Mary Ellen walked the old woman out to the car and helped her in. She decided right then that if Eddie didn't tell Sonny about the attempted exorcism, she didn't need to tell him either.

EDDIE ROLLED HIS aching head to focus on the tick of the clock. Four o'clock. Four in the morning or four in the afternoon? He listened. No sounds from down the hall. He wheeled out front and yanked at the string on the lobby light. The bulb hummed and whispered "Yaaaasss."

He raked the beaded curtain to his studio aside and picked up a pencil. He winced at the clawing and screeching of his colored pencils on paper. The sound ripped raggedly across his dream-like state. The eyes had to be right. Blazing. Not yellow, not red. On fire. Maybe Sonny would do the ink for him. Shit. Was that his dad that was in his room yesterday, or the day before? Shit.

The howling face of Satan watched Eddie from the paper while Eddie added his Lucky Eddie logo to a slitted pupil.

1945, New Orleans, Louisiana

"MRS.—UM—" THE pudgy, oatmeal skinned doctor glanced at the file on his desk.

"Lafontaine."

"Yes." He touched the pencil lead to the blank pad. "So, Edward is your son?"

"Stepson. He lost his leg at Pearl Harbor. It should all be there."

"Yes. Two amputations. Second to clean up some—putrefaction. And he has pain?"

"That's what he says."

"Of course. Mood swings? Is he despondent?"

"Well, I didn't know him before, but I'd say yes. I wonder if you can prescribe something for pain. He's getting worse."

"Worse than?" The doctor folded his hands atop the notepad and looked kindly at Mary Ellen. He knew what she was getting at. He knew exactly what was worse. He'd talked to a hundred wives, sisters, mothers, brothers. He knew this woman was trying to save face.

"Worse than when I first met him, four years ago," she said.

"What does your step-son do for a living?"

"Eddie and his father tattoo. We have a studio. He's still doing good work. He's an artist. But then he disappears. And the other day, his father found . . ."

The doctor blinked slowly. He knew what was coming.

". . . heroin." Mary Ellen ran the hem of her dress under a fingernail.

"This is not uncommon, Mrs. Lafontaine, I promise. Some of these boys will do anything for morphine in the hospitals. The army doctors—well, they are liberal with it. To keep things quieter."

Mary Ellen touched a knuckle to her upper lip to keep from sniffling. "I think he had a girlfriend who was a nurse."

"Yes. That happens. Sneaking morphine out is easy enough. It's not accounted for in most of the VA hospitals. Then, I'll bet, one day she couldn't send more. So."

"So, his father just found out. And Eddie looks—"

"Mrs. Lafontaine, do you think he'll come in? There is nothing I can give him without seeing him."

"Dr. Gaston, I'll pay for the treatment. I just want him to stop what he's doing."

Gaston folded his hands again. "Mrs. Lafontaine, I'm going to tell you something. Your stepson has to make the commitment to stop using heroin. If you pay, he's not responsible for his own actions. It's a choice he has to make."

"I heard that if someone's addicted, they have no power of their own." Mary Ellen took a tissue from her purse and blew her nose. "That's why I came to talk to you about your treatment."

"Mrs. Lafontaine, if someone says they have no power over their addiction, that's someone who wants to remain an addict. I have treated those people. Some more than once. Honestly, they don't all recover. My treatment helps, but it's really up to the patient. So, if this stepson of yours wants this, I'll help him. If you pay, he's off the hook. He can say you and his father made him come here."

"I understand. I'll try to get him to come see you."

The doctor stood and leaned across his desk to shake her hand. Mary Ellen stared for a second at the doctor's stained shirt cuffs. Maybe coffee. Maybe scorched by a too-hot iron. The doctor smelled of clove cigarettes. "I can help, if he's ready to kick the habit."

"That would be . . ." She inhaled slowly. She gathered her handbag and turned to go. "Thank you." She let herself out of the room, nodding to the receptionist. Splintered ceiling fan blades thrashed the humidity like a bird with broken wings.

EDDIE WAS IN the studio, staring at a sketch when she found him. "Hey, Mary Ellen, you like this? See, the tulips go over to the ribs, but that gal that wants this has no idea how that's gonna hurt. Think if I go to here with it, and just do one flower on the ribs, the rest on her back, she'll like it? See? More on the shoulder, and just this one that goes down to the"—He added a leaf to the stem—"see?"

Mary Ellen picked up the sketch. "That's for Wanda that drives the bus?" Eddie dipped his head once. "Looks good. She coming this afternoon?" He nodded again.

Mary Ellen pulled up a stool and sat beside Eddie. He glanced up at her curiously, then added a pale red highlight to a flower. "You need somethin'?"

"Yes. I saw a doctor this morning."

"You sick?"

"No. But you are." Mary Ellen's voice dropped into a whisper. "It's legal. It might help."

"I'm fine." He snapped his paint box closed and shoved a pencil behind one ear.

"Eddie. You are not. I see it. Your dad, I don't know why he didn't see it before, but he does now. You look like hell."

"You think I don't have a mirror?" Eddie lit a cigarette.

"Will you try this? Please?"

"I'm busy."

"Day after tomorrow. Nine in the morning. Will you? I can drive you."

"I got a car."

"Will you go? Here's his card." She touched the card to his hand, and he opened his fingers. Eddie's ink-stained thumb and forefinger closed on the card. "I just want—"

"Yeah OK. I got work to do. You're a good woman, Mary Ellen." Eddie's eyes welled. "I'll go." He let out a notched breath and touched his pants where they folded over his stump: where he'd forgotten to put the safety pin at the fold. Eddie tucked the card into his shirt pocket. "I will."

Mary Ellen smiled weakly and went out front to answer the phone.

the hell you will, buddy boy. The monkey groaned and chucked a green stream of burning bile into Eddie's throat.

Eddie rubbed his neck and patted his shirt for another cigarette.

Pressure

"THAT'LL LOOK GOOD," Eddie told his dad's old friend, chief of police Dole Fancher, "Want the skirts to move?" Eddie held the sketch of two hula dancers that would frame Dole's bicep and made the paper undulate.

"Oh, hell yeah."

"Flex for me." Eddie made an ink mark on either side of the muscle. "Hey, Dole, how about I make the hula skirt so it moves on this one, and this one, I bend her at the waist, make her tits swing. See, like this."

"Oh ho ho ho," Fancher chortled, "my old lady'll meow like a cat when she sees it."

"She won't like it?"

"Naw, she'll love it."

"Gimme a couple minutes to draw it right. Coffee? Mary Ellen's got coffee on."

"Naw, I'm good. Hey, Eddie. I'm retiring next month. Before I do, I want something on this other arm. My shield and the dates. Something like that."

"Yeah?" Eddie kept his head down while he drew. "Man, you been on the force a long time. What we gonna do without ya, Dole?"

"I need to tell you, Eddie, the guy taking my place is a hard ass. He came in last week to, you know, get a feel for stuff, have me show him who's who. He's setting up to get Tom Stang."

"Yeah? Tommy? Huh." Eddie added a lei that draped over a hula dancer's breast. "How come?"

"Eddie, don't play dumb, okay? Jesus. Rufus Sinclair told me when he fixed up that car that other Stang kid left here, there wasn't nothin' in it. Not a speck. No way he didn't have nothin' in it. You get the stash, Eddie?"

"Jesus, Dole, been what, three years, four since they hauled him in?" Eddie swabbed Fancher's arm with alcohol. "I can't remember everything."

"Eddie, I knew damn well what that Casey Stang was up to. And I know you been buyin' from Tommy. Or somebody Tommy knows."

Eddie laid the stencil over the arm in two pieces. "Flex again."

"This new guy, he'll be sniffin' around and once he nails Stang and whoever else in his band is movin' goods, he's gonna be after Stang's customers. I don't want that."

Eddie transferred ink to Dole's arm. "Your wife's a brunette, right? I'll make this one girl brunette."

"You think I don't know, son? My guys leave you alone because of me, but if that new guy gets a bug up his ass to bust addicts in the district, you're in trouble."

"I ain't an addict." Eddie squinted through cigarette smoke. He filled ink pots and loaded the first one. "Ready?"

"Yeah, you are, Eddie. There's this new thing they're doin'. They call it Methadone. It keeps you from havin' shakes I hear. A doctor over in the market district. One of the fire chief's sons is there. Says it's helpin'. He tried before and couldn't quit but this Methadone got him over the hump."

Eddie gassed his lungs and exhaled. He stuck two fingers into his shirt pocket for the card Mary Ellen had given him. "Dr. Nevel Gaston?"

"That's the name. You know him?"

"Naw, Mary Ellen gave me his card. Jesus. I'm fine."

"Eddie. Listen. You ain't fine. You listen to me. This new department guy, he's gonna nail you. Do this for me. Just go see that doctor. Before you get your ass thrown in the pen with that queer Stang kid."

"What? Casey ain't queer."

"Pretty as he was, he is by now."

Eddie started the machine and Fancher looked away. "You're a good friend, Dole. Just for you I'll go see the guy, okay?"

"Yeah." Fancher sucked in and held his breath. He never had gotten good at getting tattoos.

"MR. LAFONTAINE, MAY I call you Edward?"

"Eddie. You can call me Eddie." Eddie picked at the scab in the crook of his arm through the sleeve. He was itching like a whore with crabs.

tell him to stick it up his ass and give us the goodies, the monkey grumbled. Eddie mentally rapped the monkey on the head. It moaned and coughed.

"I have room now if you're ready to start treatment. You'll be staying on the upper floor of this building. You'll share a room with another man. My wife cooks two meals a day and sets out sandwich fixings for lunch. My brother-in-law helps here too. He's a registered nurse, in case there's a problem."

"What kind of problem?" Eddie pawed a cigarette out of the fresh pack in his shirt pocket.

"Well, Methadone's no walk in the park. You may be really sick. Those who have used it say it feels a lot like heroin. But it's easier to wean you off Methadone, once we get your body adjusted to it."

"Yeah, well I got work to do, so can you just give it to me? I got cash. I'll do it myself." Eddie tapped his cigarette on the edge of the ashtray. The monkey hung limp around the back of his neck, kneading the skin under Eddie's collar.

"No, Eddie, we don't do that."

"I don't think I got time for this—how long did you say it takes?" Eddie put the cigarette to his dry lips.

"You might get through the initial transition in two weeks. Depends on how your body reacts. How long did you say you've been using heroin?"

"I didn't say."

we hate this guy don't we, buddy boy? tryin' to break us up. let's you and me go home.

"Well, Eddie, how long did you use morphine?"

"Couple months. Couldn't get it after that. V.A. ships ya out with twelve aspirin and a roll of bandage. Ready or not."

"And then you needed something." The doctor folded his hands to listen.

"I had a customer. High school kid. High roller. He carried for another guy. Then he got arrested."

"So where are you buying now?"

"What are you, a cop? I'm not tellin' you that. Jeez."

"I don't report these things, Eddie, but I'm not going to have anybody visiting you who'll bring heroin into a heroin addiction treatment facility."

"Yeah. Well I'm not invitin' anybody." Eddie blew a fan of smoke to one side. "How much does this cost?"

i need outta here, buddy boy. let's go, go home, before this asshole kills us both.

"One hundred dollars for the first month. If you need to stay longer, we'll work with you, as long as you're making progress. That includes your room, meals, and the two weeks of Methadone treatment. I do a brief examination daily before each treatment, otherwise you'll mostly be in your room at first. Richard, my brother-in-law will be with you to monitor your condition. The next few weeks is about helping you stay clean."

"Jesus."

"There is some Jesus too. We find that prayer is powerful once a man reaches the bottom. Are you at the bottom, Eddie?"

"No, I'm not. We done talkin', doc?"

"Eddie, how's that arm right now? You're bleeding. Vein blowing out? I'm going to tell you, the bottom's not too far. I know addicts."

"Yeah?"

"Yes. I know by looking at you, you had a little hit before you came down here. And you probably have a little hit to roll out in the morning. Another at night. I know how it works, Eddie."

"Yeah, well, been nice talkin'. I got work to do." Eddie backed his wheelchair away from the desk. Dr. Gaston rose and walked to the door, opened it, and clapped Eddie's shoulder as he rolled out.

"If you decide to do treatment, I have a bed for you now."

"Yeah. I'll let ya know." Eddie rolled past the receptionist. She smiled and went back to her typing. Eddie yanked the door open and stopped in his tracks. Dole Fancher was standing across the street, leaning on a lamp post, watching the door. Eddie raised a hand to his pop's old buddy and reversed his wheelchair.

Dr. Gaston stood at the end of the hallway. "Your stepmother said she'd bring some clothes. I'll call her."

"Shit."

shit shit shit shit shit. The monkey puked down Eddie's sweating back.

Methadone

WITHDRAWAL GOUGED THROUGH Eddie like battery acid. He never knew, rushing to the toilet, which end was going to explode first. Gaston's brother-in-law Richard may have been a good nurse, but Eddie hated him, the way he came in to check on him and his roommate Till, always checking his blood pressure. Shining a light in his eyes.

bunch of shit, ain't it, buddy boy? the monkey whispered weakly.

TILL WAS FROM the Garden district. Frat boy. College educated. Tennis and polo and sailboats. Daddio had a brokerage firm. Till's father told him he had to get clean or he was out of the will. Till had shot up in his neck after his arm got infected, and he clawed at the vein when he had nightmares. His monogrammed silk pajamas were rust stained at the collar.

Till talked big about getting rid of his dad's third wife once he got out. One of the guys in the group session asked him why he hated her so much, and Till said she was a gold digger. Just waiting for his dad to die.

"What about you?" the guy asked. "You'll get a shitload of money when he dies."

"Hey, I deserve it."

"All you did was you were born. That gal had to put out for your old man. Bet she earned every dime."

"I wouldn't know. I just hate her guts."

Richard, the nurse leaned forward. "Because she told your father you were using heroin?"

"Oh, like she was little Miss Perfect. She was just a high-priced hooker. She thinks I don't know. I know. She's trying to get me out of my dad's will."

EDDIE TOLD WHAT he remembered about being on the deck of the Oklahoma when the first planes hit Pearl Harbor. He told about the long-faced nurse with doe eyes who brought extra morphine and snuck syrette packages out of the hospital for him.

"Did you love her?" one of the guys asked. "I had a nurse like that. Had tits like nobody's business. Man, I loved her."

Eddie glanced at the man's prosthetic leg. "You in the war?"

"Naw, motorcycle wreck, but I was supposed to ship out the next week. If I'd shipped out, I'd still have my leg."

"Maybe." Eddie rubbed at his stump.

The man raised his pant leg. "You oughta get you a leg like this. You don't have to be in that chair, you know."

Eddie glared at him. "Piss off."

"Eddie, why do you stay in the chair?" Richard the nurse turned toward Eddie.

Eddie's eyeballs felt like hot ash had landed on them. "Just easier."

"Easier for what?"

Eddie didn't have a bone to pick with Richard. The guy was just doing his job, walking the hallway, opening doors to make sure nobody was lying on his back vomiting, choking, wrapped up in sweaty sheets. "I dunno."

rickie dickie don't know the good shit. we don't quit the good shit. The monkey was barely breathing.

THE END OF the second week one of the guys who'd been there four weeks left to live in a halfway house.

"He'll be back," Till said. "He was here first time I was here."

"You been here before?" Eddie offered a cigarette.

"Third time's a charm." Till reached for his own smokes and snapped up the collar of his starched shirt. "I'm not letting Irene, that's my dad's wife, get my money. I'm getting clean. You helped me, Eddie. You know that?"

"Yeah? How's that?"

"God, Eddie, look at you. You work with your old man. I hate my old man. You come from the other side of the tracks, no offense. My old man is rich. But you have something you're good at. One of the other guys told me you're like a master tattoo guy. I want to learn to do something. Maybe my old man would let me work with him if I could do something."

"Yeah, well, don't be blowin' smoke up my ass, Till ol' buddy. You're not gettin' a free tattoo."

"See, Eddie, you're all tough, and you don't want anybody to like you. But you're honest. Except that you're an addict. Yeah, I'm an addict too, but I think about my friends, and I don't think I have one that would stick by me, unless I was paying for drinks. I bet you have friends. Real friends."

"Not really."

"I'm out in another week, and my father says there's a job at his brokerage for me. I'm going to do it. Because if you can earn your own way, so can I."

"Yeah, you're full of shit," Eddie said, but he smiled for the first time since he'd been at the clinic.

"So are you. And, Eddie, when I get out, I know a doctor who makes custom prosthetics. I'm going to send him here and get you fitted."

"I dunno. Sounds expensive."

"I'm paying—no, don't hold your hand up at me, I'm paying. You can pay me back with a tattoo. I want one of those hula girls. But with Irene, my dad's wife's face. And you can make her fat and ugly. Oh, she'll just shit in her fancy panties when she sees it."

"Maybe. I dunno."

"You don't know about the tattoo? Or you don't want to walk again?" Till watched Eddie roll over to the window to press his forehead on the reinforced glass.

"I can do the tattoo. You bring a picture. Maybe the VA can fix me up with a leg."

"Maybe, but they also got you hooked on morphine, and here you are."

"Yeah."

"So, I'm going to send the leg guy. I'll clear it with Gaston. And I'll see you at your shop when you get out. Hey, lunch in ten minutes. You ready?"

"Go on, I'll be there." Eddie watched Till go out the door. He pushed his chair into the bathroom, ran some water into the sink, and shaved. The monkey hadn't made a peep in five days.

Matilda Returns to Lafontaine's

1945, Early June, New Orleans, Louisiana

"HEY, BILL, ROSA and me are goin' to town. Need anything?" Matilda waited, her green canvas tote over her shoulder, for her husband to look up from his toolbox.

"You look nice. Goin' to see your tattoo guy?"

"Yeah, then we'll go see my grandparents and the kids."

The two women sprinted across Gentilly, laughing as traffic came to a screeching halt for the raven-haired beauty in the snug fitting red blouse and shorts and the apricot-haired giraffe limbed woman whose tattoos peeked around her yellow halter top and white shorts.

Matilda pointed at the street where her family lived as they walked, and the market, and the café, and finally they were in front of Lafontaine's. Mary Ellen was out front as always, chatting up a customer.

"Hey, maybe Eddie'll have time for both of us." Matilda pulled the door open.

Rosa pretend-slapped Matilda's arm. "You go right ahead, hon. I like my hide just like it is."

"Well, my goodness, look who's here." Mary Ellen came around the counter to embrace Matilda, then shook hands and introduced herself to Rosa. "Oh, yes, I remember you and those horses. Wonderful. We were planning to come Friday. Or at least I was."

"Eddie here?" Matilda's face slackened when Mary Ellen shook her head "no." "I'll wait if he's coming back."

Mary Ellen placed her hand on Matilda's arm and indicated the studio where Eddie usually worked. Matilda tipped her head at Rosa to come along, but Rosa was headed for the pile of new magazines.

In the studio, Mary Ellen whispered, "Eddie is in a facility getting well. He'll probably come home in another week."

"Oh. He sick?"

"Sort of. I don't know how much you were aware of when you were coming here—"

Matilda sighed. "Oh, you mean about the heroin? Yeah, I knew. 'Cause that guy I came in here with that first time got arrested. I knew. He in trouble?"

"No. The doctor at the place where he is says he's doing good. Really good. I'd tell you to go see him, but he can't have visitors except family."

"That's okay. I brought him something though." She presented Mary Ellen with a tightly rolled tube of paper. "You can look."

Mary Ellen was already unrolling the new circus poster.

"Oh, Matilda, look at you. There you are, the star!"

"Well, Rosa too, and the elephants. But yeah."

"I'll take this to Eddie when I visit Sunday."

"Well, you tell Eddie I said hi and to get well and get back to work."

"Hey, why don't you sign this for him?"

"Oh. Okay." Matilda rummaged in her bag, then took the pen Mary Ellen offered.

MATILDA AND ROSA linked arms as they walked toward Matilda's grandparents' house. Rosa leaned close enough that a puff of Matilda's pale orange hair brushed her face. "That's where you got your first tattoo?"

Matilda chuckled. "My first six or seven. Eddie's the best. Mary Ellen, that's his step-mom."

"Oh. He was gone, huh?"

"Yeah. Don't tell everybody this. Eddie has him a heroin problem. He's gettin' fixed up, I guess. Mary Ellen told me. But if you met him, Rosa, you'd see why I like him."

"Matilda, you weren't sweet on him were you?"

Matilda fired off a staccato laugh. "No, no, nothing like that. I was just hooked on the tattoos. Isn't that something? I'm hooked on tattoos. My tattoo guy's hooked on heroin. Lord."

Rosa stopped walking and tugged on Matilda's arm. "Well, honey, I'm hooked on good looking men. We're all hooked on something."

MARY ELLEN FRAMED the poster and hung it in the lobby of Lafontaine's for everyone to see. She proudly showed the inscription: "To Lucky Eddie, the best tattoo guy I know. Your friend always, Tattooed Matilda." It would be another two years before Matilda saw Eddie again.

The New Eddie

1945, December: Christmas Cards

    Hey, Kiddo!

       Ha! I beat you to it, got this Christmas Card in the mail before Christmas this year. I was sort of out of commission when you came by, but I'm a lot better. Hey, I got me a new leg. Kinda hurt at first but they finally got it to fit and I'll be dancing like Bojangles Robinson next time you see me.

Hope you're good, guess you're in Sarasota, that's the only address I had. Come see me when you're in town.

Your favorite tattoo guy,
Lucky Eddie

Hello Eddie,

Bill dropped the mail behind the sofa last week and I just found the Christmas card from you. I've been painting the kitchen and have paint in my hair and might have to cut some of it to get it all out.

Sorry I missed you last spring. I'm glad you're doing good. So am I. I'm learning a lot of new stuff on the trapeze. It's hard, but not as hard as it used to be. The guys take good care of me, like big brothers would I guess. You practice your dancing. I want to see that.

Your friend,
Matilda

P.S. they call me Tattooed Matilda in the show, just like on the poster I dropped off.

1946—New Orleans, Louisiana

SONNY WORRIED FOR the first year that Eddie would slip back to using. Mary Ellen asked Dole Fancher, who, in his retirement from the police force had taken to having two-hour breakfasts and lunches at the café, to keep an eye out for trouble. Dole said he hadn't seen a thing.

Two years of Eddie sober, two years of Eddie walking instead of rolling. Two years of Eddie showing up in a clean shirt. Sonny Lafontaine had his son back. Business was good. Mary Ellen scheduled interviews for a new tattoo artist.

The woman named Kat whose father's tattoo shop on a side street off the Quarter had closed was the first person they interviewed.

'I like her work, but don't you dip your dick in the cash register, son,' Sonny signed when Kat showed her designs to Sonny and Eddie.

Kat watched the exchange. "You tell your dad I know what he's saying, so no hand flapping."

"Pop, she don't want any secret talk, OK?" Eddie signed and said aloud.

'You tell her what I said then.'

"He says he thinks you'd be good for business, and he hopes some of your customers come in."

"Thanks. I think they will. I could put a sign in the window where we closed so my customers know where to find me."

"She says thanks, and her customers will come in," Eddie said, but signed, 'She's hot for me, Pop, what can I say?' Sonny read lips while Eddie signed and grinned.

'Let's give her the job.'

They set Kat up in the back room. The sailors asked for extra ink when Kat worked on them. She was experienced, she worked quickly, and she was spectacular to look at, especially when she wore the halter dress that showed off her upper chest, shoulder, and full sleeve tattoos.

When Mardi Gras rolled around, Mary Ellen showed people into rooms for Sonny, Eddie, and Kat until five-thirty in the morning. When the last customer went out the door they locked up and walked to the café for breakfast.

Two cops who'd been on the force with Dole Fancher until he'd retired came in and sat near the Lafontaine crew.

"Hey, Eddie," one of the cops said, "you hear? Dole had a heart attack last week. Dropped dead right in front of the bakery on Ninth."

"Aw, damn." Eddie signed the news to Sonny. Sonny shook his head slowly in disbelief.

'I liked Dole. He was a good man. He kept you out of jail because we were friends,' Sonny signed to Eddie.

"What's he sayin'?" the cop asked.

"He says he'll miss him. We knew him a long time."

'You are such a lying sack of shit,' Sonny signed. Mary Ellen signaled for more coffee.

"Hey, boys," Kat said to the cops, "Sonny says you boys oughta come in for some ink. On the house." Eddie laughed out loud and signed to Sonny what she'd said.

'Charge these assholes double,' Sonny signed with a grin. Mary Ellen dumped cream into her coffee to keep from laughing. She hadn't known this side of Sonny before Eddie had gotten clean, but she sure liked it.

Expecting
1947—Early June, New Orleans, Louisiana

MATILDA TALKED ABOUT writing to her grandparents to tell them she and Bill were expecting before they got to New Orleans in June but hadn't gotten around to it. Bill needed to set up, so he walked Matilda to Gentilly, hailed her a taxi, and sent her off with a kiss.

She had the cab driver take her to Liuzza's By the Track where she requested a table for one. When she asked the familiar looking waiter with the soaked prune face if Gabriel Durand was in the kitchen, the waiter leaned backward to look through the top half of his glasses.

"Matilda? Oh, my goodness, look at you. Look at you. Yes'm, he's in there. Come with me," and guided the very pregnant Matilda to the kitchen. "Gabe! Look who I found."

Gabriel glanced up over the steaming pot, put his spoon on the counter, and slapped his hand over his heart.

"Lord, child. Lord, lord. You sit right down there, child." Gabriel pointed to the staff table at the end of the long kitchen. "Vince, get her some of that pasta. Here, you need—"

"Gran-pap, you got some gumbo? Nobody anywhere knows how to make roux." Matilda lowered herself laboriously to the wooden bench.

Gabriel ladled up a big bowl and watched his granddaughter's eyes close when she put the first spoonful in her mouth.

Gabriel pointed at the fryer and said to the woman putting beignets in the basket, "You put in four more for my granddaughter, will you? She's eatin' for two."

CHEREE WEPT WHEN she touched her granddaughter's cheek, and the littlest kids stared at the woman with tattoos on her arms and legs who looked like she'd swallowed a basketball.

"Honey," Cheree touched Matilda's arm, "you got so many pictures on you, they's no space left."

"I got space left. Hey, Gran-pap, you been over to Lafontaine's?"

"Yes, yes I have." He pushed his sleeve up to show a heart with "Cheree" in the middle. "That Eddie, he got him a wooden leg since you last saw him. He walks around that shop like nothin' ever happened. And 'Tilda, they got a woman workin' there."

"Yeah, he said he got a leg in his Christmas card. Miz Lafontaine, she was there before."

"Well, she's still there, but they got a woman who does tattoos. Can you imagine? Pretty woman, too."

"She do nice work? I might want something while I'm here. Big like this, I don't want to take off my clothes for—" Matilda stopped short when Cheree rapped her knitting needles sharply on the chair arm and pointed to the kids.

"How long can you stay, honey?" Cheree asked.

"Just came by to see you. And bring these tickets for you and the kids. I read fortunes for now, 'til the baby comes."

"Oh, good." Cheree put her arthritic hand to her chest. "I'm glad you're doing something safe, not all that crazy stuff some of those people do."

"Gran-mim, up 'til I was five months along I rode an elephant, and I did stuff on the trapeze." The kids' eyes got wider, and they stepped in closer.

"Can we see the elephants?" Four-year-old Evangeline, with their mother's high forehead and long flaring nostrils, edged toward Matilda.

"Sure. They like if you bring 'em an apple."

"Gran, can we go right now?" Dallas piped up.

"Now, honey, your sister just got here. All you kids, you go fetch that lemonade from the ice box. Louie, you get some glasses. Off you go now." Cheree turned back to Matilda.

"We saw your mama opening day at the races. She's back workin' the windows. Lives in one of those rooms they rent over by—"

Gabriel slapped his knees. "Cheree, let's not talk about this right now. We gonna be great-grandparents. How about that?"

MATILDA DRANK SO much lemonade she had to excuse herself to the bathroom three times in the two hours she sat telling her grandparents and siblings about when Sally Fiscalini slapped the farm boy in that little town in Texas and nobody came to the next show, and how in California they took the elephants to the beach. She told about Bernice and how her show name was Madame Volumptia, and she sounded Russian or something, but she was really from Arizona, and how she made the prettiest costumes. She told them about Maurice who talked like the king of England but looked like he was straight out of Africa, and Sam and how he loved those elephants and how he sang to them while he rubbed gallons of oil on their skin. About the night Giovanni Fiscalini was on the mechanic rope and pulled her off the elephant at the wrong time when he had a stroke, and how Milana took care of him now and hardly ever came outside anymore.

The wall clock struck five. Matilda rocked forward and got to her feet. "I best be getting back. Here's those tickets for tonight." She playfully picked up Louie's hand and turned it over to look at his palm. "I'll read your fortune, Louie. I've got a crystal ball."

"Like the witch in the *Wizard of Oz*?" he asked hopefully. Matilda laughed and made claw hands in front of her face.

"I'll drive you back. No arguments, missy." Gabriel rattled the car keys. Matilda nodded gratefully. The baby had been kicking and punching around like it was juggling wildcats and she was worn out.

Matilda wanted to be back in the railroad car, in the rocking chair Bernice and Tony had brought from their car for her. She wanted Bernice to feel the squirming elbows and knees that poked sharply at her insides and tell her that was the way it was supposed to be. She wanted Bill to put his hand on her belly and talk to their child and tell it to settle back down the way he'd done the last three weeks. It would all be better once she was back home on the train.

Reunion

1947, New Orleans, Louisiana

"LUCKY EDDIE! THAT you?" Eddie Lafontaine turned toward the fortune teller's booth and looked blankly at the long narrow face of the woman under a lime green turban who sat with a crystal ball in front of her. He glanced around at the other people hurrying by. Eddie told the woman with him to save him a seat.

"Yeah?"

"'S me. Matilda." She slid an oversized caftan sleeve up to show the vine and bird tattoos on one arm.

"Well, son of a bitch."

Matilda stood and steadied herself. "Look at you. Lemmie see that new leg. Look at you. You look fine."

"Well, son of a bitch. Matilda."

Matilda set the turban on the chair and shook her mass of curls into a familiar mop. She took off the caftan and pulled the curtain on the Madame Matilda Fortunes of the Future booth closed behind her. Eddie patted her shoulders, grinning ear to ear.

"You got fat, or you havin' a baby?" He chuckled. "It's good as hell to see you."

"Baby. Maybe in a month but fine with me if it was any time. Dang, Eddie. You look—" She didn't know how to say she'd never seen him look good before.

"Clean livin'. Meet my leg." He rapped a knuckle on the shin, and Matilda laughed. "Hey, you comin' by the shop? We did some more fixin' up. That poster of you is hangin' in the lobby. Hey, we got a gal workin' there now. Man, she does some nice work. Her own designs too. Real nice. She's here with me."

"I saw her go by with you. She's pretty, Eddie. She your girl?' Matilda arched her eyebrows.

"Naw, we just work together. Stop lookin' at me like that. How about you? Same guy?" Eddie eyed some work on her arms that wasn't his.

"Same guy. Bill's in there working." She cocked her head toward the tent. "I'm doin' this because ain't nobody wants to see this big ol' belly up in the air. It's sure good to see you, Eddie. You at the shop tomorrow? Maybe I'll come before the matinee."

"Yeah. Come see us. I want Kat, she's that gal, to see that banana thing. She saw the sketches. Doesn't believe me that I did it for real."

"Okay. Hey, Eddie, I'm sure glad to see you. Last time . . ." She let the words fall to the grass.

"Yeah. Hey good to see you too, kiddo." Eddie grinned.

Circus Train Baby
1947, Between Baton Rouge and Lake Charles

BERNICE PATTED MATILDA on a knee and set her satchel of baby-birthing supplies at the foot of the bed. "Let me take a look—looks like you're having this baby right now."

"That'd be good," Matilda gasped when she was able to unclench her teeth. "Sum-bitch feels like he's eatin' his way out."

"Bill, you stay up there with Matilda." Bernice waved Bill away. "This isn't your mama's milk cow havin' a calf. Don't need you to faint or something. Good. Hold her hand. You okay, Matilda?"

Matilda groaned she was fine and bore down when Bernice told her to. The baby was the size of a barn cat and just as scrawny, but he cleared his lungs and belted out a holler the elephants answered from two cars away.

"It's a boy. Honey, you did so good. Didn't even tear you." Bernice reached for the towel in her bag. "Bill, run back to my place. Tony's got water on the stove. Go on. I have this part."

"He sure is little for as big as he felt comin' out." Matilda sighed.

Bernice scooted to the head of the bed with the baby. "He's a little early, honey. He'll be fine."

MATILDA AND BILL lay together on the bed, staring in wonder at their son as the train rolled into Lake Charles, Louisiana.

Matilda was at breakfast in the pie car the next morning with the baby in a sling she'd fashioned from one of Bill's work shirts. She spent most of breakfast pulling back the shirt for everybody who came by to see little Billy Kazarian. Billy had his father's dark hair and eyebrows, and his mother's tawny complexion and amber eyes.

MATILDA ASKED THE tattoo artist in El Paso, Texas for a red heart outline above her left breast, beside the cross and flowers, with "Billy + Matilda" inside the heart.

"For you, and him both," she told Bill when she got home and peeled back the bandage for him to see.

"That won't make the milk turn red or taste like ink, will it?"

"Oh stop, you sound like an old lady, Bill."

"What if he doesn't want to be called Billy later?"

"Honestly, Bill, when did you get to be a worry-wart?" Matilda pulled her blouse open to feed Billy. "Why wouldn't he?"

"He's good lookin', don't you think?" Bill touched the boy's black hair.

"Sure he is. I think he's smart too."

"How do we know?"

"Good lord, Bill, stop fretting. You sound like my grandmother. He's just fine. He's growin' fast. I can tell when I pick him up. Might need to get him on a bottle. I don't have enough boobs for your kid the way he's eatin'."

"Should I ask Bernice?" Bill's eyebrows raised into an inverted V.

"Oh, for Christ's sake, Bill, stop worrying. I know how to do this. I raised my brothers and sister, remember?"

BILLY WAS FIVE months old when the train circled back to Florida for the winter. Bill came into the bedroom one morning with coffee for Matilda and a bottle for their son and told Matilda he'd get a regular job if she wanted, and they'd stay right there and have a real home for their boy.

"What? I'm working next season. No, don't you shake your head at me, yes I am." Matilda pulled her nightgown off over her head and dug for a bra in the chest of drawers.

"Circus is no way for a kid to grow up."

"The hell. He'll be fine. He'll probably be doin' an act soon as he's walkin'." She hooked her bra and turned to look in the mirror. "I gotta start doin' sit ups or something. Hey, I got his show name."

"Billy Kazarian isn't much of a show name," Bill said.

Matilda tapped at the heart and names tattooed on her chest. "Billy Matilda is."

PART 6
On With the Show

Four Seasons Later
1950, December: Christmas Cards

Hey Eddie,

I got a card from Mary Ellen and Sonny, and what the heck, you didn't sign it? Or did you forget to send cards out before Christmas again? Bill broke a finger the day after we got home, so I guess that was good timing, because the practice tents stay up here so he doesn't have to put them up.

They fired three clowns for always mouthing off to everybody. But none of the little ones, and one of them is the worst. I guess they keep him because he matches the two women. Sometimes we play cards, but they always want to play for money, and I don't like to lose.

I hope you have a nice Christmas. Here's a picture of all of us. Can you believe Billy is four years old? You ought to get married and have a kid, Eddie. I never thought I'd want one, but I wouldn't trade this kid for all the money in the world.

Your favorite tattooed person,

Tattooed Matilda

Hey Matilda,

You guessed right. I forgot to mail cards last week. Then I got busy. I put your card on my board in the studio, and everybody asked what kind of Christmas card has palm trees on it. That's a pretty cute little kid you got there. Me get married? Are you kidding? All the women in town would be heart broke.

It's all good here. We are so busy my dad is thinking we need another person working. Maybe we do. Or maybe we just need to charge more.

You guys have a good Christmas. See you when I see you.

The best tattoo guy you'll ever know,

Eddie. That's Lucky Eddie to you. Ha ha ha.

1951, Sarasota, Florida

FOUR CIRCUS TROUPES wintered in the Sarasota, Florida neighborhood around Bill and Matilda's cozy bungalow.

Matilda dropped Billy off rehearsal mornings at the home of a set of grandmotherly spinster twins who'd been retired from circus for so long no one remembered exactly what their act had been. The children of a dozen performers played, made up their own shows in the unfenced yard and screened porch, were served peanut butter and jelly sandwiches and Kool-Aid for lunch, and were picked up late in the afternoon after rehearsals were over. From October until March the circus children's lives were as close to normal as they'd ever be.

Horses were traded and sold, dogs gathered and trained for acts, and when tempers flared in the rehearsal tents around town, acts went looking for new employment.

NED BENTLEY TOLD Gio and Tony he'd worked with exotics and showed a photo of himself posing with a lion. He showed another photo of him standing with zebras beside a train. He said he knew they didn't have cats or zebras, but he could work with Rosa, since they'd worked together back in the old days. Rosa was lukewarm to the idea, given she'd only worked two shows with him and remembered that his oral resume' had not matched his skill set.

Ned wormed his way onto Rosa's good side by being an extra set of eyes for Rosa and Schatz when they rehearsed the duo roman riding act. Rosa bought a white Arabian gelding that had a propensity for rearing and had toyed with the idea for trick horse act she could use for a filler. Ned worked up a short act where he'd cover himself with a blanket, and the horse, lying beside him would steal the covers. Hardly standing ovation stuff, but it would get a few laughs and would give Rosa and Schatz time to get ready for another act.

Sam, the elephant trainer told Gio he'd heard from a friend on an east coast circuit who'd worked with Ned on another show that Ned had been drinking one night and put a trick riding saddle on the wrong horse and the terrified horse had run down a woman and two kids, one of whom got a broken nose and the other a broken arm. "Just what we need, Gio, a drunk. We have enough problems with some of the clowns already."

"I'll watch him, Sam. Hopefully he's cleaned up. So don't be a bitch."

"Oh, screw you too, Gio, I'm not as big a bitch as Rosa will be if he makes a mistake like that with one of her horses."

"Okay, okay, Sammy. If you see something, I know you'll be the first to tell me."

"I will," Sam waggled his hand, pinky finger extended, "and if I'm right . . ."

"Let's hope you're not. And work up something new before we head out. We're playing a bunch of places we've been every year."

"Yes, yes, we have something new, just you wait and see." Sam patted Gio's shoulder affectionately. "Don't you be a bitch either. I don't suppose we can have Matilda for something, can we?"

"How about using that new girl Polly? The redhead? I just auditioned her to juggle and slack wire. She's nice looking, and she's game for about anything."

"If you can get her to stop chewing gum, I can use her," Sam said with an exaggerated sigh. "Think she could juggle pins on an elephant?"

"I'll send her over. You tell her about the gum. If it doesn't work, I'll put her back with the clowns. She's a good kid. I want to give her more to do."

"Oh my God, Gio, are you tapping the little gum chewer?"

"Get an elephant ready. I'll send her over. Her name's Polly."

"Oh, you are. Oh, wait 'til I tell Maurice. This is delicious." Sam grinned at Gio and jogged back toward the elephants, flapping his hands at his sides.

THE NEXT MORNING Matilda and Billy watched the auburn-haired Polly juggling pins while she sat on Marta's neck.

"Sam!" Matilda called out. "How come you don't have a pad on that elephant?"

"Oops. I bet her little pooter's getting pricked." Sam sneered.

Maurice cast a doleful eye at his lover. "Tilda's right, Sammy. She needs the pad. I told you."

"I'm running this act. I'm not here to cater to whoever's sleeping with the boss."

Polly caught her pins, and sat, round eyed, holding pins in both hands. "May I come down now?"

Maurice tapped Marta's foreleg and the elephant lowered herself. Polly slid off with a grimace. Matilda saw the ragged edged rash from the elephant's bristling neck hair on the girl's inner thighs.

"Shame on you, Sam. You ain't no better than anybody here."

Sam plopped his hands onto his hips. "Oh, aren't we all high and mighty now, missy, now that you're the feature. I gave you a start here, don't you forget that."

"Sammy, honey, what is *wrong* with you? Why are you being so mean?" Maurice touched Sam's arm.

"Oh, and you, you big ugly nigger, don't you question me."

Maurice took two steps back and stood stock still. His eyes filled with tears.

"Sammy? What's gotten into you?"

"Oh, God, Oh God, what have I said?" Sam put his hands over his face. "I didn't mean it. Oh God. Maur, please forgive—"

"Come on, Sammy, you're tired. Let's put these girls up." Maurice led the elephants out of the ring, and Sam followed, looking remorseful. He stopped and turned back to the two women. "I didn't mean—I—please forgive me." He hung his head as he followed Maurice out the open tent flap.

"Polly, you come with me," Matilda said. "Bernice has a cream that'll fix you up and we'll find some heavy tights. And I'll make sure that elephant has a pad on it next time." She shot a warning look at Sam's back.

"Maybe I should go back to the clowns."

"No, you're doing great. I'll make sure Sam treats you right." Matilda glanced around at her son, where he sat on his step stool. "Hey Billy-boy, you want to go see Aunt Bernice? She's got cookies."

"Yes yes yes," Billy chirped, dusting off his pants. "Mama, what's nigger?"

Matilda shook a finger at her son. "Something you don't ever say, Billy."

Eddie Lends a Hand
1951, New Orleans, Louisiana

DR. NEVIL GASTON stopped by Lafontaine's shop four years after Eddie had gotten clean. "Eddie, how about coming over on Tuesday night to talk to the guys in treatment? You'll inspire some of them."

"Me? Shit, Doc, why don't you get that college boy, that guy who's dad's a stockbroker? What was his name?"

"Till. His name was Till. He died of an overdose three years ago."

"Aw, hell." Eddie arranged inks on a tray. "Damn shame."

"Yes, it is. Come over Tuesday. You might be the best person to help these men, because once you decided to get clean you did it. Will you do it?"

"Maybe. Damn shame about Till."

"Eddie, Till did that to himself. But I want you to tell the guys about him. Tell them you were friends, that Till had everything going for him, and he let heroin take it all from him."

Eddie didn't respond.

"Three of the six patients are on their second treatment. It's important they hear that they're not immune to being just like Till."

"Damn, doc."

"I knew you'd agree. See you Tuesday."

". . . AND THAT WAS kinda it. When that guy told me I was feelin' sorry for myself, in a wheelchair and all, well, it pissed me off, but I laid awake thinkin' about it, and the next day, right in this room, what that guy said, was what woke me up." Eddie looked around the circle of men. The doctor sat listening.

A skeletal-looking man with a shock of bushy red hair lit a cigarette. A pale man with a face like an uncooked donut coughed. Eddie glanced around the six patients until he saw a flicker in the eye of a distinguished-looking mulatto man whose trousers had a laundry crease.

The man cleared his throat and looked straight at Eddie. "Sir, why did you come in here tonight? Do you think we feel sorry for ourselves?" The man spoke in musical cadence. "Because I don't feel sorry for myself. My wife thinks I'm sick. But, as you can see," he stood and twirled before doing a little soft shoe routine, "I can still dance, and I can still sing, and I have never missed a show. I'm here only to make her happy."

"Why?" the square-faced, broad-shouldered man across the circle said. "Why spend all this money? Why not quit and show your wife you can?"

"'Cause he's an addict like I am and like you are. And you, and you, and you too." The balding man beside the dancer gestured around the circle.

"Because, she thinks I can't quit," the dancer said. "But she'll love me for coming here, and the rewards are," he put his middle finger to his thumb, "heavenly."

Two men chuckled.

"Yeah?" Eddie flashed a smile then dropped it. "Sounds pretty good. Maybe you oughta go pack your stuff. Wait out the rest of the time in a nice hotel, and just tell her you were here. She'll never know." Six heads swiveled toward Eddie, the war veteran who'd lost a leg, gotten hooked on heroin, and had beat it right here and now he was telling this guy to ditch treatment. "Save you a lotta dough, not payin' for Methadone."

The dancer continued staring at Eddie for a few seconds, then his face went slack. "Because she'd know. And she'd leave me for good."

"So?" Eddie rocked back in his chair. "Dames are a dime a dozen. You could have any woman, good lookin' guy like you. Dump that bitch and find you one that won't boss you around." The room was still. Eddie heard the paper burning when the red-headed man sucked his cigarette. One man looked nervously toward Dr. Gaston. Gaston's expression never changed when he set his clipboard on the floor.

"You peg-legged asshole, you never had a good woman before. What would you know?" the dancer blurted.

"You think you have a good woman? For all you know she's bangin' some big coon down at that cheap club where you used to work." Eddie folded his arms.

The dancer jumped to his feet. "You don't talk about her like that. She loves me. She loves me. You don't know her." The square faced, big-shouldered man across from the dancer drew a breath and let out a low whistle. The dancer turned and glared at the whistler. "Have you got something to say, you big ox?"

"You're pretty sure of yourself, aren't ya? If it's all so good, why are you even here?" The square faced man glanced at Dr. Gaston then turned his attention back to the dancer.

The chiseled face of the dancer sagged as he lowered himself into his chair. "Because I don't want to lose her."

"Why would you lose her if it's all so good, except for one little thing?" Eddie said quietly.

"Because I got fired at the club. And I took something of hers to get a fix."

"You didn't have money? Big time song and dance guy like you, and you stole from your woman?"

"I sold a bracelet of hers. I didn't think she'd miss it."

"Who paid for you to be here?"

"She paid. She sold her pearls and a ring from her grandmother. She loved those pearls." The dancer's voice was barely audible. "She'll leave me if I use again."

"Screw her then. Get your money back for the rest of the time here. Go get high. You deserve that, if she's that dumb to sell her stuff to help you," Eddie said.

"You don't know her. She's a good woman."

"I do know she's with a heroin addict, and he's gonna keep stealing, and she's gonna be glad when he's dead."

"Screw you, you sonofabitch."

"Screw you too. Hey, Doc, can you give him his money back?"

"I don't want the money. I want to kick this for her. I want my Zoe."

"Well, that ain't good enough, pal." Eddie kept his eyes on the dancer's face. "Because if she leaves you anyway, then what? If you ain't doin' this for you, there's no reason to do it."

"You go to hell."

Eddie laughed. "Been there. Danced with your mama. She's a good kisser. You know, I can't stand guys like you."

"Then don't come here anymore, because I'll still be here next week." The dancer's voice weakened again. The man beside the dancer reached out to touch his shoulder, then put his hand down to grip the side of the chair. The dancer's face softened into a wrinkled blob, and he began to cry.

After the patients had cleared the room, Eddie and Gaston remained in their seats. "Eddie, I think something broke loose tonight for him, and I'll admit, I was wondering what you were thinking, but it worked. How did you know how much you could push him?"

"I didn't," Eddie said.

THE DOCTOR PAID Eddie to come once a week. Clinic patients came and went. Eddie listened, let them get mad at him if that's what they needed, walked over and planted himself right in front of the tough guys, if that was what it took. And sometimes he sat beside them with an arm around their shoulders.

"How do we know if they stay clean when they get outta here, Doc?"

"I have a few people on the street who keep an eye on them for me," Gaston said.

"Damn. You have one of them on me?"

"Of course. That's how I knew I could count on you."

Tatts That Show

1958, Fayette, Missouri

WHY DID YOU sell the house? I loved our house. I was gonna paint Billy's bedroom and I told him he could paste animals on the walls when we got home. How come you didn't tell me?

"Matilda, you prob'ly heard me tell your momma. I had to sell the house. There's lots of nice folks helping us while we're here, but there's some big hospital bills. I'm looking for some part time work, maybe at night."

Well for God's sake don't sell the car and trailer, Bill. We need the car and trailer to go back to work.

"It's a good thing we got the car and trailer. Now, they say when you get better, you could move to a nursing home for a while, but your momma and me said no. We can take care of you and work on getting you . . ."

Nursing home? Did I get old? How long have I been here?

". . . better. Two months has been a long time for you to be here hasn't it, honey? I told the doc and the nurses that they don't know you like I know you. And I know you're going to wake clear up. I know you are." A little bit of desperate clots Bill's voice.

Wait. Do I have what Sam had? Is that what happened to me? No, that can't be right.

1951, Sarasota, Florida

MATILDA SHOWED BILL the new birds and flowers and flying faeries the tattoo artist in Sarasota had added to her calf. Bill whistled through his teeth. "Hey, this one with the red hair even looks like you. He do that on purpose? Looks great."

Matilda went back to the shop in Sarasota twice more for vines and tendrils that brushed the top of the Josephine Baker banana skirt tattoo.

"BERNICE, I NEED something that covers boobs, cooch, and butt crack, and let the rest show." Bernice came up with a taupe sheer that held everything together but looked naked under the lights. While Matilda rehearsed in it, Bernice watched with an eagle eye.

"I'm going to have to add something inside on those top edges so you're not popping those nippies out when your arms go up, sweetie."

"Can we glue it?" Matilda asked.

"We could. The bottom needs a little more material too. We can't be showing your—"

"What if I shave so we can glue it?"

Bernice tugged at the measuring tape on her neck. "Might have to. Your husband's gonna either choke me or love me for this one."

BILL DIDN'T HAVE any more say in what his wife wore for her act than whether the horses left road apples on the way to the ring. He ran Matilda's mechanic for every rehearsal. He helped Gio lay out new posters to send ahead to towns up the line. The artist drew two versions of the poster: one with their trapeze flier "Tattooed Matilda" in her taupe nude sheer to show her ink, and the tamer "Magnificent Miss Matilda," in full torso coverage for bible belt cities.

SAM INSISTED GIO pull Maurice from the pre-show strong man stage and let them do the elephant show together. The new act they showed Gio and Tony had Maurice running in mock terror from the elephants while they trotted around the ring after him. Marta caught him with her trunk, then explored under Maurice's leopard print loincloth. She backed away and trumpeted. Gio shook his head. "Might be a little risqué."

"Good Lord, Gio, have you seen what your flyer is wearing?"

GIOVANNI FISCALINI SR. hardly came out of his private car anymore. Marina helped him to his armchair by the windows where he could see preparations and pulled the blinds when he'd watched enough. Tony and Gio talked to Marina about hiring a full-time nurse for Giovanni, but she'd have no part of it.

1952: Billy On the Rails

BILL AND MATILDA'S son Billy, at five years old had a perpetual look of wonder on a round face framed with black curls. Bernice altered one of Ignacio's old clown costumes for Billy so he could run around in the ring with the clowns. One clown started picking him up and tossing him to another clown as they ran. Bill pulled they guys aside out back, telling them if they dropped his son, they'd be looking for another job, less some teeth.

Matilda told Bill to stop worrying. Nobody was going to let Billy get hurt.

Cranial Anomaly

1952, Between Shows

"YOU CAN SEE it more clearly in this one. The x-ray shows a mass here." The beak nosed doctor poked a long finger at the film. "It may be why you're having these headaches." Sam sat on the end of the exam table. Maurice and Gio stood to the side.

"What does that mean, a mass?" Sam peered at the image.

"Could be a blood clot from an injury. Mr. Sanger, have you had a blow to the head recently? No? Loss of vision? Headaches? How about change in personality?" Maurice and Gio nodded in unison.

"I'm healthy as a horse. Just look at me."

"He has headaches almost every day, and they are worse in the afternoon." Maurice's sonorous voice sounded too big, too loud for the tiny exam room. "He has to lie down with a cold compress to make them stop. Sometimes during our show, he forgets what trick we're supposed to be doing."

"I see." The doctor scrawled a note on his clipboard. "Mr. Sanger, you didn't tell me this. I'm trying to help you, but you have to help me—"

Maurice glanced sideways at Gio. "Doctor, Sam doesn't remember the headaches and—"

"Don't listen to Maurice, he's always been against me." Sam slid off the end of the exam table.

Gio shifted his stance. "Doc, Sam has worked for me for years. He hasn't been himself. No, Sam don't shake your head. We're here to help you. Sit down."

Sam yanked the gown off and stood naked in front of the doctor with his hands on his hips. "Do I look sick to you, Doc? These bastards are lying. I'm telling you, they're full of shit."

The doctor looked grimly toward Maurice and Gio. "Will you help Mr. Sanger get dressed? A colleague of mine who specializes in cranial anomalies will be in his office in about an hour. I'd like him to see the radiographs. We have coffee in the waiting room, might have some pastries if my receptionist hasn't eaten them all."

Sam wept like a child while Maurice and Gio helped him into his clothes.

SAM STOOD LOOKING at the picture on the waiting room wall. "That's my favorite Winslow Homer painting. It's called The Storm. That man in the boat reminds me of you, Maur. Except the sharks will not get you, will they?" He turned his head slowly and Maurice patted his arm. "Those sharks. Homer knew about sharks. Terrible creatures. Don't get in a boat, Maurice. Don't ever do that."

"Let's sit down, Sam." Maurice pulled Sam gently toward a chair.

Gio looked up from a magazine at the print on the waiting room wall. "Sam, that's a picture of a wagon and horses."

"I know that." Sam sat down and closed his eyes.

April 7, 1953

Dear Eddie,

I hope everything is going good there. I heard my grandfather went to your place to get him another tattoo and my grandmother about had a litter of kittens over it. She won't tell me what it looks like, so you have to tell me.

Things have been kind of sad around here. Remember the elephant trainer? He has a brain tumor and it's changed him. I mean, he was not always nice all the time to begin with, but now he's mean. His boyfriend, that great big negro that was the strong man has had to take over the elephant act. I don't know if Sam, that's the elephant trainer is going to quit the show, or what. He can't do it anymore.

It really made Bill and I talk about what we'd do if we couldn't do this anymore, I mean, if you couldn't tattoo any more, what would you do? Good lord, don't answer that, because you can't quit. I want you to do banana ankle bands and I'm not letting anybody else do it.

Bill says in the fall when we get back to Sarasota we might get on a bus and go spend some time with my family. That's a long way off, but I sure want to see them all. Funny, back when I first got married, I couldn't wait to get away from them, but now I miss them.

And don't let it go to your already big head, but I miss you too. Sam being the way he is now made me think of you. And no, not just because Sam is kind of an asshole now. Just that everybody needs a friend.

I'll let you know if we do come up in the fall. I miss you.

Your friend,

Matilda

April 30, 1953

Hey Matilda,

Man, I'm sorry to hear about your friend. I sent this to your grandparent's house, in case you see them before you come over here in May or June. Or I hope you guys are coming. If you let me know when you'll be somewhere maybe I can answer general delivery. Like getting fan mail wherever you go. Except from somebody who knows you. Otherwise this is kind of one way.

Oh, and don't you forget you knew me first. I feel real bad about your friend, but don't you forget I'm your favorite asshole.

Hope I see you.

Your favorite asshole Eddie

1954, Tulsa, Oklahoma

SAM'S OUTBURSTS OF questionable behavior and language became so frequent that Gio forbade him to go in the ring for shows. Maurice and Polly did the elephant act while Sam watched through the screen in the curtain. One night as the act ended in Tulsa, Oklahoma, instead of opening the flap to let the elephants out of the tent Sam stepped into the ring with no pants on.

Sam fainted as Bill hurried him back around the curtain. Maurice carried Sam to the truck, and Bill drove them to the hospital. The emergency room doctor looked at Sam's pupils and checked his vitals.

Maurice held Sam's limp hand. "What can you do?"

"Given what you have told me, nothing. It seems the tumor has hemorrhaged. He's unresponsive. It won't be long now. Does he have family?"

Bill bowed his head to wipe his eyes with a handkerchief. "He does. Can they come see him, Doc?" He stayed up through the night and drove members of the troupe to the hospital to say their goodbyes.

Sam died in the morning. Gio arranged for burial in Tulsa, since there were no blood relations Maurice or anyone else knew of to contact.

"I AM GOING to remain here, boss," Maurice told Gio. "Someone needs to tend to Sam's grave."

"Maurice, I need you. Marta and Eloise need you. Sam would want you to take care of the girls." Gio put his hand gently over Maurice's.

Maurice let out one more muffled sob, then put his fingertips to his lips, and touched the fresh earth and the metal frame that held the paper grave marker one more time before he went back to the train to load the elephants.

Natty Ned Bentley

1954, Chickasaw, Oklahoma

"I'M HAVING BENTLEY come over to work with you two," Gio said. "Maurice, I need you to help him get the elephants working for him in the ring. You are my main guy. You know that. But—well, you know."

"Sure, Gio, I understand. You can say it. You need a white man. Sammy's costumes are in the car. They'll fit Ned." Maurice glanced over at Polly who was leaning over Matilda and Bill's six-year-old Billy, looking at the coloring book he'd brought to the ring. "Shouldn't we ask Polly, though?"

Gio cleared his throat. "Polly, got a minute?" Polly patted Billy's head and walked over. Gio told her what he'd told Maurice. She looked back and forth between the two of them.

"Are you sure, Gio?"

"I want to get the act back to three people. And Bentley says he's worked with elephants."

"Rosa told me she thinks—"

"Rosa's opinion counts for the horse acts. He's been a good citizen as far as I'm concerned. We've all made mistakes."

"Boss," Maurice said, "if you want Ned to come work with us, I say yes if Polly says yes."

Polly sucked at the inside of her cheek. "Sure, Gio, whatever you want. But he works with us a couple of weeks before we do a show." She turned to Maurice.

"Yes, boss, she's right."

"Sure. Thanks, Maurice, thanks Polly. See you at dinner." He started out of the tent, then turned back. "Hey, Billy, Rosa has a new pony. She might need you to ride it."

"Oh boy!" Billy left his coloring book to run after Gio.

MATILDA AND BILL were walking arm in arm from visiting Giovanni and Marina when they saw Billy trotting to catch up with Gio.

"Hey, where you goin'?" Bill asked.

"Gio said I can ride Rosa's new pony." Billy's face shone under his heap of black curls.

Bill tilted his head. "Is that so. Gio, is that pony safe?"

"Oh, for God's sake." Matilda pulled on Bill's arm. "Will you stop? He's fine."

"I'll be right there, Bill," Gio said. "Promise."

Matilda stood with her husband and grinned at her black-haired son, who whooped with glee, then charged ahead to walk beside Gio to the horse pens.

THE CHUNKY BAY pony with four white socks and the broad back of a draft horse took to the ring like he'd been cantering circles on a lunge line for years, which was most likely what he'd done at the riding school where Rosa had bought him.

"Here you are. I need a brave boy who can hang on." Rosa motioned for Billy to come into the ring. "You hold with both hands right here." She tapped the two handles mounted on the surcingle. Gio lifted Billy onto the pony's back.

Rosa eased the pony into a jog. "Hey, now you push on those handles. Don't pull. Pulling pulls you off over his head. Push. There you go." She smooched and the pony lifted into a slow canter. Billy's face shone. "OK, now take one hand off the handle. Just one."

When he did, he grappled at the handle he was still holding, and tipped forward. The pony stopped with a jolt, and Billy toppled off with a startled look.

"Oops. Come on, you're okay. Back up you go." Rosa legged him back up and started the pony at a trot before the boy could change his mind about riding.

Billy smooched to the pony and it cantered. He whooped and laughed. Rosa raised one elegantly arched eyebrow at Gio.

Billy Matilda

1958—Fayette, Missouri

OH MY GOD, have I been asleep? Where's Billy? Where's Bernice? She has to have him. Tell me Bernice has our boy. He hasn't seen me all broke up, has he?

An anguished cry escapes her lips as she wakes in the night, after Bill has gone for a shower and a few hours' sleep.

1954, Kearny, Nebraska

"MATILDA, HOLD UP." Rosa jogged across the backlot in Kearny, Nebraska.

"Hey, Rosa, what's up? Need me to come get Billy? He gettin' in your way?"

"No. Just come with me."

Billy Kazarian, seven years old and wearing a mechanic rig, stood in the center of the ring looking over his shoulder when Rosa and Matilda came in. Schatz started the rosinback horse at a canter. Rosa hopped into the ring and trotted alongside it, then swung up and stood. Billy waited until Rosa whistled, then sprinted to the vaulting ramp, pounced, and landed sitting on the horse well in front of where Rosa stood on the horse's rump. He stood with one smooth movement and held his arms high, eyes and cheeks shining.

"Well, look at you!" Matilda laughed and clapped. "Look at you, Billy!"

Rosa whistled again, and Billy did a credible dismount with the help of the mechanic. Schatz made a purring sound to the horse to ease him to a stop.

Rosa raised a penciled eyebrow. "What do you think?"

"You want to do an act with my kid?"

"Yes. We'll keep a mechanic on him. He'll only ride with me for now, but, Matilda, he can stand up on that pony, too and it's cute as hell."

"Mama, can I?" Billy bounced on his toes.

"Far as I'm concerned you can. Your daddy has to say so too." Matilda walked into the ring as Rosa swung her leg forward to dismount. "Bill know yet?"

Rosa shook her head.

"He'll want to see. You know how he is. You asked Gio yet?"

"Yes, he saw yesterday. Says it's up to you and Bill." Rosa tousled Billy's hair.

"Okay. Billy-boy I'll be right back. You wait here. Want to do that again for your daddy?"

"Yes ma'am! Mama? Schatz says I need a name. You know, a show name."

"Yeah? Well I got one for you." She pulled her collar aside and showed him the tattoo with Billy + Matilda inside the heart shape.

Billy thrust his little chest out. "Oh boy. That's my name. Billy Matilda."

BILL PULLED SCHATZ to the side of the ring and looked over the mechanic rig. "Nothing personal, Schatz, it's just that—"

"No, Bill, I understand. If Billy were my son, I'd double check too. I promise I double check everything every day."

"I know you do. But I have to, just like I check for Matilda. They're everything to me." Bill looked across the ring at his wife and son, while he fingered the mechanic rope. "Everything."

"I know. If you don't want Billy to ride, it's fine. But he lives on a circus train, my friend. He's going to be in the ring. Better with Rosa than runnin' around with my clowns."

Bill clapped Schatz's shoulder. "God forbid."

Bill watched the act, told Billy it was great, and said they'd talk about it. Matilda told her son to wait with Aunt Rosa, and flashed Rosa a smile. "We'll be back."

"I JUST DON'T know, honey. What if he gets kicked or hits a pole when he falls?"

"Bill, Schatz won't let that happen. You can run the mechanic if you want. But let him do something. Let him be in the ring."

"I don't know, Matilda, he's only six."

"Seven. Come on, Bill."

"But what if—"

"Bill, has anything ever happened to me? No. You make sure nothing does. Come on, Bill. Don't break his heart."

"I don't want him to break his leg. Or his head."

"He won't. We'll all keep an eye on him. Otherwise, while we're in the ring, he's out in the backyard with the rousties and clowns. Come on, Bill." Matilda put her hands on his arms and ran her long fingers from his forearms to wrists.

Bill caved. He always caved to Matilda.

Eddie and Kat

1954, New Orleans, Louisiana

KAT HAD BEEN tattooing part time at Lafontaine's for five years and six boyfriends when she gave up her apartment and rented a room in back of the shop. Eddie had passed the seven-year sobriety mark. Business and life were good.

Mary Ellen had watched Kat and Eddie's friendship all those years, and saw that regardless of who they were dating, they always went to lunch at the café together.

"Eddie, you think you'll ever get married?" Mary Ellen said one morning while Kat was out picking up a newspaper and doughnuts.

"Married?"

"Yes, married." Mary Ellen's tone softened. "Kat's a good friend, right?"

"Yeah. So?"

"Because, Eddie, that's the best reason to marry somebody. That you like each other." Mary Ellen set coffee mugs on the counter.

"Yeah? What if she says no?"

"What if she doesn't?"

The bell at the front door dinged, and Kat announced she was back. She came in and set a box of doughnuts on the sketch table.

Mary Ellen went for the coffee pot from the front room and came back right as Eddie said, "So, wanna get married?"

"Sure." Kat picked up a jelly donut. "You want the other jelly?"

August 2, 1954

Dear Matilda, and Bill and Billy too,

I know you're probably still out somewhere but guess you'll get this when you get back there to Florida. Look here, at this thing in the newspaper. I got married. Yes, to that good-looking gal that works for us. And you will laugh at this. The other day, she said to me "Hey, I still like you." Isn't that a hoot?

We're so busy now we have me and Kat and another guy working, and my dad is still working too but he's slowing down. I see your grandpa once in a while, he comes by just to sit with some of the guys in the front room since he cut back on hours. Oh man, I guess you knew that. Didn't mean to spill the beans if you didn't.

Anyway, wanted you to know I got married, so you can quit having a crush on me. Haha. Don't tell me it was just the tattoos. Kat is sitting right here and told me to cross that out. I told her no way, because you'd laugh.

Remember your old buddy Casey Stang? He got out of prison and him and his brother Tommy who had that band both moved across town. I heard about a month ago Casey got stabbed and bled to death. Hey good riddance. Just thought you might want to know. Being an asshole never pays. I told you he was no good.

Anyway, got to get back to work. Kat says to say hi and she wants to do a tattoo on you next time you're in town.

Your friend,
Eddie

November 1, 1954

Dear Eddie,

They really should call you lucky Eddie for real because why else would a girl that pretty marry you? I sure was glad to see your letter when we got in last week.

I've been taking Billy to the beach every day since we got home and that little booger can swim like a fish already. Oh and you tell Kat I laughed at that part you wrote. Sorry, it's the tattoos, my friend. Try not to cry too much.

Isn't that something about Casey! He sure did hurt my feelings back in high school, but not as much as that bitch Brenda whats-her-name did when I found out she was screwing him. Yeah, you tried to tell me.

We'll come see you when we get to New Orleans. You ought to have a kid, Eddie. Well I guess Kat will have to have it, but you know what I mean. It's the best thing.

I miss you, my friend, and I'm sure happy for you.

Yours truly,

Matilda

Giovanni Fiscalini's Final Performance
1956, Brevard, North Carolina

GIOVANNI FISCALINI PASSED in his sleep while the circus train ran through the night on the last leg of the 1956 season. Milana sat with her father's body until they pulled into Brevard, North Carolina in the morning, then calmly told the roustabout who brought breakfast to go get Gio and Tony.

Gio and Tony found her on the sofa hugging a framed photograph of the family at their Sarasota house. She turned the photo to show to Gio.

"Look how little we are, Gio." Milana closed her eyes and tears rolled over her fleshy cheeks.

Gio went to the bedroom and was back a few seconds later.

"Is he—" Tony took the photo from Milana.

"Yes." Gio sighed. "I'll go to a phone and find the coroner. Damn, two weeks from home."

"No!" Milana stopped crying and heaved herself to her feet. "No coroner. We take him home. He dies in Sarasota. We bury him with family."

"Milana, he's already dead."

Tony walked to the bedroom and came back tugging his handkerchief between his hands. "I'll go get Bernice."

"Not a word to anyone else. Not a word." Milana pointed at Tony's chest. She ran her hands through her black-dyed hair as Tony went out the door.

"Gio, listen to me. We keep him on ice. When we get home, that's when we call the coroner. It's two weeks. We can wait two weeks."

"That's crazy, Milana. We can't do that."

"Of course, we can. We'll use those waxed tarps. Maybe a layer of sawdust. Get blocks of ice every stop. It'll work."

"No, Milana, this is—"

"I'm not leaving him in God-forsaken North Carolina. Or anywhere. We're taking him home. If you want to put him on another train with me, and send him home, and miss your own father's funeral, you do what you have to do. But Pop's going home."

BERNICE PUT HER fleshy arms around Gio and Milana. Gio breathed in Bernice's talcum powder scent. "So, here's what my sister wants to do."

Bernice tucked her handkerchief in her apron pocket. "I have that soaking tub stored in the set-up car. We'll have the boys bring it here. We'll line it with straw. It'll work to store blocks of ice. You boys need to make a hole in the floor to drain the water."

Tony stood with his thumbs hooked in his belt loops. "I don't see why not. He'd want to be buried with Mama and Poppa. I'd want that too."

Gio sighed and looked around the circle. "You are all out of your minds."

Milana pulled the blinds. "Tony, go get that tub. Gio, you go get ice. Let's take him home."

October 15, 1956

THE FISCALINI BROTHERS circus train rolled into Sarasota with two elephants, four horses, a pony, one raven haired bareback rider, one unusually tall clown, seven regular sized clowns, three little clowns, six roustabouts, ten assorted dogs, one strong-man turned elephant handler, one auburn haired female juggler/elephant rider/trapeze flyer, one mustachioed elephant handler, one hairy handyman, one tattooed trapeze flyer, one little kid, one concessions manager, one fortune teller/seamstress, one old barrel-chested trapeze catcher, another younger barrel chested trapeze catcher/ flyer, and one frozen dead guy.

TONY AND GIO moved Giovanni's body into the winter quarters house so Milana could call the coroner in Sarasota and tell him her father had died in his own bed. Milana looked through her makeup case, chose a tone pale enough for an old man who hadn't been out in the sun much, and went to work with her sponge. Gio came in while she was standing back to check her artistry.

"Milana, have you lost your mind?" Gio looked at her incredulously.

"Well we can't let the coroner see he's been dead for a while. What else are we going to do? I told Tony and Bernice to go buy a casket and bring it here. We'll slip the funeral director a little something, so he'll let our guys dig the grave."

"Oh, good Lord." Gio put both hands on top of his head. "Tell me we're not doing this."

"You're in charge of the cemetery part, Gio. We can take Pop over in the parade wagon. Schatz can drive the grey horses. It'll be real nice."

That afternoon, the coroner put his stethoscope to the old man's chest to confirm Giovanni's death. He agreed that, because of his prior heart condition, they could forego the autopsy. He signed the death certificate. "Would you like me to call the funeral home for you, Miss Fiscalini?"

"That's all right, you've been too kind. We'll manage." Milana waited for the coroner to leave, then selected a nice shirt and tie for her recently thawed late father.

Sonny's Ink Runs Dry

SONNY LAFONTAINE HACKED blood-stained yellow junk into his napkin in the middle of breakfast the first of April 1957. He'd been coughing like a beat-up delivery truck every morning for a month before that, and Mary Ellen had gone to the drug store twice a week for cough syrup. She'd begged him to see the doctor, but Sonny told her it was nothing. That morning he looked down at the blue and white checked napkin and his face went pale.

Eddie and Kat came into the café for coffee as Mary Ellen was signing 'That's enough, Sonny, you're going to see the doctor today. Don't argue with me.' Sonny swatted his hand weakly in front of his face and went to coughing again.

'She's right, Pop, you need to see the doc. I'll drive you this afternoon.' Eddie signed, then handed Sonny his napkin. Sonny signed at Eddie that he was fine, and Mary Ellen reached up to silence his hands. Sonny waved for more coffee.

THE DOCTOR LISTENED with his stethoscope and tapped on Sonny's thin back. "How much do you smoke these days, Sonny?" he asked.

Eddie signed to Sonny, then answered. "Two packs a day."

"I'm sending your father for a chest x-ray."

In a dressing room on the second floor, Eddie helped Sonny into a gown. A nurse appeared at the door. "Mr. Lafontaine?"

Eddie put his head out. "We'll be right out. I'll go with my dad. He's deaf."

When the x-raying was over, Sonny put his shirt back on.

'Pop, you got a button wrong,' Eddie signed and reached toward his father's shirt front. Sonny batted Eddie away and fixed his buttons. 'They said it'll just be a little bit. Hey there's a newspaper. Want sports or comics?' Sonny took the sports section.

SONNY TAPPED EDDIE'S arm and signed, 'Don't tell Mary Ellen what that doctor said. He's full of shit. It's not cancer.'

'Pop, what do you think that was the doctor showed us?'

'I got pneumonia or something. It's getting better.'

'Pop, it's not better. You look like shit on a stick.'

'Thanks, kid, thanks a lot. Just don't tell her yet. I don't want her to—' He stopped his hands then pressed them over his face. Eddie heard the small choked cry and put his hand on his father's shoulder.

At the shop, Mary Ellen pressed her husband for more information and got the pneumonia story. Eddie left him to his story.

"Some hell of a pneumonia. Why are you coughing blood?" She spoke while she signed.

'From coughing too much. Doc said more cough syrup. Maybe some whiskey at night. He said more lovin' too.'

Mary Ellen signed, 'Then you are going home and going to bed so you can get well. You hear me? And no more cigarettes until you get better.' Sonny coughed, spat into his handkerchief, and looked away from his wife.

EDDIE AND KAT split up Sonny's morning appointments and made sure he was booked light in the afternoons. Mary Ellen didn't book evenings for Sonny, and Sonny didn't fuss about being home in his recliner with a paperback and a glass of sweet tea. Mary Ellen had a pretty good idea that it was time to get things in order.

"I DON'T WANT to tell everybody about your dad, Eddie, but he can't keep working. Maybe we can throw a retirement party. Then if we get a new person in here to pick up the slack it makes sense. So . . ." Mary Ellen leafed through the appointment book. "When? Next week?"

"Hang on. We gotta ask Pop what he wants to do. He might want to keep working as long as he can."

Mary Ellen turned a page in the book. She put a finger on the following Tuesday's appointments. A tear got away from her and fell, where it made a star-edged splotch on the calendar. "I want him to be home. I don't want him worrying about working. I want as long as I can get with him. Don't you want that?"

Eddie dragged the book toward him and thumbed through the pages. "Pop decides that. I'm not going to tell him what he can't do. Neither are you." He closed the book and slid it back to the spot beside the phone.

The phone rang, and Mary Ellen reached for it. "Lafontaine's—hang on, I'll check." She reopened the book. "You want Eddie or Kat? Okay, he has a four o'clock open next Wednesday. All right. See you then." She closed the book and closed her eyes.

TWO HUNDRED MEN in short sleeves and a couple dozen women in sleeveless dresses displayed their Lafontaine and Son tattoos when they attended the funeral of Sonny Lafontaine. Seven months pregnant Kat stood up and signed the words to the hymns.

PART 7
Stars and Stripes

Change of Season

1958, Fayette, Missouri

"HEY, HONEY, GUESS what? Bernice and Tony are coming through this way. Bernice says what you need is some egg salad. Isn't that just like her?" Bill says. "They may stay in town for a while. You'd like to have Bernice here, wouldn't you? She can catch you up on stuff. I'll bet you're tired of my stories."

"Yeaaah"

Bill grabs at her hand. "Did you say yeah? Yeah, you're glad to see Bernice, or yeah, you're tired of my stories?"

Matilda looks directly at her unshaven husband. "Yeaaah." One side of her mouth lifts. *She's bringing Billy with her, isn't she? I had a dream last night I couldn't find him. Will you brush my hair? I don't want Billy to see me a mess.*

1957, Springtime in the Midwest

THE ELEPHANTS, MARTA and Eloise, were plagued with creaking and popping joints from more than fifty years on the rails. Since Marta had lost vision in one eye, and Eloise had become hesitant to obey commands, Maurice was firm about keeping their act short and simple.

NED BENTLEY SAT down across from Bill and Matilda one evening after supper, while ten-year-old Billy was at the other end of the pie car listening to the clowns tell dirty jokes.

"I know you used to do an elephant lift off, Matilda. Maurice told me. So, I have this idea for an act with two angels on the elephants. I've got Polly, and I thought about using Ignacio but he's not too agile. But Billy would be perfect. I'd have Schatz taking care of Billy's mechanic the whole time."

"If my boy is in the air, I'm on the rope. Don't mention it to Billy yet." Bill touched Matilda's arm. "Let's not be planning anything until my wife and I have a chance to talk."

"Sorry, Bill, didn't mean to jump the gun. Let me know after you talk about it."

Bill rocked the bench when he got up. Matilda slapped a hand on the table to ride out the wobble and smiled at Ned apologetically.

"OH, GOOD LORD, Bill, it's not too much for Billy to do another act. You just don't like Ned, and you never have." Matilda and Bill leaned against the stoop railing outside their car, passing one cigarette back and forth.

Bill looked across the lot and flicked ashes onto the linkage between the railroad cars. "Well, I don't have to like him." He handed Matilda the cigarette.

"I know, but don't keep Billy from having a good time." Matilda passed the cigarette back.

"I just don't want anything to happen."

"Nothing will happen, Bill. You'll run the mechanic. They'll rehearse. He'll be a little star. Come on."

"If anything looks wrong, I get to say no—"

"Bill. Listen to you. It'll be fine."

"NO REHEARSALS WITHOUT me there," Bill said.

Ned Bentley saluted with two fingers on the brim of his fedora. "Of course, Bill."

"And he never gets on without a mechanic."

"Yes, of course. Now, we, Maurice and Polly and I, we talked about the ending, and we do need to put them back on the elephants after they fly around, have them ride out of the ring. So, they'll have to unclip as they go under the curtain bar, is that okay? Maurice will be right beside Marta as they go out to help Billy off. Otherwise, he'd get snatched off when the wire hits the bar."

"I know how it works, Ned. But not Marta. You put my son on Eloise."

"Sure, Bill. I was going to put Eloise in front, since she's taller, but if you insist, I'll switch them."

"You don't switch the elephants. Jesus. That's the order they've always worked. You're not putting my kid on the one-eyed elephant. Put Billy on Eloise in front."

"Yes, Okay, I can do that. Thank you, Bill. I think you'll like the act."

"All I care about is that my kid's not going to get knocked off or trampled." Bill glanced around and leaned forward. "You keep my son safe. You understand?"

"You have my word, Bill."

SIX REHEARSALS, THREE costume adjustments to keep the angel wings from snagging in the mechanic wires, and four music changes later, the new act debuted in Dubuque, Iowa.

Billy was doing three acts every show: the rosinback, riding in front of Rosa, then the three-minute bit he did on his pony with Rosa directing from center ring, and the elephant act. Between the horses and elephant performances, Billy ran to the dressing tent and did his costume change on his own.

"Tanbark in his pockets," Gio said to Matilda the second night in Dubuque as they watched Billy standing at the curtain, ready to run into the ring.

"I know. Not a shy bone in him. Bill's watching Bentley pretty close though."

Gio pressed his lips together and looked at his pocket watch. "What about you?"

"Bentley always looks like he's winging it to me, but I trust Maurice."

"If you see anything outta line, you come straight to me."

IGNACIO AND VELMA had been watching the angels-on-elephants rehearsals and had an idea to scrounge up their own angel costumes so Ignacio could chase Velma around the ring. When he caught her, he'd grab her butt, then she could pretend-slug him and he'd take a fall.

Gio asked them what the hell they were doing when he saw them rehearsing the grab and punch and Velma explained it would only be about a fifteen second deal, tops, to liven up the crowd after the dog act.

Gio said, "Okay, but not 'til after the elephants are out. And you come in and go out the side of the ring, not where the elephants come in and go out."

Ignacio said they'd do it Gio's way.

Sheriff Delgar Wells

1957, Fayette, Missouri

"NADINE, YOU READY?" Sheriff Delgar Wells wiped a dab of shaving cream off his ear with a pink tissue from the crocheted wiener dog tissue holder on top of the toilet tank. He sniffed his uniform shirt, then tapped Johnson's Baby Powder on the armpit seams before he put it back on over his bleached undershirt. "Nadine—I need to stop for gas on the way, come on."

Nadine Wells stood outside the bathroom door and re-pinned her pink pillbox hat while she watched her husband of forty years fussing with his shirt. "I swear, Del, you primp more than Mayor Lawson before election day."

Delgar slid his black comb into his pocket along with a clean white handkerchief. "Luther Lawson don't get to go mingle with the stars of the circus like we do. You look right nice, 'Dine."

At the fairgrounds, Gio Fiscalini pumped Wells' hand heartily and kissed Nadine's rosy cheeks. After fifteen years of the circus stopping in Fayette,

Delgar and Nadine looked forward to the Fiscalini family coming more than they looked forward to their own children coming home to visit.

Nadine slipped away from the men to peek into the back of the main tent, hoping to find Bernice Fiscalini. Nadine always brought Bernice a jar of her grandma's recipe loganberry jam, or a 7-Up pound cake from the supply she made every couple of months and kept in the freezer to take when she went calling.

"HEY, NOW, WHO'S this little fella?" Delgar asked Gio as Billy Matilda hurried by to get his pony ready.

"You remember Matilda, our lady who does the trapeze act? That's her son. Last time we were here he was doing clown acts. He's in two horse acts now and an elephant act and growing so fast it's hard to keep him in costumes. Oh." Gio produced tickets from his shirt pocket. "I have seats in front for you, or you can sit wherever you like."

"Well, Nadine will want to be in the front row. She looks forward to your circus every year."

"Fine, fine." Gio clapped the sheriff's starched shoulder. "We're glad you can be here tonight."

"Thank you. I gotta find that wife of mine. She's probably swapping pie crust recipes with somebody somewhere. And we gotta go see your sister and get popcorn. Good to have you back." And Delgar Wells meant it. Of the three circus companies that had come to Fayette in the past couple of decades, the Fiscalini bunch was the least trouble to him. And he always got free tickets for opening night. And, he reasoned, there was that tattooed gal on the trapeze. She sure was something. Even Nadine agreed she was something though she didn't much care for the tattoos.

White Doves

IGNACIO SWIPED TWO white doves from the pre-show magician's crates and showed Velma how he was going to put them in a white sack tied to his wing harness. Then, he said when she slapped him, he'd flip the sack open and the birds would fly out when he fell back.

"You ask Gio?" Velma looked around for the boss.

"He don't care. Long as it gets a laugh."

"It's bad luck, Nosh."

"What is?"

"Birds in the tent."

"Screw that."

"Matilda and Gio and Tony will already be on the platforms. Might not be good if them birds fly up there. If they got distracted—"

"Bastards been in a cage all their lives, prob'ly don't even know how to fly. I'll just pick 'em up off the ring floor. It'll be fine."

Saturday Night in Fayette

1958, Fayette, Missouri

THROUGH A DARK-EDGED haze, Matilda watches her husband come in, wearing the pants and shirt he'd worn the day before. She smells motor oil on his clothes. She thinks she's in their trailer, and he's come in from getting the tent up and she needs to get up and get dressed for a show.

He adjusts the blinds and holds the newspaper close to her face for a second before he begins reading to her. She listens to stories she can't follow and wishes he'd slow down so she can think between the words.

The doctor comes by every few days to look in her eyes. Sometimes his voice sounds sad. When she opens her eyes and moves her arms for him, he doesn't tell her she's doing "so good" the way he did at first.

It's been nine weeks.

1957, Fayette, Missouri

SATURDAY IN FAYETTE, angels Polly and Billy lifted off the elephants, flew out over the crowd, then settled back on the elephants in perfect unison. Eloise and Marta trotted out while Billy and Polly unclipped their wires. The spotlight beam swept the ring to catch Ned Bentley taking a final bow but didn't find him.

Ignacio and Velma ran in from the side in their angel costumes. Velma grabbed her butt like she'd been pinched and got a big laugh when she pretend-slapped Nosh's face. He staggered backwards, groping at his chest to free the doves. The crowd was still laughing when one bird flapped twice and landed three feet from the prone little man. The other dove headed for the partly open tent flap where the elephants had just exited.

Polly had slid down from Marta. Billy was waiting for Maurice to help him off Eloise just as he'd been taught. The dove fluttered toward the right side of Marta's face and brushed against the lashes surrounding her blind eye. Marta swung her trunk up and lurched away from whatever was touching her eyelashes, bumping Eloise's right hip with her head.

Eloise dutifully rotated around to face the in-flap, knocking Maurice down as he was trying to help Billy slide off. Maurice crawled away from the pacing feet, head spinning from the blow. He barely got out of Marta's way as she bolted out of the tent. Ned Bentley was outside the tent, congratulating himself with a snort from a well-dented flask. Marta trotted by him without slowing, trumpeting in fear with Polly in pursuit.

The light and sound man started "The Band Played On" for Matilda's trapeze feature, and the elderly Eloise, hearing a familiar musical cue, headed toward the ring with Billy still astride her neck.

"MAUR!" Billy cried out. He clung to the elephant's harness, wide eyed.

Gio looked down from the platform, then glanced to the other platform. He saw Matilda shielding her eyes from the spotlight, looking into the ring below, frozen in place.

The trotting elephant hit the ring boards with her knees and toppled over headlong. Yellow and blue boards splintered into the front seats on both sides of her. A blur of white shot out in front of the elephant, into the semi-darkness at the side of the ring. The elephant's hind legs left the ground when her forehead hit, and she made a slow somersault before coming to rest on her left side. Matilda strained against the spotlight to see where the tumble of white had gone. The crowd went silent.

A woman in the stands began to sob.

Clowns and dog handlers started pushing people toward the exits. The ring lights dimmed. A photographer from the local paper popped a fresh bulb into his camera and stepped forward to get a shot of the struggling elephant. The last thing the photographer saw before he went down was Maurice's mighty black fist.

Gio took two rungs at a time to the ring floor.

"Bill!" Matilda shouted down, "Do you have Billy?"

Her vision cleared enough for her to see her husband standing where the flash of white had landed. Bill bent to pick up the angel wings. Billy wasn't in them.

The dove on the ring floor flapped toward the top of the tent and flew past Matilda. Matilda covered her mouth with both hands and screamed.

ELOISE STRUGGLED TO rise, front left leg hanging limply from her broken shoulder. Gio shouted at the crew to get something over the elephant's head to keep her quiet. He ran to his private car and came back with a bolt action rifle.

"Boss, maybe Marta can get her up. She might be all right . . ." Maurice pleaded, tears streaming down his face. "Please, Gio."

"Maurice, I need you to get back. You know she's all broke up. You go make sure Polly has the other one caught. We don't need her loose in town. Go."

"Gio," Bill's hoarse whisper echoed unnaturally. "My son is under there."

"Under?"

Bill pointed at Eloise. The elephant rattled and grunted. Gio stared at Bill, who was still holding the wings, then looked in horror up at the platform where Matilda was on her knees, clutching the ladder.

Tony was at Gio's side, speaking in a low voice. "He didn't roll clear, Gio. He was on her when she flipped. Billy's under there."

"Hold on, Billy, we'll get you out," Gio said under his breath. Polly appeared with Marta at the entrance. "Get that elephant in here, on this side. She'll have to hold the weight long enough to get him out."

"Who?" Polly choked back tears.

"Billy. Tony thinks he's—" Gio couldn't say the rest.

He looked around the ring again, hoping the boy would appear. He'd be shaken, sure, maybe bruised and scraped, but he had to be here somewhere. He had to be fine. The little boy they'd all raised had to be getting up, dusting himself off, and trotting back to the ring to take a bow.

Marta shoved her trunk under Eloise's neck and leaned into her. The sound of Eloise's scapula splintering rang up into the top of the tent. Bill stood helplessly beside Gio and Tony, clutching the wings. Eloise made a guttural screeching sound when Polly and Maurice urged Marta to push harder. Marta dug in and heaved her wounded partner into a sitting position.

Tony and Bill reached for the arm and leg that appeared.

Tony sobbed. "Push again," and the two handlers pleaded with Marta to lean into the effort. Eloise toppled to her other side, boards breaking beneath her. The men pulled Billy Matilda away from the elephant's flailing legs.

Two shots rang through the night air. The elephant exhaled her final breaths.

Bill said Billy's name over and over, then cried out for Matilda in a voice that didn't sound human. Matilda was already beside Bill.

"Oh my God, oh my Billy," Matilda whispered.

Polly wrapped an arm over Matilda but stepped back when Matilda jerked away.

Maurice knelt and held Eloise's limp trunk, crying like a baby.

Bill looked up from his son's body and watched Maurice stroke the dead elephant's head.

"Maur, where's that God-dammed dwarf?" Polly said softly.

Matilda gawked at Polly. "What?"

"That God-damned Ignacio let those birds loose. One flew into Marta's blind side. She ran into Eloise, and—and," Polly said, and picked up the little angel wings from where Bill had dropped them.

"Where's Bentley?" Gio asked quietly. Polly pointed at the tent flap where Ned Bentley was doubled over vomiting dinner and Seagram's.

Bill lay his head on the boy's crushed chest and wept in choking sobs. Tony knelt and cried with him.

Matilda backed away from her husband and dead son. She picked up the rifle. Gio quickly stepped forward to take the rifle from her hands. She stared at Gio for an instant then walked past Bentley and out into the darkness.

1958, Fayette, Missouri

"I'D LIKE TO get the pins out of her leg this week. I think we could help Matilda with some exercises to strengthen her," Doctor McClure says, "so if and when she fully regains consciousness, she'll be able to sit up."

"And walk. You said she'd be walking," Suzette says, leaning forward.

"Recovery from her kind of injuries is never as easy as—" McClure hesitates "—as just waking up and walking. We don't know yet how much more she'll regain."

Bill is standing at the window. He's wearing the chambray shirt and jeans he wore to work on the furnace at the hospital this morning. The leaves are changing colors. He knows the circus crew is headed back toward Sarasota by now. Matilda hasn't tried to speak in close to a week, and her limbs have begun twitching involuntarily.

1957, Fayette, Missouri

TONY AND MAURICE had to hold Bill back while the coroner knelt to determine what was obvious. Some of the crowd had pushed past the crew and clowns to see a dead elephant. Ned Bentley pressed his shaking hands into his armpits while he watched the aftermath from the bottom of the bleachers. Someone in the crowd started praying.

"Shut up," Maurice thundered. He lunged toward the crowd. "Just shut up." He stopped short of the front row of people then went back to stand beside Bill. Bill was shouting at the coroner not to lay a sheet over his son.

"Let them cover him, Bill. You don't want those people to see Billy." Maurice put his hands on his friend's shoulders. Bill's arms hung at his sides when he turned to Maurice.

While the coroner helped the drivers place the child's crushed body on a stretcher, Sheriff Wells scribbled on a three by five spiral notebook, thanked the coroner, and went to stand in front of Bentley.

Bentley put his hands on his knees and looked woefully back and forth between the dead elephant and Maurice. "I go out after the elephants. After I take a bow. Because I'm the trainer. But him," he waved a hand toward Maurice, "he and that dumb red head are in charge of getting the riders off."

Wells flipped a page on his notebook. "He tells me you went out before the elephants did. Is that correct? Did you go out of the tent first?"

"I guess."

"You guess or you know?"

"I went out first, okay? I was feeling sick."

"Mr. Bentley, I can smell you."

"It was only a little nip. Just a nip. I—I—"

Delgar Wells put his notebook into his front shirt pocket. "Don't you leave here, you understand?" He turned and walked back toward the performers who stood around Bill. "Don't any of you leave town. I know this is a terrible thing for everyone, but I need to talk to all of you."

Bentley stood and walked unsteadily toward Wells and the others. "It was an accident. You all saw. It was an accident. That elephant was unpredictable. It was. You all know that."

"Sheriff," Gio leaned close to Wells, "I was on the platform. My brother and I both were. We saw most of it. We'll stay. May I let the parents go and . . ." His face tilted toward Bill.

"Yes, I can come back first thing in the morning. But please don't move anything. Can you leave some of your people to make sure nothing's disturbed?"

"Schatz, you and Gordie, you get a couple other guys. Maurice, get the other elephant secured. And don't let anybody in." Gio turned to the sheriff. "We'll do all we can." He looked toward Ned Bentley. "What about him?"

"You think he'll leave?" Wells shifted his hat from hand to hand.

Gio glared in Bentley's direction. "If you want to question a live witness, you better take him with you tonight."

Bentley stumbled to the sheriff's car and got in the back seat.

The Longest Night

"HOW ABOUT SOMETHING to eat, Bill? Egg salad sandwich? I'll be right back, okay? Tony." Bernice raised her chin toward the wire front cabinet beside the tattered sofa. Tony took two chipped mugs and the corked bottle of port from the cabinet. Bernice stood at the cotton blanket that hung between the living room and bedroom. "Matilda, honey, I'll get you two something to eat. Tony and I will stay with—" She pulled the blanket aside. "Matilda?"

Bernice walked to the roughly made bed and lifted the covers. She came back out and her eyes met Tony's. "Tony, you stay with Bill. I'll find her."

Bernice walked alongside the train. Over at the tent, two of Schatz's clowns sat in folding chairs with a lantern on a table between them, playing cards while they guarded the main entrance. She went around to the back yard where two roustabouts had their bedrolls on the ground near the fence panels. One raised up when she walked by, then lay back down with a sigh.

At the open side flap between the bleachers Bernice cupped her elbows in her hands to stare at the dead elephant. Bernice had joked to Tony that she'd quit: she'd stop sewing and telling fortunes when the dang elephants quit and now one of them had quit for good. She didn't know how long she stood there breathing the musty smell of elephant and blood coagulating on the tanbark.

BERNICE FOUND POLLY sitting with Maurice in the open door of the elephant car. Marta alternately pulled tufts of grass and rumbled mournfully in the direction of the tent. "Is Matilda here with you?"

"No, I thought she went—" Polly peered into the darkness. "I don't know."

"I'm worried about her."

"I thought she went to her car. She said she was fine."

"I don't think she'll ever be fine," Maurice interrupted, rubbing at his already swollen eyes. "How can you say she was fine?"

"I didn't mean—no, she can't be fine. She's not at her car?"

"No, she's not there, honey, that's why I'm looking for her." Bernice exhaled. "Listen, if you see her, get her back to her car. I'm going to go see if she's with Rosa."

"I'll go check with Rosa, Bernice." Maurice slid to the ground. "Polly, you stay here with Marta."

"I'll be over at Bill and Matilda's. If you see Gio, send him there." Bernice trundled back across the lot.

Egg Salad

MATILDA STOPPED TO contemplate the two men who guarded the main entrance before she climbed the steps to her car and went in. Bernice reached the door a moment later.

"I was worried about you, honey. Here, I made this fresh this afternoon." Bernice set the plate of egg salad sandwiches on the table. Matilda stood behind Bill with a hand on his shoulder. Tony poured more port into their mugs and motioned for Bernice to look in the cabinet.

Tony splashed port into the two battered tin cups Bernice set on the table. "Here, you drink this. You'll feel better." Matilda stared dully at the cup.

"Why don't you let me help you change?" Bernice said. "You boys eat, we'll be right back."

Matilda stood, child-like at the foot of the bed to let Bernice peel her costume off. "Oh, honey, look at these grass stains on your slippers. I'll take them with me and get them cleaned up. Where's your nightie, honey?" Matilda stared at the blanket that hung between the bedroom and living room. Bernice found a cotton nightgown on a hook in the closet and held it above Matilda's head. Matilda held her arms up for a few seconds, then dropped them. "How about this cotton robe, sweetie?"

Matilda swayed unsteadily while Bernice put the robe on her and tied the belt. "Let's get some food in you and have some port. That'll help you sleep. Come on. Come on, come with me."

Tony rose and pushed the chair around to the side of the table. Matilda stood, looking confused before she sank onto the seat. Tony slid the cup toward her.

She studied the inky liquid in the tin cup, then gulped half of it down. "Easy, hon, go easy on that—" He stopped when he saw Bernice shake her head. Bernice pushed the egg salad sandwiches closer to Bill and Matilda, then sat on the sofa.

Bill looked around at Bernice. "That's his bed. That's Billy's bed."

Bernice rose from the sofa and picked up the other tin cup. "I'm sorry, Bill, I didn't—" Tony motioned for Bernice to take his crate, then sat on an upturned bucket beside the door.

They were still sitting in silence, drinking port half an hour later when Gio came looking for them. "I have the guys watching the gates and left two in the . . ." He trailed off when he looked at Tony's face. He picked up Tony's cup and knocked back the rest of the port before he gave it back.

"We're going to stay here with Matilda and Bill—" Bernice started.

"No, Bernice, you don't need to." Matilda stood. "But if you see Billy, tell him to get home. It's too late for him to be out."

Bernice brushed her hand over Matilda's before she looked to her husband and brother-in-law for help. "Let's get you to bed," she said quietly.

Matilda turned her blank stare at Bill. Her eyes didn't follow Bill when he stood and shambled toward the sofa. Ancient springs under horsehair stuffing groaned as he slumped to his side on the worn fabric.

"Where could he be?" Matilda asked the three Fiscalinis. "Look what time it is. He's in trouble when he gets home."

"Matilda, honey," Bernice said. "Why don't you get some sleep?"

Matilda blinked at the people around the table, then walked to the window and pulled the muslin curtain aside. She pressed her forehead against the glass to look both ways. She turned toward the bedroom curtain and felt her way through. The bed springs emitted a low, drawn-out moan, then went silent.

Bernice motioned at Gio and Tony to go. Bill lay listlessly on the couch.

Bernice went to the bedroom and leaned down to kiss Matilda's cheek before she lay down beside her. "I'm right here, hon."

Matilda put her head on Bernice's pillowy bosom and lay, staring into the darkness while Bernice slept.

Wake Up Call

"MORNIN', SON." DELGAR Wells carried a tray into the jailhouse. "My wife, well, I told her I'd ask if you wanted breakfast, but she'd already made a plate."

Bentley groaned, sat up on the edge of the cot and wiped his face with a grimy hand.

Delgar set the plate on the shelf at the meal tray slot. "You were pretty drunk last night. Your boss thought it was best I brought you here."

Bentley looked down at his black socks. "Are my boots here?"

"Yes, I pulled those off when I brought you in. They're in a locker with your belt and your tie. You understand. Just protocol."

"You got some aspirin? I think I hit my head trying to stop that elephant."

"Prob'ly got a bottle in my desk. You better eat something first."

Ned Bentley rose, took the plate from the shelf, and sat back down on the cot. He picked up the white plastic fork and scowled.

"Am I under arrest?" Bentley stirred the grits into the scrambled eggs.

"Not at the moment. But as long as you're here, I need to ask some questions."

"You hauled me to jail for having a drink after I finished a show?" Bentley lifted a glob of grits and eggs to his mouth.

"Son, I have to interview everybody involved. I brought you here because your boss thought it was best for your safety last night."

"So those miserable bastards are blaming me?" Bentley wiped his moustache on his sleeve. "It wasn't my fault. I—"

"Son, I'm doing my job. But I could take you back out to the fairgrounds right now. Up to you."

Bentley picked up a strip of bacon. "No, I'll wait here."

Sheriff Wells was pretty sure this hungover guy in the cell wasn't directly responsible for the tragedy at the circus, but he was going to make some phone calls to see it there was a warrant out on a Clarence Dever from Tampa. Because that was the name the drunk elephant trainer from the circus had given him last night.

"HEY, CROWDER, DELGAR Wells here." Delgar used the turquoise living room phone since it was the furthest from the jail door. "Yeah, you too. Oh, Nadine's just fine, how's Lucy? Good. Hey, can you look something up for me? Yep. A name. I just got a hunch about a guy I brought in. Oh sure. I know, I never have a pen when I need one either."

Delgar Wells frowned at the grounds in the bottom of his cup and set the receiver down to get the coffee pot from the stove. He picked up the receiver.

"Tom?" Crowder wasn't back yet. Wells wiped the bottom of his cup with his handkerchief and poured his third cup of coffee.

There was a thump and shuffling of paper in the receiver. "What's the name?"

"Dever. Clarence Dever. Maybe from Florida. Maybe not."

"Hold on. Dever, Dever . . . yeah, there's a Dever. Clinton Dever. How old's your guy?"

"Maybe forty. What you got on your Dever?"

"Forgery, breaking and entering, petty theft, drunk and disorderly. Guy's been around," Crowder said.

"Got a picture?"

"Yeah, there's a picture. Nice lookin'. Looks like his nose has been broken. Square jaw. Says black hair, brown eyes. Scar on his chin, right side. Five-nine. One-fifty. Says here he's—hang on, lemmie subtract—this guy would be thirty-nine."

"Got any aliases?" Wells blew on his coffee.

"Oh dang, Delgar there's another sheet here under the first. Gol-dang. Whole dang list of 'em. Clinton Denver. Denver Clinton. Clarence Denver, Clinton Bentley, Ned Deveraux. Clarence Bentley."

"How long you there, Tom? Okay. I'll be by in a little bit."

SHERIFF WELLS DUMPED his coffee cup and drove across Fayette to Tom Crowder's office. Crowder opened the door on the second knock. "Here, I found another sheet on that guy."

Delgar Wells studied the picture. "This is our guy. Oh, hell yes. Occupation: dock loader. Tour guide. Animal trainer. Circus performer."

"Look at this," the clerk said. "Nate Bentley. Hit a pedestrian in Tampa, Florida. Drove off. Witness who said they knew him identified him as Dever. Victim died the next day. Felony hit and run."

"Christ Almighty. Thanks, Tommy. I'll call the Florida guys tomorrow. But you go home. I mean it."

"Where'd you find him?"

"At the circus. You hear what happened last night?"

Crowder walked to his desk and picked up the newspaper. The front page showed an elephant on its side, and a crowd of people around it. "Terrible. Says a midget got crushed under the thing."

"It was a little kid. Son of two of their people. Terrible. This guy I got—might be negligence, but this," he held up the rap sheet and warrant, "damn. Thanks, Tommy. I'll call 'em tomorrow. Don't tell Lucy this guy's a wanted felon. She'll call Nadine and it'll be all over town."

Eight and a Half Weeks

1958—Fayette, Missouri

"BROUGHT YOUR SCRAPBOOK in, honey. Here. I'll turn the pages."
He rests the bottom of the book on the bed rail.

She raises her atrophied arm and lets it drop. Her other arm jerks up and
she touches a newspaper photo of her riding an elephant on a beach.

"I like that one too," Bill says.

"Ehh—Ehhl—uh."

"Yes, that was Eloise." He waits for her hand to move and turns the page.
His heart feels like razor blades. He knows her condition is not improving.

1957—Fayette, Missouri

"MR. KAZARIAN, THANK you. I know this has been—well, very
hard." Delgar Wells set his dulled pencil on his notebook while the grieving
father across the table in the pie car refolded a bleached napkin for the
fourth time.

"What about Bentley?" Bill's voice crackled like dry wheat stalks. "You ask
him where he was?"

"I'll be interviewing Bentley. You have my word."

Bill nodded, stood, and left.

Rosa came in next. She and Schatz were putting horses away, she said, had
seen Ignacio and Velma run by with their angel wings flopping behind them,
then heard boards breaking and the crowd shouting. They'd finished securing
horses and had run in through the side flap, she said. She'd held the canvas
aside for Polly when she came back with the other elephant.

Schatz was the next to talk to the sheriff. "Broken-down old things. Both
those elephants. No wonder that one did like it did."

"Is that how they'd normally do that? For the barrier to be back up right
after the elephants go out?" Wells watched the lines in Schatz's face deepen.

"Oh, yeah, it always goes back up. And there's always someone with
the elephants while they help riders off them. But I wasn't there so I don't
know what happened in there." Schatz added he'd never really trusted those
elephants since one of them had knocked him down and rolled him under her
feet his first year on the show, twenty-five years ago.

"Would you say Mr. Bentley is a competent trainer?"

"Bentley isn't a trainer. He makes up shit and tells a good story. He never
trained elephants. Maurice is the trainer. Bentley should've been there though,
to help Maurice. What's everybody else say?"

"Mr. Schatz, I'm not at liberty—"

"Right. Well, I wasn't in the tent when it happened. I didn't see Bentley until after it was all over, when he was pukin' over by the bleachers, shit faced. I know he was drunk."

"You've seen him drunk before while he was performing, or on his own time?"

"After-hours, I guess. Sometimes he plays cards with us. He always has a flask."

"Is that against the rules?"

"No. You gotta have a drink once in a while to live like we live. But not while we're working. We just don't."

"Of course. Now, the two little clowns you saw run by while you were tending horses, did you see where they went?"

"No. I mean, it was kind of strange they were running like that, but they're kind of goofy anyway. Then we heard all the commotion and went to, you know—"

"To the tent?"

"Yes, sir. I didn't think about those two again. Well until this morning. One of 'em didn't show up for breakfast."

"Which one was that?" Wells had his pencil ready.

"Nosh. Ignacio. You were here Friday? You saw him. Dwarf, 'bout three feet tall. He and Velma did the short gig in angel costumes, after the elephants."

"Is that act the same every time?"

"Pretty much, but last night, little bastard stole two doves from the magician act. Magician's one of my clowns, you know? Does the pre-show, you know? We all got more than one job. Anyway, he stole the doves. Turned 'em loose in the tent. That sawed-off asshole knows better. From what I heard last night, that caused the whole thing. That bird flying into that elephant's blind side." Schatz rested his forearms on the table, leaned forward, and bowed his head.

"Anything else, Mr. Schatz?"

"Not that I can think of. Bentley should have been there. I don't like the guy, but it was the elephant that killed the kid. And it wouldn't have happened if Ignacio hadn't turned the damn birds loose."

"Know where I might find him? Ignacio?"

"Well, he's prob'ly afraid to show his face. Might ask Velma. She does that act with him. The other little gal used to, but she works concessions. They all shack up together. You know."

Wells could see bits of face paint at the man's hairline. He wondered if the paint ever came completely off.

"AND YOUR LAST name?" Delgar Wells asked the bow-legged three-foot tall woman who'd heaved herself onto the bench across from him. Her face was red and puffy, and she blew her nose loudly on a rag she produced from a pants pocket.

"Just Velma."

"All right, Velma. So, tell me what happened."

Velma told the sheriff how they'd worked out the act they'd do to follow the elephants before the trapeze act started. She told him how Ignacio would grab at her behind, and she'd pretend to punch him, and he'd go down. She said she'd told Nosh she didn't like the idea of the birds. She started to tear up and mopped at the corners of her eyes with the grimy rag.

"He wouldn't listen. And we barely got outta the way before that stupid elephant comes runnin' back in. That little boy was screaming for help. Then the thing flipped over and rolled on—" She started gulping air. "On the kid. He was just a little kid." Tears spilled onto her shirt front.

Wells pocketed his pencil and offered one of the five handkerchiefs he'd loaded in his pockets. "And where did you and your partner go after the accident?"

"We—we—were scared. Ignacio and me—" She blew her nose again. "Sorry. Well, I didn't know what to do, and Nosh, he says somethin' like 'Oh shit, Vel, run,' somethin' like that."

"And you ran out of the tent?"

"Yeah. I was scared shitless. Everybody was yellin', and the elephant was makin' this awful sound, like a dying' cow. And I followed Nosh. We went and hid. We were both scared."

"Where did you hide?" Wells put his knuckles against his cheek, as though he really cared where they'd hidden. He needed time to think about what he'd do. There was some blame here, for causing the accident, for the birds being turned loose, for one of the handlers being outside and not there to keep an elephant from running into another elephant, or to stop a confused old elephant from charging back into the tent. He just couldn't see how to put it on any one person.

"We hid under a trailer, then Nosh says, 'Go back to our car.' He says he'll make sure nobody's following. So, I did. But he never came back. And I can't find him this morning. I think Bentley must've done something to him."

"Why do you say that, Velma?"

"Bentley hates his guts. Hates mine too. He's an arrogant jackass. Sorry. But he is. Hates us for being, well, the way we are." She wadded up Wells' handkerchief and shoved it into her pants pocket.

"Anything else, Miss Velma?"

"Are we gonna get fired? What the hell are we supposed to do? What happens to people like us if Gio puts us off the train?"

"I'm afraid I don't know, Miss." But Delgar Wells was pretty sure that before this was over, somebody might get fired and put off the train. He just hoped Fiscalini waited until another town down the line to do it.

GIO, TONY, MAURICE, and Schatz walked the perimeter of the fairgrounds, then pulled the tarp off the trailer where Velma said she'd last seen Ignacio.

"I wonder if he just ran off." Gio turned his head toward Maurice. "Did you check the clown dressing tent?"

Maurice came back with a pair of threadbare trousers that measured a foot from top to bottom, and a miniature-sized shirt with rolled-up cuffs.

The four men looked at each other. "Velma thinks Bentley had it in for Ignacio," Maurice offered.

Tony folded his arms. "But Bentley was drunker than Cooter Brown and the sheriff hauled him in. Velma didn't see that. Bentley wasn't even here."

"So, the little bastard ran off, and good riddance." Schatz glanced around. Maurice looked to Tony, to Schatz, then to Gio. He bent to pick up a couple of popcorn bags and stuffed the shirt into one of them. He handed Schatz the pants and other bag. Schatz followed his lead.

Maurice cleared his throat and spoke softly. "I'd say Ignacio has flown the coop. Do we all agree?"

"Maurice." Gio looked around to confirm no one had wandered closer to listen. "He ran off in his costume? If you know something, you need to tell me."

Schatz folded the top of the bag. "He's not missing if nobody misses him. Nobody but Velma, and she'll get over it."

Gio ran a hand over his hair. "I'd back any one of you. You know I would. But—"

"There's no but about it, Gio," Schatz said. "If I'd known what happened when I saw him run by me, I probably would've grabbed him and choked him 'til his eyes popped. But I didn't. And you didn't and Tony didn't and Maurice didn't."

"And Rosa was with Schatz, and Polly was out catching the other elephant," Tony said. Maurice raised one eyebrow, then looked at the toe of his shoe. Schatz slid both long hands into his back pockets and rocked on his heels.

Maurice took the popcorn bag from Schatz. "Well, I need to get to work. We've got a mess to clean up." He dropped the bags in the trash barrel on his way to the elephant car.

THE MORTUARY OWNER in Fayette provided a casket. Nadine Wells said the boy could be buried in her family's plot on the home farm, where she could tend the grave. On Tuesday morning, a dozen folks from town drove their cars out to take circus performers to Nadine's family's farm for the funeral.

Bill and Matilda stood in silence, not touching while the Presbyterian minister spoke of God's will and the importance of prayer. The train pulled out Wednesday morning for Clarksville, Tennessee.

AFTER A COUPLE of weeks of letters and phone calls, two officers from Tampa extradited Clinton Dever, a.k.a. Clinton Denver, Denver Clinton, Clarence Denver, Clinton Bentley, Ned Deveraux, Clarence Bentley, Nate Bentley and Ned Bentley to the Florida justice system on a five-year-old felony hit and run warrant.

Nine Weeks

1958—Fayette, Missouri

HER ARMS FLING backward as he swings her around. When he lifts her over his head, she's taller than all the other dancers. The drum is too loud. The sound is all wrong. But her daddy has her, and he squeezes her while he spins across the dance floor. Too much, Daddy. You're squeezing too much. You're making it hard to breathe, Daddy. He says something but she can barely hear him over the drum. She wants to see him. Her eyes are clenched so tightly her cheeks hurt.

"Matilda, you're waking up from anesthetic," the nurse says. "You're going back to your room."

"Baby, Momma's right here." Suzette walks beside the gurney.

Bill is on the other side, holding the rail, watching his wife's face. He wishes Suzette would shut up.

1957, Clarksville, Tennessee

WHEN MAURICE UNLOADED Marta in Clarksville the crew put up a screen of tarped panels to keep curious circus goers away. Maurice and Polly took turns coaxing her to eat, but she mostly picked at the grass in the circle around her stake and made mournful sounds.

Gio stopped at the elephant car on his way to get the crew on double time putting tents up. "Polly, do you think you can do something with Billy's pony? Like, tricks? We need to put in some time. I can't send Matilda up right now."

"It'll stand on a platform. I can get it to rear or something. What do you want me to wear?"

"Something that gets their attention. Fishnets. We have some tall gaiters that look like tall boots in a trunk. I think Bernice has a short white coat Matilda used to wear. Know what I mean?"

She did.

"You and Tony, what are you going to do? Swing back and forth and look at each other?"

"We can do a couple things. I don't know much else we can do."

"Why don't we use that big grey horse and do that lift off from the horse? Pass me once and put me back on the horse, or on the floor. Like Matilda did from the elephant."

Gio scratched his jaw for a moment to think. "Okay. But you have Maur and one other guy on the mechanic rope. And Rosa is in the ring, and that horse is on a lunge line." Polly nodded in agreement. "And Polly? No chances. None."

Tony's job was to pull Betty out of concessions and put her back in the ring with Velma. "I need you gals to work up one of the longer acts. We need a good four minutes. Keep it clean."

Velma fumed. "Screw you, Tony, you're givin' Matilda and Bill time off. What about me?"

"Hey, Velma, you're on thin ice with everybody right now, so why don't you shut that big mouth of yours?" Tony put his hands on his hips and glared down at her.

"Oh yeah? You and who else is gonna make me?"

"Knock it off, Vel." Betty pulled at Velma's arm. "It ain't Tony's fault Nosh ran off. Tony, we'll be ready."

"Good. Thanks, Betty," Tony walked toward the horse pens. He had plenty to figure out so they could all get through what was going to be a tough weekend in Clarksville.

ROSA FOUND MATILDA sitting on the sofa, staring at the tattered pages of a copy of *Tom Sawyer*. "Brought you some magazines, 'Tilda."

Matilda blinked at Rosa as if startled. Rosa sat down beside her and took her hand. The two sat silently, Matilda looking at the hand holding hers, Rosa looking at Matilda's profile.

"Sweetie, is there anything you need right now, anything I can do for you? Want to call your grandparents? I saw a payphone outside the store, 'bout a quarter mile from here. I'll walk with you."

"That'd be—yes—I need to get dressed."

"Yes, you do. How about I bring back a bucket of hot water and you can clean up, too?"

Matilda raised an arm and sniffed the robe she'd been in since right after Billy's funeral. "Oh lord, Rosa, I stink."

"Yes, you do." Rosa patted Matilda's leg.

Matilda followed Rosa out the door and stopped on the stoop. It dawned on her then, she hadn't been outside the car since Tuesday afternoon, and this was Friday morning. She squinted at the sunlight hitting the top of the tent and pushed her matted hair back with both hands.

Rosa brought back a bucket of hot water, soap, and a fresh towel. Matilda took the bucket. "Thanks, Rosa. While I clean up can you go ask Bernice if my red sequined thing is fixed? Otherwise, I gotta wear the old green one and the top doesn't stay put."

"Matilda, sweetie—"

"I know, I heard Gio tellin' Bill I wasn't workin' this weekend. But I need to do somethin'."

"Matilda, I think—"

"Will you see about the red sequins? I'll be ready in ten minutes."

"Okay, we'll go to the phone, but don't you think—?"

"I think, Rosa, I think I'll go crazy sittin' in this car for one more day."

BILL KNELT IN front of a gear trunk, sorting cables and ropes. Nothing was in the right place. Schatz worked just outside and waved to Matilda and Rosa as they walked toward the road to town. Marina went in the tent to see Bill.

"I'm doing great, Marina. No, really, I am," Bill snapped. "My son is dead. And my wife hasn't said two words to me since we buried him. And some jackass put the slack wire cable God knows where and used the mechanic rope to tie a tarp down. I got two hammers I need missing. So, I'm dandy."

Marina raised an eyebrow at Schatz on her way back to her concession trailer.

Schatz listened from the other side of the canvas while Bill uttered curses at the roustabouts who'd broken down the tent Sunday morning. Schatz waited for quiet before he went in.

"Bill, can I help you get this stuff straightened out? Sorry it didn't all get done right. I was in charge, but I thought they knew how to put it up. I didn't check it—"

"Nobody checked nothin' last week, did they, Schatz? Where was everybody when they should have been checkin' on stuff?" Bill yanked coils of trapeze wires out of the trunk and dropped them. "Can you tell me, Schatz? 'Cause I was in the tent workin' while Bentley got plastered, and I was here workin' while Nosh was stealin' birds, and I was here when somebody was supposed to be out there and get my boy down and clear, and nobody was doin' their job. Nobody was doin' their job, Schatz. Nobody was . . ." He let the lid of the cable trunk drop shut and sat on it, his forearms on his knees. He gazed into the top of the tent, then at his feet.

Schatz sat beside Bill. After they'd stared at the tanbark for half a minute, Bill cleared his throat. "God, I'm sorry. You, Marina, you're trying to help. Everybody is. But what do I do about my wife? She just—"

Schatz decided not to tell him that he'd just seen Matilda headed to town with Rosa. It didn't matter that much right now. What he needed to do was to get Bill to let the rousties help him. They'd know where they put everything. But what he did was put his lanky arm around Bill's shoulders, and sat with him for a few more minutes, while the rest of the world inched by.

1957—New Orleans, Louisiana

CHEREE DURAND WAS in her chair with the reading lamp pulled close, peering through coke bottle glasses to crochet a border on a hand towel when the phone rang. "Matilda! Honey, I'm so glad you called. I have good news. Your mama's come home she says for good. Isn't that wonderful?" Cheree listened to her oldest granddaughter for a moment. "Oh, my sweet, oh my sweet. Honey, you come on home. You need your fam'ly."

Matilda clutched the payphone receiver five hundred and seventy-five miles away. "Grand-mim, I can't come home right now. Because—no, listen, because. I'm sorry I didn't call. But it was—Yeah, I know. I know. Well, Bill's doing all right, I guess. I'll tell him you said that. Okay, I'm outta change. I'll call next week."

Rosa had gone to sit on a low brick wall in front of the store and walked over to the phone booth when she saw Matilda replace the receiver. "You okay?"

"I know I shouldn't be, but I am. Are you hungry? I'm starving."

IN THE PIE car they rummaged around the pantry shelves for the last of the peach cobbler. Rosa poured two cups of lukewarm coffee and the two sat side by side, eating out of the corner of the baking pan while they watched Maurice driving tent stakes.

Matilda rested her chin in a cupped hand. "You think Maurice will ever find somebody again?"

"Oh, I think he has."

"Since when?"

"Since a month ago. You didn't know? Polly moved into the elephant car."

"Whaaat? Three weeks ago, I saw Bentley's mustache wax on the back of her blouse. Lord, she gets around. How did I not know?" Matilda watched Maurice.

"I think she wanted to keep it quiet about Maurice, him bein', you know."

"Well I guess Maurice wasn't as 'you know' as we thought."

"Schatz thinks they'll get married."

Matilda picked up the empty baking dish and walked to the sink. "That ain't gonna happen."

Rosa picked up a piece of cobbler crust from the bench beside her and dropped it in the last half inch of coffee in her cup. "Well, they're kind of sweet together."

"I think he's just been lonely." They watched Polly walking toward the elephant car. "And Maurice told me a long time ago his mother would just die if he married a white."

"Hey look." Rosa leaned over the table to peer out the window. "There she goes now. What's she got on that hanger?"

"Hey. That's my old yellow costume Bernice made me for the lift-off. Remember?"

They turned in unison to look at each other.

"WHAT ARE YOU doing? I'm not using the grey." Rosa put her hands on her hips. Schatz looked up from tightening a surcingle on the Percheron mare.

"Gio wants Polly on her."

"For?"

Schatz pulled the surcingle three holes tighter. "I'm just following orders."

"So, Polly's doing a lift-off with one of my horses?"

Schatz tucked the billet into the loop. "She'll be fine."

"Oh, and you're lunging her? Or am I, and nobody's told me?"

"I will if you don't want to."

"I'll lunge her. But when's Gio planning to announce Polly's doing Matilda's old act? Not to mention in her costume. Use the other bridle. No, the blue one."

"He doesn't want Matilda on the trapeze this weekend."

"He hasn't said a word to Matilda about *this* though. And she and I just saw Polly coming from Bernice's with one of Matilda's costumes. That's how Matilda knows."

"Gio had to fill the show."

"I know, but that's not the point. He could have told Matilda first."

"I guess he didn't think—"

"No, of course he didn't think. Do you guys ever think?" The horse flicked her ears while Rosa straightened the browband.

"What are you mad at me for? It wasn't my idea." Schatz sighed.

"Do this for me, please. I'll take this horse over and get Polly set up. But you tell your buddy Gio he needs to tell Matilda himself."

"You want him to do that, you tell him. Don't make a big deal out of it and it won't be a big deal."

"It's a big deal, Schatz. He didn't ask me for the horse, and he didn't tell Matilda." Rosa measured the side reins before she looped them back to the bit and led the horse out.

Schatz closed the tack trunk and ambled toward the main tent.

BILL FOUND MATILDA in front of the mirror in the bedroom, putting the last pin-curl in her freshly washed hair. He sat on the bed and watched her. She smiled, tight lipped, in the mirror at him.

"Hi. I needed a bath. And I went and called my grandmother."

She dropped her robe on the floor, dug around in the trunk at the end of the bed, and pulled on a high cut leotard. She glanced at the alarm clock on the bedside crate, then pulled on a pair of shorts before she went to sit beside her husband.

"So, everything's back where it should be?" She let her arm rest against his.

He ran a hand over his stubbled cheek. "Yeah, but it was all a mess. How's your grandparents?"

"Grand-mim cried. Wants me to come home."

Bill watched Matilda's reflection in the mirror.

"But I'm not going. I need to work."

"Honey, Gio has it all covered this weekend. He's got Polly doing a lift—"

"Yeah, Rosa and me figured that out."

"Why don't you go over and help Polly?"

"She'll be fine." Matilda lay down on her back, legs dangling over the side of the bed. Bill did the same. They stared at the tongue and groove ceiling.

Bill cleared his throat. "You know, Nosh ran off that night, looks like. Never came back before we left Fayette."

Matilda rose, pulled a white scarf from a nail beside the closet, tied it around her hair, pushed the hanging blanket aside, and went to the front of the car for her shoes. Bill was still staring at the ceiling when she went out the door.

MATILDA STOOD IN the shadows with Maurice while Rosa and Schatz fitted Polly's mechanic. Gio was already on a platform, watching his uncle climb the other ladder.

"We'll do the lift and set down on the horse a time or two."

Tony paused climbing. "If it doesn't work to put her back on the horse, put her back on the floor."

"Or on the platform," Matilda said half aloud.

Polly unclipped the mechanic and walked over to Matilda. "Should I start on the horse, or vault on?"

"Vault. Looks better." Matilda raised her face toward the platform where Gio stood. "That okay with you, Gio?"

"Polly, you want to try that? Vault, lift, I pick you up from the middle. Put your arm out to the right. I'll get you on the backswing."

Polly looked to Matilda, who nodded. "Keep your elbow a little bent when you reach, and don't lean out or you'll pull off to one side."

"Thanks. I wish it was you doing this."

"Naw, it's fine. You can do it. Push a little to the right when he hits your arm. The mechanic will help." She turned to Maurice. "You do her just like we used to do this, Maurice. Don't you let Gio yank her arm outta the socket like they used to do me."

Maurice smiled. "I'll take good care of her."

"Tell you what, Maur, I'll go up on the platform and help Tony catch her."

"I've got her, Matilda, I promise," Tony and Gio exchanged a quick look.

Gio peered into the shadows, then mouthed "hold on" to Tony. "Hey, Matilda, you don't need—" But Matilda was already ten rungs up the ladder.

She stared across the top of the tent at Gio when she got to Tony's platform. "Let's get this show on the road."

"You okay, hon?" Tony whispered.

"I've been better."

ON OPENING NIGHT, Polly, who'd asked to be introduced as Paulina, vaulted onto the horse, did the lift and pickup and was sent to land on the platform.

Matilda, dressed in tights and a tank leotard just like Gio and Tony wore, caught the bar and held it while Polly, now Paulina, and Tony held hands and took a bow. While the applause rang out from below, Matilda launched off toward Gio.

"You gonna catch me or not?" she said as they passed each other. He caught her on the next pass.

"Damnit. Rotate. I'm gonna put you back on Tony's platform."

"Oh, yes, with your new star. Thanks for telling me." She rotated and looked to Tony. He made room for her to land. She raised her arm, flourished a bow, then took Polly's hand. "Take another bow."

Bill was at the bottom of the ladder as the three of them came down. In the ring, a clown in Bill's Borneo Wild man costume chased Betty and Velma, who were dressed in coconut shell bras and grass skirts.

"Guess we're both replaced," Matilda said, and walked out of the tent.

ROSA WENT TO Bill and Matilda's car Saturday morning after she was sure Bill had gone to breakfast. "Matilda, if you don't answer this door, I'm coming in."

"Then come in."

"I told Schatz to tell Gio he needed to talk to you before they even rehearsed that—"

"I shouldn't a done that, though."

Rosa eyed her. "Let's get you dressed."

"I'll get dressed later." Matilda flopped onto the sofa with her arms folded.

"Bernice has a new costume for me, and I want your opinion before she sews on the skirt."

"Bullshit. You don't need my opinion."

"You're right, I don't. But I want you to go with me anyway. So, put on some clothes and let's go. Come on, get up." Rosa rummaged through the pile of laundry on the end of the sofa.

"No."

"Yes. Look, I know it hurts, and I know I can't fix it, and nobody can bring—"

"Don't you say it. Don't you say his name."

Matilda took the trousers, bra, and blouse Rosa handed her. She stood to pull the pants up under her nightgown, then let her arms drop to her sides.

"It was my fault, Rosa." Matilda's voice cracked. "I talked Bill into it. He never trusted Bentley and he never trusted the elephants. I talked him into it."

"Oh, honey," Rosa sat down between Matilda and the laundry. "It wasn't your fault. It was Nosh and Bentley. I hope Bentley stays in jail forever. Might, if what that sheriff told Tony and Gio is right."

"I wanted my Billy to be happy. He wanted—" Her voice dropped to a broken whisper. "He wanted to be a star. He wanted to be like me."

Rosa swallowed hard. "He was like you. He was stubborn and wild. He was a star."

Matilda peeled the cotton gown off and put on a wrinkled shirt before she ran a hairbrush over the top layer of curls.

"Okay, Rosa. Let's go see Bernice."

1958—Fayette, Missouri

MATILDA CATAPULTS INTO consciousness. Bill's bristly arm rests against hers.

"Honey, here's some ice." A spoon touches her open lips. Tiny ice chips slide through them. "There ya go. Want some more?" She opens her eyes and sees Bill clearly for the first time in two months.

"Well, I see you're awake, young lady." Dr. McClure moves closer. "You gave us a scare with that seizure. We removed a blood clot, and you should be feeling a lot better soon." Matilda blinks at him. Bill spoons more ice into her mouth.

The ice slides out onto her pillow when she croaks "thank you."

Two Donkeys in a Cow Pasture
1957—Fayette Missouri

TWO MONTHS AFTER the elephant had fallen on the little boy at the circus and six weeks after Sheriff Delgar Wells had turned the elephant trainer who'd gone by the name Ned Bentley over to the Florida authorities, Bart Penrose, the farmer who owned the field north of the fairgrounds called to tell Delgar he'd better come out to his place and see something.

"RIGHT THERE, IN that tall grass. Cows won't eat over there. I came out to see why. Del, you think that's a kid?"

"What the hell happened to his head?" Delgar held his handkerchief over his nose and mouth while he inched closer to the battered body in the deep grass.

"Them donkeys, they keep coyotes and dogs outta the pasture." Penrose jabbed a thumb at two shaggy headed donkeys that stood nose to tail in the shade of a tree. "They catch one once in a while. Reckon them donkeys killed him?"

"Jesus, Bart, that isn't a kid. It's that guy that went a-wol from the circus. That there's that dwarf."

"Think them donkeys did that to his head?" Penrose turned his head and reeled sideways.

Wells took two steps backward from the rotting corpse and tried to spit the stench out of his mouth. "Maybe."

"Gosh, Del, what do I do? Do I have to shoot my donkeys?"

"No, don't do that. But I gotta get somebody out here to get this body. Can you be here and make sure your donkeys don't go after the coroner?"

"Sure, Del. I'm real sorry if they did this."

"I wouldn't worry about it, Bart. If they did, they might a done somebody a favor."

SHERIFF WELLS FILLED out a report, stating the little man wearing the torn remains of a white robe was believed to have been kicked to death by a cow or a donkey when he went into the pasture and startled the farmer's livestock. There were plenty of cow and donkey tracks in the soft ground near the body to back up the theory.

The county coroner had made a note on the death certificate when he noticed what looked to him like longish triangular depression wounds in the shoulder and skull. "Blunt-force trauma apparently caused by animals" was what he wrote.

Wells put on his reading glasses. "Yeah, prob'ly cow hooves made them marks. Don't you think?"

"Your call if you want me to change it, Delgar."

"So, what would you say those marks look like?" Wells shook out a white handkerchief and wiped his nose. "Off the record?"

"I'd say a maul, or a hammer. But I already wrote down the other. We good?"

"We're good."

The coroner didn't argue when Delgar took custody of Ignacio's body to be buried in the family plot beside Nadine's uncle she never did like.

An Elephant's Future

MAURICE CRIED INCONSOLABLY while Marta touched his head and arms with the tip of her trunk. Polly sat on an upturned bucket behind Maurice and stared dully at Gio.

"Maur, it's the only thing we can do. If word gets out—"

"Marta only did what any animal would do. She was afraid, boss. She didn't—"

"I know, and you know. But if people find out, the newspapers will crucify us. We can't take a chance. With Eloise gone, we have to let her go. Vargas wants her. She'll be with other elephants. She'll be better off." Gio's voice became less steady when Maurice put his head in his hands.

"What about Ringling's farm, Gio? She could live there with other elephants," Polly said.

"They just retire their own."

"Then give her to them when we get to Sarasota. So, they can retire her." Maurice stroked Marta's trunk tenderly. "Please don't sell her to Vargas. They'll hurt her. Please."

"I can't give her away, Maurice. Vargas will pay six hundred for her."

"I have six hundred dollars, boss. I'll buy her. I'll take care of her until we get to Sarasota."

"Maurice, you've been saving that money for a long time to go see your mother."

"I don't care, boss. I can't watch Marta get on another train. She doesn't—" Maurice started crying again, and Polly rested her cheek against his massive back.

"Maur, we don't even know if Ringling would take her."

"Then I'll pay them to feed her. I'll send money for the rest of her life. Would you sell Tony because he's old, Gio? Or Bernice?"

"Oh, for God's sake. Don't do this to me Maurice."

"Don't you do this to Marta. She's been in the show longer than you have, Gio." Maurice rose and planted his bulk between the half blind elephant and Fiscalini. Polly rose to her feet and stood at Maurice's side. Maurice glanced down at Polly, then refocused on Gio's face.

"Okay, okay." Gio breathed a long sigh. "I'll talk it over with Tony."

"Okay, boss. And, boss? Marta wants to tell you something." Maurice stepped back to touch the elephant's shoulder. When he did, Marta raised her trunk and chortled softly.

MARINA COOKED SUPPER on her double hot plate for the Fiscalini family meeting. It was agreed that since Bernice had been part of the family longer than Marina and Gio had been alive, that she would also vote on the fate of Marta. Gio regretted that decision as soon as it was made.

Gio reminded them six hundred dollars would go a long way toward buying a few more horses, and maybe hiring another aerialist. Tony poured a second glass of wine and drained it before he spoke.

"That's good money for an old elephant. But we have two deadbeats off the payroll we're not feeding anymore, and one less elephant to feed, and I hate to even say it, but one less boy to feed if you're counting. So, we'll save that much by the end of the season in food and salaries, right?"

"That doesn't mean we can afford not to sell that elephant." Gio's glass clattered as he set it on the table. "And I called Emilio Vargas. He'll take her."

Bernice shifted in her chair and leaned toward Gio. "Can you afford to lose Maurice and Polly?"

The two men swiveled their heads to look at her.

"Polly? Why Polly?" Gio asked.

"What is wrong with you?" Bernice put her hands on her hips and shook her head at her nephew. "How do you not know about those two? If Maurice leaves, and much as he loves that elephant, he will, Polly's liable to go with him. I'll bet Vargas would love to hire Fiscalini's strong man and elephant handler and guy who can do about every job in this show. And they'd get Paulina or whatever she calls herself now, too."

"She's right," Marina added.

"We'll vote," Gio slugged back the rest of his wine, "but I can see already it's going to be a draw."

"No, it won't be a draw, Gio," Tony said. "Bernice is right. We let Maurice have the elephant."

"But he says he wants to buy it."

"No." Bernice and Marina spoke in unison.

"You want me to give it to him and lose money."

Bernice drew a slow breath. "You lost money when you shot the other elephant. No, now I know you had to, Gio. But that sweet old elephant has been with us for fifty years. And Maurice has been with us for close to twenty. Let's not break any more hearts this year." As Bernice placed her time worn hand over Gio's, her voice softened. "And stop worrying about it. That old girl can perform the rest of the season. Maurice and Polly won't let anything happen. We'll advertise her retirement in every town and get a sponsor to bring a big cake. We'll sell tickets to an after-party the rest of this year's shows, and people will pay to eat cake with an elephant. There's your money."

Tony looked at the woman he'd adored all these years and knew, all over again why he loved her.

PART 8
End of an Era

Starting Again

"I DON'T KNOW if I want a trailer. I like our old rail car just fine." Bernice sat on the sofa in Gio's house and took the plate of marinated olives and cheese squares her sister-in-law offered. Marina set a plate of risotto on the coffee table and plopped down beside Bernice.

"The trailers are just as nice, honey." Tony patted his wife's leg. "And we'd have a car so we can go do things."

"So, we're off the train next year for sure?" Marina turned to Gio, who looked more like their father every year.

"We can fit all the gear and tents in two trucks, and the horses can go in a horse van. We can make bunks in another two trailers for rousties and clowns, unless any of them want to get their own trailers."

"What if somebody has trouble?" Bernice wrapped the teabag string around the bowl of her spoon. "Or gets lost?"

"Honey, we'd caravan." Tony smiled in earnest. "Everybody's going to trucks and trailers. Unless they have elephants. And now we can go places trains don't go."

Bernice picked up two olives and a square of cheese. "Gio, what are you going to have Maurice do? If he doesn't have elephants, what does he do?" The air seemed to suck out of the room while Gio filled his glass.

"Ringling's trainer looked at our elephant and says he can use her. They have others as old as she is. Maurice asked him for a job."

The four of them avoided each other's eyes. Bernice set her saucer down and got up from the sofa to walk to the window. "Did he tell you that?"

"No, Ringling's trainer asked me for a reference. Asked me about the elephant too. I told him what happened. I had to."

"And what about Polly? Her too?"

"I don't know, he didn't ask about her when he asked about Maurice."

Marina went to stand by the window. Matilda and Polly walked by outside, heads together, deep in conversation.

Tony cleared his throat. "Maurice told me he wants to work elephants. Ringling will pay him better than I can, and they'll take Marta." He glanced at Gio. "You gave him that elephant. So, if you tell me now that you want to sell it to Ringling, that's wrong."

"Tony, that was when he wanted to retire it. Now he's getting on the train with them, and they'll make money on it."

"Gio, you are my nephew and I love you like my own son, but sometimes all you think about is money. We made our money on Marta for fifty years. Let her go. She's Maurice's now. Just let her go."

THOSE WHO HAD homes in Sarasota moved in for the winter, and the roustabouts that worked odd jobs until spring got situated in rented rooms and tent camps.

Matilda moved her things from the rail car closet and trunk into the house, then packed her satchel, and told Bill she needed to go to New Orleans. "I need to be with my family, I think. Can you take me to the bus station?" She sighed when she saw his shoulders slump. "I'll be back in a week. I just need to do this."

1957, New Orleans in the Fall

"GRAND-PAP? HI, it's Matilda. I'm at the bus station. Okay, thank you. See you in fifteen minutes." Matilda replaced the receiver and breathed deeply, welcoming the memory of her old neighborhood into lungs that hadn't felt the blunt, brackish air in far too long. Mildewed phone book pages begrudgingly separated at "L" and she found the number for Lafontaine's.

"Hello, Mary Ellen? Oh, this Kat? This is Matilda Chevalier. Yes. Is he? I'd love to talk to him if he has a minute, but—oh, that's awful nice. Thank you. I'll hold."

She rattled her pocketbook open for the pack of cigarettes she'd plucked out of Bill's work shirt the day before. She shook a soggy crumbling cigarette out, peered into the pack, and threw the whole mess in the trash can.

"Well, there you are. Where the hell you been, kiddo?" Eddie's voice washed over Matilda and she choked on what she'd planned to say.

"Hey, Eddie. I'm in town for a few days. I've been—well, I got to Florida a couple days ago, and decided to come see my fam'ly. But I'll come by and see you."

"Good. Good. Kat and Mary Ellen want to see you too. Bill with you?"

"No, I came—"

"You bring Billy up to see your mom and the kids?"

"No." Matilda felt the gust of damp November against her back as she closed the phone booth door. "I'll come see you. You busy tomorrow? How about ten? Naw, you don't need to do a tattoo, I just need to see you."

GABRIEL FRIED UP a pan of porkchops while Cheree and Suzette cooked collard greens and cornbread. Matilda's sister Evangeline, now thirteen, showed Matilda to her room where she offered Matilda her bed. She pointed to the bed she'd made herself on the floor. "Honey, don't let me put you out of bed. I'll take that nice pallet. Or if you want to share the bed, I'd like that." Matilda found herself staring at the sister she'd barely seen in the past eleven years. Evangeline was a spit and image of her except for the hair.

Cheree said an extra-long grace over the food on the table and Gabriel pointed sternly at the boys when they shuffled their feet before the prayer ended.

They talked about the new traffic lights on Gentilly Avenue. Grand-mim asked Matilda if any women who came to the circus wore pill box hats these days, because she'd been shopping and couldn't find a decent pill box anywhere in JC Penney's. The boys talked about school and Evangeline chimed in about tryouts for the Christmas pageant.

After supper, at the sink, Cheree put her hand on Matilda's soapy wrist to stop her from clattering the dishes. "You and Bill okay, sweet?"

Matilda shrugged and smiled weakly. "It's been hard, Mim. We don't talk a whole lot."

"Don't get used to that, baby girl. You two need each other like your grandfather and I need each other. Don't let what's happened break another precious thing."

"I know. It's just—he doesn't say anything, so I don't."

"He hurts as much as you do. I pray extra for you ever morning and ever night."

Matilda picked up a dishtowel. "I'm glad you do that, Grand-mim. I think I forgot how."

THE FRONT WINDOW of Lafontaine's had been repainted with a fan of playing cards. Flowers and flying dragons wove in and out of the lettering: Lafontaine Family Tattoo Artistry.

Eddie snatched the door open when he saw Matilda standing at the front window. "Hey, no loitering on my sidewalk. You get your skinny butt in here."

Matilda met him at the door. "Hard to get through the door with you standin' in the way."

She ducked under the arm that held the door open.

"Mary Ellen's in back doing the books. Kat's got the pukes this morning. She says she's not preggers, but I say she is. Hope she has a boy this time. Too many dang women around here."

"God, if she has a boy, he'd be just like you. Poor Kat."

"Damn it's good to see you. I got coffee on in the studio. Don't say you already had coffee. You'll sound like my wife."

EDDIE SET THE percolator down soundlessly and watched Matilda's hands while he let what she'd just told him sink past the lump in his throat.

". . . and we buried him in somebody's graveyard in Missoura. I don't even know how to get there for sure, because I was—"

"Oh, kiddo." Eddie slumped onto his rolling stool. "I didn't... God."

"I have a picture. Of him."

"Yeah? Lemmie see. Ah, hell, he sure looks like his dad here. Oh Matilda, I'm so sorry." He slid the much-handled photo back toward Matilda and watched her wrap it in a handkerchief and place it back in her pocketbook.

"Maybe someday I'll get a tattoo of him. What do you think?"

Eddie breathed out and rotated his coffee cup a half turn. "Maybe."

"Maybe? Why maybe? I asked what you think. Maybe isn't an answer."

"I'm sorry. I don't have an answer. How's Bill doing?"

"I can't tell. He used to try to talk about it. I don't want to talk about it, not even to my family. The people we work with, they have their own crap. It's like they go right on, and we don't get to. I asked God one time if he'd just bring him back. I was dead serious. I guess God said no. I didn't hear back from him."

"Yeah. I don't know about that prayin'. I tried it when Pop got sick. Didn't change a thing. Want that coffee warmed up?" Eddie flicked the rim of her cup.

"It's okay. I didn't come all this way to drink lousy coffee. I just needed . . ."

"Yeah. I know. I'm glad you came to see me."

The two friends stared across the sketch table at each other for a few seconds.

Matilda inclined her head toward his cup. "Your coffee's gettin' cold."

BILL PICKED OUT a used Airstream for himself and Matilda the day before she got back from New Orleans. He saw a '55 Ford Woody Wagon for sale in front of a house near theirs and knocked on the door. The bearded lady who answered the door went to get her remarkably skinny husband, who came to the door in a painting smock, and told Bill he'd take $475.00 for it, since it had new tires. Bill told him he'd seen two threadbare tires and he'd give him $400.00.

When Bill pulled up at the bus station, Matilda walked around the car and gave a nod of approval. At the house, he opened the trailer to show her the inside. Remembering what Eddie had said about how nice it was that Kat appreciated things he did, Matilda kissed Bill's cheek.

THE NEXT AFTERNOON Matilda took the photo of Billy in the little ringmaster costume he'd worn for his pony act with her to the tattoo parlor in downtown Sarasota. The artist traced the child's image and went to work adding it beside the outline of the red heart on her chest.

Matilda looked at the progress with a hand mirror.

"Can you change this heart to blue?"

The artist leaned back, said he could do it, but it would be pretty dark.

"That's fine."

THAT NIGHT MATILDA put on her nightgown and instead of turning her back to Bill to go to sleep, she placed her hand on his bristly cheek.

Bill touched the curve of her face in the semi-darkness. "I should've shaved."

"I should've too." She slid an unshaven leg over his.

Back To Work

January 1958

RINGLING DIDN'T OFFER Polly a job, which was fine with her. She'd gotten over the novelty of Maurice. Plus, Polly had already set her sights on the single male co-owner of the Fiscalini Brothers Circus.

GIO NOTICED HIS uncle Tony moving slowly at rehearsal one day. "Hey. Tony. You okay?"

Tony turned his head, and Gio saw a blank look on his face for an instant, then it was gone.

"Yes, yes, I was just thinking." Tony went up the ladder.

Polly and Matilda arrived to rehearse a few minutes later and headed up the other side. They had been practicing their own catches, for no other reason than to cause some gasps from the audience when a girl caught a girl. Polly told Gio they wanted to show him the catch. "Just watch. If you don't like it, we'll work up something else."

Matilda went up Tony's ladder. "Honey, you're the star," Tony said under his breath while they got rosined up. "You should be the flyer and let Polly catch you."

"I'm stronger, Tony. And taller. It's fine." Matilda bounced on her toes and launched away. Polly sprang away from the other platform. Gio watched closely. Polly wasn't bad, she just hadn't been remarkable. Maybe, he thought, he needed to give her a chance and build up her confidence. If Matilda could work with her, they'd have two strong female flyers, just like back when Marina and their aunt Gloria were still on the trapeze.

Gio snapped to attention when he saw Tony had taken the other bar and was in the air.

"Tony? No—"

Tony was watching Matilda as he swung, then glanced at Gio. Tony's face went dark. He turned on the bar and dismounted on the platform.

"Oh, sorry, I forgot for a—sorry."

Matilda gave Gio a questioning look when they were on the ground and glanced back at Tony, who'd waved and gone to watch a new slack wire act.

"He's not all right," she whispered.

Gio whispered, "I know."

GIO WENT TO Marina's house with his calendar and address book. "I need you to call this one, and this." He pushed his book with toothpick-marked pages across her kitchen table. "This one, remember him? Only gave us two dates? See if you can get three." He waited while his sister made notes. "We're going through Alabama and Arkansas. We'll go a little south." He traced a route through Shreveport, Louisiana, then on to Texarkana, Mount Pleasant, and Sulphur Springs, Texas. "We haven't done Dallas or Weatherford in years. Time to change that." He drew pencil circles around towns. "Abilene, Midland, then in New Mexico: Carlsbad, Artesia—"

"Is there anything there? Artesia?" Marina scrutinized the map.

"There's oil there. Good money. Every seventy-five or a hundred miles if you can. If it has to be a couple hundred in between, then sit us down for more days so we pay for fuel."

Marina replaced the toothpicks with strips of paper. "Are we going north of Denver?"

"Let's see how Nevada and Utah shape up. We can go to Grand Junction and go south, go to Canon City, Pueblo, couple little places between there and Wichita. Let's get to some towns before everybody else does. We never could do that on the train."

"Gio, you know, we need more people who can drive. Half our clowns don't drive."

"I'll figure it out. You work on this part. We can do this, 'Rina."

"I know we can, but I worry about Bernice and Tony. They're getting old, Gio. Bernice is really worried about Tony. Has she told you?"

"Told me what?"

"She's told me he forgets what day it is, and the other day he came in all worked up because he'd been looking for Sam and couldn't find him anywhere.

And she said last week Tony told her he needed to talk to Giovanni about something."

"Maybe he meant me."

"You know he didn't."

Gio nodded solemnly. "I'm going to call our cousins. Bobby and Robby catch and fly great and I think they still tightrope. Maybe they're ready for a change."

"I heard that whole act's been fighting. Maybe the twins want out anyway. What are you going to say to Tony?"

"I don't know yet." He leaned his forehead on one callused hand. "I'll think of something."

1958, Fayette, Missouri, Ten Weeks After

"THEY SHAVED MY hair." Matilda's voice is still unaccustomed to making words. Her mother holds the hand mirror above her face. Matilda studies her reflection: the shorn scalp, the dented place where her cheekbone shattered. "Momma,"

"You done lookin'?" Matilda looks away from the mirror and Suzette sets the mirror aside.

"Did Bill say if Bernice has Billy?"

Suzette takes Matilda's hand. "Honey, you got hurt and the doctor says it's normal for you not to remember things. I know Bill told you yesterday, but Billy's been with the angels for a long time." She watches Matilda's face for a glimmer of comprehension.

"He—" Matilda reaches toward the bedside table and touches a photo of Bill, Maurice, and Schatz.

Suzette presses a finger to the corner of one eye. "Bill took me to his grave, honey. That nice sheriff and his wife keep the grass cut around it."

"Bill didn't bring a picture of our Billy. That's why, isn't it? I hoped I was rememberin' all wrong. I—damn it, why can't that be somethin' I can't remember?" Matilda clenches bony hands on the sheets.

"I wish it was that way. Just not remember some of that stuff we wish never happened. Maybe the good Lord needs us to remember the bad stuff so we remember to pray."

"Prayin' won't fix it, Momma."

"Maybe. But when I pray, at least I feel like I tried." Suzette leans forward to put her face against Matilda's arm. "I pray for you every day. I know. I know. Me, your heathern momma. But I do. And here you are, talkin' again. So maybe it worked."

"When can we go where Billy's buried?"

"If you're ready to go, 'Tilda I'll work on that."

Matilda runs a thin hand over her shorn head. "Have Bill bring me a scarf from the trailer."

New Flyers
Early Spring 1958, Sarasota, Florida

GIO AND MARINA'S twin cousins on their mother's side, Bobby and Robby Salvato drove across town to meet with Gio and Tony about joining the act. The boys would take one car and share a trailer, which left one of them to drive an equipment truck when the troupe headed out.

Bernice convinced Tony she needed him managing their folder of state maps instead of driving, and he could sleep or read a book aloud to her on the long stretches of highway. Sometimes Tony rode with Bobby, thinking Bobby was Gio. Bobby told Bernice one evening when she apologized for her husband's confusion, that if his uncle Tony thought he was Gio, it didn't hurt a thing.

Betty and Velma decided to bunk with the roustabouts and clowns until they could decide if they wanted their own car and trailer and rode most days with one of the Salvato brothers. Polly seemed content to take a space in the same bunk trailer with the little women.

Bill and Matilda invited Polly to ride with them, which she did for the first two states. Then she started riding with Gio and a couple days later, moved out of the bunk trailer.

WITH THREE MEN and two women in the air, Antonio Fiscalini didn't need any convincing to let the trapeze act go on without him. Tony had been a key performer with the family's circus for sixty-three years. Long enough. He told Gio and Milana he'd finish the year helping where he could, then he and Bernice would decide if they wanted to stay on the road or settle down in Sarasota.

Bernice told Gio he'd stayed single long enough. It was time to find a nice girl and get married. Instead, Gio married Polly.

Polly
Late Fall 1958, Fayette, Missouri

"HEY, GOOD NEWS, honey," Bill says. "The doctors both say you're ready to do therapy to help you get to walkin'."

Matilda raises her arms and studies her two different sized forearms.

Bill struggles to smile. He's been making plans to take her home. The doctor has warned him that after the trauma of the accident, she might have a hard time re-adjusting to life out of bed.

Late Spring 1958, Kansas City, Kansas

MATILDA WAS PULLING a full sleeve leotard over tights for rehearsal before the first Kansas City show when Polly knocked at the door of the trailer. "Matilda, you in there?"

"Yeah." Matilda adjusted her too-loose bra under the blue leotard and pushed the door open on her way to the refrigerator. "Come on in. Want some iced tea?" She stopped dead in her tracks when Polly stepped through the door.

Polly Fiscalini had bleached her dark auburn hair almost white and had pulled it into a tightly rolled chignon. Her formerly straight brows were drawn in heavy arches. The spaghetti-strapped silver leotard topped with a filmy white ballet skirt accented the stark whiteness of her hair.

"Holy cow. For a minute I thought—" Matilda stammered.

"Sally Mills Fiscalini, right? I found some pictures of her. She was so beautiful," Polly gushed, coming into the trailer.

"Has Gio seen you yet?"

"Not yet, but he will at rehearsal. What do you think? I think it'll be great. You being, you know, the coloring you are, and whatever you wear, and me all in silver and white."

"Really. I'm not sure Polly. I think Gio wanted us matching."

Polly admired her fresh manicure. "I think you're jealous of me, Matilda."

"Jealous? What are you talkin' about?"

"Well, for all I know, you had a crush on Gio before Bill married you."

"Good Lord, Polly, Bill and I got married the first day I was on the train. What's got into you?"

"It's Paulina. And I just think it's time to change the act, that's all. I like to look pretty. And you don't even care how you look anymore. Gio's doing new posters. And I'm going to be on them."

"Well, all he has to do is use the old posters with Sally on them. Same hair. Same eyebrows. Why would you want to look like her?"

"She was gorgeous. Have you looked in a mirror at all this year? When was the last time you cared how—" Polly stopped and watched three roustabouts going by with armfuls of rope and cable.

Matilda leaned on the table. She knew what she looked like. She wasn't going to cry. She wasn't. But she wished she'd feel something. Nothing but empty came up from her heart to her head. Everybody said it would get better. It wasn't getting better. She heard a faraway voice, and realized it was Polly's voice somewhere in a fog, somewhere in a pond, somewhere behind a billboard on the highway, someplace where the music wasn't music, but it was loud and hideous around Polly's words.

"Hey, Matilda, I didn't mean to hurt your feelings. But it's time I got to be the star."

Matilda slid her hands over her mass of pale apricot-colored hair and blinked at the platinum-haired woman across the table. "Bein' a star might not be all you think it's gon' be, hon."

"How would you know? All you ever did was show those tattoos and let your hair look like a poodle," Polly snapped.

"Huh. Well, I made it without sleepin' with the boss. You want the spotlight, Polly? You go right ahead. But you earn it. I had to." Matilda exhaled. "Don't you be comin' in my trailer waggin' that diamond ring either. Don't' mean nothin' here."

Polly's eyebrows knitted together. "I'm a Fiscalini now. Don't you forget that."

"Well, you are now. Sally was too. Couple others, from what I hear. Look, I don't care what name you give yourself. But as long as I gotta do this show with you, you might wanna remember I was here first. And I'm not goin' away because of what happened."

Polly stood and leaned across the table. She put her hand on Matilda's shoulder. "You poor thing. I know it's been so hard for you—"

"Be on the poster, Polly. People only care how we make 'em feel, sittin' in the dark for a little while because they think it's special. We're not that damned special. Nobody cares after the music stops and nobody gives a shit who was on the poster." Matilda patted the table with both hands. "Okay?" She spoke louder as she stood. "You look real pretty, Polly. Oh yeah. Paulina. Now, I got to get ready for rehearsal. That all right with you?"

Polly closed her painted lips over her imperfectly aligned teeth and stood. "See you at rehearsal." She hurried to Gio's trailer to freshen her lipstick before she went to find her husband and tell him how concerned she was about Matilda. She practiced her worried expression on the way.

GIO LISTENED INTENTLY to Robby and Bobby's ideas about a new act. "Sounds good, but we don't add anything 'til we've run through it perfectly for two weeks. Especially if we're advertising we're working without a net."

"We get it, Gio," Robby said, "but you know darned well we all improvise every night. Like last night when Polly came out earlier than we rehearsed, and we had to figure out how to make that train wreck look good."

"It's Paulina." Polly scowled at Robby. "And I came out to save you two from making asses of yourselves. Your boy-boy back and forth thing you were doing was boring."

"Dear, what Robby is saying, and what I'm saying is, we don't change the basic routine. We don't have accidents that way—"

"Yeah, Polly. Think we should let you do whatever the hell you want?" Bobby waved his hand. "Maybe we put the net back up to catch people because you don't want to do what we rehear—"

"It's Paulina. And don't you dare talk to me that way! Gio and I are trying to save this act, aren't we dear?"

Matilda watched Gio coolly, then looked to Bobby and Robby with a half-smile. "Save it from what?"

"You see, Gio?" Polly waved a hand toward Matilda. "Every change I try to make, I have to put up with these three trying to sabotage me."

"No one is sabotaging you, dear. The boys and Matilda and I have been doing this longer, and we know what can go wrong if—"

"And I know the audience wants to see new stuff!" Polly shouted.

"It's a whole new show, with three new people to these audiences, Polly." Matilda leaned back, shaking her head.

Polly jolted from her seat and stood with her hands on her hips. "Fine. If all you people want to do is the same act, do the same act. You wouldn't know a good idea if it slapped you."

"What we want," Bobby Salvato set his closed fist on the table with a soft thud, "is to live to see our kids grow up."

Bobby looked across the table at Matilda, cringing with regret at his choice of words. He mouthed "I'm sorry." Matilda forced a smile.

"As long as I'm the senior member of this troupe, and as long as my family name is on the trucks, I'll decide what new ideas we use." Gio didn't look at his wife of three months. He was beginning to regret not listening to his uncle Tony who'd once told him to never marry a girl in the act.

The Anniversary

Fayette, Missouri—1958

BILL AND MATILDA stood shoulder to shoulder, looking at the ten by twelve-inch marble stone: Billy Matilda Kazarian 1947-1957—R.I.P.

"Nice of them to do that," Bill said. "I don't remember anything about the day we left him here."

Matilda knelt to touch the sun-warmed stone, then rose slowly. "I wish I didn't remember."

A cow lowed from somewhere beyond a blackberry vine covered fence line. Another answered.

"Bill . . ." Matilda trailed off as Bill watched her profile in the afternoon sun. Her eyes were bright as topaz as she kept them fixed on Billy's gravestone. "There's something' I gotta tell you."

MATILDA HUDDLED AGAINST the passenger side door.

Bill gripped the wheel with both hands and stared at the freshly mowed cemetery.

"Honey, why didn't you tell me this before?"

"I didn't know if it happened, or it was a dream." She stared, glassy eyed across the cemetery. "It wasn't 'til I heard somebody sayin' it was just as well, he run off, 'cause somebody prob'ly would've killed him anyway. Then some of it started comin' back."

"I would've." Bill kept his eyes on the uneven grass along the fence line. "I would've killed him." He wrapped a work roughened hand over the gear shift knob.

"But you didn't."

"And you don't know if you did or didn't either."

Matilda raked long fingers through her curls. "I know I had your ball peen hammer in my hand. I know 'cause I was holdin' the ball end of it." She turned her head. Her eyes met Bill's. "And I was sure Polly was runnin' right beside me. I don't remember swingin' that hammer. And then that donkey or whatever it was came at me. I remember getting' away from it but not comin' back to the train. I asked Polly later, but she told me she wasn't even there. I thought I was goin' crazy. Maybe I did."

Bill looked at Matilida's hands. "Maybe that little shit got up and ran off. Somebody would've found him if he was out there."

"I don't think that's what happened." Matilda clenched her hands on the dash and rested her chin on them.

Bill stared out the windshield for a few seconds, then started the car and backed up. The car jolted to a stop against the bumper of Sheriff Delgar Wells' patrol car. Bill threw the car in park and jumped out.

"Afternoon." Wells stepped out, looking unconcerned. "Don't worry, that bumper's like a railroad tie. Me and Nadine figured you'd come out. Hope the stone is right. We—well, the town pitched in for that."

"It's real nice, Sheriff. Thank you." Bill touched both bumpers. "I'm sure sorry. I should've been lookin'."

"No harm done. Say, Bart Penrose offered his pasture next to the fairgrounds for extra parking. He just had some cows and a couple donkeys in there and moved them over to another place. He said he'll mow it good today. If you want to have your people put some signs up for parking, it'll be ready."

"Gosh, that's awful nice of him."

"Oh, and I don't know if Mr. Fiscalini told you, but we did find that little clown that went missing. Looks like the cows or donkeys might have kicked him or stomped him to death. Hard to tell. It was a few months before Bart found him."

"Oh, that's terrible." Bill said.

Matilda leaned toward the driver's side to peer through the open car window. The top of the door frame blocked the view. She watched the two men from belt to chest.

"Well, from what Bart tells me, those donkeys'll go after anything bothering them cows and calves. You never know what animals . . ." Wells let his words trail off, remembering the dead elephant, the crushed child, the eyewitness accounts of the accident. "Well, listen, I just wanted to check on you. If Nadine and I can do anything else for you—"

"Thank you. And thank you for the headstone, Sheriff. It means a lot."

Matilda wondered if Bill would shake the sheriff's hand. If he might lean close to whisper, "Listen, my wife just told me something."

THE TENT WAS going up when Bill and Matilda got back, and Bill hurried to supervise the roustabouts while Gio moved equipment trucks. A tractor and mower churned in the field alongside the fairgrounds to the south.

MATILDA SANK TO the folding chair in front of the dressing mirror, tied her hair back with a yellow scarf, and smeared cold cream on her face and neck. She unbuttoned her blouse and shrugged out of it, watching her reflection.

The tattoo of her Billy was fading. She had to think for a bit to remember it was only six months ago she'd taken the photo of her son to the parlor in Sarasota. The flowers and vines around him were bright and clear. So was the little emerald hummingbird that had been her first tattoo that night she'd danced with Casey, Casey . . . what was his last name? She remembered the scent of his hair oil and the cigarette smell of his car, but not his last name. He sang to her while they waltzed. He bought that first tattoo for her and she never even kissed him. Casey's last name had faded away. Now her son's face was fading from her skin.

Matilda stood, unzipped her skirt, and let it drop. She traced fingers over the banana tattoos Lucky Eddie had designed to make a skirt that circled her now boney hips. The images on her thighs looked strangely wrong. She grazed her hands over them to see if something had happened to her legs. She pushed the slackened skin on her right thigh with one hand. The tiger's head seemed too big for its crouching body. Was it always like that? With the skin pulled taut the tiger's eyes were bright with flecks of yellow. Now the tiger watched her in the mirror while she touched its face. A blue bird's wing flicked on her arm, and the tiger's eyes darted toward the movement, then came back to stare at her. Matilda froze looking at the reflection of eyes fixed on hers in the mirror.

Matilda scooped up a handful of cold cream and swiped it over the tiger. She pulled her cotton robe on. The fabric clung to the layer of cold cream when she wrapped it tight and tied the belt. She began to brush her hair.

She heard a soft whir at her collarbone, pushed the gown aside, and touched her index finger to the hummingbird's finely feathered green wing tip. On the other side of her chest something shifted. She stared at the blurred face of her son. The little face was congealed into a grimace. Matilda touched the fading pink cheek with her thumb. His eyes were on his own reflection in the mirror and then watching hers. She could not bring herself to put cold cream on him.

She slid into sleep sitting at her dressing table. The images of Billy and the birds and the tiger that had been with her that night raced across her dreamscape. She was running out of the back lot, pushing strands of barbed wire apart to slip between them. She was chasing the white figure running in front of her. Someone's voice, not her voice, was shrieking from somewhere. The figure in white, face-down in the grass. Something shoved her aside and she staggered to keep from falling. A guttural sound, then thudding sounds while she stood there holding something hard in her hand. She couldn't see all of the white figure, as though there was a shadow over part of it. The groans she heard didn't sound human.

And then she was back outside the tent, and Schatz was directing his crew to keep watch. She looked at her hands and they were empty.

And now, a year after losing her son, her choked breathing still yanked her awake before the dream was finished. Matilda woke wishing she could dream about her Billy instead of this replay of the run through the cow pasture.

She opened bleary eyes to watch the thin, tattooed woman in the mirror who wore her cotton gown. Matilda wondered if she'd been replaced with another woman with apricot orange hair and amber eyes. Another woman with tattoos that undulated and watched her and whispered, "We saw . . ."

ROSA AND POLLY, dressed in trousers, long sleeved blouses, and broad brimmed straw hats held parking signs while Schatz wired them to the fence. They waved cheerfully at the farmer who mowed his way across the pasture.

"Awful nice of that guy to mow his pasture for us," Schatz noted.

"Whole town's been nice," Rosa added. "Some ladies came out with plates of baked stuff for the set-up crew earlier today. And that sheriff came asking for Bill and Matilda."

From the middle of the pasture a sound like two gunshots rang out. Three fenceposts away from Rosa, Schatz, and Polly, something cracked against the fence. "He must've run that mower over a rock." Polly walked toward the still vibrating wire. She scanned the grass around the fencepost. Saw the splintered hammer handle partly held together by frayed traction tape. Saw the yellow paint. Saw the letters B Kaza—. She didn't pick it up.

The farmer stopped the tractor and raised the mower cowling to look under it. He waved at the three of them. "Everybody okay?" Schatz made the OK sign.

Polly started back toward Schatz and Rosa and stubbed her toe against something hard. She looked down to cuss the offending rock, and her face went as cold as if she'd stuck it in an icebox. She put her foot over the object for a moment to think, then shoved the sheared-off, wedge-shaped head of the blacksmith hammer into the taller grass under the barbed wire.

WHEN THE THREE of them finished hanging signs, Schatz said he'd wait for the farmer and invite him to lunch with the circus cast and crew.

"I'll wait for him. You two go on back." Polly flapped her gloved hands at Schatz and Rosa, smiling sweetly.

"You sure?" Schatz wiped his brow with a faded blue handkerchief.

"Sure. Hey, leave me that gunny sack from the tool bag. I'll pick up trash while I wait."

When Rosa and Schatz had gone around the end of the row of cars and trailers Polly started down the fence line, purposefully picking up every bit of trash she found on her way back to the broken handle and blacksmith hammer head. She dropped them in the sack.

Off the Rails

MATILDA OPENED THE refrigerator. "Iced tea?"

"Sure." Polly swiped the seat with her hand before she sat at the Formica topped table while Matilda wrestled the ice cube tray and poured tea.

Matilda set the glasses down and sat across from Polly. Polly placed the burlap sack between them with a clunk.

"What you puttin' that nasty sack on my table for?" Matilda frowned.

Polly picked up the sack by the sewn end and let the contents clatter onto the table. An ice cube shifted with a minute but clear cracking noise.

Matilda stared at the pieces of her husband's formerly missing blacksmith hammer. The wedge-shaped end had made a dent on the tabletop. Dried mud had rolled out where the handle was broken.

"It's Bill's, right? It got kicked up when that farmer mowed the pasture. Wonder how it got out there." Polly watched Matilda's face. "Oh, did you hear? That farmer found Ignacio. He didn't run off after all. He was out there in that cow pasture all that time, dead. Velma doesn't know yet. She still thinks he's in town and might show up. Poor thing."

Matilda thought about reaching for her glass of tea but changed her mind. "I heard. Sheriff said a donkey or maybe a cow kicked—"

"Matilda, I *saw* you run after Ignacio." Polly tapped her painted nails beside the broken handle. "I went back to the tent because somebody was calling for me, but you ran off into the dark after him. I saw you."

"I could swear you were with me out there."

"Now, honey-bunny, we all know you're having a hard time with what's real. And that night, I probably didn't realize what you were up to, because we were all thinking about—"

"Don't you say his name. Don't you dare say my son's name. You got no right."

"None of the rest of us knew that poor little ugly dwarf was missing 'til the next day. But you know what happened to him, don't you, Matilda?"

Matilda listened to the hiss of blood surging past her eardrums. She felt the dull throb of veins in her neck, then her arms, then the backs of her knees. "Why are you doing this?"

"I'm Gio's wife. I need to protect our circus. And Gio, you know he's soft. He just doesn't want to hurt your feelings."

Matilda looked into Polly's face. And if not for the broken hammer on the table, and her uncertainty about what had happened that night a year ago, she'd have told the little hussy to stick it up her ass. "Hurt my feelings?"

"I hate to see a good act ruined, 'Tilda. But the act is looking sloppy." Polly patted a strand of hair into place at the nape of her neck. "I'm a Fiscalini now. So, I'm not taking second billing. Time to have a beautiful star up in the lights again. Are we clear on this?"

Matilda stood and picked up Polly's untouched glass of tea. She backed up to the drain board and set the glass down. She'd have laughed right now if that girl hadn't dropped that broken hammer on the table.

"Clear?" Matilda spoke softly.

"The sheriff hasn't seen this yet. I could keep it that way. I don't want Bill mixed up in this, do you? I mean, his name's right there on it. If he gets accused, I guess it would make sense he'd have killed the little bastard. They could hang him for that, you know. But Bill was in the tent," Polly looked into Matilda's eyes, "wasn't he?"

"The sheriff said a donkey—"

"See you at rehearsal, right?" Polly put the hammer pieces back in the burlap sack and twisted the top into a knot. She stood and put her hand on the door latch. "And, Matilda? Gio invited the sheriff and his wife to come watch rehearsals. Try to look good for the local law, will you?"

Matilda watched Polly cross the lot. The pounding in her chest could have been her heart, but she was sure she heard the beating of hummingbird wings.

MATILDA DRESSED IN her long sleeve blue leotard and blue tights for rehearsal. The Salvato twins exchanged a wondering look when she entered the tent and headed up the ladder. The sheriff and his rosy-faced wife had taken seats close to the entrance.

Sheriff Delgar Wells had come, hoping for a daytime look at those tattoos on that slender caramel skinned gal, when Nadine wasn't watching him, of course. The leotard and tights were his secret disappointment. Nadine wondered half out loud to her husband where the girl who'd been in the show on the elephant last year was, and stopped mid-word when the platinum-haired Polly, in a low-cut white leotard, white tights, and a short silver skirt tied at her waist walked in. Polly glanced up at the twins and Matilda, then bent over to greet the visitors with air kisses.

Matilda watched Polly lean close to the sheriff's ear. Watched the red lips moving. Watched the sheriff lean backward. The sheriff spoke back to Polly. The sheriff raised his lined face toward the platform where Matilda waited, then nodded.

Polly started up the ladder and flashed Matilda a smile as she reached the platform. "You look nervous, hon." She turned to face the Salvato twins across the ring. "Either that or you just look like your usual hell."

For the first time since she was eighteen years old, Matilda hesitated at the push off. She didn't fly to Bobby on the first pass, and she always flew on the first pass.

"Okay?" Bobby mouthed when she approached again. She met his eyes and he caught her. "What are you doing with your left leg?" he whispered. She snapped her feet together. Robby came out to catch Polly. Polly had never left her bar on the first pass before, but she did that day.

The two women locked eyes as they passed each other.

"I wish we still had that elephant," Polly whispered.

Now Matilda hung by her feet from Bobby's hands, and Polly from Robby's. Now Polly was to be sent to Matilda for a catch, and there would be three on one bar for a pass before Polly went back to Robby again. Polly's voice carried across the top of the tent.

"Don't pass me to her. Something's wrong."

The twins improvised.

Matilda kicked higher and dismounted at the platform. Without looking back she climbed down and walked out of the tent. Nadine and Delgar Wells clapped and cajoled at their luck to get to see a real rehearsal. Bill followed Matilda and found her outside, bent over at the waist with her hands on her boney knees.

"Honey, you all right?"

"Could you hear Polly talkin' up there? Did you hear what she said?"

"No, honey, I didn't hear. What did she say?" Bill touched Matilda's ribcage, then rested his hand on her back.

"She told the guys somethin' was wrong with me. She said she wished we still had an elephant."

"Damn her. You two have a fight or something?"

Matilda spat twice before she stood. "She came to the trailer and . . ."

"And? What happened?" Bill's coarse hand was on Matilda's elbow. He looked back at the tent. "Honey, you tell me. I'm not puttin' up with this anymore."

"She—" Her mouth crumpled. She put her hands over her ears. Bill looked at her helplessly.

"Let's get you out of the heat—"

"Bill, I--" her voice sounded frantic when she gasped his name, like the muffled rustle of trapped bluebird wings. She wanted to peel the leotard down and let the birds fly away. She closed her eyes against the late morning sun.

BILL LED MATILDA toward the trailer. Nadine Wells stood watching them from the shade of the tent flap with her pink pocketbook tucked under her arm. She went back in to sit beside her husband.

"Matilda all right?" Delgar asked in a low whisper.

The clowns were running through a bicycle stunt with one of the little women on the handlebars and the other on the shoulders of the clown who pedaled. Nadine smoothed the lap of her cotton dress.

"Delgar, I think that poor girl is still heartbroken."

"That other gal said she might have to do the act alone tonight, bein's how upset Matilda's been. Says she's not right in the head. Damn shame. The whole thing is a damn shame."

"If it was me, Delgar, I think I'd just go crazy. I'm gonna pray for that poor girl."

"You do that, Nadine. She probably needs a prayer."

Release

1958, the hospital, Fayette, Missouri

DR. HARRIS FROM St. Louis sat with Bill and Suzette in Dr. McClure's office, shuffling Matilda's discharge papers.

"Since you can have her on the bed in the trailer, I think she'll make the trip to New Orleans all right. You'll ride back there with her, you say?"

Suzette affirmed she would, and Bill said he'd stop every hour to check on her. Suzette made an exasperated sound and reminded Bill she could wave from the front window of the trailer if there was a problem.

"Doctor, my daughter keeps asking what happened to her. Don't you think we ought to tell her?"

The doctor folded his hands in front of him. "Mrs. Chevalier, her brain is still healing, and it will be for a while. I'm not saying to lie to her but let her remember what she can as she's ready. It's a lot of trauma for her. Let's let her do this on her own time."

Bill watched his mother-in-law take a tissue out of her pocketbook to blow her nose. "He's right, Suzette. It might be just as well for now that she doesn't know, and you weren't there to tell it right anyway." Suzette frowned at him.

Doctor Harris slid his pen into the pocket of his shirt, straightened the files on the desk, and wished he were somewhere else.

1958, Summer, The fairgrounds, Fayette, Missouri

"BILL, YOU KNOW I can't have rehearsals go like this." Gio glanced around for eavesdroppers.

"Gio, how can you not see what Polly's doing? I swear it's like having Sally all over again." Bill faced Gio beside the concession trailer, his hands on his hips. Gio kept his tanned arms crossed.

"Now, it's not that bad. Polly just likes the spotlight. Can't Matilda share? Help me out here, Bill. I have to give my wife something."

"It's not about the spotlight. Polly said some pretty mean things to Matilda."

"What did she say?"

"Polly told the guys something was wrong with Matilda and she wished we still had an elephant."

"Well? I've been a little worried about her too. And the elephant thing was a good act back when—" He stopped and lowered his head.

"Look, Matilda's having a hard time being here, in this town as it is. Polly doesn't say stuff where everybody can hear it. Just to Matilda. It's mean." Bill's voice sounded airless.

"Bill, do you think Matilda needs to skip the show tonight? If she's not up to it, we can work it out."

"She can do the act." Bill's ruddy face went a deeper shade of red. His jaws tightened. "But this deal with Polly looking like and acting like Sally—"

Gio glowered at him.

"Gio, please don't tell Matilda to skip the show. If she's not up to it, let her be the one who says so."

"Okay. I'll tell Polly to be careful what she says. She prob'ly didn't mean it like Matilda took it." Gio rubbed his forehead wearily.

"That might be. Hard to tell with women."

"Don't you know it?" Gio extended his hand.

BERNICE HELD A wet washcloth on Matilda's neck while Matilda leaned over the sink. "You feel like you'll throw up some more, sweetie?" Matilda shook her head slowly. "Okay. Let's get you out of that hot leotard. I'll open some windows. Why're you wearing those long sleeves and tights anyway?"

Matilda knew she couldn't tell Bernice that it was to make the voices stop.

"I have some egg salad in my fridge. I'll make you a sandwich. You can't feel good with no meat on your bones." Bernice patted Matilda's elbow and headed for the door. "You just rest a while. I'll get you fixed up."

Bill met Bernice outside the trailer. Bernice motioned for him to walk with her. "I don't want her to hear us. She was throwing up. She looks awful, Bill. Like she hasn't slept. Does she sleep?"

"Hardly. Since we got to this damned town she's been staring off like—I don't know, like she's not even there. And that damn Polly said some stuff to her at rehearsal."

Bernice put her hand on Bill's arm while they walked. "Come on in. Tony should be up from his nap. He'll be happy to see you. I'll make Matilda a sandwich and go talk to her."

SHERIFF WELLS AND his wife stood beside their car after rehearsals ended. Polly stood with them, her hands in Nadine Wells' hands. Bill waved when the sheriff glanced up at him. Polly leaned close to Nadine and said something to the sheriff's wife, who gently patted Polly's arms and shook her head. Polly turned her face toward Bill and smiled. Bill didn't smile back.

BERNICE WAS BACK at Bill and Matilda's trailer in fifteen minutes with an egg salad sandwich, a pickle, and cookies. Matilda sat in front of her mirror, showered, and dressed, working tangles out of her hair.

"Well, my goodness! I'm happy to see you feeling better." Bernice put the plate on the dressing table. "If you have ice, I'll fix us something cold."

"Iced tea in the fridge. Might be ice cubes." Matilda set her hairbrush down. She pulled her mass of curls into a loose pile atop her head. "Think I should cut my hair? Something really short?"

Bernice drank iced tea while Matilda cleaned her plate. "Honey, Bill's worried about you, you know. And I see Polly elbowing her way around. Like if she changes her name to Paulina, and bleaches her hair, now she's all of a sudden special."

Matilda mopped up the last of the egg salad with a crust. "Maybe she'll get over it when she gets tired of touchin' up those dark roots."

"I came over to talk to you about taking a little time off, just for this show." Bernice raised both hands to keep Matilda from answering. "No, listen. But I'm not going to do that. I know you, honey. I know you can do your show just fine. But not when you're all covered up like you were today. Let's bring out that new sheer thing of yours I just finished. You wear that tonight. You show those tattoos to these people in this town. You hold that pretty head high and you do the best show ever. Do that for me. And that little Billy boy of yours. Honey, we don't talk about him because we don't want you to hurt. But he's your angel now and he'll be so proud of his mama."

Matilda's face was expressionless for a moment, and then she reached for Bernice's hand. "I love you Bernice. I'm going on. For Billy."

"I love you too, honey. Now. Where's your scissors? I got an idea for your hair."

Matilda's Night

TEN MINUTES TO showtime, Bill went to Gio. "Matilda's going on. She wants 'The Band Played On' for her music."

Gio ran both hands through his graying hair, watching the crowd come into the tent. "Bill, you're sure?"

"I'm sure. Of all times, Gio, this is where she needs what she knows."

Gio trotted over to alert the sound and lights man. "But you have the other music ready," he warned. "The whole thing could still change."

The house was oversold for opening night. Milana sent some roustabouts for an extra set of risers for the side entry to seat fifty more. "If we can get 'em in, sell 'em a ticket."

Rosa and her new rider trainee did a roman riding act where the new girl started on Rosa's shoulders, and they traded places. The second horse act ended with the girl doing the bareback ballerina act while Rosa changed costumes. When Schatz took the bareback horse out, Rosa came in with the dog act, which she'd taken over.

The clowns did the Keystone Cops gag, ending with a busty nurse chasing a clown in a police uniform with a flapping streamer of bandages.

Rosa's protégé took the stocking legged bay pony into the ring to walk on its hind legs. The pony bowed, then sat up like a dog, and children lined up to come into the ring one at a time for a photo with the pony. Schatz took the photos, which he told them would be for sale for a dollar during intermission. Everyone knew Matilda was going to come out and do the show, despite the aborted rehearsal. Everyone except Polly.

Polly huffed when the recorded drum roll began, and the spot wasn't on her. Bobby Salvato jerked his clefted chin toward the other ladder, grinning. Matilda was climbing in the dark. Polly muttered something under her breath. The lights came on in the tent top as Matilda stepped onto the platform, and the spotlight swung to meet her.

She stood with one arm raised over her close-cropped head. The sides of her hair were slicked back, held in place with a yellow headband. A single, shining Josephine Baker spit curl lay on her smooth forehead. But it was the costume that drew gasps. What fabric there was, was dyed to match her skin tone, and the sheer panels that held the top and bottom together disappeared in the lights. The effect was that she was nude, with only her tattoos to cover her, save for the flutter skirt Bernice had fashioned from banana-shaped pieces of sheer yellow silk, to accentuate the Josephine Baker-esque banana skirt tattoo. The audience went wild.

"Robby, just you and me." Matilda shot a look across at Bobby, who held his bar, nodded back sharply and improvised with a pose.

"What the hell is she doing?" Polly clenched her teeth.

"Polly, for once, just stop." Bobby held his arm aloft and flashed his bright white smile.

"Who do you think you are?" Polly snapped, her chin high, snarling through ruby red lips.

Robby looked at Bobby for a bar to be passed, switched bars, and landed on the platform with Bobby and Polly.

"I can have both of you fired," Polly said while she blew kisses to the audience.

"Go ahead." Robby grasped the bar and took off again. Matilda sailed away from her platform like a tattoo-covered bird with a ruffle of yellow feathers, then flew above Robby. Robby smiled as their eyes met.

She snapped her knees upward, somersaulted, and hung, untethered in the air for what seemed to be an eternity before her ankles were in Robby's grasp. The crowd bellowed and hooted. It was like old times.

"Ladies and gentlemen, boys and girls," the sound man ad-libbed, lowering the music level. "From the city of New Orleans, here to thrill you tonight." He cued the symbol crash on his second turntable and brought up Matilda's music again. "Taaa-toooed Maaa-tiiilll-daaa."

The roar of the crowd rose to the top of the tent and embraced her. The cables vibrated with the sound. The scents of tanbark, popcorn, horses, and greasepaint hung in the vapor in the top of the tent. She was home again.

Robby followed her lead when she called out moves. Three minutes into the act, she called to Bobby for a bar and he sent it her way. Robby released her and she floated like a long- limbed bird toward the familiar heft of the bar, then caught it. Matilda landed on the platform with Bobby and Polly. As she landed, she flashed Bobby a mile-wide grin.

"Go." She laughed. Bobby chuckled and sailed out to meet his twin.

"How dare you." Polly's harsh whisper fouled the air around the platform. Matilda didn't turn to look at Polly, all dressed up in her silvery costume and platinum chignon with no place to go. Matilda stood, feet slightly apart, skin glistening in the light.

"Just needed a little rest, baby doll," Matilda said, watching the twins. "You get that bar from whichever of them comes in to land."

"You are done in this circus." Polly's blazing cheeks showed through her makeup.

Bill was at the bottom of the opposite ladder, looking up, half in horror at the improvised act, half in joy that Matilda was her old self. Matilda looked down at her husband. Her glossy lips pulled into her old smile. She was back.

Matilda saw her husband beaming, shaking his head in amazement. Now, their eyes locked for an instant. Now, his face turned to a look of horror. Now his arms were reaching toward her. Now he was lunging over the boards and across the ring. Now, she couldn't feel the platform under her feet. Now, she was in the air with nothing to grab. Now, the tanbark rushed toward her.

"LIGHTS! 'STARS AND Stripes'!" Gio shouted toward the sound booth. He ran, bile rising in his throat, toward Bill, who crouched on the tanbark, shielding Matilda's twisted body.

Polly held the ladder and leaned over the boards to look. The sound man had turned toward the entrance to look for Schatz, because he couldn't see Gio, and when he turned, his arm hit the spotlight, and the light swung toward the platform from which Matilda had come tumbling down.

When the spot illuminated her, Polly put her hands on both sides of her face and opened her mouth as though she were screaming. Bobby landed on the platform, barely missing her.

"You evil bitch. I saw you," Bobby rasped, then scrambled down the ladder.

The sound man cued "Stars and Stripes" and turned to his mic. "Ladies and gentlemen, please remain calm, and make your way to the exits. Give them room, please," and then he lost his announcer voice, and sobbed, "Oh God, oh God."

Nadine Wells clutched her rose print purse in her ample lap. "Oh, my Lord, Delgar, did you see that?"

"I saw. Good God. Stay here. No, go to my car and call for an ambulance." The sheriff started toward the side of the ring where Matilda lay in the center of a gathering crowd of circus performers. Nadine's face went white, and she hugged her purse closer. "Go, Nadine. Just hold the button and talk. Jesus Christ. Tell them to hurry."

Bobby Salvato jumped the last two rungs, landed running and ran smack into the sheriff, who caught both his arms.

Wells' voice was low. "Stay at this ladder. Don't let her come down and get away."

Little Betty came running, tears rolling over her greasepaint and stopped beside Bobby. She peered up into the darkness at Polly standing above the melee.

"She do this, Bobby?" Bobby nodded. "Then I get her first."

The ambulance took twenty minutes to get there. When it pulled out, the driver didn't turn on the lights and siren.

Trapped

"PLEASE, SHERIFF, YOU don't need to handcuff my wife in front of everybody." Gio stood at Sheriff Well's side.

"Son, these people all saw what she did."

Gio called for Rosa to bring something from the dressing tent for Polly to put on when she came down. Rosa regarded Gio sadly for a second, shook her head, and walked out of the tent. One of the new acrobats said she'd go get Paulina's wrap. She came back with a wrap, slip on shoes, and the burlap sack. "This was all her stuff on the hook." She held the sack by the knotted top. "Feels heavy."

"Miss, it will be a lot easier if you just climb on down." Delgar Well's voice filled the muffled silence of the big top.

While the sheriff watched Polly on the narrow platform, Gio opened the sack and pulled out the broken hammer pieces. He looked at the flat end and the wedge-shaped end of the three-pound farrier's hammer, then at what was left of Bill's name on the shattered handle.

"You need to come down, Polly." Gio's voice sounded dull in the air. He called to the light and sound man, "Can you cut that spot?" He looked back up at the woman on the platform who'd just pushed his star performer off. "Polly, come down. Don't make me come up there."

Polly's face remained mask-like as she looked around the ring below. The sheriff glanced at Gio's hands, saw that he held a broken hammer. The discussion he'd had with the coroner nine months ago when the battered body of the little man was discovered came back like a breath of fetid air.

"Miss, come on down." Wells spoke more quietly to Gio, who stood beside him looking distraught and confused. "Son, will you put those things back in the sack? I'll need to take them with me."

Polly kept her eyes on the platform opposite her.

Wells whispered to Gio, "Do you think she'll jump?"

"If she does, she does." Gio looked toward the open tent flap.

Rosa stood in the shadows of the bleachers with Schatz. "Jump, Polly. Do us all a favor." Betty and two other clowns murmured in agreement.

"I need you to come down now, miss." Wells kept his eyes on Polly while he whispered to Gio, "Tell your other people to clear out."

"All of you get back. Please, let's not have another—" Gio hesitated as Polly put her hands on the ladder. "Good girl. Come down slowly."

Polly began the descent as though nothing had happened.

"Please step back when she gets to the ground," Wells warned.

Gio did.

Wells took Polly firmly by the elbow. "Let's go."

Polly glowered at the sheriff and then her husband. "Why? Why am I being arrested? Because of that sack? That's Matilda's sack. She was hiding that hammer. It's the murder weapon."

Schatz stepped from the shadows. "That's the sack I gave you yesterday out of the tool kit. You said you needed it to pick up trash."

"Murder weapon?" Gio looked at his wife and then Wells.

"Matilda used that hammer to beat that shithead dwarf to death. I was there." Polly's face reddened with rage.

"Polly, Ignacio was killed by a donkey or a cow. What are you talking about?"

"I saw her! I was with her!" Paulina tried to twist away from the sheriff's grip.

"Paulina Fiscalini, you are under arrest for assault." Sheriff Wells clicked a cuff onto one of her wrists.

"You can't prove anything!" Polly shrieked.

"Shut up. Just shut up!" Gio bellowed. "Don't you even know what you've done?"

On the way back to town Nadine Wells sat silently beside Delgar and never once looked back at the platinum-haired assassin behind the mesh.

The Lights Go Down
1958, Somewhere Outside Fayette, Missouri

SHE COULD HEAR her bones moving. Her head was filled with a terrible, grinding sound. She fluttered her eyelids open and her eyes hurt like they'd been left out to dry in the sun. She closed them again. She wanted her daddy. She wanted him to dance with her so she wasn't twirling and whirling all by herself.

The last thing she heard was a voice pleading, "Baby, don't you leave me."

WITH HIS DEPUTY as a witness, Delgar Wells took a statement from Polly Fiscalini. Polly denied shoving Matilda off the platform but admitted to hitting Ignacio with the hammer because he infuriated her when he ran from her. She confessed that she'd run back to the train and changed out of her bloody costume and had lied about where she was that night. She hadn't known what had happened to the hammer until the mower had run over it, and she'd found it in the grass.

In the morning Wells took his spiral notebook back to the fairgrounds. The crew was taking down the tent. He found Schatz and asked if he knew where the hammer with Bill's name on the handle had come from. Schatz replied that he was sure it was one of the two hammers Bill had found missing after the elephant accident a year prior.

"What kind of hammers did he say were gone?" Wells asked.

"A two-pound ball peen and a three-pound flat peen farrier's hammer."

"The ball peen ever show up?"

"As a matter of fact, yes, about a month after all that happened, I found the ball peen hammer in a trunk. Somebody must have put it in there, you know, by mistake."

"Did it have anything like blood or hair on it when you found it?"

"Gosh, no, Sheriff, Bill keeps his tools clean as a whistle."

WELLS ASKED THE coroner to revisit his notes about the wedge-shaped depressions on the dead man's back and skull.

The coroner adjusted his eyeglasses. "Well, I thought back then it looked like it was from something like a hammer."

"You reopen that file, will you? Looks like we have a murder weapon. Have you got pictures of that guy's head?"

"Yep. Looks pretty bad, but I got pictures."

THE NEXT EVENING, based on her confession, and clinched by the autopsy photos, Polly Fiscalini was charged with the murder of Ignacio Lopez.

Gio called a family meeting, and they all agreed that the best thing he could do for the good of the circus was to be shed of Polly. He called the family's lawyer, and in a few days had divorce papers served to Polly by the sheriff while she waited in the Fayette jail.

"I GIVE HIM everything, and this is what he does?" Polly raged. She flung the petition back through the bars at Delgar Wells.

"Mrs. Fiscalini, I'm just the delivery boy in this matter."

"Then you release me right this minute so I can go take care of this."

"Ma'am, I can't do that, you're under arrest for murder."

"That crazy tattooed bitch jumped. You saw her. She wanted to die, she—"

"Mrs. Fiscalini, we all saw you push her."

"You can't blame me for Matilda killing herself. She'd gone insane. Ask anybody."

"Ma'am, you probably need to hush now. But I'm gonna tell you something because you seem pretty confused. You were arrested for assault that night. A couple days ago you confessed to killing that poor little feller in the cow pasture."

"Oh, so now you're saying I committed two murders?"

"No, ma'am, I didn't say that. Now you need to hush up. I have your confession for one crime, and eyewitnesses for another. You'd do yourself well to be nice. You'll get an appointed attorney if you can't afford one. That's who you need to talk to."

"My husband's family will get their lawyer to take care of this!" Paulina shouted.

"Ma'am, you don't have a husband anymore, so I don't reckon they'll be providing—"

"Why, you God-damn hick, how dare you talk to me that way."

"Now you just settle down, miss. I'm just trying to help you understand the seriousness of the charges."

"But I didn't kill Matilda!"

Wells started toward the heavy outer door. "No, you didn't."

DELGAR WELLS ADDED a note on the case file per Gio Fiscalini's request that anything on record or to the press about the woman who'd be tried and sentenced for the murder of Ignacio Lopez should be under her maiden name, Polly McCormack.

Sheriff Wells was glad for Bill Kazarian that he wouldn't be adding another murder charge to the file for the woman formerly called Paulina Fiscalini. But he'd never hoped for the death sentence for a prisoner until that day.

PART 9

Another Life

Back Home
1958, Fall, New Orleans, Louisiana

BILL, SUZETTE, AND Matilda's siblings moved Matilda from the trailer to a secondhand wheelchair, then to the hospital bed a neighbor had found for them. Bill dragged sofa cushions from the trailer to put on the floor beside her.

Matilda opened her mouth for soup and rice pudding when told and smiled at Bill when he spoke. Bill warned the family to brush her hair carefully around the scars and tell her she looked pretty. Not much else changed for the next two months.

BILL TOOK A part time job as a groundskeeper at the racetrack their second month in New Orleans. He was sleeping four hours a night at best. Suzette watched the calendar, wondering what to do come November and race season. If she went back to working the betting windows, she told Bill, they'd need someone to watch Matilda, since Cheree was going blind.

The nurse next door knew a woman who hadn't finished nursing school, but knew the basics, and was willing to sit with Matilda from eight in the morning until three in the afternoon when Evangeline got home from school, for two dollars a day.

In December, Matilda began fiddling with the dial on the radio Suzette had placed beside her bed and hummed along with the music. The next week, the almost-nurse reported excitedly that her charge had tried to brush her own hair.

Good Intentions
1959, February, New Orleans, Louisiana

"LOOK HERE, HONEY, you can grab on to this and pull yourself up any time you want." Bill tapped the wooden frame with a trapeze bar on cables he'd built to span Matilda's bed.

She stared at the apparatus. "What's that?" She extended a pale hand toward the bar and touched it with one finger.

"It's like a trapeze. To help you get stronger."

"What for?"

"So you'll be strong again." He searched for words. "Like you used to be. Remember how strong you were?" He adjusted the bar a few inches lower.

"Why?"

"So you can pull yourself up. You'd like that, wouldn't you?" He touched the wheelchair. "You could use it to get in your chair by yourself."

"You can put me in the chair. I don't need that thing."

"I'm sorry, honey, I was just thinking—"

"Why are you doing this?"

"Because you're my wife."

"Because you want a wife that can walk."

"Matilda, the doctor says—"

"Why? Do I have somewhere to go?" She stared at the ceiling above the mock-up trapeze. "Why do I want that thing now? I must have been lousy at that trapeze thing, because I'm all broke up now. Why the hell would I want that thing to remind me?" Her mouth crumpled but she didn't cry.

"Sweetheart, you didn't fall. You didn't. Don't you remember?"

"What?"

"That night. Remember going up?" Bill watched Matilda's face for a glimmer of recognition. "Remember when you were doing the act? The Salvato twins were catching. You had a new haircut and a new costume." Bill sat back and waited for her.

She furrowed her brow at him. "I remember them. They wore those red and blue things, like—like—I remem—Drum majors. No—like tin soldiers. Gold cloth buttons."

"Yes. That's what they wore that night. You remember that better than I do."

"I don't remember." She looked away.

"I think you do, if you know what the boys were wearing. What were you wearing?"

"I don't know."

"It was brand new."

Matilda closed her eyes for a moment. "Bernice had just finished that costume and she cut my hair. I looked like Josephine Baker."

"Yes, you sure did. Go on."

"And the boys and me—were makin' it up as we went to get back at Polly for being . . ." She looked up at the trapeze bar over her bed. "Did they drop me—because we didn't rehearse?" She stared at the ceiling beyond the bar. "Was it my fault? For changin' the act?"

"No, baby." Bill cleared his throat. "You were on the platform." He waited and prayed silently in those seconds Matilda scanned the ceiling for answers.

"I was on the platform. I was wearin' the new costume and—" She turned her head toward Bill. He nodded. "Bernice. She made it. Did she make me a skirt too? Yeah, a skirt. Yellow. Wasn't it? Yellow. Like—like—ba—bananas."

Bill nodded and fought back tears. "Go on."

"I was—on the platform, and the light—the light was on me. Me and Sally—no, it wasn't Sally."

"No, it wasn't Sally. Who was on the platform with you?"

"No. It wasn't Sally, but she was all in—sil-silver like Sally, wasn't she?" Matilda screwed her face up and touched her fingers on the bar above her head. "Polly. Polly—that girl from—North Carolina or somewhere. She was wearing that silver—not Polly—was her name Paulina? Naw—it was Polly."

"Yes." Bill scooted the chair closer. "It was. See, I knew you could remem—"

"Polly was on the platform with me." The words tumbled out like water. Matilda's eyes widened. "Did I—fall off the platform? No. How would—no, that can't be right. I was on the platform watching the boys. I was smiling at you, wasn't I?"

"Yes. You were beautiful, even when the light wasn't on you." He reached for her hand and kissed the backs of her fingers.

"She said—she was going to make me regret—yeah, that was it. She was mad because I changed the act. I was mad at her too." Matilda stopped abruptly. "She told me I killed Nosh. She came to the trailer—with a broken hammer. But it was the wedge lookin' hammer, not your ball peen hammer. And I knew that night I had that ball peen—I was running with it."

Bill pulled out his handkerchief.

"I was in a—a field. I was chasing Nosh. Polly was with me. How did I forget? She had a hammer too. It was your hammer—that wedge hammer. Polly said—" Matilda put her long fingers over the bar above her. "Lemme at that sonofabitch. That's what she said. And she hit him. Then a donkey was making that sound and started kickin'—and I ran. Oh my God. Sally—no, Polly—Polly told me I was the one who did it. I was so mixed up. She told me that, and I believed her. Why did she do that?" Matilda choked out a sob, and Bill offered his handkerchief. "No. And Polly—then she said she'd tell the sheriff I killed Nosh. But I didn't. She killed him, didn't she?"

"That's what the sheriff said. He said she confessed after . . ." He let the rest of the words fall to the floor.

"After she pushed me. She pushed me, didn't she."

"Yes, she did."

Matilda touched the scar on her scalp. "Bitch."

"Yes."

"After she pushed me, what happened to Polly?"

"She got arrested for assault. Because everybody saw what she did. And she confessed to killing Nosh."

"To the sheriff? That nice sheriff? He and his wife came to the hospital, didn't they?"

"Yes. Polly confessed to him. She got charged with murder."

"Really? Is she in jail?"

"Yes. She got the death penalty."

"Really." Matilda blew her nose and handed Bill his handkerchief. "So, she's dead?"

"No. Something in the paper said they'd move her to a women's prison. But she'll never get out. It was in the paper. She looked terrible in the mug shot."

"What happened to everybody else?"

"Well, Gio got a divorce. Bernice and Tony came and sat with you. You weren't awake then. Rosa and Schatz are still with 'em, and Betty and Velma, I guess. When they come here in early summer we can go see them."

"Does the circus come here?" Matilda asked, frowning.

"Yes, they come to New Orleans same time every year. We'll go see them."

"No."

"Okay, we won't."

Matilda put both hands on the bar and wriggled her fingers, then let her arms fall to her sides. "I miss all them though." She blinked at Bill and extended her hand toward his face.

"I miss them too. I've missed you too." He sniffed and looked toward the open bedroom door. "Hey, time to eat. Evangeline made gumbo. Your grandma says she makes roux as good as your grandpa's."

Matilda reached for the bar over her head and pulled weakly.

"That's a start," Bill said.

Time Marches On

1959, Spring, New Orleans, Louisiana

WHEN THE RACE season at Fair Grounds ended, Bill asked the track manager if there was any other work for him. As a matter of fact, the manager told him, they were looking for a full-time track superintendent. Bill took the job.

Suzette declined an early offer from Churchill Downs to come work their race season. She told the family that night at supper that she wanted to be home with them and would find off season work somewhere in town.

Gabriel's back had been aching from years bending over the cutting boards and pots at the Fair Grounds clubhouse restaurant, and Liuzza's in the off season. "I'm gonna have to cut back to one job before I get so stove up I can't lift a frying pan, so it's a good thing the rest of you are workin'."

"What about me? I want a job." Fifteen-year-old Evangeline glowed with excitement.

"Evange, you're just like I was." Matilda fiddled with the brake on her wheelchair. "I did ironing for the neighbor lady when I was fourteen, fifteen. Then I was a waitress."

"*You* were a waitress?" Evangeline eyed her half-sister suspiciously.

Matilda bobbed her head. "Gran-pap made me wear long sleeves to cover my tattoos when I went to ask for a job. Remember that, Gran-pap?"

"Did they hurt?" Evangeline put her elbows on the table and locked eyes with Matilda.

"Don't you get any ideas, little missy." Cheree shook a gnarled finger at her granddaughter.

"Hurts like hell when they first start." Matilda ignored her grandmother and leaned toward Evangeline.

"Why'd you do it then?"

"Because I saw this picture and then there was this boy. He danced with me and he took me to Lafontaine's, and he bought me a tattoo. This one." She pulled her blouse open to show Evangeline the hummingbird.

"Don't you do that at the table, that's trashy," Suzette scolded.

Matilda snorted and laughed. "Oh, Momma, good Lord. Look who's talkin'."

Suzette laughed right along with her.

MATILDA TOLD EVANGELINE stories of life on the rails, because Evangeline begged her to tell.

Bill asked Evangeline to help Matilda do the physical therapy exercises Matilda had only begrudgingly done.

Evangeline eyed the bar above her sister's bed. "Hey, can I use your bar to practice? I might want to work in a circus."

"Better get your grip right then. It's like this." Matilda pulled herself upright.

But when it came to what the doctor had prescribed for regaining her strength and balance, Matilda told everyone, "Just leave me be. This is how it is now."

Gabriel's End
1959, Early Fall, New Orleans, Louisiana

GABRIEL'S FRIENDS FROM the neighborhood and the restaurant where he'd worked until the day a heart attack dropped him to the floor with a spoon in his hand, poured out into the street to walk behind the band that played a funeral march, then "When the Saints Go Marching In." Cheree wore a pale blue veil over a black pillbox hat, and her black and white polka dot dress, because Gabriel had loved that dress. A grandchild walked on either side of her, holding her by the arms.

Eddie, Kat, and Mary Ellen Lafontaine walked with the funeral procession to the cemetery. Eddie handed their two-year-old black-haired, pink-cheeked daughter to Kat, and sent them home. He scanned the crowd for Matilda.

He saw a teenage girl who reminded him of the girl who'd come in all those years ago and had sat without a whimper for a tattoo of a hummingbird below her collarbone. The girl stood talking quietly to some boys, then made her way to sit with the widow Durand.

"Gotta be a sister," Eddie said to himself.

CHEREE DURAND PEERED through thick-lensed eyeglasses at the nice-looking white man beside her at the table in the basement of the parish hall and smiled. "Thank you, sweet. So nice of you to come. Did you go to the racetrack? Or the restaurant? It seems my husband knew so many people."

Eddie affirmed he'd been to the track, had eaten at the clubhouse.

"These here are my grandchildren," Cheree said. "All but one of 'em's here. We thank you for your kindness."

Eddie decided it best not to bring up exactly how he knew Gabriel and Cheree's celebrated, tattooed granddaughter.

The Craving
1959, Fall, New Orleans, Louisiana

"WHAT'S THIS ONE? This boy dressed like a soldier?" Evangeline sat on the edge of the clawfoot tub, dabbing a washcloth on her sister's chest. Matilda steadied herself with a hand on the faucet.

"That's a drum major costume. My Billy. You know, he died."

"I know. You must miss him, huh."

"I remember everything about when he was little. When he got older, it's like some of the years are gone. I have pictures of him somewhere, but I can't . . ."

"Bill says sometimes you got a new tattoo whenever you felt sad."

"He said that? I guess I did sometimes."

"That why you have this one of Billy?"

Evangeline put the washcloth on the side of the tub and traced her finger over the blue heart tattoo beside the image of the boy. "How come this one of Billy is lighter than the other tattoos?"

"Hand me that mirror. Well, hon, it's fading. I need to get it touched up."

"Won't that hurt?" Evangeline waited until Matilda handed the mirror back. "Why would you want it to hurt again?"

Matilda's eyes widened as she grabbed Evangeline's wrist. "Because he was mine and it's all I have left of him. He was all I had. I know you can't understand that. You never lost nobody."

"Gran-pap. He died. We both of us lost him." Evangeline used her fingers to loosen Matilda's grip. "Let go."

"I'm sorry, Evange, didn't mean to hurt you."

"Well at least you're gettin' stronger."

"I want to get Billy touched up. Will you take me?"

"Take you where?"

"Lafontaine's. Where I got my first tattoos. I got some money in that box in my room. I'll pay you a quarter to push me over there."

"Two quarters," Evangeline countered.

"You're *just* like me. Okay two."

"BUT SHE REALLY wants to go. I'll be real careful with her. I promise," Evangeline pleaded. "I'll take her and stay with her the whole time."

Bill looked at her dubiously. "What if they're busy? It's not like it's just walking over there and walking back."

"I looked 'em up in the phone book and called. Hey, they knew her. The lady I talked to said 'Tattooed Matilda? We'll be so glad to see her.' That's what she said." Evangeline rocked on her heels.

"Did you tell them about her though? That she's, you know, not the same?"

"'Tilda was with me when I called. I couldn't tell that part with her right there." Evangeline was crestfallen. "Want me to call them back?"

"Give me the number. I'll call. You're a good girl to want to help."

Evangeline ducked her head and smiled to herself. She didn't mention she was making fifty cents for pushing her sister's wheelchair over to Lafontaine's.

"HI, EDDIE, THANKS for coming to the phone." Bill clutched the receiver in the phone booth at the track. "It's about my wife, Matilda. Yeah, thanks. Well, she's talked about you too. You're that same Lucky Eddy, right? Okay, I just need you to know something." Bill slid the door on the phone booth shut.

"Matilda had a bad accident last summer. Yeah, it was real bad. Thanks. I didn't know if you knew. I knew she always sent you a Christmas card. Well, I sold our house in Florida, so we live here now. Right. Well, it was a broken leg and hip and an arm, but she had a bad concussion too. It took her a long time to get any memory back, and she's still—yes, she's—" He listened for a few seconds. "The doctor tells us it's what helps somebody not give up: not remembering right away. We lost our son a year before that. Oh. She didn't tell me she'd told you. Thank you, it has been, well--" He listened again. "Her leg and arm are healed, but she's still in a wheelchair, and—you were too? Gosh, I'm sorry to hear that. Matilda never told me that." He looked across the racecourse while he listened on the phone. "Oh. Pearl Harbor. Well, I'm sure sorry. Wow. I'm—"

Bill listened for a full minute to a man who'd known Matilda before he'd ever met her. "So, you know the problem is she won't even try to—right. Yeah, that's it. And I've tried everything." He pressed the phone tightly to his ear to listen again. "Well, sir, I'm glad you're walking now. That might be what Matilda needs. Somebody to get tough on her. I can't do it." He listened again.

"Thank you, Eddie. I don't know how that will go, but if it doesn't, and I owe you anything for your time—well, thanks—that's nice—I sure hope so. All right, then. Her little sister will bring her. Yes, tomorrow. Thank you."

Bill set the receiver in the cradle and stood in the closed phone booth for another minute, staring at the dial, the coin return, the mildewed phone book. He saw that his hand shook when he checked the return slot for a coin. Old habit.

He hoped to God he'd done the right thing.

Eddie's Old Customer

EDDIE LEANED ON the counter next to Mary Ellen.

"Those posters I'm having printed are going to go there and there." Mary Ellen indicated the newly spackled and painted walls. "Hey, I took an appointment for Matilda Chevalier. Guess somebody's bringing her in, 'cause they needed directions. Today at two."

"I know. Her husband called. She had a bad accident last summer. She's pretty messed up, sounds like. I'll see what she wants done." Eddie looked at his watch. "I got time to run to the corner for a Dr. Pepper. You want one?"

EVANGELINE'S FACE WAS flushed by the time she'd pushed the wheelchair the six blocks down, two blocks up the wrong street, found the right street, and then the final three blocks to the shop.

Mary Ellen and Eddie watched the skinny teenager and the pale-skinned ginger-haired, hollow-eyed woman in a wheelchair crossing the street.

"She looks like death warmed over." Mary Ellen sighed. "Did her husband say? I mean, Eddie, she looks like . . ." Her voice dropped.

"I'm gonna find out. Put her in the back room. Leave her in that wheelchair. You take the little sister with you. I'll come in after you all are out of there."

"WELL, I'LL BE go to hell, if it isn't Matilda, come back to see me." Eddie strode into the back parlor and plunked onto his rolling work stool.

Matilda's eyes glistened. He stuck out his hand. She shook it.

"Been a long time, hasn't it?" she said, "I was tellin' my little sister about my first tattoo. Remember that? Little hummingbird? That boy paid for it."

"Hoo-boy, I remember that. I was so mad at him for bringin' you in here, underage and all. Runnin' around at night with a guy like that. Your granddad should a skinned you alive."

"I know! Lord, Eddie, it's nice to see you."

"Yeah, likewise. So, what can I do for you today?"

She pulled at the neckline of her peasant blouse. "This one here, got it somewhere else. It's faded real bad. Can you fix it?"

"Yeah, you asked me to do that and I didn't want to, last time I saw you." He watched her face for a glimmer of recognition. She blinked twice and opened her mouth, but nothing came out. "What's this cross one beside it? Nice work. What's that, a Silver Cross?"

"My dad got a Silver Cross in France. A guy that knew you did that one. Did I show you this before?"

"Yeah, but it's still nice. This other one is shitty work. And this is what you want touched up?"

Matilda twisted her mouth to one side and give him a short nod. "My Billy."

Eddie leaned back and folded his arms. "Can't work around that blouse. You gotta put the kimono on, kiddo." Matilda pressed her lips together tightly as she leaned forward to pick up the kimono.

"Turn your head then."

Eddie grabbed the kimono from her. "Ut uh. You get on the chair here like everybody else."

Matilda narrowed her eyes and looked toward the closed door. "You gonna help me up?"

"Nope."

"Evangeline!" she shouted.

Mary Ellen pushed the door open a second later, and Evangeline poked her head in.

"No." Eddie pointed at them.

Mary Ellen guided the girl back to the waiting room.

"What the hell? How am I gonna get up there?"

"You want a tattoo, you get on the chair. That's the rules."

"You don't know how bad this hurts!" Matilda's voice rose, quavering.

"Don't I?"

The clocked ticked four seconds, five, six, seven. "Why you bein' like this? Can't you just do it over here?"

"Nope."

"Why?"

"Why do you think?" Eddie picked up a pencil and stuck it behind his ear. "Huh? Your lips are moving, but nothin's comin' out."

"Think? How the hell do I know why you're doin' this. Get my sister back in here. I'm goin' home."

"Oh, don't you pull the pity-party with me, Matilda. Yeah you. Now it's you that's in a wheelchair. It's the shits, ain't it?" He crossed his arms and watched her face. "You know, I have you figured out. I know what you want. Do you know what you want?"

"I thought we were friends. I'm goin' home now."

"Yeah, you want to run home because I'm not gonna help you? That what you want? You come in here and tell me you want me to fix something I didn't even do. Kiddo, all I can do is make it hurt again."

Matilda's features crumpled with confusion. "I know it hurts. Jesus H Christ, Eddie, you don't think I know tatts hurt?"

"Oh, see, now we're getting' somewhere. Let me ask you somethin'. You gonna cry?"

"No, I'm not."

"Why not? You oughta be mad enough to cry. Why not? Oooh, I got it. You don't cry because that might show you got feelings. Everything in your life hurts. And you know what I think? No, don't you answer this time. You listen first. Are your listening?"

Matilda swallowed her rage and scowled at him.

"Good. I think you're an addict, Matilda. Hey, hey, don't get all big eyed and lip flappin' on me now. I know addicts. I was one. Did you know I was an addict?. Oh, I was. Me and your boyfriend were smokin' heroin that night you got that first tattoo. Damn, I did good work even when I was high."

Matilda stared at Eddie for a few seconds, then looked away. "I knew somethin' was wrong with you. You were always goin' out for a smoke and you came back nicer. Maybe you need to start doin' that again."

"Really. I kicked that nasty habit. Why the hell would I go back to doin' that?" Eddie shoved his seat over to the worktable to get a notebook. "So, ol' buddy, what is it you really want today?"

"I—I told you. Fix this one tattoo. That's all I want."

"No, now you know better than to lie to me. That's not all you want. You want a fix. That's what you want," he said coolly. "And it won't fix what's wrong."

"I don't take drugs. Why are you *saying* that?"

"Oh, you think I meant *drugs*? No, you listen to me. See, I been doing this a long time. You know why guys come in here and get a new tattoo on Saturday night? Pick a reason. Girlfriend broke up with 'em Friday. Lost their job. Got a job they hate. Shippin' out to some damn war. They're scared. But they're all tough so they can't cry. But you know what I can do for 'em?"

Matilda swallowed and shook her head slowly. Her throat ached the way it used to ache in high school when she watched Casey walk into a room and drape himself over a chair. When she saw Brenda kissing him. She could feel the pain as sharply as it had felt when she was fifteen.

Eddie's voice softened. "They need the pain. That's what they need. And I punch that ink in and it reminds 'em they felt something. That ink lasts forever, and they can look at it anytime they want to remember. They're addicted. Just as much as I was to heroin. They're addicted to the pain. And to hangin' on to whatever sent 'em here."

"I just like tattoos," Matilda whispered hoarsely.

"No, you got your heart broke by your daddy dyin' when you were just a kid, and then by your momma leavin' you here when she took off, and again by that no-good pretty boy after that night he brought you here and you got your first tattoo. And those jerks at school were mean, and life was a shit storm all the damn time. But, by God, you still got all those tatts to remind you how much it hurt, don't ya? No, don't shake your head at me like that. I know."

"You don't know what it's like." Matilda fought to keep her voice steady.

"The hell I don't. You think it was a piece of cake losin' my leg? But you know, one day I figured out the pain I was tryin' to kill smokin' and shootin' heroin wasn't where my leg used to be." Eddie stood and tapped a finger over his heart. "Listen to me. It was where my heart used to be."

"Well, that's not me." Her voice barely cleared trembling lips.

"Sure it is." Eddie pressed the knuckles of both hands into the red chair between them. "That's why you got that medal from your daddy tattooed on your chest there, and that's why you got that little boy of yours right beside it. Anytime you need to hurt and feel sorry for yourself, all you gotta do is look at those tattoos."

"If I can get up there, will you fix this picture of my—" A sob escaped her lips. She put her hand over her mouth and recomposed her trembling voice. "Of my son."

"I don't think you can get up here."

"I hate you."

"Bullshit. You know I'm the best in town."

Matilda pressed her hands on the arms of the wheelchair.

"Better put the brake on." Eddie watched her face.

Matilda repositioned her hands and leaned forward. The arm that had been broken in four places buckled. She pushed harder on the good arm.

Her legs shook so hard she thought her teeth would rattle when she threw herself forward to grab the far side of the chair with both hands. She didn't look at Eddie. She didn't want to know if he looked concerned or was laughing at her.

She wished she'd practiced more, pulling herself up with the bar Bill had hung over the bed. Bill was always doing something he thought would help. She didn't know why he kept doing that. She'd wondered, while she lay in the hospital bed in her old bedroom, when Bill would grow tired of trying to get her up and walking again. Maybe now that she had her mother and Evangeline to take care of her, he'd leave her. He could go back to work for Fiscalinis. Or go back to California. He could leave her just like everybody else she'd loved had done.

She didn't know how long she'd half-lain over the tattoo chair when she felt a soft tap on one of her hands. She raised her head and caught her breath. Her face and neck were wet.

Eddie was eye to eye with her. She watched his lips move and felt his whisper rumble in her pounding ears. "Okay, kiddo. You been cryin' all over my nice chair long enough. Stand your skinny ass up."

Matilda gulped air into her lungs and welcomed the twinge of her lungs expanding. She gasped in surprise when shards of pain shot down her hip and leg. The wheelchair skidded against the brake when she braced her good foot on the footrest. She heard birds, she thought, or was that music, or was that her own voice?

Matilda took the first deep breath she'd taken in a very long time. The agony was exquisite. It wasn't the dull throb it had been for so long. It was razor sharp, and fresh. At the crest of pain, a pinpoint of warmth opened behind her eyes. She looked down at her hands. She inhaled again and felt a dozen pings as her ribcage spread apart to let life back in.

"Atta girl. How's that feel?"

"Hurts. But better," she whispered.

"Sit down here and tell me when you're ready," he whispered back.

"I'm ready."

"I'll step outside. Get the God damned kimono on like I told you in the first place."

MATILDA STARED AT the reflection of the fading tattoo of her son with a hand mirror.

"Still want me to touch this one up?" Eddie sat back and tapped his pencil on his sketch pad.

She put a finger to the image. "Maybe I don't need this one to hurt anymore."

"No, I don't think you do."

"I get what you're sayin'. It doesn't have to be a bad thing for me to want ink, though. Maybe I just want somethin' new."

"Well, if you want me to do somethin' else, I will." Eddie picked up his sketch pad and flipped a page. "Look here."

She took the pad from him. "It's . . ."

"I drew that a long time ago, after that first time you were at the circus and they put you in that act with Bill."

"I love it. You pick where."

AN HOUR AND a half later, Eddie held the door so Matilda could shuffle into the waiting area pushing the wheelchair. Evangeline whooped and clapped her hands. Eddie hugged Matilda for the first time in the seventeen years they'd known each other.

"If you weren't such an asshole I'd kiss you," Matilda whispered.

"You just want me for my tatt machine. Get outta here before I change my mind and charge you. Now get in that chair. That's enough showin' off for today. But next time you show your face here—"

"Matilda, can I get a tattoo when we come back?" Evangeline asked breathlessly.

"Nothin' doin'," Eddie said. "I don't tattoo kids."

AFTER THE CHEVALIER sisters were on their way, Mary Ellen brought two ice cold Dr. Peppers into the parlor.

"I was right outside, you know. I heard what you did. I didn't know what you were up to. How did you know how much you could push her?"

"I didn't." Eddie clinked the pale green bottle against Mary Ellen's. "To gettin' on with life."

And The Band Plays On

EVANGELINE RAN MOST of the way home, both of them laughing and shrieking when the wheelchair bounced over warped sidewalk breaks.

"Wait'll you see!" Evangeline squealed when Suzette and Bill got back from work.

Matilda put her forearms on the sofa back and tediously dragged and pulled herself up until she was standing. Suzette sputtered and cried while she described to her nearly blind mother what Matilda had just done. Bill carefully put his hand on Matilda's arm.

"Don't I get a hug or something?" Matilda asked, wrinkling her brow.

Bill grabbed her and held her against his chest.

THAT NIGHT, AS Bill sat on the edge of the hospital bed in their room, Matilda touched his stubbled cheek. "I guess I been gone a long time." She traced the creases in his face. "I'm sorry for how I've been."

"Shhh. You're back."

"You never once got mad at me this whole time."

"Who says?"

"Must not have been that bad, or you'd a left me here and gone back to Fiscalinis."

"Who says?" He took her hand.

"If I said things, you know, bad things, I'm—"

Bill kissed her fingers. "Honey, I love you. I never would have left you. God only knows why."

"My momma said she loved me too, but she left me."

"Maybe she did, but when I called, she came straight to the hospital. She was there with you almost the whole time."

Matilda squinted at Bill's serious tone. "I wonder why."

"Because she loves you. And you could be glad she's here, or you could keep on wondering if she'll leave."

"She did before," Matilda said quietly.

Bill rocked his head back, then put his forehead against Matilda's. She stared into his almost black eyes until the closeness became unbearable.

"What?"

"You want your mother to stay? I'm asking you."

"I guess. You're not planning to leave, are you?"

"You know, when I first saw you, I promised myself right then I'd do anything just to be with you. So why would I leave now?" He eased his forehead back from hers a few inches. "Why?"

"You might." Matilda's mouth slackened.

"Stop that. And stop it about your momma."

"Okaaay."

"Okay what?"

"Okay, you won't. Momma might not either."

"Stop."

"Okay. She won't. Can you get up on this bed with me? I want you right here when I wake up." Matilda pressed toward the far bed rail to make room.

"What if I hurt you?"

She kissed the end of his tanned nose. "You won't."

Indelible Link

1959, November, New Orleans, Louisiana

THE NEW TRACK supervisor at the Fair Grounds Race Course in New Orleans drove back to the rented house next to the house with Chevalier on the mailbox, on the side street just off Gentilly Avenue after he lined out everything for opening day of racing.

His mother-in law came out of her house dressed to the nines and thanked him for opening the car door. He was closing the rear door when he heard the musical bells at his own front door and turned to watch his tall, stately ginger-haired wife walk across the lawn with just a trace of a limp. She took his offered hand and slid into the front passenger seat. She was to start her first day working at the betting window next to her mother.

MATILDA AND HER mother wore sweaters against the chill of November for the first two races. As the sun warmed the big windows that overlooked the saddling paddock, Matilda pushed up her sleeves.

And while the third race was running, and there was a lull in the betting, Matilda looked down at the newest, finely worked art, compliments of Lafontaine Family Tattoo Artistry. Lucky Eddie had known exactly what another kind of addict needed to remind her that love and pain weren't the same thing.

She touched the image Eddie had drawn and tattooed into her skin from bird-like wrist bones to elbow. The image of the heavy browed, hairy man carrying a caramel skinned girl in a blue and orange striped blouse and blue apron over his bulging shoulder made her smile. The Borneo Wild Man, running with his mouth pushed permanently into a circle, as though he were hooting for joy was forever at full stride. The girl's arms would eternally flap toward the cotton candy tray that would remain frozen in the air just out of her reach. The explosion of apricot-colored hair would stream around the girl's face for the rest of time.

Matilda traced the image with her little finger. She couldn't remember the sting and burn. But for once, she didn't need anything to hurt for her to feel the memory.

As the racegoers who'd win or lose bets hurried to watch the next race, Matilda slipped out of her sweater. She still knew how to draw a crowd, even if it was to the betting window at a racetrack in New Orleans, instead of the ticket window of a little one-ring circus. Tattooed Matilda quietly hummed her old favorite song and smiled at the gift of memory her best friend had inked on her arm. Her next round of customers formed a line.

SOMEWHERE, OUT ON the road, in a circus tent, the rigging was checked and double checked. Horses were tacked up, and a rosinback rider pulled her corseted costume a little tighter. Clowns patted a final coat of powder over their makeup.

A new trapeze flyer dressed in tights and a leotard painted to imitate the full body tattoos of the former star of Fiscalini Brothers Circus was in the wings, ready to take the spotlight when the sound man cued "The Band Played On."

Juni Fisher is a multi-award-winning singer, songwriter, and producer. The IWMA Entertainer of the Year, four times Female Performer of the Year, (IWMA and AWA), four-time Song of the Year winner (IWMA and WWA), and two-time True West Magazine Best Solo Musician, she was the first woman to win the National Cowboy Museum's Wrangler Award in 2009 for her CD, Gone for Colorado, which was also the 2009 IWMA Album of the year. Her songs have appeared in feature and documentary film soundtracks and have been recorded by various award-winning music artists.

Before writing her 2019 Willa Literary Award Finalist, *Girls From Centro*, she'd been published in *Equus Magazine, The Trout Unlimited Newsreel, The Western Way,* and *True West Magazine.* When she's not on the road or writing her next novel, she's riding her cutting horse, or fly-fishing.

Visit Juni's website: https://www.junifisher.com

Just aim your phone camera at the QR Code